ReGina Crawford

I0662368

Snake
Chaser

Published by True Meditations of the Heart
A division of G Styl Productions Incorporated

About the Author:

ReGina is a 45 year old divorced mother of three children 2 girls and 1 boy, ages 22, 18, and 7. She has been writing since the age of ten; beginning with poetry and short stories. Her first book, a romance novella, Triple Threat, hit the market in June 2008 with her second book, Food From The Heart, hitting the market in March 2009, and the response was overwhelmingly positive. Heart Body and Soul, her third novel, was released in April 2011. Snake Chaser is her fourth release, and she is hopeful that it receives the same positive response as her first three releases. She has had poetry published in five National Library of Poetry publications, and has also performed as the feature poet at open mics in Cleveland and Columbus, OH, as well as, appeared on stages in Detroit, MI and Wheeling, WV. She was featured in Who's Who in Black Cleveland in 2004 and 2009, and has received numerous awards for her contributions to the Cleveland Community, as well as, promoting entrepreneurship.

You can check her out on the world wide web at GStyl.com, Facebook.com/GStyl, and Facebook.com/TrueMeditations.

Cover Design by SYRE Arts & Entertainment, Cleveland, OH
SyreGrafix@gmail.com or facebook.com/frostbyte76

Acknowledgements

I once again have to thank my children for standing beside me as I completed this novel. Their unwavering love sustains me more than they will ever know. And now I have a grand dude to share my life with. I love you all!

To my fans who have once again patiently waited for me to complete another novel, thanks for your patience and support and for the badgering to "Get It Done". I love you all as well.

Although I said it in my last novel, it warrants being said again. To the many brothers and sisters whom have adopted me, and whom I have adopted as well, thanks for your love, support, and encouragement over the years. I love you all so much.

To Frost, my little brother and designer of all my book covers, you came through once again with a dynamic cover and I can't thank you enough. Love Ya Bruh

Peace Time: In Ottawa, Canada the Peace Tower located at the House of Parliament houses one of that country's most famous clocks. On May 28, 2006 the clock inexplicably stopped working for one day, displaying the time of 7:28 to the confusion of many, sparking news stories often called the day that time stood still.

Stephen's Time: The official name for the tower that houses Big Ben in London, England, is St. Stephen's Tower. Big Ben is the name of the 13-ton bell that strikes on every hour. On May 27, 2005, the hands of Big Ben stopped moving twice, once at 10:07 and then a second time 10:20 local time.

.

Snake Chaser

Prologue

Sixteen year old Sylvia Williams is called into the headmaster's office, and upon her arrival she sees two officers with blank expressions but she knows by the way they are dressed they are not there to deliver good news. She instantly knows that something tragic has happened to one of her parents who are both Marines. What she wasn't expecting to hear the officers' say was that both of her parents had been killed in action while on a routine intelligence mission in Russia. She didn't even know that they were on the same mission as married couples were not allowed to be on the same mission together.

"How were they on the same mission together," are the first words she speaks.

"They weren't on the same mission. Unfortunately their separate missions lead them to the same location," states the female officer.

"What went wrong," asks Sylvia

"We are not at liberty to disclose any details about their mission," states the male officer. Sylvia takes a defiant stance and gets an angry look on her face, but before she can say a word the officer speaks again, "Ma'am, I'm sure you have a lot of questions, and if you will come with us to headquarters our superiors will be able to answer them for you."

"Fine," bites out Sylvia.

"You will be excused from school until after your parents' funerals," states the headmaster. Sylvia simply nods in her direction. "My condolences on your loss. If you need anything, please call me."

"Thanks Ma'am. I will," responds Sylvia before following the officers out of the school building.

Once at headquarters Sylvia is taken straight to the Lieutenant General's office. Once she is seated and the other officers leave the office closing the door behind them, the Lt. General leans forward before speaking, "I know the news you received is shocking and I know that you have a lot of questions, but I also know that you know I am not at liberty to give you the details you would like." He pauses to assess Sylvia's reaction to the words that he has just spoken as he has known her from the day she was born, and he knows how volatile her temper is when she doesn't get what she wants, as well as, her determination to get what she wants. When she shows no outward signs of reaction to what he has said, a little red flag goes off in his mind for this is not a good sign but he continues anyway, "As you know, I am to become your guardian in the event that both of your parents are no longer able to care for you, so we will get your things in order and moved into my home as we handle all of the plans for the memorial services for your parents." Again he pauses and again he sees nothing in Sylvia's eyes, face, breathing, movements that indicate what she's thinking or feeling. He thinks to himself, "*Maybe I was wrong. Maybe Massanutten is the best place for her. She used to be such a hot head, but now she seems rather controlled. But I'll be keeping a close eye on her anyway for this could be the calm before the storm.*"

2

Snake Chaser

"We have a lot of work to do, so let's get started," he states as he rises from his chair and walks around his desk to where she is sitting. Without so much a word, Sylvia gets up and follows him from his office.

*****

Upon arrival at the house she shared with her parents when they weren't on missions and she wasn't away at school, Sylvia sees that the Marines have been hard at work packing up her parents' belongings. She heads straight to her room, and breathes a sigh of relief when she sees that they haven't touched a thing in her room. She says to herself, *"I'm sure Uncle Chappy made sure they didn't come in here."* Uncle Chappy is what she has been calling Lieutenant General Raymond Chapman since she could speak, and now he would become her guardian for the next two years. That thought made everything real for tough-as-nails Sylvia, and she flings herself to her bed and cries herself to sleep. That's how Chappy and her brother find her two hours later, sleep in her bed with tear tracks visible on her face. Chappy leaves Chance to wake and console his sister concerning their parents' death. After Chappy leaves the room, Chance just stares at Sylvia trying to figure out what his next move should be. He hasn't seen her in over 2 years as his life as a Marine has kept him away from home, and he hasn't had to deal with any real emotions in all that time and has become known as the Barracuda among his fellow Marines. Deciding that there is no easy way to deal with the situation, he gently wakes her and when she sees him she launches herself at him and a fresh wave of tears begin to stream from her eyes. Unaccustomed to dealing with this much emotion, Chance holds her until she finally stops crying. When she lifts her head and looks in his eyes he simply says, "Death is a part of life Sy. I know this is hard for you, but if you plan to be a top notch Marine you'll have to learn to deal with the loss of life without becoming overly emotional."

Stunned by his words, Sylvia pushes out of his arms and simply glares at him before turning her back on him to begin packing her belongings. "I should be done shortly," she states in a terse tone.

Not knowing what else to do, Chance joins Chappy downstairs to wait for Sylvia to come down with her things. Chappy is aware of Chance's emotional detachment from the situation, and doesn't say a word as they wait for Sylvia so that he can take her to his home.

*****

Over the next five days, they get Sylvia's belongings moved to her new room, take care of the funeral arrangements for her parents, and get her adjusted to life without her parents. There were a few touch and go moments when Chappy saw the old uncontrollable, headstrong, and rebellious Sylvia emerge, but he was having none of it. She had come too far after her first two years of military school, and he was not about to let her backslide into her old behaviors. She has two more days before she has to return to Massanutten, and he plans to make sure that she knows what he expects of her.

*****

As they arrive home after the funeral services and repast, Sylvia attempts to make a beeline for her room but Chappy takes her hand and leads her into his study. He motions for her to have a seat in front of his desk as he takes the seat behind it. "I know that you have had a lot to deal with over the last week," he begins. "Actually, you've had a lot deal with your whole life with your parents being damn fine Marines, and being called away quite frequently. However, I want you to know that I will not have you becoming unruly, and I'm sure you are quite aware that the consequences will be severe if you cross me," he makes a slight pause for effect. "So let's avoid all of that by you returning to school and continuing on the path that you have been on the last two years. You have made great strides in controlling your temper and curbing your rebellious nature, and I have no doubt that you will make a damn fine Marine in the future. Do we have an understanding," he asks.

"Yes Uncle Chappy, we have an understanding," she responds. "I'm just feeling like I'm without family since my parents were only children, and Chance appears to want to be a Marine more than a big brother."

"I know Sylvia, but you still have a life to live and I know that you are going to make the best of it. I will be with you all the way, okay?"

"Okay."

"Go ahead and relax for the rest of day before you return to school tomorrow."

Sylvia nods her head before getting up and heading to her room. Once there, she contemplates what she is going to do with the rest of her life. She makes the decision to honor her parents' lives and their dedication to the Marines by being the best student she can, and then joining the Marines herself upon graduation.

*****

Two years later, Sylvia graduates at the top of her class and is one of the Marine's top recruits. She excels in all of her military training, especially in marksmanship and stealth and camouflage. She so impresses the top brass that she becomes their go-to Marine for all their high priority missions. Chappy watches her career very closely, and is extremely proud of the woman and Marine that she has become under his tutelage.

*****

Six years later Chappy has a major heart attack, and Sylvia rushes to his side. His prognosis is bleak, and Sylvia is devastated as he is the second father she has lost in her lifetime, and she hasn't seen her brother since the death of their parents. Within a week Chappy passes and she is once again neck deep in funeral arrangements, and feeling the weight of the world on her shoulders. Tired of losing the people that she loves for she feels like her brother has been lost to her since he became a Marine, she makes a vow to never get too close to another human soul for fear of losing them. Once Chappy is laid to rest, she returns to work as a Marine and becomes even more determined to be the go to person for all of the most critical missions for the Marines is all she has left that she loves.

Snake Chaser

First Encounter

Four years later Sylvia reaches El Carmen, Bolivia just as night falls, and joins up with the other Marines assigned to her latest mission which is to gather Intel about a human trafficking ring. This is strictly a fact finding mission, there is to be no engaging of any of the suspects, and it is her superior abilities of camouflage that are needed for this mission. She hasn't worked with any of these Marines before and they have no idea who she is, at least that is what she believes until she sees her best friend's brother in the briefing. After the briefing is complete, she heads off to complete her mission unaware that one particular Marine is watching her very closely.

"Why is Sgt. Williams on this mission," asks Qasean Richardson Junior Gunnery Sergeant of his commanding officer Master Sergeant Robert Evans.

"Williams is the best at stealth and camouflage, and one of the best marksmen that we have if needed," responds Evans. "No one knows too much about Williams, and it would be in your best interest to leave Williams be."

Just as Qasean is about to speak again, Evans quirks his eyebrow signaling Qasean to leave it be. Qasean goes about seeing to the tasks that he's been assigned without letting anyone know that he knows Williams on a personal level, at least he use to. He assigns himself a mental task of finding out why she's treating him as though she had no idea who he is, for he was like a big brother to her when they were teens.

*****

Sylvia changes into her specially made camouflage gear as she tries to rid herself of the nagging feeling that Qasean is determined to know why she didn't acknowledge him during the briefing. It is this sixth sense that has saved her life on many a mission. Her ability to feel someone's interest in her is something that she has found interesting and disturbing all her life. Determined to focus on the mission at hand, she dismisses the feeling, and sets out on her mission to discover who the major players are on the wrong side of the playing field she finds herself a major player on.

She checks the coordinates on the map she has of the compound she is approaching, and double checks the longitude and latitude on her electronic compass. Confident that she is where she wants to be, she pulls her night vision binoculars out of one of the pouches on her jacket to survey the compound for points of access and to determine where the sentinels are located. After watching the compound for five minutes she determines that the best way to gain access is underground, so she heads back to her quarters to gain an underground layout for the compound.

Once she has secured herself away, she accesses the computer software she helped design to determine what, if anything, is under the enemies hideout. She is not surprised to see that they have a complex set of tunnels underground, and is in fact glad that they do. Now all she has to do is find out how well these tunnels are monitored, and which one is the best one to use to gain access inside the compound. She spends the next hour virtually accessing the tunnels to see what security measures she needs to circumvent, and working out different scenarios using the software to see the best ways she can enter and exit the hideout. Once she is confident that she has a good plan laid out, she returns to the camp to inform Sergeant Evans of her plans to ensure that they are in alignment with the tasks the other Marines will be executing while on this mission.

As she enters the tent that serves as Evans office, her sixth sense picks up the interest of someone nearby so she scans the camp and locks eyes with Qasean who seems to be watching her intently. Determined to ignore his interest for the moment, she enters the tent.

"Williams," greets Evans.

"Why is your junior gunny so interested in me," she asks.

Not at all surprised by the question as he is used to her uncanny ability to detect interest in her and to her blunt way of speaking, Evans answers, "He doesn't like working with people that he doesn't know. He doesn't know you, and he will make it his mission to find out who you are," unaware that that is not his interest at all.

"Did you tell him that his quest will be futile as no one knows any more than I want them to know?"

"I told him to let it go, but like you once he gets something in his mind it's hard to get him to let it go."

"Just make sure that he doesn't interfere with my mission," she responds. After a brief pause, she informs him of her plans for the following evening. "I'll report back my findings the following morning."

"Good enough. God Speed Snake Chaser."

Sylvia nods before turning to leave the tent. As she exits the tent, the junior gunny is standing directly in front of her. She looks him in the eye before making a move to step around him, and go about her business.

He anticipates her move, and takes the same step that she makes. She cocks an eyebrow at him while giving him a look that would make a lesser man stand down. However, Qasean is not intimidated by the look he receives, and cocks an eyebrow of his own. "I know you have the reputation of a lone wolf, however, I don't like being ignored," states Qasean.

"Personally I don't give a damn about what you like or don't like, and I'm here to do a job and not rekindle old friendships." She pauses briefly before adding, "Now gunny I suggest you move out of my path before we draw any more attention to ourselves."

Qasean looks around and sees a few of the other Marines are trying to discreetly watch their exchange. Not wanting to explain himself to Sergeant Evans, Qasean steps to the side and lets her move on. However, his gaze stays with her until she is out of sight. He is determined to solve the puzzle that is Sergeant Williams. He is also determined to find out why he is so intrigued with her after all this time. He has known her since she became his sister's best friend when they were fourteen, and although he hung out with her and his sister he's never given her this much personal attention before. Once she has entered her quarters, he heads back to his own quarters still confused by the affect Williams is having on him.

As he enters his quarters his best friend Vince pulls him back out the tent and off to the side. "Let it go man, for your own good," states Vince. At the cocked eyebrow, Vince continues, "She is no one to tangle with man." He pauses and looks around to make sure that no one is around to hear what he is about to say, "If you haven't heard the stories, let me enlighten you. She is deadly! And does not like to be interfered with," he states in a heated whisper.

"What the hell are you talking about," Qasean asks in a fierce whisper of his own.

"Williams. I've seen you watching her, and I saw the exchange between the two of you when she came out of the Sarg's tent. Whatever you're thinking concerning her, let it go."

"Why is everyone so content in letting her have her way?"

"Maybe because anyone who hasn't let her have her way has found themselves caught up in her wrath which has lead to some very unpleasant assignments for them," he pauses while double checking that no one has moved any closer to them. "And I've heard that she is very close to the President, and he has given her an all access pass to the world. So let it go for your own good."

That bit of news takes Qasean by surprise, but instead of squelching his interest it only piques it. Not wanting to upset his friend any further, Qasean responds, "Fine man. I'll let it go, but I'm not happy about it."

They both head back inside the tent to lay it down for the night. Vince is not completely convinced that Qasean will let go of his interest in Williams, and plans to keep his eyes and ears on the situation. Qasean now knows a little bit more about her reputation as he has not had any contact with her since she graduated from military school, and knows that he must be that more discreet when trying to talk to her in the future.

*****

Sylvia walks to her quarters fully aware that Qasean has not taken his eyes off of her, and she is determined to dissuade him from the notion that he has the right to know anything about her. She is also determined to ignore the old familiar sensations that she felt while being in his presence. During her life as a Marine she has constantly been in close quarters with men most of her life, but none of them have evoked any types of feelings within her before. As she settles in for the night, she can't seem to get Qasean off of her mind even though she hasn't thought of him in years and is for once in her life at a loss as to how to proceed.

Snake Chaser

Mission Critical

The next morning, Sylvia rises early and heads to her make shift hideout to get ready to make her entry into the compound's underground tunnels.

She knows that she needs to find the main line to the security system protecting the compound so that she can access the security cameras, and make copies of the feeds, as well as, rig the motion sensors so that they appear to working correctly but won't detect her movements. After changing into her specially made camouflage gear, she makes her way to the compound to put her plans in motion. After capturing the video that she needs and taking care of the motion sensors, she decides to access the tunnels to see what more she can find out about what is taking place inside the compound. She inserts the earplugs in her ear that work with the beta parabolic mic that she has been tasked with testing, and walks the path of tunnels that she believes will take her to what she believes is the office of the man in charge of the compound. As she gets closer to the area she is interested in, she picks up a conversation between two men.

"Boss, I've just heard something that I think you will find very interesting," states an unknown voice.

"What is that?"

"It seems that there are US Marines in the area, and the word is that they are going to try to storm the compound and take out our operation."

"Really? And they think that they have the ability to do that?"

"Apparently."

"Well won't they be unpleasantly surprised when their mission fails," he states before a sinister laugh leaves his throat.

Sylvia is not exactly surprised that they have learned of the Marines presence, but she plans to make sure that the mission doesn't fail. With that thought in mind, she heads back the way she came so that she can alert Sgt. Evans that they must move up their timeline if they wish to capture their prey. After changing out of her gear and into her normal fatigues, Sylvia heads to Sgt. Evans' tent at the Marine compound.

After being granted permission to enter, Sylvia informs Evans of the conversation that she overheard and they put together a plan to breach the enemy compound without the proof that there is illegal activity taking place there. Once they are satisfied with their plans, Sgt. Evans calls together his troops to let them know that they will be making a move on the compound come dusk. Gunny Richardson knows that he cannot question the orders that he's been given, but can't help but wonder what Sylvia told the Sarg that has made him alter the mission. Once the mission has been laid out, Sylvia heads back to her hideout to change back into her camouflage gear and wait for dusk as she will be the first to make an entrance into the enemy compound. What she doesn't know is that Qasean will be right on her tail.

At dusk, Sylvia makes her way back to the compound and just before she enters the underground tunnels, she feels the presence of someone close by but is confident that she can't be seen. Instead of entering the tunnel, she takes up position near a tree to wait for the person or persons to reveal themselves. She doesn't have to wait long before she see a lone figure in camouflage gear similar to her own stealthily making their way towards to the tunnel's entrance. As they walk right past her, not knowing if they are friend or foe, she quietly snakes out and takes them down. As she looks into the eyes of her taken down prey, she recognizes the eyes as belonging to Gunny Richardson.

"I'm not sure why you're here and I don't have time to figure it out now, so just quietly follow me in to the tunnel so that we can complete this mission," whispers Sylvia close to his ear.

Knowing that she is right and that he doesn't have time to figure out how she knew he was near, he nods his head in agreement but he's determined more now than ever to have that conversation with Sylvia.

She turns him lose and they make their way into the tunnels. He watches closely as she checks to make sure that the safe guards she put in place regarding the cameras and motion sensors are still in place before they proceed further into the compound. She finds it rather strange that the boss and his henchmen are not hunkered down in his office developing their strategy to take down the Marines, but she doesn't have time to contemplate that little detail at the moment. Sylvia and Qasean make a sweep of the compound with their heat sensing goggles, and locate a room with a large number of warm bodies in it and a couple of guards in the hallway outside the room. They send the signal back to Sgt. Evans that the compound is ready to be breached, and let him know where the bodies are located so to speak.

Once they receive the signal that the troops are in place to breach the compound, Sylvia and Qasean make their way back out of the tunnel to join the other Marines. The breach is made, and the women are rescued. However, the head boss and his right hand men are nowhere to be found. Only a handful of guards are arrested during the sweep of the house.

After the hostages are seen too and the criminals are taken to lock up at the Marine base, Sylvia informs Sgt. Evans that she needs to speak with Gunny Richardson privately. Not sure what is going on Evans quirks an eyebrow at her, however, he lets her have her way.

Evans walks out of his tent only slightly surprised to see his Gunny posted up near the entrance. "Sgt. Williams would like to have a word with you Gunny."

"Good, because I have a few words for her as well," is his response.

"Tread lightly. Her call sign might be Snake Chaser, but she packs a powerful venom of her own."

Surprised by the warning, Qasean quirks his eyebrow at his sergeant who simply turns and walks across the encampment to the supply tent.

Qasean walks in to the Sarg's tent and finds Sylvia perched on the edge of his desk, and a strange sensation washes over him.

However, before he can analyze what he feels she moves off the desk with a look on her face that lets him know she is about to sink her fangs into his hide. "I don't know nor do I care why you were out of position on the mission today, but I do care that you could have jeopardized the mission," she begins in a deadly calm voice. "I don't play with other people's lives nor do I play with mine, and in the interest of everyone's safety everyone needs to take up their assigned posts and efficiently execute the tasks they are assigned," she continues. "I do not

16

have time to babysit hot shot soldiers who do not think they need to follow the orders they are given," she adds.

At this point she is standing directly in front of him, and he is fighting hard to focus on her words as the heat from her body is having a bigger effect on him than he anticipated. He suddenly realizes that she has stopped talking, and is looking at him with her eyes in an evil squint.

"Are you paying attention Qasean," she asks in an angry tone.

It takes him a minute to process the question as he is so focused on the movement of her lips that words they spoke have to be pulled from his subconscious. Before answering her, he mumbles under his breath, "Probably more attention than I should be paying." In his normal tone of voice he says, "Yes, I'm paying attention." And then suddenly remembering the dressing down she gave him upon entering the tent, he adds, "My mission was to cover you in the event that someone tried to get the drop on you." Seeing she was about to speak, he takes a step closer, places a finger across her lips, and continues, "I know you are believed to be some type of super soldier, but I've learned that when dealing with criminals in their own country they always keep an Ace up their sleeve that they reveal at the last minute. And I couldn't watch your back while you were in the tunnels if I was above ground, so I decided to follow you inside. And speaking of that how did you know that I was following you?"

As he removes his finger from her lips to allow her to answer the question, she places her own fingers across her lips as she can still feel the heat from where his finger rested against them. So focused on the foreign sensation that she feels, she forgets that he is waiting on an answer to his question and she walks right past him and out of the tent.

Stunned by the turn of events, Qasean just stands there staring at the spot that she occupied just seconds before. "What the hell," he growls a few seconds later. Needing answers, he follows her out of the tent but she is nowhere to be seen.

Snake Chaser

Foreign Territory

Determined to find out what the hell happened in the Sarg's tent, Qasean makes it his mission to find her and continue their discussion. However, before he can get too far, Sergeant Evans walks up to him and asks, "What the hell did you do to her?"

"I have no idea what happened, but I intend to find out," responds Qasean. "Where did she disappear too," are his next words.

"She left the encampment. Said she needed space."

"What? Where could she possibly go?"

"Williams' skills allow her to disappear without a trace which is why she is called in when recon is required in unknown territory. If she doesn't want to be found, trust me you won't find her." He pauses before continuing, "Why do you want to find her Gunny?"

"To be honest, I'm not sure," begins Qasean. "I just know that I need to find her, and find out what happened back at the tent," he pauses as he replays the events that took place a few moments ago. "She went from being a viper to being a church mouse in a matter of seconds," he continues. Then it hits him, he placed his finger across her lips and felt them tremble. At first he thought that the tremble was a result of her anger with him, but what if it was due to something else . . . "Sarg, I really need to find her. Where could she have gone?"

Not sure if he is doing the right thing, but feeling as though the two of them have something to resolve, Evans gives him the only information that he can, "You'll have to use your superior tracking abilities to find her," he states. "I'm sure she is close by, but more than likely she is underground. That's all I can tell you Son," he adds as he starts to walk away. He then stops and turns around, "Gunny, good luck on your mission."

Qasean heads back to his tent to change into his specially made camouflage before taking off into the woods surrounding the encampment in his quest to find the elusive Sylvia. He knows that she has to be somewhere between the encampment and the compound that they just raided, so he starts out on the path they took earlier that day. It isn't long before he senses someone else's presence, and his instincts tell him that it's Sylvia's. Not wanting her to get the drop on him again, he heads into some dense foliage to scan the area for her.

Sylvia senses his presence before she sees him, and she too heads into dense foliage to figure out just where he is. Using her uncanny ability to pick up on the heat emitted from another person, she locates him just five steps from where she is located in the foliage. Sure that they are the only two in the woods, she speaks, "Why are you here?"

Not at all startled by the sound of her voice, he responds, "We need to talk."

"We have nothing to talk about."

Snake Chaser

"I beg to differ," he responds. "I need to understand what happened back at the Sarg's tent."

"Let it go Qasean."

"Wish I could, but I can't." He locates her through her voice, and walks over to where she is crouched in the bush. "I know you feel it too, so let's figure out what it is and what we plan to do about it."

Feeling like she's in foreign territory, she's not sure what do. However, needing answers of her own, she acquiesces and heads in the direction of her underground bunker quite certain that he will follow her lead. Once they are securely inside, she begins to remove her camouflage gear for she feels that this will not be a quick discussion. Once she is down to her basic gear she turns to him, and is not all surprised that he has removed his camouflage as well. She takes a seat behind her make shift desk, places her elbows on the desk, and rests her chin on her steepled fingertips. "What is it that you think we need to discuss?"

Qasean takes a seat on the edge of the desk before speaking, "What happened in the tent? Why did you just walk out?"

"Wish I could answer that for you Qasean, but I honestly don't know," she answers.

The confusion that he sees in her eyes lets him know that she is telling the truth, and only adds to his confusion. However, that feeling is being overridden by the need to touch her. Now he's just as confused as she is since he's never reacted this strongly to a female, ever. He lifts her chin with his index finger so that he can look deeper into her eyes, and notes the surprise she's feeling in them. Compelled by some unknown force, he moves his finger to trace her lips and feels them tremble again. Shock registers in both of their faces at her reaction to his touch, but he is determined to ignore it and leans forward to kiss those same lips. He tastes her innocence on her lips, but doesn't let that deter him from tasting her deeper. As the kiss continues, he lifts her out of the chair at the same time that he stands up. The kiss is only broken by their need to breathe. She buries her face in his chest and he wraps his arms tighter around her as he tries to understand why he feels overwhelmed from just kissing her.

She feels the rapid beating of his heart against the lips that he has just kissed so thoroughly, and knows that her own heart is beating just as rapidly. As he continues to hold her, questions are running rampant in her mind. Why him? Why now? What is going on with her body? What is she going to do with what he is making her feel? She knows that she needs to get her body under control, and feels the only way that she can do that is to separate her body from his. He feels the change in her and figures she plans to move back from him, but he is determined that that won't happen so he tightens his hold on her.

She looks up at him at that moment, but before she can say a word he shakes his head no. Then he speaks, "I sense this is new territory for you, but I refuse to let you retreat. We are going to figure this out together."

He sees the uncertainty in her face and determined to put her at ease, he turns them and takes a seat in her chair pulling her down into his lap as he does so. He then kisses her again until he feels her body soften in his arms. Once he breaks the kiss, he says, "This is new territory for me as well, but I can't seem to stop myself from exploring what is happening between us." He pauses and wipes a hand down his face before continuing, "I have no idea why I am reacting so strongly to you, but I don't think that I could stop myself if I wanted to." With that said he kisses her once again, and he feels her complete submission to him and the kiss.

Snake Chaser

He breaks the kiss and rips her T-Shirt from her body. The sight of her breasts encased in a lacy barely there bra nearly takes his breath away, and he takes a finger and circles the nipple on her right breast. She sucks in her breath as her head falls on his shoulder, and her nipple hardens even more under his touch. Needing to have the taste of her on his tongue, Qasean places her on the desk as he takes the nipple in his mouth and circles his tongue around her nipple through her bra. Unable to stop herself, she moans from deep in her throat. The sound of her moan makes him shiver, and he moves his mouth to her other breast and she continues to moan as foreign sensations take over her body. Wanting no barriers between his tongue and her breasts, he tells her to place her hands on his shoulders as he goes about removing her bra. Once her breasts are free from their confinement, he cups both of them in his hands before dipping his head to suckle them. The heat from her skin damn near singes his palms, but he doesn't stop devouring her breasts. Before he knows it, he hears her cry out as an orgasm crashes down upon her from the attention that he is lavishing on her breasts. The sound makes him pause for he senses that it is the first time she has ever experienced an orgasm, and he looks up at her. The surprise in her face, lets him know that he is right and that takes him by surprise. Instantly he wonders if she is a virgin.

He gives her time to recover, before asking, "First time?"

Slightly embarrassed that it's obvious that she is virgin territory, she closes her eyes as she nods her head.

"Open your eyes," he says. When she doesn't comply, he gently says, "Look at me." This time she complies. "It's nothing to be embarrassed by, and in no way impacts what I'm feeling." He then shakes his head before saying, "That's a lie. Yes it does, but not in a negative way. It makes me want you even more." He notes the surprise that registers in her face, and smiles the most devastating smile she has ever seen. She helplessly smiles in return. Taking her smile to mean that she is willing to undertake the mission that he is silently proposing, he reaches down to unlace her boots. Once her boots and socks are removed, he is surprised to see the scarlet red nail polish on her toes and looks up at her.

"I am still a woman," she states, "and I still like to feel like one under my uniform."

"Yeah, I kind of gathered that by the lacy bra covering your lush breasts," he states. He smiles at the blush that appears on her face, before standing and lifting her off the desk to place her on her feet. He proceeds to remove her pants, and feels the muscles of her abdomen tremble as his fingers brush across them. He also feels his manhood surge in his pants in anticipation of gaining entrance into her lush body. As her pants hit the floor, he is floored by the sight of her matching lace panties, and the scent of her arousal. He takes a deep breath inhaling the essence of her, and feels his tongue tingle in anticipation of tasting her. He hooks his thumbs into her panties from the leg opening up to the waistband, and pulls them down her gorgeous legs. As she steps out of them, she is surprised to see him put them up to his nose and take a deep breath before placing them in his pocket. However, before she can say a word, he picks her up and places her back on the desk. He takes a seat back in her chair moving it closer to the desk as he places her thighs over his shoulders, and buries his tongue in the place it wants to be most. The sound of their combined moans fills the room.

Snake Chaser

Friendly Invasion

Overwhelmed and unsure what to do, Sylvia grabs a hold of the edge of the desk in a near death grip as he proceeds to devour her. She bites her lip to keep from releasing the moans building up in the back of her throat, however, that proves to be unsuccessful as another orgasm crashes down around her and she screams loud and long. Fueled by the strength of her screams, Qasean buries his tongue deeper inside of her as he strengthens his hold her hips to keep her positioned exactly where he wants her. He continues to feast until another orgasm takes over her body. Once her body stops trembling, he stands up and lifts her off the desk to carry her over to the cot that he noticed earlier. After laying her down, he steps back to remove his own clothing and she watches him through love dazed eyes.

The removal of his shirt reveals a well-toned chest and abdomen covered by a fine layer of hair that narrows as it enters the waistband of his pants. As he bends down to remove his boots, she takes in the definition of the muscles in his arms, shoulders and upper back. His physique is wreaking havoc on her senses, and she feels her nipples harden even more and the moisture flow between her legs increases. As he stands to remove his pants he picks up the scent of her increased arousal, and his nostrils flare as he stares in her eyes. Completely undressed, he moves up her body from her ankles, placing fleeting kisses on her legs and thighs. As he makes a move to place a kiss on the lips between her thighs, she grabs the sides of his head to stop him. He looks up at her and smiles before grabbing her wrists, and removing her hands from his head and holding them hostage as he kisses the place he plans to make his in a short while. As much as he would love to bring her to another orgasm with his mouth, he knows that he would reach his own release if he did so he continues up her body after only give her a few kisses in that area. When he reaches her breasts, he pays them a brief tribute before positioning his body over hers.

He stops before entering her and looks into her desire laden eyes, "Are you sure you're ready for this?"

Not sure of anything, she shakes her head no while whispering yes. He laughs at her contradictory response before kissing her senseless, at the same time as he makes his initial foray into her body. Despite how wet she is, she is still tight and he is not able to make a complete entry. He pulls back and makes another attempt, going a little further inside. He feels her muscle pulsing around his manhood and trembles before pulling back and then surging forward with enough force to gain complete entry. He absorbs her small gasp of pain in his mouth as he breaches her virginity, and he then freezes giving her time to get over the pain and adjust to the feel of him inside her body.

When he feels her body relax, he breaks the kiss and looks into her eyes once again. The smile she gives him takes his breath away and causes his member to tremble inside her body reminding him of where it is buried. The flexing his manhood causes her inner walls to involuntarily clench him, and he sucks in a deep breath as a result of how she feels gripping him. He pulls almost completely out of her before surging forward in an aggressive and deep thrust which causes her hips

26

to rise up of the cot and grind against him. The movement sends him over the edge, and despite wanting to be gentle with her this first time he vigorously makes love to her. In no time at all, they both are shouting out their release. Not having anywhere to go and not wanting to crush her with his weight, he holds his upper body up on his arms. As he holds this position he watches her emotions play out on her face, and feels himself harden while he is still buried deep inside her body.

She feels it too, and opens her eyes and finds herself looking directly into his. What she sees in his eyes, causes her breath to catch in her throat and her heart begins beating rapidly. His eyes tell her that he is nowhere near done loving her, and as if on cue he pulls his lower body back only to deeply dive back inside of her as he proceeds to make love to her again. He doesn't break eye contact with her as he takes his time exploring her womanly cove with his manhood. She sees the sweat breakout on his forehead and chest as he fights his desire to take her has voraciously as he did the first time, so she decides to take matters into her own hands and lifts her hips on his next downward thrust. The unexpected contact sends him over the edge, and he lowers his upper body as he takes her hips in his hands and loves her for all he's worth. Not wanting to miss a single sensation, Sylvia instinctively wraps her legs around his waist and grinds her pelvis against him. Qasean increases the tempo of their loving until they both find themselves caught up in the throcs of another powerful release.

This time he's too weak to hold his body up, so he collapses on top of her while trying to regain control of his senses. Feeling like he is too heavy for her, he rolls off the cot onto the ground and not wanting break contact Sylvia rolls as well so that she is on top of him on the floor. She lays her head on chest as she tries to gain control of her breathing, and slow the rapid beating of her heart. He recovers first, and lifts her head off his chest so that he can read her thoughts through her eyes.

ReGina Crawford

The first thing he sees when she looks at him is surprise, and he quirks an eyebrow at that and then a blush creeps into her face. She tries to hide her face in his chest, but when he won't allow her to lower her head she closes her eyes instead.

"Uhn't Uh," he says just above a whisper, "look at me." When she looks back up at him, he asks, "Why?" He himself if not sure what question he's asking, but is willing to let her choose what question she will answer. Why is she still a virgin at age 28? Why did she give him her virginity? Why is she still surprised about everything that has taken place between them?

She chooses to answer the question that is easiest to answer, and doesn't force her to think to hard about what has taken place between them the last couple of hours. "When my parents died, I was so devastated that I became a recluse and my brother was so much of a Marine that he never thought to check on the emotional state of his teenage sister. Because of him, I learned how to become emotionally detached from the people around me except for Quintana and Uncle Chappy and then he died. Once I lost him and began taking on missions that didn't allow me to keep in contact with Ana, I never allowed myself to become emotionally attached to another person, and lack of emotional attachment creates a 28 year old virgin."

That was not the answer he was expecting, but it did give him a deeper insight into her personality and explained why she was such a lone wolf despite being a Marine. During the telling, he was able to sense the pain she experienced at reliving the deaths of the people who meant the most to her not to mention the abandonment by her brother. Sensing she needs to regroup from the telling of her story, he allows her to lay her head back on his chest and he gently strokes her back from shoulder to hip. After compartmentalizing her emotions once again, she begins to concentrate on the hand caressing her back and reminisces on what that hand has previously done to her body.

Snake Chaser

Her nipples get hard with her memories, and when the hand caressing her back grips her hip she realizes that he's picked up on the fact that she is becoming aroused.

She snakes her tongue out and flicks it across his nipple, and she hears the quick breath he takes and feels his hand flex on her hip. Encouraged by his reaction, she moves closer to his nipple and circles it with her tongue. His heart rate picks up under her ministrations to his nipple, and he transfers his hand from her and clenches it in a near death grip. Becoming bolder, she moves to his other nipple and circles her tongue around it as well. He moans and she proceeds to lick down his chest to his navel, circling it with her tongue. She feels his abdomen flex under her mouth and feels his manhood flex against her chest, and becoming even bolder she gentle grips him and is amazed at how hot his flesh feels in her hand. She looks up at him and sees him watching her every move. Without breaking eye contact, she again snakes out her tongue to circle the head of his manhood. He closes his eyes and a moan form deep in his chest rumbles past his lips. Feeling daring, she takes him completely into her mouth. He places both of his hands in her hair at the feel of her hot, wet mouth making love to him. His reaction to what she is doing makes her bolder, and she begins to devour him in the same manner that he did to her. A short while later he pulls her up his body and buries himself inside her body, not caring that they are still lying on the ground as he holds her hips in a tight grip and surges in and out of her body at a vigorous pace.

"Come! Now," he practically shouts as he feels his climax about crash down upon him. As if her body was waiting on his command, she climaxes with him. Spent, she collapses on his chest as she tries to catch her breath. "What . . . made . . . you . . . do that," he asks as he sucks in deep breaths trying to calm his racing heartbeat.

"Not . . . sure," she answers somewhat breathlessly as she is still recovering from their latest round of lovemaking. "I've . . . never . . . done that . . . before." She pauses as she takes a deep breath to calm her racing her heart, before lifting up and looking him in the eye. "I'm not sure why I've done any of the things that I've done with you in the last few hours, but I would do it all over again." Somewhat ashamed by her admission she lays her head back on his chest.

He absently rubs a hand down her back as he contemplates her sensual confession. He too isn't sure why he has made love to her for the past couple of hours, but like her he would do it all over again. Sensing that she is becoming complete relaxed, he place a gentle smack on her behind. "Come on. Let's get dressed and head back to the encampment," he states.

"You're going to have to go back without me," she states. At the lifting of his eyebrow, she continues, "I have to pack up my gear and get it ready to be shipped back to the states, as well as, erase all trace that this bunker ever existed."

"Do you need help with that?"

"No. It's covered. You go on back to camp, and I will see you there later."

"Okay," he states before pulling on his gear. Before he leaves the bunker, he gives her one more kiss. "See you back at camp," he whispers against her moist lips. She simply nods, and he turns and exits the bunker.

Snake Chaser

The Vanishing

Harboring no regrets about what she shared with Qasean, Sylvia gets dressed and packs up her gear knowing she will not be returning to the camp. She's already received her orders for her next mission, and will be heading out as soon as she's packed.

Qasean arrives back at the camp and runs into Sgt. Evans first thing, "Did you find her?"

"Yeah."

"Were the two of you able to come to an understanding?"

"I believe so," responds Qasean as he's not quite sure what happened between him Sylvia.

A few hours later, Qasean has more doubts about what transpired between him and Williams as she hasn't returned to the camp. So he seeks out Sgt. Evans to see if he can shed some light on the situation. He finds him exiting the supply tent.

"Sarg," he calls out. As Evans stops and turns in his direction, "Do you find it strange that Sgt. Williams hasn't returned to camp?"

"Not at all," Evans responds to which Qasean cocks his eyebrow. "She already received her orders, and was scheduled to ship out," he pauses and checks his watch before continuing, "thirty minutes ago."

"What," Qasean nearly yells.

"I take it your discussion wasn't over and she didn't bother to tell you that she wouldn't be returning to camp," Evans says as a statement rather than a question.

"You take it right," is Qasean's reply.

"Sorry Son, but that's how she operates. She completes one mission, and quickly moves on to the next."

Qasean merely nods, and walks away with his thoughts. *'She's never done what she did with me before,' he thinks to himself. 'And this time she has left a mission incomplete, but I fully intend to rectify that as soon as possible.'*

*****

Sylvia gets her gear packed away, and informs her next crew that she is ready to be picked up. While she awaits their arrival, she takes one more glance around the space and relives the last few hours she spent there with Qasean. She will cherish those memories forever, as she doubts she will ever embark on such a mission again in life. Just as she's done reminiscing, the crew arrives, grabs her gear, and proceeds to fill in the cavern so that no one will know that it ever existed. No matter how many times she's done this, she is always amazed at how efficient her crew is at creating and disposing of her underground hideouts.

Her next mission takes her to Yining, China a northwestern town close to Russia to investigate the illegal smuggling of uranium into Russia by a small left-wing faction of Chinamen. She has a long journey ahead of her, so she decides to take a nap on the plane that will take her to a ship that will take her to India via the Bay of Bengal. Once she departs the ship, she will have a long journey over land to reach China. This will be her most challenging mission to date, so she needs all the rest that she can get. However, her sleep is repeatedly interrupted by the memories of the time she spent with Qasean in her underground bunker. She fights the memories, and goes back to sleep.

*****

Later that evening, Qasean receives new orders and must put aside thoughts of Sylvia in order to pack his gear. Knowing he can't be distracted while on a mission, he pushes thoughts of her to the back of his mind, for now. Little does he know that his next mission will bring him dangerously close to running into her again, and neither does she.

*****

A week after her journey begins, Sylvia arrives at her destination, and proceeds to gather the Intel that she has been sent to retrieve. Despite the fatigue that she is feeling from several restless nights due to reliving the time she spent with the gunny, she executes her mission with perfection. However, after she drops the last of her Intel off to her superiors, she feels a familiar sensation on the back of her neck. She instantly pauses, and then shakes her head as she knows that it is impossible for him to be nearby.

Qasean is on his way to meet with his superiors to turn in the last of his reports on his latest mission, and feels a familiar sensation in his gut. He doesn't stop walking despite the fact that it's hard for him to breathe, for there is no way that '*she*' is anywhere in the vicinity. However, as he glances to his left, he swears he sees her in the crowd and stops walking.

As Sylvia stands there, the sensation gets stronger and she glances around the crowd, and swears she sees Qasean staring at her. She closes her eyes to clear them, and in that moment gunfire breaks out. She opens her eyes to see her crew in a gunfight with the men her Intel has labeled as the uranium dealers her government has been after. A bullet pierces her side, but before she hits the ground one of her crew scoops her up to carry her to safety.

Qasean shakes off the sensation that she was somehow hurt during the gunfight, and that is why her crew carried her from the scene. Needing to deliver his report and handle any clean up after the gunfight, Qasean doesn't have time to ponder what happened to her at the moment.

*****

Once on the outskirts of the crowd surrounding the gunfight, Sylvia and her crew vanish from sight. They know they need to get her to a medic to determine how badly she has been injured, for she appears to have lost a lot of blood. In the underground bunker, they determine that the bullet has exited her body but she is bleeding profusely. They call in support that gets her out of the bunker and into a helicopter that takes her back to the ship in the Bay of Bengal that brought her here. The doctors there perform emergency surgery on her,

Snake Chaser

removing her spleen which was damaged by the bullet. Once she is in stable condition, she is transferred to a military hospital in DC to recover from her injury.

*****

Qasean delivers his report, and is told that he will be returning to DC to receive some specialized training. He doesn't question his orders, however, he is curious as to what training he will receive and why. After delivering his report, he packs his gear and heads to the plane that will take him back home. Little does he know that shortly after his return there the object of his dreams will be arriving there as well.

ReGina Crawford

Reunion Part I

Upon his arrival in DC, Qasean stores his gear in the room he's been assigned at the bachelors housing bunker before heading over to his parents' home for a visit with them and his sister. His twin sister Quintana, that he affectionately calls Ana, is the only one at home. When he walks in the door, she runs to him and jumps into his arms. He hugs her tightly and when he feels wetness on her cheek as their faces come in contact, he pulls back to look at her. Seeing that she's been crying, he asks, "What's wrong," all the while praying that it has nothing to do with their parents.

"Sylvie was hurt on her last mission," she replies, "she should be at the medical center in a couple of days."

"Damn," Qasean whispers fiercely. "I wondered if she had gotten hit."

Quintana pushes out of his arms, and glares at him while asking in a near yell, "You were there? You didn't protect her? Why didn't you stay with her?"

"Calm down Ana. I was there, however, I didn't know she was there until just before the gunfight broke out. I wasn't close enough to her to protect her, but I doubt she would have wanted me to. And I'm not with her because her people whisked her away, and then she is a master at hiding. I've been trying to find out about her for the past few days, and no one will tell me anything." After answering all of his sister's questions, he thinks back upon something that Sylvia had told him in her underground bunker and states, "I didn't know that you two kept in touch with each other."

Ana drops her eyes as she quietly states, "She doesn't keep in touch with me, however, Chance does." At Qasean's cocked eyebrow she continues. "Even though he's not in direct contact with her, he has been monitoring her career as a Marine and has actually been responsible for most of the training that she has received." She pauses before adding, "He's the reason you are here for the training you're about to receive."

"What," Qasean yells.

"Calm down," states Ana. "He has been tracking some master criminals all over the world who have their hands in quite a few pots of illegal activity, and he's putting together a specialized team to track them down and put a stop to them. He has handpicked the people to be on the team, and you and Sylvia are two of the people he's picked."

"What," yells Qasean once again.

Confused by his reaction, Ana asks, "What?"

Qasean runs a hand down his face as he paces and thinks over what his sister has just told him. After letting him pace for a few minutes, Ana steps directly in his path. Knowing she wants to know why he's so upset, he stops his pacing and says, "I don't think Sylvia is going to be too happy about seeing me or Chance."

"Of course she will," states Ana. However, the look on Qasean's face gives her pause, and she asks, "Why wouldn't she be happy to see the two of you?"

"She and Chance have not been in direct contact with each other since their parents' death, and she feels like he has abandoned her so I'm not so sure she'll be happy to see him," is Qasean's response hoping she will overlook the fact that he has made no reference to himself.

No such luck as the next words out of Ana's mouth are, "And the reason she wouldn't want to see you?"

Deciding that telling her part of the truth was the best way to get her to back off, he replies, "We were recently on a mission together, and although we got along okay I don't think she planned on seeing me again after the mission was over." Ana squints her eyes at him not sure if he is telling her everything, and so he adds, "We had no idea that the other one was on the mission, so we were both surprised to see each other, we completed our mission, and went our separate ways on amicable terms."

"Okay," states Ana but the look on her face says that she's not entirely sure that she has gotten the whole story.

Wanting to distract her from asking any more questions, he asks, "Where are the folks?"

"They should be back any second now. They ran to the store."

They catch up while waiting for their parents to arrive to join the reunion. After the arrival of their parents, the four of them catch up on each other's lives as they prepare and have dinner together. Then Qasean heads back to the bachelors bunker for the night.

Snake Chaser

He has trouble sleeping as he alternates between reliving his time with Sylvia, and pondering how she will react to being on a special team with him and her brother. He wonders if he should try to break the news to her before her brother does, and then decides that's a bullet he would prefer to dodge. He finally drifts off to sleep with thoughts of Sylvia still floating through his mind.

*****

A couple of days later Qasean is at the medical center having his inoculations updated when a recovering Sylvia is wheeled past the waiting room he's sitting in. She doesn't see him although she does get the familiar sensation on the back of her neck, and she is too tired from her journey to even care where he is located or why he is even there. Qasean discretely follows her so that he will know what room she will occupy during her stay. Once he has the information he is seeking he goes back to the waiting room to wait for his next round of shots, however, once those are complete he plans to pay Sylvia a visit.

A couple of hours later, he is easing himself into her room. Her eyes are closed but he notices the slight hitch in her breathing as he enters the room. She makes no other movement, so he gathers that she is going to pretend to be asleep in hopes that he will leave the room. He thinks to himself, '*There's no chance of that happening Sweetheart.*' So he sits in the chair beside the bed to wait her out. He doesn't have to wait long before she opens her eyes and glares at him.

"Why do you keep popping up wherever I am," she asks in an irritated voice.

"I was wondering the same thing," he states as he gives her a lazy grin.

She rolls her eyes at him, before asking, "Why were you in China?"

"I suspect the same reason you were there, on a mission for our country."

She nods at his response before asking, "Why are you now here in DC?"

Not sure how to answer that question for he doesn't want to give anything away if she doesn't already know about the special team they will both be on, he ponders what he what he will tell her if anything at all. Then he decides to give her an answer he believes she won't question, "My orders after China were to return to DC for some specialized training for the next team that I will be joining."

While he was pondering how he would answer her question, she was pondering a few things as well, "Why do you not seem surprised to see me in the hospital," she asks.

"I thought you might have been injured during the gunfight in China, but I wasn't sure until Ana told me when I arrived home a couple of days ago."

"Ana?" Something akin to pain flashes across her face before she asks, "How did Ana know that I had been injured?"

"Chance."

His one word answer causes that flash of pain to settle in her face, and she turns her head away from him. He doesn't say another word. He just simply waits for her to turn his way again. Even though she knows he's waiting on her response to that bit of news, she keeps her face turned from his as silent tears course down her face. He continues to wait.

Snake Chaser

However, before she has gotten herself together enough to look in his direction, the person in question walks into the room. Qasean stands at attention at the entrance of a superior officer.

Reunion Part II

"At ease soldier," states Chance.

Upon hearing her brother's voice, Sylvia snaps her head back around. However, before she can utter a word, Chance says, "Hey Sis! How are you feeling?" Still shocked by his presence in her room, Sylvia is unable to answer the question, and her surprise is evident on her face. "Do I have to pull rank in order to get an answer out of you," he asks around a smile.

Not at all in a jovial mood, Sylvia responds, "Since when have you ever given a damn about how I feel?" She then turns her head from him.

Sensing that they need time alone, Qasean heads for the door figuring he and Sylvia could finish their conversation at a later time. "No need to leave Qasean," states Chance. "I get the feeling she would rather have you in here than me." He pauses as he runs a hand down his face, "Look Sy," he begins. However, before he can continue, she snaps her head back in his direction with an evil glare on her face. Not at all afraid of his little sister, Chance continues, "Even though I haven't always shown it, I have always cared. I have followed your whole career and have even been instrumental in some of the assignments you have been given." She's still glaring at him, so he figures he might as well give her what he believes she will consider bad news. "Which is why I'm here now. You and Qasean have been assigned to a special forces team that I am putting together, and I wanted you to know before you showed up and was surprised to find me as your mission leader." True to form, Sylvia just maintains the glare on her face until Chance leaves the room.

Once the door closes behind Chance, Sylvia looks at Qasean, "Did you know about this?"

"Yes. I found out after I returned state-side and before you even think to ask me why I didn't tell you, you know that I couldn't."

Knowing that he is right, she lets go of some of her anger, "I know you couldn't. It was just such a shock to see him after all these years, and then to know that I will be under his command . . .," she states before her voice trails off and a fresh wave of tears glisten in her eyes.

Unaccustomed to a woman's tears, especially this woman, Qasean mutters, "Aw hell," before walking over to the bed and taking her in his arms and letting her cry it all out of her system.

Once she feels like she has her emotions back in check, she pulls back from his embrace while saying, "Thanks. I'm good now."

Knowing showing weakness is not something she is accustomed to, Qasean releases her and stands. "No problem. That's what friends are for." At her arched eyebrow, he whispers, "That's what lovers are for as well." At the blush that steals across her cheeks, he laughs out loud before saying, "Get some rest. I'll come back and see you tomorrow, and I'll bring Ana." His smiles widens at the unexpected smile he sees on her face at the mention of his twin.

He leaves her to her thoughts, and knows that she will never be far from his. He has no idea why he suddenly feels this deep connection to her, but decides not to question it and to follow it wherever it leads.

*****

The next afternoon Qasean and Quintana enter Sylvia's hospital room to find her standing and staring out the window. They know she heard them enter the room, but she doesn't immediately turn around to greet them so they wait. Five minutes later she turns toward them, and immediately tears stream down her cheeks. Ana crosses the room to her, and envelopes her in a big hug.

After a few minutes of just holding her friend, Ana leans back and while wiping the wetness from her cheeks whispers, "I love you Sylvia." This starts a fresh wave of tears from Sylvia, and Ana holds her tighter until they subside. "I've missed you girl," states Ana a short while later.

"I've missed you too," replies Sylvia. "I didn't know how much until I saw you just now."

"Well now that you're here in DC we'll have to catch up on each other's lives."

"Yes we will."

Qasean clears his throat to remind the women that he is in the room. They both turn and look at him, to which he shrugs his shoulders. They both fall out laughing at his antics. "Hello Qasean," greets Sylvia.

Snake Chaser

"Hello Sy. I take it your feeling better." At her arched eyebrow, he adds, "You're up out of the bed."

"I was fine yesterday. I just didn't feel like getting out of the bed." Now it's his turn to cock his eyebrow, to which she responds, "I was feeling out of sorts yesterday thinking that I would have down time, and not sure what to do with myself as this would be the first time in years that I wasn't on a mission." She shrugs her shoulders before turning back to Ana, "So tell me, what have you been up to while I've been away?"

The ladies spend the next twenty minutes catching up while Qasean stands at the window that Sylvia was standing at earlier. Having had enough of being ignored, Qasean turns towards them just as Sylvia looks in his direction. Their eyes lock in a heated stare, and Ana looks back and forth between the two of them for a few minutes before saying, "I'm going to give you two a few minutes." When all they do is nod without breaking eye contact, she heads out the door to take a seat in the waiting room.

They hold eye contact without speaking for several more minutes before Qasean breaks the silence. "Sy we need to talk about what happened between us, especially if we are going to be assigned to the same team."

Sylvia breaks eye contact and sighs before responding, "I know, but I don't want to have the discussion today, in this room, or anywhere else we could be overheard. So it will have to wait until I'm discharged from this place."

"Okay, but know that I will not be dissuaded from having this conversation."

"I have no intentions of dissuading you from anything, I just would like to keep the ears listening in to a minimum."

He nods his consent before saying, "So where will you stay when you are let out of here?"

"I keep an apartment here," she responds to which he quirks an eyebrow. "I like the idea of having a permanent residence even if I'm never there."

"When's the last time you've been there?"

She tilts her head to the side while she tries to remember. She finally shrugs her shoulders, and then states, "Probably three years or more."

"Really," asks a shocked Qasean. "Are you sure it's fit for you to occupy once you leave here?"

"I'm sure it is, but you would probably fair better asking your sister that question as I left her in charge of the place the last time I left."

Qasean makes a mental note to talk to Ana about Sy's place when they leave the hospital. "We've been here long enough. You need rest, so back into the bed with you." When it appears that she is about to protest, he shakes his head as he ushers her back to the bed. "Be a good girl and humor me, at least until I leave," he adds as he flashes her his devastating smile.

Unable to resist the smile, she climbs back in the bed and lets him tuck the covers around her. He kisses her on the forehead, and she closes her eyes at the gesture and the feel of his lips on her skin. He steps back from the bed, and leaves the room.

Snake Chaser

Missing Years

As Qasean and Ana exit the hospital, Qasean begins his inquisition of his sister about Sylvia's life since he left town years ago.

"I understand that Sy has an apartment in town that you have been taking care of," he states.

Quintana looks at him sideways as his statement has come out of the blue, and even though it was a statement and not a question, she responds, "Yes she does, and yes I have been maintaining the place in her absence just in case she ever needed some down time." She pauses as she thinks about her long time friend, then absently says, "It's a shame she had to get shot in order to come back here. I've truly missed her."

"So the two of you remained close even after she graduated from military school?"

"Yes we did. For the first two years or so after graduating Sylvia stayed here while undergoing specialized training for the role she planned to play as a Marine. She has studied various weaponless fighting styles, various languages, and became an expert in stealth maneuvers," states Quintana as she reminisces on those years. She suddenly breaks out laughing as memories course through her mind.

"What's so funny," asks Qasean.

Still chuckling, Ana replies, "I was remembering when Sylvia was assigned to watch a young lady from Africa who was in high school at the time."

"What's so funny about that?"

"Her parents were African Art Historians and had spent a lot of time in Africa prior to her birth, and I guess some of the natives there thought that her parents were royalty. Anyway, an exchange student from the country where her parents lived saw Zamora at school and exclaimed that she was some long lost princess and all hell broke loose. There were a couple of kidnapping attempts, and Sylvia became her protector but he girl was a handful and frustrated the hell out of Sylvia by trying to lose her on occasion." She pauses as she chuckles some more, "I remember her actually getting away from Sylvia, and Sylvia being so mad she could have chewed nails."

"Wow! Seeing how serious she is about her assignments, I can see her getting real pissed about being given the slip by a high school girl." He chuckles a little himself before asking, "What else was Sy up to during that time?"

Quintana suddenly remembers another high school student that Sylvia was involved with saving, "If I recall correctly, there was some high school kid who was being bullied into hanging with the wrong crowd that Sylvia also saved." She pauses as she tries to recollect what exactly happened during that time. "I think Sylvie busted him painting graffiti on government property, and something about his demeanor caught her attention and she made it her mission to see if he was really a

48

bad kid. Turns out he wasn't, but the other boys in the foster home he was living in were. They forced him into doing things that he didn't want to do, and eventually Sylvia got all of them busted but saved the one kid."

"Saved him? How?"

"I believe she got Chappy to be his guardian, and they both sent him to military school. I think the last time that Sylvia mentioned him, he had received an art degree but was still in the service working as an agent."

"Wow! Seems Sy has been saving people all her life."

After thinking back on Sylvia's life, Quintana responds, "I guess she has. Just make sure she doesn't have to save yours."

"I think she may already have," Qasean says somewhat under his breath.

"What was that?"

"Uh . . .," stammers Qasean, "Nothing." Quickly wanting to change the subject, he asks, "When's the last time you went by Sy's place? Should we go make sure everything is ready for her when she leaves the hospital?"

Never having thought about that, Ana replies, "Oh my God!! I didn't even think about that! We need to go to the grocery store and make sure she has the basics on hand." She smacks herself in the forehead, "What in world was I thinking?"

Qasean reaches over and squeezes her hand, "You were thinking that your friend was home, and you wanted to make sure she was okay and catch up. No need to be hard on yourself."

Quintana leans over and gives him a kiss on the cheek, "You're a great big brother." Then she settles back in her seat for the ride to the grocery store, however, she can't help but be saddened a little about the fact that Chance isn't a brother to Sylvia like Qasean is to her. She then shrugs her shoulders, and chalks it up to the fact they are twins and even though they are not identical twins they still bonded during their nine months in their mother's womb.

*****

After getting the basics from the grocery store, they arrive at Sylvia's apartment and open the windows to air out the place and stock her fridge and cabinets with the food that they have purchased. Qasean helps Quintana make the bed, and he vacuums while she dusts. Once their tasks are complete, they head back to their parent's house where Qasean drops off Quintana before heading to gym to work out.

Snake Chaser

Release

A week after her arrival at the medical center, Sylvia is cleared to be released and Qasean happens to be in her room when the news is delivered.

"What time will she be ready to be wheeled out of here," asks Qasean before Sylvia could open her mouth.

"The doctor is writing up her discharge instructions right now, so I would say that she should be ready to go within the hour," answers the discharge nurse.

"Great! I'll leave to move my car around to the entrance in about forty-five minutes, and then you can bring her down. Okay?"

"Sounds good to me. See you shortly."

At first Sylvia was stunned at how quickly Qasean spoke up, but now she's furious about the conversation that took place between him and the nurse as though she wasn't even in the room.

Qasean turns towards Sylvia with a big smile on his face to ask her if she needed help with anything while she waited for her discharge papers, however, the scowl on her face quickly wipes the smile from his. He rushes to her side, "What's wrong Sweetheart," he asks concerned that maybe she's not quite ready to be discharged.

Seething, Sylvia states between clenched teeth, "What gives you the right to make arrangements for me?"

Slightly confused by her anger, Qasean tilts his head to the side as he studies her face and it's not long before his own anger rises. He moves till he is nose to nose with her before responding, "The fact that I'm you're first and only lover gives me the right, not to mention you're my sister's best friend and she would blister my ears if I didn't make sure you got home and settled in."

Not one to ever back down, Sylvia maintains her anger and her position when responding to his comments, "It was only one time. Don't make it seem like it is more than it really was, and I had planned on calling your sister to pick me up and take me home."

Not wanting to debate the importance of her giving him her virginity, he decides to skip over her first statement and concentrate on the second. "We can call Ana once we get you settled in. She and I already aired out your place and stocked it with groceries the other day, so you shouldn't need anything for a few days. And since we need to have that conversation you keep putting off, I think it would be better if it were just the two of us when we get back to your place." He looks at her with a challenge in his eyes knowing that she would never back away from it.

"Fine," she states through her clenched teeth knowing that he knows he backed her into a corner. She sits there on the bed stewing in her anger as she waits for her discharge papers and the wheelchair that will take her to freedom.

Snake Chaser

Qasean lets her stew, but he fully intends to have that talk regardless of how much Sylvia wants to avoid it. He looks at his watch and sees that it's time to move his car around, so he looks at her as he says, "Don't try anything sneaky while I'm getting the car." Sylvia rolls her eyes, and Qasean laughs as he exits her room.

As if perfectly timed, the nurse is wheeling Sylvia out of the door just as Qasean pulls up to the entrance. While the nurse is helping her into the car, Qasean puts her belongings in the trunk. Once he's back in the driver's seat, he looks over at her and asks, "Ready?"

She glares at him while mumbling, "Would it matter if I wasn't?"

"No," responds as he puts the car in gear and pulls away from the hospital, and Sylvia continues to glare at him.

They make the drive to her apartment in silence, each lost in their own thoughts. She doesn't want to think about let alone talk about what happened between them in her hideout in South America, and that's all he can think about. When they arrive at her place, she lets out a sigh of relief as she believes she has figured out a way to avoid talking to him. She will play like the journey to her apartment was a bit much, and that she is tired and needs to rest. He too lets out a sigh of relief as he is finally going to have her alone, and he has no intentions of letting her blow him off.

He helps her out of the car before grabbing her things from the trunk, and helping inside. Once inside, Sylvia puts her plan into action by wearily sitting on the couch, and giving a fake yawn. He ignores her while he takes her things to the bedroom, and then he sits beside her on the couch to have that talk.

However, before he can say one word she lets out another yawn before saying, "I didn't realize that I would feel this worn out from so little movement."

Knowing what she is trying to do, Qasean pretends to play along. "Well then, let me help you get comfortable so that you can rest," states Qasean as he reaches down to remove her shoes and socks. The electricity that sparks between them as he touches the bare skin of her ankle is hard for either of them to ignore. He looks her in the eyes as she emits a small gasp at his touch, and desire instantly springs to life in both of them. Not able to stop himself, Qasean leans in to kiss her and she helplessly moans at the contact. As if on cue, Qasean's tongue enters her mouth to absorb the next moan she releases. Before either of them knows it, he has her stretched out on the couch kissing her for all he's worth. Unconsciously, Qasean begins removing the sweat pants she wore home from the hospital, and Sylvia is unable to stop him for she is overwhelmed by his kisses. He picks up the scent of her arousal as he pulls the sweats off her feet, and it's an aphrodisiac he can't resist. So he begins placing kisses up the inside of her left calf, and as he reaches her inner thigh he takes a deep breath inhaling a healthy whiff of her scent. It's like a siren's call that he can't resist, and he runs a finger over the center of her and discovers that her panties are drenched. Needing to get a taste of her, his tongue follows the path his finger just traced. Sylvia moans as her hips involuntarily lift off the couch bringing her center closer to his mouth, and he takes advantage of the offering by stroking her with his tongue through her panties.

Realizing that that's not enough to satisfy his craving, he removes her panties in a swift move and plunges his tongue deep inside her. Again her hips lift off the couch giving him full access to her, and all she can do his grip his head as she moans out her pleasure. In no time at all, she is screaming his name as an orgasm crashes down her with the force of a

Snake Chaser

tsunami, but that doesn't stop him. He continues to make love to her with his lips and tongue until she finds herself caught up in another earth-shattering climax. Once the tremors of her body subside, he places a kiss on her inner thigh before looking up at her and saying, "That's twice. So do you consider me your lover now?"

Even though she is still caught up in the sensations he invoked inside of her with his loving, she responds, "No."

Little does she know that is the response he was hoping for so that he could love her some more, and he dips his head once again to partake of the taste that he has suddenly begun to crave. Sylvia is once again overwhelmed by the heat of his mouth, and makes no move to stop him from feasting upon her body. In fact that only movement she feels capable of making is thrusting her hips closer and closer to his mouth. As the tempo of her movements increase, Qasean moans out, "Yes baby . . . feed me . . . Hmmm." Having reached one orgasm already, it seems Sylvia's body is not ready to release the second one as quickly as the first, so Qasean lets his fingers join in the fun. Feeling his tongue stoking her clit while his fingers dip and swirl inside her causes Sylvia to increase the movements of her hips and tighten her grip on his head. Her actions only increase Qasean's desire to bring her to release once again, so he boldly adds another finger to her hot center as he increases the suction on the bud of her womanhood. He feels the tremors begin as another orgasm begins to take over her, and increases the stroking of his fingers and sucks her deeper into his mouth. The scream that she releases as she climaxes is pure music to his ears.

As she rides the waves of her latest orgasm, Qasean lifts his head to watch the sensations play out on her face. Once she feels as though she has finally landed back on earth after floating helplessly on love's passion, she opens her eyes to find him watching her. She tries to speak, but her throat is slightly

55

raw from all the screaming she has done as a result of his lovemaking. "That . . . wasn't . . . fair," she manages to get out despite the rawness she feels in her throat.

Smiling, Qasean replies, "Everything is fair in love, Sweetheart." And to prove his point, he begins moving the fingers that she didn't realize were still inside her. She closes her eyes and moans at the movement. "See," he asks as he continues to stroke her with his fingers while moving his thumb to stroke her clit. She raises her hips, and he asks, "Like that?" Her reply is simply a moan to which he responds, "I like it too. In fact I love it." She continues to writhe her hips to the rhythm of his fingers for he his giving her nothing but pure bliss. As her movements increase, so does the stroking of his fingers as he watches her be swept away by the sensations overtaking her body. "That's it baby. Let go. Give me one more, and I'll let you rest," he whispers as he feels her climax approaching. Unable to do anything but let go, Sylvia gives in to the orgasm and Qasean swallows her scream in a kiss that is as hot as the center of her.

Snake Chaser

Fair Play

As Sylvia recovers from her final orgasm, Qasean holds her until her breathing becomes even. When she finally opens her eyes to look at him he can see how tired their activity has made her, so he places a kiss on her forehead and tells her to rest. Sylvia simply nods at his words even though she has no intention of doing anything of the kind. Qasean gets up from the couch and heads for the kitchen to make her something to eat so that she won't have to when she wakes up.

Sylvia waits mere seconds before she leaves the couch to head in his direction, and when she enters the kitchen she finds him lounging in a chair with his head laid back against the back of the chair. It's quite obvious that he hasn't recovered from their session in the living room, and as a trained Marine she quietly walks over to him and runs her hand across the bulge in his pants. He sucks in a deep breath from her touch and opens his eyes, and the look of desire in them almost takes her breath away. Not planning on being deterred from her mission, she continues to stroke him through his pants.

Seeing her intent, Qasean grabs her hand before saying through clenched teeth, "What do you think you're doing?"

"Returning the favor," she replies as she strokes him with her other hand.

He grabs that hand as well, and that's when he notices that she is completely undressed. The sight of her bandaged waist from her surgery sobers him quickly despite what seeing her nude is doing to his throbbing manhood. "Sylvia," he says in a cautionary voice, "You are in no condition to carry out what you're contemplating."

She leans over him brushing his face with her breasts before placing her lips against his before she responds, "You didn't have a problem with my condition a few minutes ago."

"Sy," he whispers against her lips, "Don't."

She runs her tongue across his lips tasting her essence on them, and he sucks in a deep breath giving her greater access to his mouth and she takes advantage by sweeping her tongue inside. Qasean helplessly tangles his tongue with hers, and in the process lets go of her hands so that he can bury his fingers in her hair and take over the kiss. With her hands free, Sylvia proceeds to unfasten his pants and places her hand inside to caress him free of any barriers. He moans deep in his throat, and she increases the rhythm of her strokes. He takes his hands out of her hair to grab her wrists but before he can stop her, she breaks the kiss and immediately takes him in her mouth. Lost in the feel of her hot wet mouth on his throbbing member, he buries his fingers in her hair once again as she strokes him with her tongue and lips. Before he knows it he is ready come, and once she feels him on the brink of an orgasm she increases the strokes of her mouth.

He screams her name as a massive orgasm crashes down upon him. She savors of the taste of him on her lips and tongue as he watches her watching him. The smoldering look in her eyes reignites his passion, and his manhood begins surging back to

Snake Chaser

life. As she watches him expand and lengthen, she smiles as she gets up and walks from the room confident that he will follow. She's not disappointed as she looks over her shoulder to see him following behind her, and removing the rest of his clothes as he does so. Once she reaches her bedroom, she lays down on the bed with her head propped up the pile of pillows behind her. He pauses in the doorway as he just takes her in laid out on her bed for he is stunned at the intensity of his desire for her. He's never craved the feel and taste of a woman this much, and he's known her most of his life.

"Are you just gonna stand there and stare at me or are you going to join me," she asks.

Her voice shakes him out of musings, and he walks over to the bed and lies down beside her. He runs his hand over the bandage on her waist, gently fingering the white gauze. He doesn't say a word, just continues to caress the bandage and the flesh surrounding it.

"I'm fine Qasean," she whispers.

"I know you think that you're fine, but you had a serious injury Sy and I don't think we should do anything that could jeopardize your recovery."

"My time here in the hospital was just a way to keep me from over doing it when I first returned home."

"And you don't think that making love with me qualifies as overdoing it," he asks with his eyebrow cocked.

She smiles and says, "Oh I know it will qualify as overdoing it, but I've never felt this way before and I don't know how much time we'll have to be together like this once we begin training. And I for one would like to take advantage of the time we do have, despite my injury." She then leans up and runs her tongue across his lips.

That was all the encouragement that he needed. He immediately takes possession of her mouth, and kisses her with the hunger of a starving man. She returns his kiss with the same intensity, and he loses all control. He trails kisses from her lips across her cheek, and down her neck to her breasts. Her taste is driving him crazy as he sucks her plump softness into his mouth and plays with the hardened bud with his tongue. As she begins moaning from the attention he is giving her breast, he moves on to the other one to give it the same attention. It's not long before she begins gyrating her hips as her core gets hotter and wetter from the attention he is lavishing on her breasts. Her movements capture his attention, and he begins kissing a trail down her stomach to the area of her body that is craving his attention. Realizing his attentions and knowing that's not what her body wants or needs at this point, in a quick maneuver she flips him on his back and straddles his hips positioning her womanhood over his manhood as she takes in the startled look on his face.

She smiles down at him as she begins lowering her body, "This is what I want," she states as she takes him inside her body. "This is what I need," she breathlessly states as he fills her completely. She moans from deep in her throat once he is completely buried inside her body. Wanting to savor the feel of him, she remains motionless except for her inner muscles that rhythmically clench and release his manhood.

Unable to remain still any longer, Qasean grabs her hips and begins moving her up and down his throbbing member. "This is what I want," he states between clenched teeth, "What I need." Sylvia immediately takes over and begins swiveling her hips along with the up and down motion of her body, as well as, grinding her hips against his body when their bodies make contact. Afraid that he might grip her too tight, Qasean lets go of her hips and grabs the sides of the bed instead. "That's it baby . . . take what you want," he says. When he feels another orgasm coming on, he reaches between their bodies and caresses the bud of her womanhood with his thumb as he practically yells, "Come! Now!"

Unable to refuse the command or the sensations that are overtaking her body, Sylvia comes while yelling his name and he does the same. The orgasm that slams through his body is powerful, but not powerful enough to stop him from flipping her on her back and making love to her again. He becomes lost in all that he's feeling while buried inside her body, and places her legs on his shoulders as he holds his upper body off the bed on his arms. His hips pound into her body at whiplash speed as he tries to get as deep inside her as he can go. It's not long before another orgasm crashed down on both of them, and they let go again screaming each other's names.

Completely drained, Qasean falls to the side and pulls her into his arms. She lays her head on his chest as they both try to regulate their breathing and heart rates. Qasean is the first to speak, "You didn't play fair."

"Everything is fair in love Sweetheart," is her response.

Realizing those were his words to her in the living room, all he can do is smile and shake his head. "You need to rest," he states as he pulls her closer to him. In no time at all she is fast asleep. He continues to hold her close to his heart as he contemplates what he is feeling. Never has he had this reaction to a woman before, and he can't for the life of him figure out why he's having it with Sylvia.

ReGina Crawford

Revelations

Needing to analyze what is happening between himself and Sylvia, Qasean gets out of the bed and places her under the covers. He then heads to the kitchen to retrieve his clothes, and get dressed. Knowing that she is going to be hungry when she wakes up, he proceeds to make her something to eat before he takes his leave of her apartment since he didn't get around to it the last time he entered her kitchen.

Once inside his car, Qasean looks up at her apartment windows before laying his head on his steering wheel. '*What the hell is going on with me,*' he thinks to himself. However, before he can answer his own question, there is a tap on his window. Startled and a little embarrassed at being caught like this, he snaps his head up with force while sending an evil glare to the person intruding upon his thoughts. However, once he recognizes the intruder as his sister, he relaxes somewhat and rolls down the window.

"Are you okay Qasean," asks Quintana.

Heaving a weary sigh, he responds, "Yes, I'm fine."

Knowing her twin almost as well as she knows herself, Quintana is not buying his response. "If you are fine, why do I see worry in your face," she asks. Upon further inspection of

Snake Chaser

his face, she adds, "And some guilt as well?" However, before he can respond to either question, she asks a third, "Did you upset Sylvia?" She further adds, "Damn, Qasean! How upset is she?"

"I did not upset Sy," he replies. "In fact I left her sleeping rather soundly."

Quickly interpreting his meaning and the guilt and worry she sees in his face, she smiles before saying, "She finally got you, huh?"

He quirks his eyebrow at his sister before asking, "What do you mean she finally got me?"

She shakes her head while saying, "Men are so dense. She's been in love with you since we were fourteen, and has been waiting for you notice her all these years."

"What," he practically yells.

"Sorry to spring it on you like this bruh, but it's the truth. And I know she will never tell you since she doesn't want to become too attached to anyone with her track record of her loved ones either checking out on her or dying."

"Shit," he all but yells. "What the hell am I supposed to do now," he asks more of himself than his sister.

"Tread lightly would be my advice." Not wanting or liking her advice, Qasean turns an evil eye to his sister. She laughs before saying, "Don't give me that look! I didn't get you into this mess, and I hope you put together a well thought out plan to keep yourself from getting into hot water with her."

He drops his head back to the steering wheel, mumbling, "Shit! Shit! Shit!"

"Go get some rest brother. I'll go upstairs and make her something to eat for when she wakes up."

"I've already taken care of that," Qasean says absently.

Now it's Quintana's turn to quirk her eyebrow, "Really now," she says as more of a statement than a question.

"Don't start Ana," is his response.

"Go on home. I'll check in on Sylvia a little later since she probably needs her rest."

Qasean doesn't say another word, puts his car in gear, and heads to his parent's home instead of the barracks as he needs some quiet time to process everything that has taken place today. Quintana watches him drive away before going up to Sylvia's apartment anyway. She knows that Sylvia is going to need someone to talk to when she wakes up, so she'll read the book she brought along until that time.

*****

Sylvia wakes up several hours later not at all surprised to see Qasean missing from her bed, so she dons a robe and heads for her kitchen. However, she stops short when she sees Ana on her couch reading a book. "Ana," she begins, "I didn't expect to see you here."

"I just bet you didn't," replies Quintana around the smile she is unable to stop from spreading across her face.

"What's that supposed to mean," asks Sylvia as she heads towards the kitchen for she is starving.

Snake Chaser

Instead of answering Sylvia's question, she states, "Qasean left you meatloaf, potatoes, and green beans on the stove."

Sylvia stops dead in her tracks. She looks over her shoulder at her friend, and based on the smile on her face she knows that her friend knows what transpired between herself and Qasean. Deciding that she needs a full stomach to have the conversation that she is sure that Ana wants to have, she continues on to the kitchen to make herself a plate of food.

Quintana follows her into the kitchen, and takes a seat at the table while Sylvia fixes her plate. Sylvia chooses to ignore her while she eats her food, and Quintana is perfectly content to wait for her to finish eating before they have their talk.

Once Sylvia has finished her meal, she pours her and Ana a glass of wine before sitting back down at the table. "Okay, go," is all Sylvia says before taking a long sip from her glass.

"Go? That's all you're going to say? Go."

"Yep! That's it. Nothing more."

"Fine! How did you and Qasean end up having sex today? How did he react to you being a virgin? Are you still a virgin? Are you two getting together? Or was this a one night stand so to speak?"

Sylvia shakes her head at the barrage of questions that flow from Ana's lips. "See now why I said go?"

Ana laughs at herself, "Okay! Okay," she states as she hold her hands up in mock surrender. "You got me! But we haven't talked since you got back, and when I saw Qasean as he was leaving his face gave away that you two had slept together and that he was battling his feelings . . . ," her voice trails off as she remembers what she said to Qasean outside.

"I know that look Ana," begins Sylvia feeling a sense of dread overtaking her. "What did you say to Qasean?"

"Um . . . Uh . . . Er . . . I'm not sure how to say this."

"Just spit it out!"

"Okay," responds Ana in a desperate voice. "I told him you've been in love with him since you were fourteen," she states. Then adds on a rush, "I'm sorry. It just came out."

Sylvia simply drains her glass of wine and pours herself another. She takes another long drink from the glass before speaking, "Well I guess I don't have to worry about him coming back here now."

"Why would you say that," asks Ana.

"One sure way to make a man turn tail and run is to tell him you love him after only sleeping with him twice, and I don't think it matters that it didn't come directly from my lips."

"Twice? So this wasn't the first time?"

"No. We slept together when we were on assignment in South America, and yes I was a virgin, and yes he was surprised that I was a virgin the first time."

Ana blows out a long breath before taking a drink from her glass, and then says, "I don't think you have to worry about him turning tail and running. He seems to be struggling with his feelings after he left here, and I know once he figures them out he'll be back."

"I know you two are twins and all, but I don't think you know what you're talking about."

Snake Chaser

"We'll see," is all Ana says before taking another drink from her glass.

Question

Not wanting Sylvia to dwell on what Qasean's next move would be, Ana starts asking questions about what Sylvia has been up to since they last saw each other and it is effective in getting Sylvia's mind off of Qasean. After an hour or so of conversation, Sylvia begins yawning and Ana can tell that she needs rest.

"I think it's time you went back to bed and got some rest, so I will see you tomorrow," states Ana as she gets up from the table.

"Sorry girl. I guess I'm a little worn out. Thanks for hanging out with me. I have missed you." They hug before Ana heads for the door and Sylvia heads for her bedroom.

However, before she can get in the bed, she hears a knock at her door. "Who in the devil could this be," she asks herself. "Ana has a key so it can't possibly be her," she adds.

"Who is it," she asks as she reaches the door.

"Qasean," states the voice on the other side of the door.

Shocked that he has returned, she snatches the door open. "What are you doing back here," she asks in a voice a little harsher than warranted as she wonders if Ana saw him returning.

Instead of answering her question, he walks in the door forcing her back into the apartment. He closes the door behind him and locks it before he says one word. "Ana didn't see me, and she won't see my car," he states as though he is completely aware of what is irritating her for he is sure that it's not him. Once he gives her his full attention, he realizes that she is wearing a robe and nothing else and to make matters worse her nipples are hard and pressing against the satin fabric of that robe.

Unable to stop himself, he leans in and captures a nipple between his lips. Unable to stop herself, Sylvia moans from deep in her throat as she grabs the sides of his head. Neither is sure if she intends to push him away or hold him place. Deciding that he doesn't want her to push him away, he sucks her breast deeper into his mouth without even pushing the robe aside. Deciding she doesn't want him to stop either, she frees her other breast from the robe hoping he will switch to it so that she can feel the heat and pull of his mouth on her bare flesh. He doesn't disappoint. While he's focused on the breast she bared, Sylvia unbelts the robe and lets it fall to the floor. Qasean welcomes the freedom to explore her bare flesh from head to toe, and wastes no time doing just that. Before either of them knows it, he's stripping himself out of his clothes and picking her up off the floor. She instinctively wraps her legs around his waist, and he backs them up to the nearest wall as he impels her hot wet flesh with his hard throbbing flesh. He loves her fast and furious up against the wall until they are both screaming each other's names.

Weak from the explosive orgasm she just experience, Sylvia lets her legs drop from his waist and as her feet hit the floor he has to hold her up to keep her from sliding down the wall to the floor herself. Once he has regained a semblance of strength, he picks her up and carries her to the couch and sits placing her in his lap. They sit in silence as they attempt to calm their breathing and heart rates.

Qasean is the first to speak, "Is what Ana told me true?" Sylvia takes a deep breath as she buries her face in his chest. She doesn't answer, she just nods her head. Even though she knows there's no point in denying it, she can't bring herself to say the words. Qasean lifts her chin so that he can look in her eyes, "Say it," he whispers. She closes her eyes, and he whispers again, "Say it." When she doesn't open her eyes or a say a word, he gently says, "Open your eyes." When she doesn't immediately comply, he softly says, "Look at me and say it."

She opens her eyes and finds herself looking into the depths of his eyes and she feels compelled to respond. "I love you. It seems as though I have loved you forever."

Overwhelmed by her words, Qasean is unable to do anything but capture in her lips in a slow, mind drugging kiss. The kiss doesn't last long, and when he lifts his head he asks, "How did I not know this?"

"I didn't want you know," she responds in voice that hints at that that should have been obvious.

"Why not?"

"Qasean you know why not," she begins. At the arching of his eyebrow, she adds as further explanation, "I can't handle another emotional roller coaster." His eyebrow remains arched, so she continues, "You're a Marine. At anytime you could go into battle and never return, and that's something that my heart and mind can no longer endure. I lost my mother and father in battle, my brother to The Core, and then Uncle Chappy. I cannot, will not suffer another emotional loss, so I

70

Snake Chaser

have keep my feelings for you locked deep inside me," she pauses briefly before continuing. "And had I known Ana would spill her guts, I never would have told her."

Processing all that she has said, Qasean remains silent and simply stares in her eyes as though he is trying to explore her soul. When she tries to close her eyes to prevent him from looking deeper inside her, he grips her chin a little tighter. After a few more minutes, he softly states, "I'm glad I know." He places a gentle kiss on her forehead. "You effect me like no one ever has, and I'm not sure what that means but I want to find out." He pulls her into his body and holds her close as he adds, "Since we connected in South America, you're all I can think about. I'm not sure where we are headed, but know that I will be there beside you every step of the way."

He feels her trembling in his arms, and leans back to look at her face and sees the trail of tears that are cascading down her face. He kisses each one away knowing that she's just as scared as he is of what the future holds for them. Once her tears stop flowing, he pulls her back into his body and just holds her until she falls asleep. He then carries her to the bedroom and puts her to bed, and he gets in beside her content to just hold her close to his heart while she sleeps.

An hour or so later, she awakens to find herself still wrapped in his arms and he's still wide-awake. "Hi," she shyly states.

"Hi," responds.

"What are you thinking," she asks as he simply stares in her eyes.

"How at this moment you are so different from the warrior I saw in the jungles of South America."

"Different in what way?"

"I'm seeing a softness and gentleness that you did not display in the jungle. I can also sense that you are unsure of yourself when it comes to me."

"I've never been involved with a man before, so I'm not sure how this works."

A small smile appears on his lips as he remembers that she was a virgin the first time that he made love to her. "For someone who's never been involved before, you seem to know exactly how to bring me to the heat and height of passion very quickly. How is that possible?"

She gives him an answering smile before replying, "I'm not sure. I do know that my body has never reacted to anyone the way it has reacted to you. Do want to explain to me why that is?"

"I'm not sure why that is," he responds. "Maybe our bodies are trying to force our hearts and minds to face the fact that we have an intangible connection to one another, and that we should stop ignoring it, avoiding it."

"And how do you propose we do that if we are working together in the same unit?"

Qasean is silent for he had forgotten that they would be a part of the same unit once she's cleared for duty. "I'm not sure," he states, "but we'll find a way to make it work." He remains quiet for a while as he thinks, then he states, "Right now, all I want to do is hold you and cherish the feel of you in my arms." He then hugs her a little tighter.

As Qasean holds her in his arms, Sylvia snuggles closer to him and the movement of her bare flesh against his causes his body part that is all male to awaken and she feels it flex against her stomach and her muscles quiver in response. When Qasean makes no move to make love to her, she asks, "What do you plan to do about him?"

"What would you like me to do about him," asks Qasean in return with detectable humor in his voice.

Instead of answering, Sylvia reaches between their bodies and takes him firmly in her hand while caressing the head of him with her thumb. Qasean is stunned and unable to resist her touch. When she receives no words of protest from him, Sylvia assumes that he is surrendering to her, and before he knows it he's flat on his back and her mouth is consuming his throbbing manhood. He lets her have her have her way, and simply grips the side of the bed to keep from burying his hands in her hair while biting his lip to keep the moans he feels building up in his chest from escaping. However, despite being a novice, she soon has him losing all control as his orgasm crashes down on him and carries him off on an uncontrollable wave of passion and he screams her name.

Loving the sound of her name rolling of his lips, Sylvia is close to her own climax and impels herself with his manhood which instantly comes back to life. He grabs her hips to guide her down the path of orgasmic bliss. Spent Sylvia collapse on his chest and is soon sleep. Qasean wraps his arms around her, and is soon sleep as well.

Back To Work

Over the last week, Qasean and Sylvia spend as much time together as his schedule allows getting to know each other all over again while she continues to heal from her injury, and now it is time for them both to report to duty with Sylvia's brother Chance.

They both show up at the training facility at the same time, and find it hard not to show how close they are to the rest of the team. Chance introduces each one of the team members outlining their special skills and why each one was chosen for the team. Qasean and Sylvia are both surprised to learn that they possess some of the same skills, and will be working closely with each other.

Chance then proceeds to brief them on the team's purpose, and the type of training they will go through before entering the field. The next order of business is to familiarize the team with the country's most wanted criminals since that's whom they will be 'hunting' on their missions. The next six hours are spent going through video surveillance and audio of conversations captured of the criminals so they are able to identify them via sight and sound.

Finally Chance calls an end to the day and tells the team they may leave the facility, however, he asks Sylvia to remain behind. Not wanting to give anything away, Qasean files out of the room with the rest of the team, however, he is deeply interested in why Chance wants Sylvia to remain behind. He sincerely hopes that Chance doesn't upset his woman. *'Whoa!'* His mind screams. *'When did you start thinking of Sylvia as your woman?'* He has no idea when the transition occurred, however, he's not backing away from it. With his mind made up, he heads to Sylvia's place instead of back to the barracks with the other members of the team.

"Sgt. Williams," begins Chance, "how is recovery coming after your injury?"

"I am fully recovered, and quite capable of fulfilling my duties on the team if that's what you're worried about."

"That's good to know for these missions will be quite gruesome, and there will probably be little time for down time in between them. Once one major player is taken down, the others usually start scrambling for cover just in case they are next on the list for a taken down."

"I understand, and I believe that I am up to the tasks at hand."

"Great! I'll see you in the AM with the rest of the team."

Knowing that she's been dismissed, Sylvia turns and leaves the facility.

Chance watches her go, and wonders about the distance between them emotionally. He recently did a self-evaluation and found himself lacking in the area of personal involvement with others. His whole life has been centered around being a Marine, however, he has found himself in need of human companionship lately and wonders if he can reconcile with his sister as she is the only family that he has left.

Sylvia too is wondering if she and her brother will ever be anything more than team members in the Marines, however, she is not going to dwell on their relationship for she knows that no answers will be forth coming.

When she arrives at her apartment, she is somewhat surprised to see Qasean leaning against her door. However, she doesn't say a word and just opens the door, and walks inside knowing he will let will follow and let her know what's on his mind once they are inside.

Qasean closes the door behind him, and asks, "So what did Chance want?"

"He just wanted to make sure that I was capable of handling my duties on the missions since they will be grueling and there will be little down time between them."

Qasean nods his head, and then asks, "How do you feel about us working closely together on these missions?"

"We are Marines. We know how to push our personal feelings aside and carry out our duties. I have no qualms about us working together."

"Are you sure that we will be able to be in close proximity to each other without your body reacting to mine," he asks with humor in voice.

"Are you sure that you will be able to be in close proximity to me without your body reacting to mine," she asks as her eyes catch the growth that is emerging behind his zipper.

He simply smiles at her as he walks in her direction with mischief glowing in his eyes, "I guess I'm just going to have to get my fill of you before we embark on these missions," is his response.

Snake Chaser

She shakes her head at him, and when he stops in front of her she caresses his growing manhood while asking, "Are you sure that's possible?"

He starts undressing her as he says, "There's only way to find out."

They undress each other and they embark on a déjà vu love making session as he takes her up against the wall before taking her to the bedroom and making love to her again. Once he's able to breathe normally again, he tells her to get some rest and then leaves for the barracks. Feeling like a limp rag doll, Sylvia doesn't complain and simply goes to sleep.

*****

The next morning, they are back at the training facility and learn that they will be undergoing some mock drills on the terrain they will be covering during the missions. Qasean and Sylvia change into their camouflage gear and head to the training site where they find themselves traipsing through some dense rainforest foliage, and the temperature is eighty degrees and it's raining cats and dogs. They must maintain their cover and tread silently so as not to alert anyone to their presence while maintaining their footing. The ground is slippery and muddy, but they are able to navigate it with their specially made shoes. They successfully complete their mission, but are a muddy mess when they arrive back at the training facility.

"Good job today Marines," states Chance. "Go get cleaned up, and I will see everyone in the AM for the next mock drill." Even though he doesn't say it, Chance is truly impressed with his sister and her ability to perform her duties.

After getting showered and dressed, Sylvia heads home. As she approaches her door, she is surprised to see someone leaning against her door. When she realizes that it's Chance, she's even more surprised. She doesn't say a word as she opens the door and enters her apartment knowing that he will follow her inside the same way that Qasean did yesterday.

Once inside, she asks, "Why the visit?"

"You're my sister. I can't come visit?"

"I'm not saying that, but you haven't paid me a visit in over ten years. So excuse me if I'm a little surprised by the visit," she responds somewhat sarcastically.

Chance lowers his head for a second before looking her dead in the eyes, "I'm sorry about that," he begins. "But even though I haven't come to see you personally, I have kept close tabs on your every movement. I am very proud of the woman and Marine that you have become, and I know that Mom and Dad would be just as proud. As well as, Uncle Chappy."

The mere mention of the three people she loved most in this world causes a stream of tears to cascade down her face. Chance wastes no time in gathering her into his arms and rocking her while whispering, "I didn't mean to make you cry." When she begins to cry harder, he pulls her closer and just stands there holding her until her tears stop. "Are you okay," he asks as he leans back to look at her face.

"I'm sorry about that," she states as she backs out of his arms while wiping her face with her hands. "No one has mentioned them to me in years and you're the one thread that connects me to them, so I just became a little overwhelmed at you saying they would be proud of me." Her voice trails off as she heads to the kitchen to grab a cold beer from the fridge. When she

Snake Chaser

sees him standing in the doorway to her kitchen, she holds up the bottle and asks, "Want one?"

"Sure," he replies as he walks in the room and takes a seat at the table. He opens the bottle and takes a long swig before asking, "You don't think that they would be proud of you?"

"I don't think that I've ever thought about it," she answers. She takes a drink from her bottle before saying anything more. "After Uncle Chappy died, I think I shut off all of my emotions and just concentrated on being the best Marine that I could be. It seemed that was all that I had left."

"Whoa," states Chance. "I was still here."

"I couldn't tell."

Chance once again drops his head, this time in shame for he realizes for the first time that his sister didn't believe that she could come to him. "I'm sorry that I wasn't there for you over the years," he begins. "I had a plan for my career as a Marine, and was determined not to let anything distract me from accomplishing my goals," he continues. "It wasn't until recently that I took stock of my life, and realized that I have no personal connections to anyone. But know that I have always loved you and watched over you. I am so very proud of you Sis," he concludes. He sees tears forming in her eyes again at his words, and sits his bottle on the table before getting up and going to her. He pulls her into his arms as he says, "It seems everything I say makes you cry."

Second Chance

"I don't think I've cried this much since Chappy died," responds Sylvia. "Having you near, talking with you is making me realize how so much a like we are in terms of how we have structured our lives," she continues. "I too have remained emotionally unattached from people with the exception of Quintana. She's the only person who I feel has been a constant in my life."

"Quintana?"

"Qasean's twin sister."

"Ahh. That explains the closeness I sense between the two of you."

"Excuse me," she states as she steps out of his embrace and takes her seat. Her legs are feeling a little shaky as she wonders just what he has detected about her relationship with Qasean.

"You two seem to be very comfortable with each other, and I know that you have only been on one mission together so I was wondering how the two of you could be so in tune with each other so quickly," he states. "But if you are close with his twin, then it makes sense that you would be close with him as well, especially if they are very close with each other," he adds.

"Yes they are very close, and he was always around when I went to visit Ana," she states in hopes that he will leave it at that and not try to delve deeper into her connection to Qasean. She would hate to jeopardize either one of their careers by revealing too much of their relationship to her brother since he is also their commanding officer.

"Well I'm glad that you have had someone in your life that you have been able to bond with. I unfortunately haven't done that in my life, and now I'm beginning to wonder if I did the right thing." He stops talking and appears to be contemplating his life. "I think that's why I took up command of this special team," he begins again. "Sitting behind a desk for the past six months had me in a state of flux since I didn't have anyone close to me to spend time with. My entire life my time has been spent with the men in my unit or under my command, and I never took the time to cultivate personal relationships with any of them." He pauses again, contemplating his next words. "That's also why I'm here today, I would like to get to know you personally. Not as someone under my command, not as a Marine, but as my sister."

Again tears flow from Sylvia's eyes, and Chance finds himself going to her and pulling her into his embrace. "Are you going to spend the whole time crying," he asks light heartedly.

Sylvia laughs through her tears while shaking her head no. "I would very much like to get to know you as my brother and not just my commanding officer."

Chance squeezes her close while saying, "Thanks Sy." They step out of their embrace, and Sylvia arches an eyebrow at the use of her nickname. "Although you may not be aware of it, I've always called you that."

"I had no idea," she says with the sound of tears in her voice.

"I'm going to quit talking if everything that I say is going to make you cry," he says while smiling.

Sylvia laughs as she says, "I'm sorry for being such a cry baby, but I'm just overwhelmed by you being here and us talking like this. I've wanted this for so long, and I never thought that it would happen."

"I'm sorry it's taken this long for us to get here," responds Chance with a sober expression on his face.

"Don't be sorry. We made it here, and that's what counts," replies Sylvia with the same sober expression.

They sit back at the table, and catch up on each other's lives for the next couple of hours.

*****

Shortly after Chance leaves, there's a knock on Sylvia's door, and she wonders if Chance has returned. She looks through the peephole, and sees Qasean on the other side of the door. She opens the door, but before she can say a word Qasean is asking, "What did Chance want?" She arches her eyebrow at the gruff way he asks the question. "Sorry . . .," he begins but his voice trails off as he notices the puffiness of her eyes and knows that she has been crying. He closes the door behind him with a slam. "What the hell did he say to make you cry," he asks in an angry tone.

"First you need to check the tone of your voice," responds Sylvia in an equally angry voice. "Second, you have no right to question me about anything, and especially what occurs between my brother and me."

She takes a deep breath before speaking again, however, Qasean speaks before she can. "The hell yeah I have the right to question my woman about anyone who makes her upset," he says at a near yell.

"NO . . .," begins Sylvia but her voice trails off as what he has said registers in her brain. "Your woman," she asks in a near whisper.

Qasean pulls her into his arms and holds her tight before looking in her eyes, "Yes, my woman. You have taken over my heart and mind and now you are mine, and I will not tolerate anyone upsetting you. No One!"

His words effectively dampen her anger, and Sylvia smiles at him before speaking, "Well you'll be happy to know that they were tears of happiness. He wanted us to get to know each other as brother and sister, and not as Marines."

"Really," asks Qasean surprised by her words.

"Really."

He pulls her tight against him once more before saying, "That's great Sweetheart. I'm glad he wants to start a relationship with you outside of being your commanding officer."

"Me too. I wanted that for so long but never thought that it would happen, but it seems as though it will now." She takes a slight pause before continuing, "It seems we both have been living our lives devoid of emotional attachments, and he has reached a point in his life that he wants to have a close relationship with someone who is not just a Marine to him. So he came here to ask me for a second chance to be my brother."

"I'm happy for you Sy," he states before capturing her lips in a breath-stealing kiss. Consumed by the heat of the kiss, they immediately begin removing each other's clothes and make love at a frantic pace.

Snake Chaser

Love vs. Family

The next day as they are going through their training at the compound, Qasean has to fight hard to keep his feelings for Sylvia from showing on his sleeve or on his face. Accustomed to keeping her feelings under wraps, Sylvia has no problems with not giving away her feelings for him and it rubs him the wrong way. At the end of day, before Qasean can approach Sylvia, Chance asks her to have dinner with him and she agrees. Qasean leaves the facility slightly pissed that Chance got to her first.

Sylvia and Chance have dinner before going back to his place to pick up a gift he has for her. When they arrive at his apartment, Chance tells her to have a seat on the couch while he goes in the back room to retrieve her gift. He returns with what appears to be a shoebox, and Sylvia cocks her head to the side confused by the box. "There are no shoes in the box sis," he says on a chuckle.

Sylvia blows out the breath she didn't know that she was holding before chuckling herself. "That's good to know," she says on another laugh. "I was a little nervous when I first saw the box."

Chance, still chuckling, sits down beside her and removes the lid from the box and reveals a photo album. Sylvia lifts the album from the box, and flips it open. She lets out a small gasp as she sees a picture of her parents on their wedding day. She loving runs her hand over the photo before flipping the pages, and they reveal a time line of her parents' lives together, as well as, the births of Chance and herself. As she continues to flip through the pages, silent tears run unchecked down her cheeks. Chance's face is moist from his own tears as his sister looks at the pictures that he has had years to peruse at his leisure.

When she reaches the last page, she turns to him and mouths the words thank you. Understanding the emotions that she is feeling, Chance takes the album from her lap and places it back in the box before pulling her into a huge hug. "So as you can see I have tried to preserve as much of our lives as I was able," he states while holding her. "That album is yours and I have an identical one."

"You have no idea how much this means to me," states Sylvia while still encompassed in his embrace. "I have no pictures of any of us, and Mom and Dad's images have long faded from my mind so this is truly an awesome gift."

"I'm glad that I could give it to you."

"It's getting late, so I should probably be heading home," states Sylvia still slightly overwhelmed by the gift of the photo album.

"Yes it is, and you have a hectic day ahead of you tomorrow," responds Chance.

They hug once more, then Sylvia places the lid back on its box before picking it up from the table and heading home. Once she arrives there, she finds Qasean leaning against the door to

Snake Chaser

her apartment. "Am I always going to come home to find you leaning up against my door?"

"Only when I don't come home with you," he states as she stops in front of him. Looking in her face, he notes that she has been crying again. "Why is it that every time you spend time with Chance I find you with red puffy eyes from crying," he asks with a tinge of anger in his voice.

Not liking the tone of his voice and not wanting to argue with him in the hallway, Sylvia unlocks her door and walks in knowing that he will follow behind her and close the door. She set the box down on the table before turning to him with her hands on her hips, "Why is it that every time Chance comes up in conversation between us, there is always a hint of anger in your tone," she asks with eyes flashing.

"Because he seems to always make you cry and I don't like it!"

She takes a good hard look at him and sees that he seems to be struggling with his emotions, so she squints her eyes at him as she asks, "And just why do you just assume that they are tears of sadness instead of tears of joy?"

"Because I know how much you cried for him when your parents passed."

"What," Sylvia yells. "How do you know that?"

"I would over hear you when you would cry on Ana's shoulder about how you had no family, and how you longed to have a brother just like she did. Why do you think I never minded when you hung out wherever I was?" He pauses before adding, "I wanted to keep you from crying, just as I want to keep you from crying now." His words effectively douse her rising anger, and a fresh wave of tears run down her cheeks.

He pulls her into his arms and cradles her head on his chest. "Sssh! Sssh! Why are you crying?"

"Because," she responds around the knot in her throat, "that has to be the sweetest thing you've ever said to me."

"Baby, I love you and never want to see you cry unless they are tears of joy." Sylvia goes instantly still which causes Qasean to lean back and look at her, "What's wrong Sweetheart," he asks as he sees the look of shock on her face.

"Wh . . . wha . . . what did . . . you just . . .say," stammers Sylvia.

Instantly aware of what has caused her to go into shock, Qasean lifts her chin with his thumb and forefinger, looks her dead in the eyes, and repeats his earlier words, "Baby I love you."

As the tears continue to flow down her cheeks, she whispers his name before kissing him. He accepts her kiss with all the love that he has for her, but when he feels his manhood coming to life he pulls back because she hasn't said how she feels or why she was crying before she arrived.

Stunned that he ended the kiss, Sylvia looks at him with a confused look on her face. He caresses her cheek while saying, "Sweetheart, I just confessed that I love you but you haven't said how you feel."

She covers his hand with hers before stating, "Sweetheart, I love you as well. I thought you knew that."

"I know that you had a school girl crush on me as a teenager, but I have no way of knowing if that has grown into love now that we are adults." He pauses before adding, "Unless you tell me."

Snake Chaser

"I have never stopped loving you, and yes I loved you even back then."

Qasean kisses her while lifting her off her feet, and carries her to the sofa. When the need to breathe is paramount he releases her mouth, and as he looks in her eyes he remembers that she had been crying prior to reaching her front door. "Why were you crying before you arrived," he asks in a gentle voice.

Sylvia removes herself from his embrace, and reaches for the box that she placed on the table earlier. As she removes the photo album from the box and opens it, she states, "This is why I was crying." She continues to flip through the pages, and fresh tears run down her face as she does so. "I didn't have any pictures of us prior to tonight, and the fact that Chance kept these pictures and made us matching photo albums really touched me. And that is why I was crying."

Qasean is so moved by the gesture that he pulls Sylvia into his embrace and kisses the tears from her face while saying, "Well I am glad to know that they were indeed tears of joy this time."

"They were." She pauses before asking, "So will you stop showing so much animosity towards Chance?"

"That's easier said than done, Sweetheart. One photo album does not make up for all the years that he was not there for you."

"But he's trying now. Doesn't that count for something?"

"Only time will tell."

"I'm trying to get to know the only blood family that I have left. Can't you understand that?"

"I understand. I'm just not ready to forget his neglect as easily as you seem to be."

Sylvia dislodges herself from his embrace, "He had his reasons for not being there in the past, but he's trying to make up for it now."

"There is no reason or excuse to neglect one's family, especially when they were left all alone by a tragedy."

"Are you serious," Sylvia asks with a glare on her face. Qasean simply stares at her without saying a word. Sylvia runs a hand down her face, "Maybe you should head home now," she states.

Unable to believe the anger that she is showing him, Qasean stands and heads for the door as he states, "Maybe you're right." He then walks out the door slamming it behind him.

Snake Chaser

Stubborn

"The nerve of him," Sylvia yells to the empty room. She begins pacing back and forth as her anger builds. "I've wanted this closeness with Chance all my life, and he knows that! You would think that he would be happy for me instead of pouting like a spoiled brat! UUUUGGGHHH! MEN!"

She then heads to the kitchen and grabs a beer from the fridge. She guzzles half the bottle in one drink. Pissed that the night has ended on such a sour note, she heads to the bathroom to take a long hot shower before going to bed.

*****

"Damn," Qasean nearly shouts as he leaves her apartment building. "Why does she have to be so stubborn? Doesn't she know that I just want to protect her from being hurt by him again?" Qasean asks himself these questions as he gets into his car. He knows he's too pissed off to go to bed so he heads to his parent's home hoping that his sister is awake.

Quintana is just walking to the front door when Qasean pulls into the driveway, and turns as she hears his car pulling up. She waits at the door for him to get out of the car, and when she sees the look on his face she knows that she will not be going to bed as she hoped. As he reaches her side, she opens the door and then grabs his hand and leads him to the kitchen. She grabs him a beer out of the fridge, and a bottle of wine to pour herself a glass. As she sits down at the table she says, "Okay, spill it." When he cocks an eyebrow at her, she responds, "Obviously you're upset about something, so spill it."

He takes a long drink of beer before speaking, "Why doesn't she understand that I don't want to see her hurt again?"

"He's her brother, and she has always wanted to have a close relationship with him. So it stands to reason that she's going to take advantage of this opportunity to get to know him, and for him to get to know her."

Not surprised that his twin knows exactly what he's talking about, he takes another swig of beer before saying, "I know what you're saying is true, but I just can't shake this feeling that she's headed down the road to another heartbreak."

"Well you're going to have to if you don't want to have more nights like this." He cocks his eyebrow at her. "You said it yourself that she's stubborn, and if she thinks that you are standing in the way of her getting to know Chance she will not be happy with you."

Knowing that she is right, Qasean finishes his beer, kisses her on the cheek as he walks past her on his way to the trash can, and once again as he heads to the front door. He says over his shoulder, "Thanks Sis. Night."

"Night."

*****

Snake Chaser

The next day at the training facility, Sylvia is determined to ignore Qasean and is doing a pretty good job at it. In fact she is doing such a good job, that Qasean becomes almost enraged by the fact that she hasn't said one word to him or even looked his way. When it's his turn for the hand-to-hand combat exercise, he lets his anger get the better of him and takes his opponent to the mat rather hard.

His opponent is momentarily stunned, but Chance isn't. "Gunny," Chance barks in his direction. Qasean realizes what he has done, and is instantly contrite. Chance notices the instant change in his demeanor and calls an end to the exercise. However, before Qasean can leave the room, he calls out to him, "Gunny, my office now!" Chance doesn't wait for a response before turning on his heels and heading straight towards his office, confident that Qasean is right on his heels.

Once they reach his office, Chance perches himself on the corner of his desk as Qasean closes the door behind him. "What the hell is going on with you?"

Qasean wipes a hand down his face before replying, "Nothing and everything."

"What the hell is that supposed to mean?"

"It's personal Sir."

"There is no place for your personal bullshit in my training program. So either tell me what's troubling you, or handle it. Now!"

Qasean closes his eyes and takes a deep breath before looking Chance directly in the eye, "I wish I could tell you what is troubling me, but I think it would cause me more trouble than I'm already dealing with Sir." Chance cocks an eyebrow at him, and Qasean adds, "I will clear it before training tomorrow Sir. On my honor."

"Great! Now go handle what you need to handle." Chance then turns his back on Qasean as he rounds his desk to take his chair.

Knowing that he has been dismissed, Qasean exits Chance's office determined to find Sylvia and straighten things out between them. He sees her heading out the door to the parking lot, and takes off in a jog to catch up to her. He reaches her just as she is opening the door to her car. She turns and gives him a look that would make most men take a step back, however, he is not fazed by the look. Before she can say a word, he speaks, "I really need to talk to you." She cocks an eyebrow at him. "Please," he asks.

Hearing the anguish in his voice, she concedes. "Meet me at my place." A big smile breaks out on his face to the point that she smiles in return while shaking her head. She gets in the car, and he turns to head towards his own vehicle.

Sylvia is opening her door when he reaches her side. She doesn't say a word. She simply opens the door, drops her bag to the side of the door, and heads towards the kitchen. She grabs both of them a beer from the fridge, and takes a seat at the table. Once they both have taken a long drink from their bottles, she asks, "What do you need to talk to me about?"

Knowing that she is trying to hold on to the distance between them, Qasean swallows his anger along with another long swig from his bottle. "Sweetheart, I didn't mean to upset you last night." He pauses before saying, "I love you and what to protect you from ever being hurt again. By anyone. Even your brother." He places a finger across her lips before she can say whatever it is that she is about to say. "I know I have no right to come between the two of you, but Baby I'm not sure I could

94

control myself if he ever hurt you again." He removes his finger from her lips and takes hold of both of her hands, "Please tell me that you understand?"

"I understand your desire to protect me from being hurt, but that's not possible. At least not in this case," she pauses as she closes her eyes to search for the right words to express what she's feeling. "I've always wanted this, and now that I have a chance to have it I can't walk away even if it leads to heartache down the road. I need to embrace this chance to get to know the only family member that I have left in this world." She looks him directly in his eyes, "Please tell me that you understand?"

He stares in her eyes for a minute before responding, "Since I have a close relationship with my sister, I understand the need to be close to your only sibling. And since neither of you have your parents, I'm sure you need that connection even more so now." He gets up from the table and walks around it until he is standing directly in front of her. He takes both of her hands, and pulls her to her feet before taking her seat and placing her in his lap. He wraps his arms around her before speaking, "I love you and I'm sorry. Please say that you forgive me?"

She stares into his eyes for a long moment before responding, "I love you too, and there is nothing to forgive. I understand now that if you didn't love me deeply, you wouldn't have reacted the way that you did."

He softly whispers thank you before pulling her close to him and kissing her deeply. Before she knows it, he has stripped her naked and is making love to her on the kitchen table. Before the night is over he makes love to her in the living room and the shower, before making love to her one final time in her bed. They fall asleep exhausted.

Live Op

When they arrive at the training facility the next morning, they see a somber faced Chance and wonder if he knows that they spent the night making love. However, before they could speculate too much on what he knows, he makes an announcement.

"While I would like for us to continue the additional two weeks of training that I have planned, we have been given orders and will be shipping out in thirty minutes. Packed your jungle gear, and be on the tarmac in exactly thirty minutes. You will be briefed on our mission on the plane." After making the announcement Chance turns, and heads to towards his office.

Knowing that time is of the essence, the group of Marines heads to pack their gear without so much as a word to each other. They are in their seats on the plane in exactly thirty minutes. Once the aircraft is in the air, Chance stands to give them their orders. "We are headed to the Peruvian Rainforest in search of one the world's most formidable arms dealers," he begins as he hands each one of them their orders. "The man is as deadly and as fast as the Black Mamba, and can camouflage himself as well as the diamondback rattler. I'm telling you this because each one of you must be on ready alert at all times." Chance pauses as he takes the time to look into the eyes of all

Snake Chaser

six members of his team to ensure that they understand how deadly the man is that they are hunting. "In your orders, you will find the exact details of your duties while on this mission. Do not deviate from your orders for they are critical to the success of this mission." Again he pauses to make sure that his words have been completely received. "Last but not least, each of you must be aware that we may not capture our prey on this mission, but it is critical that we learn as much about him as possible so that we may shut down his whole operation." With that he takes his seat at the front of the plane leaving his team to read the briefs that they were handed.

They spend the first two hours reading their briefs and understanding their duties for the mission. They spend the next two hours of their flight planning their strategy for the mission based on each one's skill set, and their assigned roles for the mission. Before they know it, they have reached the naval carrier that will be their base of operations until nightfall at which time they will venture out into the jungles of Peru in search of their prey.

Qasean and Sylvia will be the first team to hit the shore as their expertise is in camouflage, and their task is to scout the area surrounding the compound believed to be the home base of the arms runner. As soon as night falls, they slip off the ship and swim to the shore. Once on dry land, they remove their wet suits and make their way to the part of the jungle where they are to build their underground bunker. It takes them most of the night to get this accomplished, and they are beyond fatigued once it's complete. They pull out their bedrolls and prepare to lay down for what remains of the night, for the next day they will begin scouting the land to determine how many people occupy the compound during the day, and to see if they can get a handle on what occurs at the compound during daylight hours.

However, before Qasean can go to sleep, he has one more mission to complete. Just before Sylvia makes a move to get into her bedroll, Qasean makes a move on her. Before she knows it, Qasean comes up behind her, secures her body to his by placing an arm up under hers and across her chest with his hand gently wrapped around her neck. With his other hand he grabs a handful of her hair and turns her head to face him so that he can steal whatever sound she was about to make with a kiss. He doesn't release her lips until he feels her become pliant in his arms. He then turns her to face him as he says, "I don't know when I'll get the chance to do this again, so I'm going to take advantage of this moment." He then proceeds to strip her naked before lifting her legs and placing them around his waist just as his rock solid manhood enters her in one swift thrust. Sylvia is unable to do anything but wrap her arms around his upper body and enjoy the ride. When he feels her inner walls start to flex indicating that her orgasm is upon her, her whispers in her ear, "Don't hold back. Let it go. Cum for me baby."

Unable to resist the pelvic thrusts he's giving her, Sylvia wraps her legs tighter around his waist, her arms tighter around his upper body, and lets her body have its way. Qasean captures her mouth and swallows her scream just as her climax crashes down around her and him. As the last shudder leaves her body, he thrusts deeper, faster, and releases the essence of himself inside her. Not trusting himself to hold his own weight let alone hers, he slowly lowers her legs to the ground before walking her over to her bedroll and placing her in it.

As he makes his way to his own bedroll, Sylvia turns his head in his direction and asks with a smile on her face and in her voice, "And just when did you strip your clothes off, and decide to take advantage of me?"

"When you walked past me to douse the lamps, I caught a whiff of your feminine scent and became instantly aroused, stripped down, and made my move," he responds as he crawls inside his own bedroll. "Now go to sleep. We have a mission to undertake tomorrow."

Almost completely asleep, all Sylvia says is, "Mmm Hmm." Then she is out like a light and so is Qasean, but they both have smiles on their faces.

*****

They awake in the morning with smiles on their faces, but neither of them mentions the activity of the night before as they get ready for the days mission.

Once they are dressed, they make their way out into the jungle to see what information they can gather about the compound's daily activities. As they reach the perimeter, they head in opposite directions to gather the Intel they were sent to gather.

*****

Sylvia's trek takes her to where the women and children gather to carry out the domestic chores of the compound. She makes note of the number of women and small children that live at the compound, and what chores they carry out. When they break for their siesta, she heads back to the hideout that she and Qasean erected the night before.

*****

Qasean's trek takes him to a make shift shack where men are crating guns and ammo. He makes note of the caliber of the guns and ammo, as well as, the number of men present. He too heads back to the hideout that he and Sylvia erected the night before when the men indicate that it's time for the daily siesta.

ReGina Crawford

*****

Back inside their hideout, they exchange the information that they have learned from the days scouting. Since they know that there will be no activity taking place at the compound for the next two hours, they too take a nap for they know that they will be repeating their day's trek to observe what takes place at the compound at night.

*****

They awaken a few hours later, get something to eat, and then work on their strategy for the night's mission. "Be careful when you're out tonight. We don't know who were dealing with or what they may be hiding," states Qasean. Sylvia cocks her eyebrow in what Qasean instantly knows is an angry manner, however, before she can say a word he speaks again, "I know you're experienced at this, but you might as well get use to me being overprotective because it's a part of who I am."

His words take most of the wind out of her angry sail, but she likes having the last word so she says, "Look here gunny, I'm very good at what I do, but I do appreciate your concern." She ends her statement with a smile.

All he can do is shake his head at her, and then they both burst out laughing. Once their laughter dies down, they get back to their blueprints of the compound and their mission notes as they need to be fully versed in everything about their surroundings before venturing out in complete darkness.

Several hours later with darkness covering the land, they venture out of their hideout to see what else they can learn about the group they've been sent to investigate.

Snake Chaser

While they don't see too much activity, they are able to get photos of some of the sentries guarding the compound, as well as, a few of the women they believe are used to appease the needs of the men in the main house. They return to their hideout at the appointed time to document their findings before calling it a night.

Strange Activity

The next morning they repeat their routine of scouting out the compound, and they don't observe anything more than they did the day before. They continue their surveillance for another five days, and nothing interesting takes place at the compound. They return to the carrier to report theier findings, and to replenish their supplies before venturing out into the jungle once again. They repeat the process for another three weeks with the same results, and after spending a month in the jungle they are beginning to wonder if they are ever going to see what the 'Boss' of the compound is really up to. That is until they see the main gate open, and three large trucks roll into the front yard. The trucks don't stop until they reach the end of the compound where the women are housed, so Qasean makes his way over to where Sylvia is hidden the brush. Keenly aware of the slightest movement of the earth surrounding her, Sylvia hides herself on the off chance that it's not Qasean approaching. Having keen vision, Qasean is a little unnerved that he doesn't see Sylvia as he approaches her location. Once she spots Qasean, Sylvia makes herself visible to him. Qasean breathes a sigh of relief once he spots her, and then takes up a position within fifty feet of her so that they can observe the activity taking place around the trucks.

Expecting to see crates of guns and ammo unloaded from the trucks, they are both surprised to see women being unloaded

Snake Chaser

off the trucks. They continue to watch as the women are lined up by the truck, and some of them appear to be teenage girls. Several well-dressed men come out of the compound to perform what appears to be an inspection of the women, and they are separated into two groups. One group is escorted into what appears to be the servant's quarters, while the other group is instructed to follow the men to the other part of the compound. One of the guards appears to pay the drivers of the trucks before telling them they may leave the compound. Qasean and Sylvia maintain their positions until the siesta is called, and are quite disappointed that they don't see any other activity taking place after the trucks depart.

Once they are back inside their hideout, Sylvia explodes, "Is that mother fucker trafficking women?"

"Whoa! Whoa! Relax," states Qasean as he holds up his hands.

Sylvia begins pacing back and forth mumbling under her breath as she tries to work through her anger, but it doesn't appear to be helping. So Qasean stealthily approaches her, and wraps his arms around her before she can strike out at him. She surprises him by instantly going completely still, but he's not fooled by her response and tightens his grip. "Now before you go all commando on me," he begins. "You need to calm down and I know that there is no talking to you when you're this pissed off, so I had to result to subterfuge to make you see reason," he adds.

"How were you able to sneak up on me," she asks in a stunned voice. "That's never happened to me before."

Now understanding what caused her to go still, Qasean puts a fake pout on his face, "And here I was believing that my mere touch had the ability to instantly calm you, and you burst my bubble by telling me that my getting the drop on you is what made you instantly freeze?"

Sylvia cocks her head to one side at his attempt to make light of the situation while still trying to deal with her own confusion as to how she wasn't able to detect his movements or his nearness to her.

Sensing her confusion and knowing that she must be set to rights, Qasean attempts to provide an explanation as to why she wasn't able to sense his presence. "First, we are in a secure location," he begins while looking her directly in the eyes. "Second, I am so much a part of you that my movements are in sync with yours, so you're unable to tell them apart," he continues. "And lastly, you are so pissed that you are a little off kilter."

Sylvia's head remains cocked to the side as she tries to process what he has said to her, however, after processing the events of the last few hours she comes to the conclusion that he is partly right. "Okay, I give you that we are in a secure location and that I was truly and thoroughly pissed, but that other part . . . I don't know about that." She pauses for a second before continuing, "I mean I was able to detect your movements when we were in the jungle after the trucks arrived."

"That's because we were not in a secure location, and your senses were on high alert."

"Maybe," she states as she continues to ponder the situation.

No longer fearing retaliation from her, Qasean loosens his grip on her and slowly leads her over to her bedroll, and lays her down. He lies down beside her, and wraps his arms back around her after placing her head on his chest. "Sweetheart, I think you need to understand something," he begins. "We have been connected spiritually for quite a few years even

Snake Chaser

though I tried to block that connection, and I was actually successful until that time we met in the last jungle we were in together. Now that we have both embraced each other and the love that we have for each other, that connection only gets stronger day after day. You will eventually get use to it, I know I have."

Sylvia lies there and absorbs his words and processes them in her mind, and eventually comes to the conclusion that he is right. She's not sure when or how it happened, but she's not gonna fight it. She just hopes that she can have both Qasean and Chance in her life, and it not become messy for she hates messy entanglements thus the reason she never became involved with anyone before Qasean.

Once she has resolved that issue in her mind, she switches gear back to their mission, "I thought we were tracking an arms dealer, what the hell is with the women," she asks as Qasean continues to hold her.

"That is a question I don't have an answer to," answers Qasean. "It is certainly an unexpected turn of events, and a situation we will have to keep close tabs on," he adds. After a brief pause, he states, "I suggest we get some sleep before we have to venture back out into the jungle to see what else our mystery dealer has up his sleeve." Sylvia nods her head, and they both drift off to sleep.

*****

Once again as darkness descends over the jungle, Qasean and Sylvia venture out into the jungle to see what activities are taking place at the compound. As soon as they get settled in their positions, they see another convoy of trucks enter the compound and this time they see what they were expecting the first time. Large crates are unloaded from the trucks, and when

105

the lids of a few of the crates are opened they see automatic weapons and ammo, and the side of the crates have words written on them in Russian. They take pictures of the cargo as the men move the crates inside the main house. Once again one of the guards pays the drivers, and the trucks leave the compound. They maintain their positions for several more hours and when they see no more activity taking place, they head back to their hideout.

The next morning they once again take up their positions in the jungle surrounding the compound, and are surprised to see a convoy of trucks already in the front yard. What's even more surprising is that trucks are covered in medical insignias and that the women of two days ago are dressed as medical personnel, and they are being loaded into the trucks with what appears to be medical supplies. Sylvia and Qasean both come to the conclusion that that is how the head of this organization gets his merchandise out of the jungle and out of the country. Knowing that they can't follow the trucks on their own, they head back to the hideout to close up shop and head back to the carrier to report their findings to Chance and the rest of their crew.

Snake Chaser

Downtime

Once they are back on the carrier, they brief Chance on their findings, as well as, turn over their cameras. Once Chance has had a chance to review the pictures and their reports, he calls the entire team together for a briefing.

"Based on the information retrieved by Qasean and Sylvia and that received from another agency watching docks and airstrips in the country, it seems that the arms dealer we're hunting has developed the perfect strategy for transporting weapons to his buyers," begins Chance. "His method of transport is going to make our job a little more challenging as we will not be permitted to search any medical cargo leaving the country. However, we can track its movements and pray that it ends up in a country that will cooperate with us in inspecting the packages and the personnel traveling with them," he continues. "As a result of these latest developments, we'll be returning to DC to await further developments on the movements of the cargo that left the compound in the jungle," he concludes.

After he walks out of the meeting room, the rest of the crew looks surprised by that statement, but knowing they have no say so in what happens next they return to their quarters to pack their gear to return to DC.

ReGina Crawford

Once they return to DC, Sylvia heads straight to her apartment as she still needs to process all that has occurred between herself and Qasean and come to grips with certain things that he said to her. However, as though he has a second sense when it comes to her, Qasean is waiting at the door to her apartment when she arrives. No longer stunned by his ability to arrive at her door before she does, she simply opens the door and walks through it knowing that he will follow and close the door behind him. She doesn't stop in the living room, and simply walks straight back to her bedroom where she drops her travel bag before heading straight to her bathroom to start her bath.

Qasean, knowing that she was expecting to have some time alone to come to grips with what is happening between them, simply follows silently in her wake. Once the tub is full, she begins to undress and he merely takes a seat on the closed commode. After she submerges herself in the water and bubbles of the tub and closes her eyes, Qasean removes his clothes intent on joining her in the tub. She feels his presence behind her, but doesn't open her eyes even when he lifts her back off the tub so that he can climb in behind her. Once he positions himself behind her and her between his widespread legs, he pulls her backward to lay her head on his chest.

Neither of them speak for quite a long time, then Qasean whispers in her ear, "Accept that our heartbeats are synchronized as though we are one. Accept that my soul is intertwined completely and totally with yours." He pauses several seconds for effect before adding, "Once you accept those two things, your mind will be at ease just as mine is." Knowing that she will not instantly respond to his words, he kisses the top of her head as he wraps his arms around her a little tighter before leaning his head back against the back of the tub. They stay that way for about twenty minutes before Qasean says, "The water's getting cold sweetheart, time to get out."

Snake Chaser

He leans forward placing them both in an upright position as his arms are still wrapped around her. He then grabs her hips to help her stand up before standing up himself and stepping out of the tub. He sees she is totally relax, so he lifts her out of the tub and grabs a towel to wrap around her. He then carries her to the bed so that he can dry her off without even grabbing a towel for himself. Once she is completely dry, he grabs her moisturizer off the dresser and proceeds to moisturize her whole body. He then pulls back the covers and places her in the bed before going to the bathroom to retrieve a towel so that he can wrap it around his waist before getting into bed with her. When he returns to the bedroom, she appears to be sleeping, and he carefully climbs into the other side of the bed.

As he pulls her in his arms to cuddle, she runs her hand down his stomach and encounters the towel. Without opening her eyes, she asks, "What's this," as she tugs on the towel.

"Me recognizing that you need rest," he replies.

She continues to tug on the towel while stating, "What I need is for you to remove this towel."

"Go to sleep Sy," is his response.

She opens her eyes and looks up at him, "Either you remove the towel, or I will."

"I don't know how you think you're going to be able to manage that wrapped up in my arms."

Instead of responding verbally, she proceeds to show him how she can manage it. Once she has thrown the towel across the room and is straddling his body, she says, "That's how." Then cocks her eyebrow at him in arrogance.

ReGina Crawford

"Nice moves Sy. Now lay your ass down and go to sleep."

"What if I want to do something other than sleep?"

"Don't start," he says as he places his hands behind his head as a sign of passiveness. He's hoping that she will accept his stance, and just lay back down.

Sylvia has no such intentions, and dips her head to his chest and circles her tongue around his left nipple. Just as she looks back up at him, she sees him closing his eyes and knows that she can quickly gain the upper hand. So she dips her head and circles her tongue around his right nipple before running her tongue down his chest to his navel, and even though he is trying to ignore her she feels the muscles in his stomach treble from the caress of her tongue. Fueled by his natural reaction, she continues past his navel as she slides further down his body and feels his manhood automatically respond to her. She then runs her tongue across the sensitive tip, and feels his body jerk from her touch. She settles herself between his legs and looks up at him just as she runs her tongue up the full length of him from base to tip.

His eyes fly open as he grits out between clench teeth, "Stop that!" Ignoring his words, she proceeds to take the tip in her mouth and flicks her tongue back forth on the most sensitive part of him. "Damn it Sylvia," he begins before she takes all of him inside her mouth, then all he can do is moan as sensations take over his body. He grabs tight to the pillow behind his head to keep from grabbing fistfuls of her hair as he surrenders to her mouth. However, when she sucks him into the back of her throat, he helplessly entangles his fingers in her hair as he is pushed to the edge and a powerful orgasm surges through his body. Once he catches his breath and is able to speak, he lifts her head to that he can look her directly in her eyes, "You know payback is . . ." His voice trails off as he cocks his eyebrow in a suggestive manner, and then in one quick move she finds herself on her back with him straddling her pinning her body to the bed.

He leans down and places a kiss on the side of her neck before trailing his tongue down her body to the place he loves burying his face the most. He places his arms under her thighs, placing them over his shoulders as he spreads them wide. He then plunges his tongue deep inside her love cove which causes her hips to jerk off the bed, however, he has such a firm grip on her hips and thighs that she's not able to lift them too high, nor is she able to dislodge his mouth from her body. He greedily consumes the nectar produced by her body until her body begins trembling signaling she's about to climax. Before she knows it, he's plunging his throbbing member inside her body the same way he did his tongue earlier, and they both climax as though their bodies are completely in sync.

Once their breathing evens out, he tells her, "That was not what I had in mind when I showed up here."

"What did you have in mind?"

"Just holding you in my arms and enjoying sleeping next to you."

"Well since I will be sleep in seconds, you can get what you wanted." He laughs out loud at her statement. After his laughter dies down, she says in a sleepy voice, "Good Night Love."

"Good Night."

They awaken the next morning to messages from Chance stating that there was no need for them to come to the training facility today as he was chasing down some leads generated by the information that they had gathered. So since they have a day of down time, they make love for the rest of the morning before venturing out to get a bite to eat and see some sights.

Snake Chaser

Another Jungle

After three weeks of down time, they learn that they will be venturing out into another jungle hoping to gain more information about the arms dealer their group was assembled to catch.

When they arrive at the training facility, they learn that the group will be traveling to a jungle on Africa's Ivory Coast. The group grabs their travel bags, and heads to the tarmac to catch their ride to Africa. On the plane they are briefed about the mission, and learn that one of the shipments from South America has turned up at their next destination. After their briefing, they settle in for the long flight.

Upon their arrival, Qasean and Zeke are paired to explore the southern region of the jungle, Sylvia and Garth are paired to explore the central region of the jungle, and Chance and Leah are left behind to set up the command center that will serve as their headquarters while they are on this mission.

Qasean and Zeke's trek through the jungle fails to provide any useful information as they find no evidence of any foreigners passing through the jungle, so they return to the command center to await word from Sylvia and Garth. However, Sylvia and Garth learn that some foreigners have set up a make shift camp in the northern most part of the jungle that has few inhabitants. It sounds to them like the perfect place to stash illegal arms, and conduct clandestine arms deals with potential buyers.

By nightfall, Sylvia and Garth are within two miles of the camp, and stop to create their hideout at that point. They know that they will not be able to gather any information at this point so once their underground hideout is complete, they go over the maps they have the region, as well as, the documents in their briefs detailing what animals inhabit this part of the world. Wouldn't do for them to encounter anything poisonous that prevent them from completing their mission. Once they feel that there is nothing left for them to cover, they settle into their bedrolls for the night.

The next morning they make a wide circle around the encampment they are watching to take note of the vegetation and animals in the area, so that they don't get tripped up when venture out in the darkness. That evening ask dusk touches the earth, they stealthily make their way close to the encampment to see what types of activities are taking place. After thirty minutes of surveying the area, they see a group arrive on elephants that appear to be equipped with rigging to carry heavy loads. After another thirty minutes of watching, they see crates similar to the ones Sylvia and Qasean observed in South America being loaded on to the elephants and then the procession files out of the encampment. Sylvia and Garth follow the elephants until they come to a make shift road, and then the crates are unloaded from the elephants and into trucks.

Knowing that they will not be able to follow the trucks on foot, they head back to the encampment to see if there is any other activity taking place. Sylvia notices that the women that are dressed up in African clothing and lined up as though they are up for sale are the same women from the jungle in South America. Sure enough, another group of men arrive on a caravan of elephants, and inspect the women standing in the center of the encampment. It appears as though their arms dealer is selling women, as well as, guns and ammo. When the caravan of elephants leaves the encampment, Sylvia and Garth head back to their hideout to gather their gear so that they can break camp in the morning and head back to the command center to brief Chance on their findings.

When they arrive back at the command center, Sylvia and Garth turn over their reports and cameras so that the pictures can be retrieved. What Sylvia isn't aware of is that Qasean is watching her intently and that he notices how agitated she is, but he knows that he will have to wait to ask her about it. He just hopes that Garth isn't the source of her agitation, for he would hate to have to take a fellow team member to task over his woman. What Qasean isn't aware of is how intently Chance is watching him, and Chance is definitely developing a strong curiosity about the relationship between his sister and Qasean. Knowing that he can't explore his curiosity at this time, Chance leaves the briefing room to process the pictures from the cameras that Sylvia and Garth turned in.

Qasean eventually makes his way over to Sylvia, and asks her what she's so riled up about. "He is selling the women that he uses to transport his guns and ammo," she begins. "That's why he's able to be so elusive. He's not using the same women over and over again, and the women he is using end up sold off to men who keep them hidden so that no one is the wiser about what is taking place. And the men he is selling the women to are different than the men he is selling the arms to, so the two groups aren't able to connect the dots together so they won't be any help in bringing him down." She pauses to take a breath. "I have to give him credit, he is very clever and that is the reason he has been so successful in his dealings. But I want to bring this bastard down."

"Calm yourself Sy," begins Qasean. "You can't think clearly if you get emotional about these women."

"But he's selling women as though they are a commodity like his guns and ammo," she grits out through clenched teeth.

"I understand your frustration, but you can't do the team or the women any good if you let your emotions have free reign."

Knowing that he is right, Sylvia takes several deep breaths before speaking, "I know you're right, but I'm pissed."

Before Qasean can say another word, Chance returns to the briefing room. "It seems that we have stumbled on to something bigger than we anticipated," he begins. "However, it's a problem that the African Government welcomes our involvement in," he adds. He directs everyone to take a seat so that he can bring them up to speed on his findings. "It seems that the women who are transporting the arms into this country are being sold off as slaves, but most of them are infected with one disease or another and the African Government wants to stop put to their sale. So, they are willing to help us stop our arms dealer if it means keeping these infected women out of their country."

"If these women know that they are infected, why are they agreeing to be sold, and sold into slavery," asks Garth.

"Because they are told that money will be given to the rest of their family that is infected, and some of them are treated and cured," responds Chance. "Others, mostly the women, are given the same promise and so that is how they have a continuous flow of women to transport their arms to other countries," he adds. "The women aren't aware that they too will be sold until they arrive in a foreign country with the weapons, and by then it's too late for them to do anything about their plight," he continues. "So now our mission has

Snake Chaser

become two fold. We must find out where these guns are ending up, but we must also find out who is buying the women as it is obvious that our dealer isn't selling the guns and ammo and the women to the same groups," he concludes.

"Since the trail of the guns and women have grown cold at this point in this country, we will return to DC for a couple days of down time and then we will return to the jungle in South America to see if we can track the next shipment of guns and women," states Chance. He sees that Sylvia is not entirely receptive to the idea, and knowing that she will not question a direct order from a superior he adds, "Your orders are to gather your gear and prepare for the flight home."

The team files out of the briefing room, and gathers their gear for their flight home. Chance sees Qasean standing alone on the tarmac with his travel gear, and seizes the opportunity to talk to him alone. "Gunny," he states. When Qasean turns and gives him his full attention, he continues, "I'm not speaking to you as your superior, but as Sylvia's older brother. Is there more to your relationship than just fellow Marines?"

Never having lied to a single soul in his life, Qasean speaks the truth, "I'm in love with Sylvia and she loves me in return."

"I see," responds Chance.

"What do you see Sir?"

"I see a life of challenges for you," he begins. "But I also see that you have the ability to make her see reason when no one else has ever been ever able to manage such a feat."

"Are you sure you see that second part," Qasean asks around a grin.

"Well, you appear to more successful at it than anyone else has been," replies Chance around his own grin. "I will not interfere in your relationship with my sister, just make sure that your relationship doesn't interfere with our missions," he adds.

"Yes Sir."

"Let's head home and regroup. I think this mission is going to turn into more than we first thought with the addition of the selling of women added into the mix."

"I agree."

The men are then joined by the rest of the team, and they head toward the plane that will be returning them to DC.

Snake Chaser

New Strategy

Once again Qasean is waiting at her apartment door when she arrives home after they land in DC, and once again she just opens the door and heads to her bathroom for her much needed bath. However, once they are in bed, Qasean notices that she is contemplating the plight of the women who are sold along with the guns and ammo, so he proceeds to distract her from her thoughts.

"Chance knows about us."

It takes her a minute to process his words, but once she does she sits straight up in the bed. "What do you mean he knows about us? Knows what about us," she practically shouts.

"He knows that I love you, and that you love me in return."

"And just how the hell does he know that?"

"He asked me while we were standing on the tarmac in Africa, and I told him the truth." Sylvia closes her eyes, and takes several deep breaths. Taking advantage of her efforts to calm herself, Qasean adds, "And he's fine with it."

Her eyes fly open, "What do you mean 'he's fine with it'," she asks.

"He didn't get all brotherly on me, and his only response was that he sees a life of challenges ahead of me."

"Oh really," states Sylvia in what Qasean recognizes as her pissed off voice. "I'll show him a lifetime of challenges," she adds.

Knowing that she is about to go on a tirade, Qasean quickly pulls her down to the bed and covers her body with his pinning her to the bed covering her mouth with his. He kisses her until he feels her sub-come to the warmth of his kiss. He ends the kiss but doesn't remove his lips from hers as he speaks, "You will not give your brother a hard time, is that understood?" When he feels her lips begin to move, he kisses her once again. When he ends that kiss, he tells her, "Just nod if you understand." She nods. "Good girl," he says as he smiles even though his lips are still attached to hers. "I'm going to hold you to that, so don't even think about reneging later on. Okay?" Instead of letting her answer, he kisses her deeply once again.

Before he knows it, she has taken over the kiss and somehow manages to flip them over so she's on top. She eventually ends the kiss to say, "I won't renege as long as you keep an open mind about he and I getting to know each other as family again."

"I'd already decided to do just that, so no worries."

Liking his answer, Sylvia kisses him again, only this time she adds more passion into the kiss. Feeling the change in her kiss, Qasean takes over and makes love to her till they both fall asleep.

Snake Chaser

When they arrive at the training facility the next morning, Chance has set up a large video monitor displaying the pictures that were taken in the jungles of South America and Africa. After everyone has taken their seats, Chance begins to speak. "We have identified some of the people whose images were captured on our last two missions. It seems this group operates worldwide, and deals in everything from arms to drugs to people." He pauses before adding, "As a result we are going to be joined by another group similar to ours that has been operating Europe, Asia, and Russia, as it was their briefings that helped us identify the people that you see on the screen behind me."

As he finishes speaking, in walks a team of four men and two women. "Meet the members of Captain Zaire Muhammed's team," begins Chance. "Captain Zaire, Joshua, Henry, Jules, Juilete, and Whitney," he states as each one walks up and stops beside him. "You all can get to know each other after the briefing," states Chance. "Right now Captain Zaire is going to brief us on what they have discovered in their scouting missions, and then we will put together a new strategy to try to put a stop to this group."

Zaire picks up the remote and switches the image on the screen as he speaks, "We believe this man is the head of this group," he pauses as he switches the image on the screen, "However, there are some that believe that this man is the head of the group." He switches the image once again which shows the two images side by side, "And there are some that believe that these men are one and the same based on the fact they are similarly built and share some of the same facial features," he continues. "Also, both men have been spotted with the same henchmen at different times." As he speaks, he once again switches the image on the screen. This time there four men on the screen, "These men have been identified as Marcus Henderson, Jason Lewis, Frank Jackson, and Marquise Redmon. They are known guns for hire, so that is why we can't be sure that the head of the group isn't two different people."

At this point Chance moves to stand beside Zaire, "So our new strategy will be to investigate these four men to try to determine if they are working for two different groups or if the two groups are one and the same," begins Chance. "It has been rumored that the men believed to be the head of the groups has a team of plastic surgeons on hand that slightly alters his appearance every six months so that he cannot be identified by any law enforcement agencies, which is another reason why he has been so successful."

"Our new strategy is to keep tabs on both groups and create a timeline for the man in charge to see if we can determine if we're dealing with two criminal masterminds or just one," states Zaire. "Chance and I are going to work on our strategy while all of you get to know each other," he adds just before he and Chance exit the briefing room.

Sylvia has been eyeballing Joshua undercover since he walked in the room for there is something familiar about him that she just can't put her finger on, and what she doesn't know is that Joshua has been keenly aware of her scrutiny of him. To appease her curiosity, Joshua walks over to her and introduces himself, "Hello Sylvia, I'm Joshua," he begins. A little perplexed that he addresses her by her first name, Sylvia cocks an eyebrow at him. He laughs before stating, "You obviously don't remember me," he says after his laughter dies down. "We met when your Uncle Chappy died. I was viewing the body alone when you walked in and interrogated me for being there."

Somewhat embarrassed by the reminder, Sylvia lowers her head for a split second before raising it and extending her hand, "Sorry about that," She begins. "I was grieving and you took me by surprise being there all alone. It's nice to see you

Snake Chaser

again." As they shake hands, she recalls that she never did get a solid answer from him as to why he was there. "You never did say why you were there, and then you weren't at the funeral the next day. Why is that?"

"I was given special consideration to say my goodbyes in private," he responds. He then lowers his voice before continuing, "I was not permitted to attend the funeral for personal reasons, of which I don't want to get into here. But maybe we can meet after the briefing, and I can explain it to you." Not crazy about the idea but wanting answers, Sylvia agrees to meet him later.

The introductions continue amongst the group, and just as everyone finishes getting acquainted Chance and Zaire reenter the room. "We don't have any leads on where our guy has gone since he completed his deals in Africa, so we'll embark in some training sessions until his trail is picked up again," states Chance as he and Zaire begin handing each of them their briefs containing the information that they covered earlier. Chance and Zaire then dismiss their teams before exiting the training facility.

Revelations II

Once the team is dismissed, Sylvia heads to her favorite coffee shop across town to await the arrival of Joshua. However, what she isn't aware of is that Qasean watched their exchange at the training facility, and knows that they are meeting. She also isn't aware that he knows who Joshua is, and that he'll be sitting outside the coffee shop in case she needs him.

Sylvia arrives first and orders her favorite coffee as she waits for Joshua's arrival. He walks in just as her coffee is set in front of her. He takes a seat, and places his order with the waitress. After she walks away, he says, "Thanks for meeting with me."

"No problem. I'm very interested in what you want to tell me."

His coffee arrives, so he waits until the waitress walks away before speaking again, "The man you knew as Uncle Chappy, I knew as Dad."

Sylvia is glad that she hadn't picked up her coffee and taken a sip as he spills that bit of information. She tilts her head to the side and simply stares at him for several minutes before replying, "While I'll admit you have similar features to Uncle

Snake Chaser

Chappy, but he didn't have any children. So you want to try again?"

Joshua simply smiles at her, "That's where you're wrong Sylvia. He has a son, me." He pauses to take a sip from his cup before continuing, "At the time of my conception and birth, Dad was involved in some very dangerous missions and he wanted to protect me and mom, so he only told a few select people about us." He pauses so that she can process what he's told her, and he still sees doubt in her eyes. "It's true, and if you remember we actually ran into each other a few times at his house when you popped up unexpectedly to surprise him. He always told you that I was the son of a very good friend whom he was taking care of for a short while." Again he pauses to let her absorb and process his words.

"I remember you," she states in a somewhat far away voice. She continues to replay those events in her mind, and then a thought hits her, "You're the Joshua he left most of his estate to," she asks.

He smiles, "Yes that would be me."

"But his will stated since he didn't have any children of his own, he was leaving everything to the one person who has most been like a son to him. Why didn't he just acknowledge you as his son?"

"Because he believed that there is still someone out there that would harm me and mother because of the missions he was involved in. He spent my whole life protecting me and my mother."

Sylvia slumps back in her chair, and the only thing she can say is, "Wow!"

"My mother understood, and in time I came to understand. Especially after I entered the military as well, and gained firsthand knowledge of how ruthless some of the criminals we hunt can be."

"So technically, we're cousins," she states before chuckling.

"I guess you can say that, but why does the thought make you laugh?"

"Because up until a few months ago, I considered myself without family. Now I have my brother and a cousin."

"And I take it that pleases you?"

"Yes! Yes it does! Welcome to the family," she states as she gets up and gives him a hug.

Qasean is shocked that she hasn't flown off the handle, but is please that she has accepted Joshua with open arms. Realizing that she isn't going to need him, he leaves to go complete some errands he needs to take care of but plans to be at her place when she arrives home.

Joshua accepts her hug, and then proceeds to remind her that no one can know who his father is. When Sylvia asks why, he responds, "Because it has never been determined if the person whom he feared is alive or dead, so the military, and everyone for that matter, has decided that it would be best if my paternity is never revealed." He takes a sip from his cup as he tries to decide if he should reveal another secret he's not told her. As he sips, he decides that he should tell her since it has to do with the mission they both are assigned to. He leans over the table as he begins to speak, "The man that we are hunting could be the very person that my father was concerned about."

"Really? Does Chance know any of this?"

Snake Chaser

"How do you think he came to be in charge of one of the teams that is hunting this criminal mastermind? Chappy made it clear that when Chance reached the level he has in the military that he wanted him to hunt down this man, and put an end to his criminal empire. And yes he knows who I am as well. As a matter of fact he was reluctant to bring in Zaire's team, but since we are already deep into our investigation he had no choice but to join forces. However, Zaire doesn't know who I am, and no one had any idea until now that the person we've been hunting is the same person that Chance has been hunting."

"This is getting more and more complicated by the hour," states Sylvia.

"Yes it is, but I have confidence that we can bring this guy down."

"I hope you're right."

"I am. Now finish your coffee so we can get out of here."

"Yes Sir," says Sylvia playfully.

They finish their coffee, and leave the coffee shop. When Sylvia arrives home, she is not surprised to find Qasean at her door. However, as she unlocks the door, she does ask, "Do you have a GPS device on my car so that you know exactly when I arrive at home?"

"Not exactly," is Qasean's response.

She turns towards him, "And what exactly is that supposed to mean?"

He laughs before responding, "When are you going to realize that now that we've unlocked our souls to each other, that I will always know when you need me by your side?"

"And what makes you think that I need you by my side right now?"

"You don't," he asks as he arches his eyebrow at her.

She drops her head because she does, but quickly lifts it as she drags him to her couch. "Uncle Chappy has a son, and it's Joshua."

"And you're cool with that?"

She notices his lack of surprise at her announcement, "You already knew, didn't you?" He simply nods his head, "I was wondering why I didn't feel you being overprotective in the briefing room. Now it all makes sense." She pauses to catch her breath and gather her thoughts, "I don't understand why no one thought I should know," she muses.

"I'm not supposed to know either Sweetheart. I stumbled across the information, and was sworn to secrecy, so there was no way that I could tell you." Still confused about her reaction to the news, he asks, "Why are you not over the top pissed about this?"

"Because I don't feel so all alone now. I have more and more people to talk to, to share things with, to relive memories with. Although it seems we'll have to dispatch this crafty criminal mastermind in order for me to do so."

"What's that supposed to mean?"

"Oh, so I know something you don't know," she asks with laughter in her voice.

Snake Chaser

Qasean gives her a sarcastic smile before saying, "Spill it!" She tells him what Joshua told her at the coffee house about the man that they are hunting. "Really? Wow! That certainly adds another element to the mission," is Qasean's reaction to the news. They sit and talk for a few minutes more, before Qasean says, "Time for bed. We have no idea when we will have to pull out of DC, and chase down this man who seems to have no regard for human life."

"Okay. I just hope our next mission takes us to a city instead of another jungle," states Sylvia as she heads for the bathroom.

"I'm thinking the jungle conceals his operations a whole lot better than any city ever could."

"I wasn't really expecting a response," she throws over her shoulder as she steps into the shower.

"Smartass," quips Qasean as he joins her.

Collaboration

At the training facility the next day, the members of the two teams are paired up based on their skill sets so that they can compare techniques and become better acquainted for their upcoming missions.

By coincidence, Sylvia and Joshua have the same skill set and spend the morning together comparing techniques that they employ when tracking "prey" in the jungle. Joshua gives Sylvia some good pointers on how to control her heart rate and breathing so that she can become better in tuned with the jungle, and will be able to better detect even the slightest change in the environment. He also gives her tips how to distinguish the various inhabitants of the jungle by sound, smell, and movement.

Qasean and Juilete have similar skill sets and are paired together. She confesses to Qasean that she would like to improve her skills in hand-to-hand combat, and that she understands that he excels in that area. He agrees to take her to the training facility that afternoon to see what her skill set is, and offer any pointers that he can.

Garth and Whitney are both equipment gurus, and compare the types of cameras, listening devices, and tracking devices that each uses in the field. Whitney has some more advanced

Snake Chaser

"toys" and she spends the whole morning showing Garth how they work.

Zeke and Jules are navigation experts so they spend the morning going over satellite maps of the areas that they know their criminal mastermind has used to conduct his sales in the past.

Lucas and Henry have superior underwater skills, and thus are paired together to compare equipment and underwater pitfalls that each has encountered in the past.

Later that afternoon, Qasean takes Juilete down to the training facility to practice moves so that he could see where her weak points are, and help her improve her hand to hand combat skills. He discovers her take down and follow-through needs some beefing up, so he coaches her in those areas. As they are practicing a new maneuver that Qasean has shown her, Jules and few other members of the team walk into the facility in time to see Juilete take Qasean down.

However, as she attempts the follow-through move he taught her, Jules runs and grabs her and pulls her to her feet. "What are you doing Juile," he yells at her. Then he turns to Qasean, who is still down the mat, and yells, "What did you try to do to her?" Neither one is sure which one should answer first, and Jules seems just as equally confused as he keeps looking back and forth between the two of them.

Finally Juilete decides to answer him, "I was practicing a new technique that Qasean taught me, that's what I was doing," she yells as she jerks her arm out of his grip. "I keep telling you that I don't need you to protect me! I carry the same rank as you Big Brother!" She walks over to help Qasean up off the mat, "Sorry bout that. He seems to think that because he's five seconds older that he has the right to play big brother every second of my life."

"Big Brother? And your twin to boot? Oh this should be interesting," quips Qasean around a smile.

"It's not funny," responds Juilete at a near yell.

"Sorry," replies Qasean. "Don't mean to laugh, but I can relate as I have a twin sister as well. So, I've been in his shoes a time or two."

"My bad man," states Jules as he walks over to shake hands with Qasean. "I tend to react without thinking when it comes to Juile."

"It's cool man, no worries."

"Thanks."

"It's not cool," comes back Juilete. When everyone turns in her direction with smiles on their faces, she throws her hands in the air in frustration and walks from the facility.

"Excuse me guys," states Jules, "I'm going to have calm her down."

No one says a word until he too has left the facility, and then Henry states, "This happens all the time during training with a new team. I don't know what it's going to take for him to stop seeing her as his sister, and as a fellow Marine who is capable of handling herself."

Qasean isn't interested in getting into a family dispute, so he asks, "What brought you guys down to the training facility?"

"We heard that you and Sylvia are very skilled at hand-to-hand combat, so we wanted to see some of your maneuvers to see if we could pick any of them up," responds Whitney.

Snake Chaser

And for the first time, he sees Sylvia leaning up against the door jam with a smirk on her face. He thinks, '*Oh shit! I'm going to hear about this later.*' But in an effort not to give anything away concerning their relationship he turns back to the others and simply says, "Cool." He then turns back towards Sylvia, and asks, "You ready Sy?"

"More than ready," she states with a smile on her face.

The two of them take to the mat to demonstrate some of their maneuvers, and a few times Sylvia takes him down to the mat kind of hard. Qasean doesn't complain for he knows that he will return the favor when he makes love to her later that night.

"Those are some great moves you two, I think I've learned a thing or two watching the two of you," states Whitney.

"Then it's been a productive day," states Sylvia as she grabs her towel to wipe her face. "See you guys in the AM," she states as she grabs her bag and heads towards the door.

Once she's out of earshot, Whitney asks Qasean, "Does she not like you? She took you down hard a few times."

Qasean laughs, "It's not that at all. That's just Sylvia. She likes to let everyone know that she is not fragile and doesn't need them treating her the way that Jules treats Juilete."

"Oh," is all Whitney says in response.

Henry, however, says, "I bet if Juilete took Jules down like that a few times he would definitely back up off of her."

The room bursts out laughing as they all head towards the door to leave the facility.

ReGina Crawford

Qasean arrives at Sylvia's about thirty minutes after she left the facility, but he knows that she's waiting for him. In fact he's so sure, he doesn't bother to knock, just simply turns the doorknob. Sure enough the door is open, and he enters to see her sitting in the armchair that is facing the door. He stops in his tracks and stares her directly in the eyes for several moments before closing the door behind him, and heading for the bathroom.

Once he completes his shower and dresses, he heads back to the living room and finds Sylvia in the exact same she was in when he walked in the door. "Say whatever it is that you want to say so that I can take you to bed."

She sits there and doesn't say a word, so he walks over and picks her up and carries her to bed. After placing her in the center of the bed, he removes her nightgown and his shorts and proceeds to teach her a lesson about slamming him to the mat the way she did earlier. He knows she has learned her lesson by the way she screams his name as a massive orgasm slams through her. He finds his release, and screams her name in return. He falls to his side, gathers her in his arms, and they both fall asleep almost instantaneously.

Snake Chaser

Tag Team Part I

A month after their last mission, they receive word that their prey has been spotted in two separate locations that they will investigate and should be ready for transport early the next morning. Each team arrives at the tarmac at 0500 to board their respective planes for their respective jungles in an effort to determine if they are dealing with one criminal mastermind or two.

Since they believe his base of operations is in South America, Chance and his team head back there to see what activity is taking place in hopes to get better pictures of the people involved, especially the man in charge.

They also have Intel that the next shipment is headed to Malaysia, so Zaire and his team are headed there to gather Intel on when the shipment arrives, who arrives with it, and who the buyers are of the shipment.

Qasean and Sylvia once again set up their hideout in the jungle near the compound, and as soon as night falls they venture out to observe the activity taking place at the compound. After thirty minutes of no activity, they observe a commotion spilling out into the courtyard. It appears one of the women decided that she will not be used to assuage the needs of one of the men, and tries to run away. Her clothing is in shreds as she runs out into the courtyard, and a large man wearing a bathrobe is following behind her with several other men following behind him.

"Do you know who I am tramp," yells the first man out the door. "I am God to you! I determine whether you live or die," he continues to yell at her as the other men grab both of her arms and handfuls of her hair so that she is forced to look at the man yelling at her. "You have no say so in what happens to you!"

The young woman stands her ground, "I am a virgin! I am but sixteen years old! I will not be raped by you," she yells back him.

He slaps her across the face before yelling, "You will give yourself to me willingly or by force, but I will have you!"

"Why can't you sleep with one of the whores you have here?"

"Because there is no way of telling if they carry disease! And I will not be infected by the likes of them!" He then looks at his men and yells, "I will not continue explaining myself to her! Get her back to my bed! NOW!" The men do as instructed by picking up the young woman and carrying her back into the main house and back to his bed.

Qasean and Sylvia assume he is the man in charge of the operation, and are grateful that they were able to get great shots of his face during the commotion although his face is distorted with anger. Qasean is extremely grateful that Sylvia did not leave her post to go defend the young woman and blow their operation, but he knows that she must be fuming mad right about now. Feeling that they got what they came for, he makes his way to where she is hidden so that he can get her back to their hideout so that she can vent her frustration without giving notice of their presence in the jungle.

When he reaches her, he can tell by her body language that she is barely containing her rage so he motions for her to follow him back to their hideout. She follows him without saying a word for she doesn't trust herself to speak with all the rage she is feeling.

Once they are safely back in their hideout, Qasean simply takes a seat on his bedroll to await the tirade he knows is sure to come and he doesn't have long to wait.

"He's raping children," she screams. "CHILDREN!" She paces back and forth in an effort to vent her anger and frustration. "If there weren't women and children in that compound, I would go back and blow it all to hell in an effort to get rid of him! Spending the rest of his life in prison is too easy for him! He deserves to die!" She continues her pacing, and Qasean simply sits quietly waiting for her to get it all out of her system.

Once her pacing slows to a walk, Qasean stands up and walks over to her to pull her into his arms. "I know it's unfair to them, and we will put a stop him Sweetheart," he whispers near her ear. "I am so very proud of you right now, do you know that?"

She tries to pull back to look at him, but he holds her closer to him so she speaks into his chest. "Proud of me for what," she asks.

"For holding your position and not running into the middle of the compound to save that young woman."

"Oh, I wanted to. Oh how I wanted to, but I wouldn't have been able to save her. I know that, but it doesn't make me feel any less helpless right now."

"I know how you feel. I wanted to rescue her myself, but I too know how futile that would have been." He kisses the top of her head before continuing, "Come on. Let's get cleaned up so that we can get some rest before venturing out in the morning."

They both go get cleaned up, however, before Qasean can zip up his bedroll, Sylvia is attempting to get inside with him. "What are you doing," he asks.

"I don't want to sleep alone," is her response.

"I don't think it's a good idea for us to sleep in the same bedroll."

"Why," she asks with a confused look on her face.

"Sweetheart my body doesn't know that we are in an underground hideout in a jungle in South America. All it knows is that it craves your touch, your heat, and when you're next me it wants to make love to you."

"Oh," is all she says at first as she processes his response, then she proceeds to continue climbing inside his bedroll.

"You like playing with fire don't you?"

"As long as you're the one providing the flame," she replies as she snuggles closer to him.

His body instantly reacts to her being close, and he refuses to deny his body what it wants so badly. So, he pulls her under him as he rains kisses over her face, neck, and shoulders as he gently rips her tank from her body exposing her breasts. He takes a dark tip inside his mouth to suckle, and feels her body buck beneath him as a moan escapes her lips. He transfers his mouth to her other breast as he removes her bottoms, so that his hands can roam freely over her thighs and the jewel that they protect. She kicks her legs free of her bottoms, and spreads her legs to give him better access to what he seeks. He instantly inserts two fingers inside her love cove to test her readiness, and finds her soaking wet and trembling from his touch. He trails his mouth down her stomach as he makes his way to feast on the sweetness he craves. He replaces his fingers with his tongue, and has to grab her hips as she nearly bucks him off of her. He proceeds to make love to her with his mouth until she screams out her release. Before she can fully recover from her first orgasm, he buries his throbbing manhood deep inside her in one swift thrust. She instantly wraps her legs around his waist, and tries to draw him deeper inside her. His adrenaline is on high and he knows he's not going to be able to hold out for long, so he growls in her ear, "Come! Now!"

She instantly complies, and he follows right behind her. Her second orgasm was just as powerful as her first, and both drain her completely. "Mmmm," is all she says before falling asleep.

Qasean's orgasm is just as powerful as hers, and he's having a hard time catching his breath and getting his body under control. He looks over at her in disbelief that she could instantly fall asleep after that, however, before he can dwell on it too long he is sleep as well.

*****

Meanwhile, back at the compound, the man is not having much luck with woman in his bed and ends up breaking her neck before he can get what he's after. He has the men who brought her inside the compound take her body out to the woods to dispose of, however, they pick up on the fact that someone has been in the woods watching the compound. So they simply drop her body, and rush back to inform the "boss" of what they have discovered. He's even more furious than he was about the girl not giving him what he wanted. He instantly makes calls to move up the time frame of his next shipment as he is not sure who has been watching the compound, or what they have learned about his movements or the shipments.

Snake Chaser

Tag Team Part II

As Sylvia and Qasean are on their way to their places in the jungle, they sense something different in the air so they take to higher ground in the trees. As they scan the area surrounding the compound, they spot the body of the young woman from the night before lying close to where they were positioned the night before. Fearing that they might be blown, they take one quick sweep of the compound, which appears to be abandoned, before they make their way back to their hideout.

They assemble their gear even though they know that they will have to remain there until dusk before they can head back to the carrier where the rest of their team is waiting for them. Once that is taken care of, Sylvia turns to Qasean and says, "I wonder if he killed her before or after he raped her."

"From the looks of it, I would say before," responds Qasean.

"I guess that's one consolation," she says. Qasean cocks an eyebrow at her. "He wasn't able to rape her, she gave her life for what she believed in. I can find some comfort in that knowing I wasn't able to save her."

"Come here," he says as he crooks his finger at her. She walks into his arms, and he pulls her close as he says, "We can't save them all. You know that right?"

"I know, but it doesn't make it any easier to swallow."

He holds her for a few moments more before coercing her into a game of cards until they can leave the hideout.

*****

Once they are back on the ship and give their report, they stand by as Chance calls Zaire to let him know what has occurred in the jungle in South America, and to be on the lookout for an early arrival of the expected shipment. He also sends along the photos that Sylvia and Qasean were able to take of the man referred to as "Boss".

*****

In the jungle of Malaysia, Zaire and his team speed up their timetable so that they will be ready if the shipment does arrive earlier than expected. Juilete and Joshua head out into the jungle to prepare their hideout near where they believe the shipment exchange will take place. Jules and Whitney inspect all the equipment, and make sure that they have all possible routes in and out of the area under surveillance so that they are not taken unawares if the shipment arrives earlier than originally expected.

A couple days after the call from Chance, a caravan of large trucks is detected on the road south of the believed exchange point. Juilete and Joshua are able to make it to their stakeout positions in the jungle just before the trucks arrive. Within five minutes of the trucks coming to a halt, two other caravans of

Snake Chaser

trucks arrive. Sure enough the man that Qasean and Sylvia identified as the head of the organization exits one of the trucks, so that is one piece of information they are able to confirm.

A man that has been previously identified as the head of a rebel faction in Pakistan exits the lead truck of one of the caravans, and walks with an angry stride towards the "Boss" from the jungle of South America. An angry exchange takes place between them, and Juilete and Joshua are glad that they have recording equipment with them as the conversation is taking place too rapidly for them to decipher. However, they assume that the argument centers around the presence of the other caravan as both men keep gesturing in the direction where the other caravan is waiting. After fifteen minutes of arguing the sale takes place, and the first caravan leaves the area with their cargo of guns and ammo.

Once that exchange is complete, Juilete and Joshua are met with a surprise as a woman exits the lead vehicle of the other caravan, and the woman has a huge smile on her face. They take plenty of pictures of her as she is a new element into the black market of arms, drugs, and human trafficking. The man from South America and the woman have a pleasant exchange before they complete their deal for the women that accompanied the arms shipment.

The South American caravan pulls out shortly after the sale of the women is complete, however, the caravan lead by the woman doesn't immediately leave as she takes the time to inspect each woman individually. Sensing that this may be a perfect opportunity to get a jump on the human trafficking trade of his business, Juilete and Joshua send a message back to Zaire and the rest of the team as they are not that far away.

Zaire and the rest of the team arrive in the area just as the woman and her caravan is about to pull out of the area, and they surround them halting them in their tracks. Juilete and Joshua join them from their locations in the deep foliage surrounding the area of the exchange. However, what no one is aware of is that the leader of the first caravan left some sentinels behind to watch the woman, and they record the capture of the woman and her crew. Once the sentinels feel that they have captured enough footage of the takedown, they leave the area to take the information back to their boss. They grin as they head back to the rendezvous point for they know that their boss will fetch a pretty penny from the South American for this information, and that they will be richly rewarded as a result.

*****

Zaire sends word to Chance about the capture of the woman involved in the trafficking of the women from South America, and lets him know that he will be taking the captives to the Operations Office they have in the Philippines. So Chance makes arrangement to have his team meet Zaire's team in the Philippines so that they too can be part of the interrogation of the captives

Two days later, Chance's team and Zaire's team and the captives arrive at the operations office simultaneously, and immediately get to work interrogating their female suspect and the women being illegally sold on the black market. They learn that the woman in charge is named Genevieve, and owns several brothels in Vietnam is which where the women she purchased were headed. She is more than willing to give up information on the man who purchased the guns and ammo after being left alone in a camp for two days not sure of her fate, but refuses to reveal anything about the man whom she purchased the women from. No matter how hard they push her, she will not reveal his identity or how they communicate with one another when he has women to sell.

Snake Chaser

The women that were being sold are also reluctant to impart any information regarding the man who has sold them. They beg and plead to be left alone for they fear for the lives of their family members that they have left behind in South America. Chance tries to reassure them that they will make sure that their family members are kept safe, but they doubt the validity of his words. After three hours of questioning and not getting anywhere, Chance decides to give the women a break hoping that they will realize they have nothing to fear from him and his men and that they will eventually become more cooperative.

Zaire is fed up with Genevieve, and walks out of the interrogation room and bumps into Chance as he leaves the conference room where the women are being held. Zaire runs a hand down his is face as he says, "This woman is working my last nerves."

"I'm not surprised," states Chance. "She seemed rather cocky and confident when you guys arrived even though she was in handcuffs and facing serious charges for human trafficking."

"Right," responds Zaire. "I wonder why she has no problem telling all about the man who purchased the guns, but refuses to reveal a thing about the man whom she purchased the women from," he states.

"There must be some strong connection between her and the South American, and she must have an axe to grind with the man who purchased the guns and ammo," responds Chance. "Let's focus our investigation on him for the moment, and see of anything about him reveals who this South American 'Kingpin' is," he adds.

"Alright let's get to it," replies Zaire.

Hidden Danger

In the meantime, the man who purchased the guns and ammo has been joined by his sentinels, and now has images of Zaire and his team. While he is elated that Genevieve has been captured, he knows that she will be happy to spill her guts about him and he fears that his organization will now be targeted by the American Military. He wastes no time converting the video footage into pictures, and informing the black market of what has taken place. He is confident that the South American will waste no time in contacting him to get his hands on the pictures so that he can take care of the American Marines to prevent them from busting up his organization, and he will gladly sell him the images in hopes that he can take care of the American Marines before they come after him.

Once the word hits the black market about Genevieve's capture and the fact that Hassan has images of the captors, the South American crime lord indeed does not waste any time contacting him to get his hands on the images of the people he believes were watching his compound in the jungle. They arrange to meet in Jaisalmer in Rajasthan, India which is not far from Hassan's camp, and close to Punjab where the South American decided to hold up while he tried to gather information on who was doing surveillance on his South American compound. He is extremely elated that he has been able to gain information this quickly for he has some major deals taking place soon, and can't afford to be compromised at this point.

The South American Kingpin has no problem paying top dollar for the pictures for getting rid of those who are trying to bring down his operation has become his top priority. Once he has the images, he focuses all his time and energy on finding out just who the people are in the images. He immediately contacts the heads of a few Mexican Cartels that he has dealt with in the past to find out who the people in the images are, and he has no problem paying top dollar to his contacts to get the information that he will eventually receive on this group of people trying to track his movements. Once he learns their identities, he's be able to put together a plan of action to get rid of them, and he knows he must take care of them before they take care of him. He utilizes his connections with the Mexican Cartels to help him rid himself of the problem, as he knows they would be more than willing to get rid of the people that could possibly plague their operations as well.

They set up a meeting on the western coast of Cuba to discuss what their plan of action will be. When the South American arrives in Cuba two days later, the heads of the Mexican Cartels have gathered and are ready to put together a plan of action to find and dispose of these interlopers.

*****

Meanwhile, Zaire and Chance conduct an investigation into the arms purchaser from the Malaysia deal whom Genevieve has identified as Hassan Awan. They discover that he has been trying to make a name for himself as a major supplier of guns and ammo to rebel factions from China to Africa, but he has been hard to pin down because he's somewhat of a nomad and no one has been able to discover if he has a home base. However, they are able to discern that he doesn't deal with too many different suppliers for the arms and ammo that he sells seem to come from the same manufacturers. Feeling that keeping tabs on him might be more costly than useful, Zaire and Chance decide to be more forceful with Genevieve to see if they can get some useful information from her concerning the South American.

They go into the interrogation room together hoping that seeing them together will make her think twice about not cooperating with them. When she sees them walk in together, she does give a momentary pause before she puts a confident smile on her face showing that she still plans to remain silent. What she doesn't know is that even though Vietnam and the US don't have the best of relationships, her government is not exactly pleased with the infiltration of South American women into their country especially since when Genevieve is done with the women she just lets them loose with the clothes on their backs and they result to criminal activity just to survive.

Before either of them can speak, she says, "My, My! Two of you this time. And such fine looking specimens, too!" She follows up her statement with a cocky little laugh.

"I like your confidence," begins Chance. "However, you may want to rethink your position after what we are about to tell you," he adds.

"You are in no position to do anything to me. Our governments are not at all friendly, and I very seriously doubt that they would be willing to prosecute me based on your words alone," she states with complete confidence.

"You are correct in the first part of your statement for our governments are not exactly friendly," begins Zaire, "however, your government is not exactly pleased with your activities either."

Snake Chaser

They notice a quick flash of fear cover her face, but she quickly replaces it with a cocky smirk as some of her government's top ranking officials utilize her brothels on a regular basis. "I assure my government is not at all concerned with any of my activities," she responds, "well at least not in a negative way." She again follows up with her cocky little laugh.

"See, that's where you're wrong," replies Chance. He pauses to let that little tidbit sink in before adding, "When we spoke to the person in charge of '*housing*' your discarded women, he indicated that he would like to put a stop to the infiltration of South American women in his country and in his prison." When he sees a fission of fear flow through her eyes, he stops talking for he knows that she is aware of her position with this particular gentleman, and she knows that he can make trouble for her.

At that point, Zaire speaks again, "It seems that once the women are of no more use to you, you turn them loose with no more than the clothes on their backs, hungry and diseased, and then they resort to committing criminal acts to survive." Zaire pauses as he walks over to the table separating them, and leans over it so that they are face to face. "So he said he would be willing to be a liaison between us and your government if it meant keeping these women out of his country, off his streets, and out of his prison."

Chance then moves to stand beside Zaire and leans over the table as well, "Now, you can cooperate with us now, or we can use our '*new friend*' to go to your government and have them interrogate you."

They both lean in closer and say, "So what's it going to be?"

This turn of events has her mind reeling, and they see a genuine show of fear in her eyes with the news they have just

149

given her. She's trying to think fast as to how she should proceed, and they can see that in her eyes as well. "Fellas, it seems as though you have definitely turned the tables on me, and I would love to cooperate with you but you don't understand who you are attempting to tangle with," she replies.

"Well, why don't you enlighten us about him," they both respond in unison in somewhat menacing voices.

She leans back slightly in her chair, "Can you guys not come at me in stereo," is her first response. When they lean back slightly, she continues, "This man killed his own brothers when he thought that they were plotting against him. He has no problem with taking out anyone that he thinks is trying to interfere with his business, so understand my reluctance to give you any information about him or his business dealings."

As though it was scripted, Chance and Zaire each perch themselves on opposite corners of the table, and Chance is the first to speak, "Lady, I could care less about your fear of this man," he starts. "What I do care about is saving these women from the likes of him and you. So either start talking or my partner and I will be going to make a phone call that will land you in place that will make you wish you were dead."

When she doesn't say anything for a few minutes, both Chance and Zaire stand up and head for the door. "Wait," she yells. They both pause and turn back in her direction, "If I tell you what you want to know, how are you going to protect me from him?"

"Protect you," they both yell in unison. She scoots back in her chair from the fear that their voice invoke in her.

"Lady we have no interest in offering you protection," states Zaire.

Snake Chaser

"If you want me to talk, I have to be given something in return since it seems that I will also be in danger in my own country."

Chance and Zaire look at each other for a few moments, and then Chance states, "We might be able to work something out so that you can stay in this country, however, you days of running brothels is over. Got it?"

"Got it," she states reluctantly but she knows she has no choice.

Secrets Revealed

Chance and Zaire sit down across the table from her, and Chance pulls out a tape recorder to record what she is about to tell them.

Genevieve takes a deep breath, and then begins talking, "The man that you are looking for is known in different circles by different names, or so I've heard. I know him as Mr. Red, but I know for certain that he is known to Hassan as The Archman. I think his name changes depending on what he's selling." She pauses when the looks on the faces of Chance and Zaire look unimpressed by what she has just told them. "I'm telling you what I know, what more do you want from me," she asks somewhat exasperated.

"We want some relevant useful information," responds Chance.

"Okay," she replies. "He deals in anything that makes him money, guns, drugs, women, . . . ", her voice trails off as the same look remains on their faces. "I take it you already know that." When they don't respond, she takes their silence as a yes. "Well what you probably don't know is that he alters his appearance through plastic surgery. Nothing drastic, but I make it my business to remember faces and every time I see him his face is slightly different," she states with confidence
152

Snake Chaser

feeling that she has given up information that they will be pleased with. However, when she's no change in their expressions, she becomes frustrated all over again. "You know that too," she asks.

Since Chance and Zaire know that she really doesn't want or need an answer to her question, they remain silent. "I'm not sure what I know that you don't already know," she states as she folds her arms over her chest.

"We want to know how he is able to travel from country to country with his illegal contraband without getting held up at customs offices, and with no one questioning who he is and what he's transporting," replies Zaire.

"Oh, well why didn't you say that in the first place," she says with a manufactured smile on her face. Once again, Chance and Zaire are not impressed with her, and are frankly losing patience with her. "Fine," she states with a little anger in her voice. "He uses the plastic surgeons who alter his face to get his cargo through customs. They are well known doctors, with credentials to get medical supplies through without going through the customary paperwork."

"How is that possible," asks Chance.

"Mr. Red provides them with funding to offer free services in the countries where he has shipments scheduled to arrive. So when they are not altering his face or ensuring his shipments reach their destinations, they are in country helping those who can't afford to see doctors, especially children and women," she pauses to catch her breath and to see if they react in a positive way to what she has said. When she sees that they plan not to give away what they are thinking in their faces, she continues, "And since they come on a regular basis, no one questions them when they arrive with crates labeled as medical supplies. Once his product has made it past customs, then the

153

doctors turn it over to him in some obscure location, and he makes his deals."

When she doesn't say anything more for several moments, Chance says, "Go on. Continue."

"Continue? Continue? What more do you want me to say?"

"Who are these doctors? Where are they originally from? Do they have active practices in their countries? Do they have family," asks Zaire.

"Each shipment in each country is accompanied by a different doctor so as not to draw attention to how frequently they are arriving in any particular country, and the medical supplies that they are carrying with them are never questioned," she states. "While most of the doctors are only used twice in a twelve month period so that it has hard to connect them to any illegal activity, there are a couple of doctors that have been detained a time or two for the frequency of their arrivals in a few countries," she stops for she feels she has given them enough information to make a few demands of her own.

Aware that she is banking on the fact that she feels she has gained some ground with them, Chance begins a line of questioning to take her back off balance. "How did you come by this information? How can we verify what you have told is true?"

"Really? You ask me to talk, threaten me into talking! And now you're questioning the validity of what I've told you! Really," she nearly yells in frustration.

"Lady you're a criminal facing some serious charges, you could be feeding us a fairytale in order to save your ass," replies Chance.

Snake Chaser

She throws her hands up in frustration before banging her head on the table a few times. When she lifts her head, she blows out a breath before speaking again. "Hassan and Mr. Red have been doing business together for years, which is how I became aware of who he is and how I came to do business with him."

"Continue," states Chance.

"Hassan was trying to appease Mr. Red for a business transgression that took place near one of my houses, and so he brought him to me to provide him with a couple of virgins being I had just acquired some new girls. Well, Mr. Red damaged one of the girls beyond repair so to make good on the damage that he caused he offered to replace her, and me being the business woman that I am I told him he had to replace her with more than one girl. He came back with a counter offer of letting him have first go round at virgins from my country if he provided me with virgins from his country to appeal to men who liked variety, thus how we became business partners."

"How often does he supply you with girls," Zaire asks.

"Every three months, but if anyone gets word of my capture he won't be willing to supply me with anything. Ever!"

"How does he contact you when he's ready to bring you new girls," asks Zaire.

"We have scheduled dates, times, and locations when the exchanges are made."

"But this time was different," begins Chance. "He arrived a couple of days ahead of schedule, and from our observation he never conducts two deals at the same time. So how did he let you know that he was arriving early and where the deal was taking place," he asks.

"I received a call from an anonymous source stating that the meeting had been moved up."

"How did you know that the call was legit," asks Zaire.

"Because we have a call and response that lets each of us know that we are in contact with the right person."

"And this anonymous caller provided you with the right response," asks Chance.

"Yes."

There's a knock at the door, and Chance and Zaire knows that means their teams have located some very valuable information about either Hassan or Mr. Red, as Genevieve calls him. They tell her to sit tight while they get up and leave the room. Out in the hall are Garth and Whitney looking very pleased with themselves.

"Spill it," bark Chance and Zaire at the same time.

"You need to see it," state Garth and Whitney at the same time.

"Lead the way," states Chance.

The four of them head down the hall towards the communications center so that Garth and Whitney can show Chance and Zaire what they have discovered.

Snake Chaser

The Next Journey

When the four of them reach the communications center, Garth and Whitney lead Zaire and Chance over to a large screen that is showing satellite images of what appears to be a compound set up in a remote location, however, Zaire and Chance aren't able to determine where the compound is located.

"Well," states Chance as they all stare at the screen.

The image changes and shows a small group of men exiting a small building on the compound, "There," states Garth as he freezes the image on the screen.

It's a bit grainy, but both Zaire and Chance are able to determine that the men are heads of various Mexican Cartels that the government has been keeping their eye on. "I'll be damned," state Zaire and Chance at the same time.

"While I would love to pursue them at the moment, Mr. Red has become our top priority," Chance states.

"Just stay focused on the screen," responds Whitney.

As Chance and Zaire continue to watch the screen they see the arrival of the infamous Mr. Red, and they notice how friendly the greeting is between him and the heads of the cartels.

"Where are they," asks Chance.

"Cuba," responds Garth.

"Cuba," exclaim Zaire and Chance in unison.

"Do the two of you have to keep taking in stereo," asks Whitney around a smile.

Chance and Zaire laugh as they respond simultaneously again, "No."

Garth and Whitney simply shake their heads, before continuing, "It seems they arrived at this compound shortly after we arrived here in the Philippines. Not sure what it means that the South American is enlisting the help of the Mexican Cartels, but it can't be good."

"Well whatever they're up to, I say we make moves to put a stop to it since they aren't aware that we know where they are and I say we do it quickly," states Zaire.

"I agree," responds Chance, "but first let's take a look at all the footage we can gather of this compound so that we know how many people they have there and what kind of artillery we'll be facing."

Zaire, Chance, Garth, and Whitney spend the next three hours reviewing the footage of the compound prior to Mr. Red and the cartels' arrival there. They discover that the cartel members arrived first with only a small band of bodyguards, but they do appear to have brought a large shipment of artillery

Snake Chaser

with them which makes Zaire and Chance very suspicious and very nervous.

Mr. Red arrives the next day with a small band of men and no women which they find odd, but continue to watch the footage to see what happens next. Later on that day, they see the arrival of some men in medical coats which leads them to believe that Mr. Red plans to alter his appearance again and plans to use the Mexican Cartels to provide security while he recovers which they too find odd with the number of people he employs. However, they quickly make the decision not to sit around and let anyone off the island, and contact their superiors to inform them of what they have learned so that they can get the go ahead to head to Cuba and for them to take over with Genevieve and the women that they have in custody.

Once they have the green light, they gather their teams together and inform them of what they have learned and let them know that they are headed to Cuba for their next mission. Since they can't get transport to the carrier that the military has in the Gulf of Mexico until the next day, Chance and Zaire give their teams some time off. So the team decides to go out to eat as they have been living off of rations for quite some time now, and they know once they arrive in Cuba it will be more of the same.

When they arrive at the restaurant they have chosen, Qasean secretly dials Sylvia's phone and once she sees who the caller is she knows that he wants some time alone with her. So tells the team that she has to take the call, and stays outside as she answers the phone. Qasean tells the team, that he's going to hang back to make sure that she is not hassled by anyone while she's on the phone. No one on the team suspects anything, so they go inside the restaurant to get a table.

Once the rest of the team is out of sight, Qasean directs Sylvia to a secluded area in the parking lot. Once he has her all to himself, he wraps her up in his arms and kisses her deeply stealing her breath. He doesn't release her lips until the need to pull oxygen into his lungs forces him to do so. He stands there holding her until their breathing is somewhat normal, and just stares into her eyes. "Sorry to ambush you like that," he begins, "but I've missed holding you in my arms." He pauses as he runs his tongue across her lips, "And I've missed the hell out of your lips." She simply smiles at him, and he says, "God, have I missed seeing a smile on those lips as well." He then proceeds to steal her breath away again with another kiss.

Even though she is enjoying the kiss, she breaks it off and says, "We better get inside before they come looking for us thinking that something is wrong."

"I know you're right, but I'm reluctant to let you go now that I have you just where I want you."

"I'm sure you will have plenty of time to have me where you want me once this mission is over," she replies. The images her words conjure up in his mind cause his manhood to jump, and she feels the movement. But as he begins to lower his mouth towards her lips once again, she pulls out of his embrace and begins laughing. "Uhn't Uh Mister! Now get yourself together so we can join the others."

"You are so going to pay for this after this mission is over," he states around a smile.

"I'm going to hold you to that," she throws over her shoulder as she starts walking back towards the entrance of the restaurant.

He pulls himself together, and then quickly catches up to her just as she is about to enter the restaurant. They join the rest of their team, and enjoy the rest of their evening over food, drinks, and laughter.

Snake Chaser

*****

The next morning they board their transport to the carrier so that they can bring this mission to a close. At least that's what Qasean is hoping because he desperately needs to have some alone time with Sylvia for he is jonesing to make love to her, and what he doesn't know is that she is jonesing to have him make love to her. While in the air the team reviews its game for when they arrive on the carrier, and how they plan to capture whoever is still in Cuba when they arrive on the island.

Once on the carrier, Zaire and Chance head to the communications room to review the satellite images of the compound to see what activity has taken place while they were in the air while the rest of the team heads to their sleeping quarters to get their gear in order and rest.

As Chance and Zaire review the satellite images of the compound, they notice that there has been little to no activity taking place since they left the Philippines which can only mean that their assumption that Mr. Red was going to alter his appearance once again was dead on. As a result, they make the decision to not rush onto the island, but to observe the compounds' activity for another twenty-four hours so that they can ensure that they will successfully capture Mr. Red and any Cartel members that happen to still be on the island.

Seizing The Moment

Zaire and Chance send word to their teams about the change of plans, as they keep a close eye on the compound. As they sit and watch the screen, they aren't seeing too much going on other than the changing of the sentinels every few hours. Since they saw no evidence of the doctors leaving the island, they assume that they are still inside the compound and wonder how cooperative they will be after the raid. Will thcy give up all they know about Mr. Red and his operation?

*****

Deciding to take advantage of the extra hours of down time Qasean seeks out Sylvia, and runs into her just as she is about to enter her room on the carrier. Making sure no one is the corridor, Qasean follows her inside. "You know you shouldn't be in here, right," Sylvia asks after the door closes behind them.

"I won't tell if you don't," quips Qasean around a smile. She simply shakes her head at him as she returns his smile. "Take a seat, I want to talk to you," he states as his face takes on a sobering look. Not sure what he's about to say but dying to find out, Sylvia takes a seat on the edge of her bed without saying a word. Qasean clears his throat as he walks to stand directly in front of her. "You know that I am head over heels in love with you, right?" Not trusting her voice, Sylvia simply nods her head. "You know there is not another woman in the world for me, don't you?"

Starting to feel a little uneasy, Sylvia clears her throat before responding, "Qasean, I know all of this. You have told me how much you love me on multiple occasions, and you know that I have loved you since I was fourteen. So where are you going with this?"

"I'm going to get to that. Just humor me and answer me one more question, okay?"

"Okay."

"You know that I plan to spend the rest of my life loving you, right?"

"Yes, and I plan to do the same."

He lets out a breath he didn't realize he was holding when he hears her answer, and then he reaches into his right pants pocket and pulls out something that fits in the palm of his hand before getting on one knee in front of her. "Sylvia Michelle Williams will you do the honor of becoming my wife," asks Qasean as he opens his hand to reveal an Emerald and Diamond engagement ring.

Tears instantly fall from Sylvia's eyes as she looks back and forth between his face and the ring that he is now holding between his thumb and index finger. She places a hand over her mouth to keep from screaming, and simply nods her head. "I need to hear you say yes Sweetheart," whispers Qasean.

Completely overwhelmed, Sylvia whispers "Yes." Then says yes again with a little more strength in her voice. Sure that she is not going to scream, she states yes once more in her normal voice as she extends her left hand in his direction.

After placing the ring on her finger, he uses the same thumb and index finger to take hold of her chin to raise her face to his before saying directly into her eyes, "I love you with all my heart, and I will love you until I take my last breath." Before she can respond, he kisses her fully, totally, and deeply.

As she returns his kiss, she begins removing his clothes. He breaks the kiss as she attempts to pull his t-shirt over his head. "Sweetheart, what are you doing," he asks as she whisks the shirt over his head.

"We are sealing this deal with more than a kiss," she replies as she goes after the buttons on his pants.

He places his hands over hers as he asks, "Don't you think that's a little too risky?"

"As long as you're quiet, no one will know that you're in here with me," she replies with a smirk on her face.

He chuckles before stating, "You just make sure that you don't get loud." He then proceeds to help her remove his clothing before he begins removing hers. He places her on the bed and cups her breasts in his palms, and admires the contrast of her chocolate brown nipples on her peanut butter complexion skin. He dips his head and draws a nipple in his mouth and suckles. The sensation causes her hips to rise off the bed, and he draws her breast deeper into his mouth. As she continues to move her hips to the rhythm of his mouth on her breast, he moves his mouth to her other breast to feast on it the same way. When he has had his fill of her chocolate treats, he slowly moves his mouth down her body until he reaches her moist center. His tongue dips into her fountain of love and he greedily consumes while looking in her eyes until he brings her to a mind-blowing

Snake Chaser

climax. He can tell by the way she's biting her lip and the surprised look in her eyes that she is just as overwhelmed by her release as he is, but he's not finished with her yet.

He slowly moves his body over hers until his throbbing manhood is poised at the juncture of her thighs. He leans down and kisses her deeply while using his legs to spread her thighs to allow him entry. He makes one deep thrust into her body that allows him to be buried completely inside of her, and then he pauses wanting to cherish the feeling. Unable to control her body's reaction to his invasion, Sylvia plants her feet on the bed and thrusts upward nearly bucking him off of her. Qasean quickly grips her hips in his hands keeping them suspended in the air as he begins thrusting in and out of her body burying himself to the hilt with every foray into her body. Sylvia wraps her legs around his hips and her arms around his neck in an effort to keep her body as connected to his as possible. She's too wet, too hot for him to last much longer, so he leans down and whispers in her ear, "It's time Baby. Come with me."

Her body instantly reacts to his voice and the feel of his breath on her neck, and he feels her body begin to convulse as her orgasm approaches. He can tell by her body's movements that this is going to be a powerful one, so he leans down and captures her lips in a kiss to keep either one of them from screaming out in ecstasy. Within minutes both of their bodies explode so explosively that they have to tighten their grip on each other to stay connected to one another. Once the spasms of their joint climax subside, Qasean collapses on top of her as they both are completely drained of all energy.

"Baby . . . I know . . . I'm heavy . . . but I need . . . a few moments . . . before I can move," states Qasean around gasps for air.

"Hmm," is Sylvia's response as she is enjoying the feel of his body on hers and is in no hurry for him to move. After a few more minutes Qasean attempts to roll his body off of hers and onto the bed, however, Sylvia is not ready for him to move so she wraps her arms and legs around him to hold him in place. "Not yet," she states.

Qasean lies there for a few more moments before saying, "Baby, I'm crushing you. Let's turn over." In full agreement with that idea, Sylvia allows him to roll to the side and he brings her with him. After he is flat on his back with her lying on top of him, he begins stroking her back as he just can't keep from touching her. "As much as I would like to stay here the rest of the night, that's not possible Sweetheart."

"I know," she states and her voice gives away her disappointment in that they can't spend the night in each other's arms.

He gives her a few minutes to wallow in her disappointment before he swats her on the behind as he says, "Alright, time for us to get up and get dressed."

Knowing that he is right, she doesn't say a word. She just gets up and gets dressed, however, the light reflects off of her ring and catches her eye, and she instantly pauses and stares at it.

Unsure why she is frozen in place, Qasean walks around her so that he is facing her and sees her just staring at the ring he placed on her finger. "What's wrong Sweetheart," he asks with a hint of fear in his voice.

"Nothing," she whispers. Then she looks up at him with tears shimmering in her eyes. "It's beautiful," she states in an awe struck voice. As the tears silently roll down her face, she looks him straight in the eyes and says, "I can't wait to become your wife."

Snake Chaser

Qasean expels the breath he was holding and pulls her into his arms. "I can't wait to make you my wife," he responds. Then he remembers the chain that he bought her to wear it on for she cannot wear it on her finger while they're in the jungle taking down their fugitive crime lord. He reaches in his pants pocket and pulls out the chain, "You can wear it on this chain when we're on a mission so that you have it with you always," he states as he shows her the chain. He then takes the ring from her finger, places the ring on it, and then puts the chain around her neck. He then kisses her forehead before they finish dressing.

"I'll step out first to make sure that the corridor is clear," she states once they have finished dressing. She opens the door and looks up and down the hall, and finds it to be unusually quiet but puts it out of her mind as she motions to Qasean that the coast is clear.

Qasean leaves the room, and too notes how unusually quiet it is on the ship. As Sylvia steps back into her room, Qasean makes his way to the main deck for the quietness of the ship has the hairs standing up on the back of his neck.

Unexpected Development

As Qasean approaches the upper deck he runs into Henry who is damn near running to his room, and when he tries to stop him he simply yells over his shoulder for Qasean to go to the communications room. Qasean does double time to the room to see what is going on. When he arrives, he finds Garth, Whitney, Chance, and Zaire in the room looking at one of the screens showing satellite images of the shore of Cuba closest to the compound where Mr. Red is currently in residence.

Chance hears someone enter room, and is surprised to see Qasean as he was expecting Henry and Lucas. However, he has a situation on his hands and doesn't have time to explain things to the gunny, so he turns back towards the screen.

Qasean moves in closer so that he too can get a good look at the screen, and he's surprised at what he sees. There are two small yachts in the harbor near the compound, and some of the men from the compound are loading crates on to them. He, like the others, believe that Mr. Red is going to try to give them the slip in the middle of the night, but how in the world would he know that they were there watching him. "What's the move," Qasean asks the room at large.

Snake Chaser

"Henry and Lucas are going to swim to the yachts and attach tracking devices to both, so that if they do manage to get away we can track them later," Zaire throws over his shoulder.

"Joshua and Juilete should almost be at the compound by now," adds Chance, "and they should be able to give us more information about what is taking place at the compound as they were dropped off in the jungle on the other side of the compound about an hour ago."

"Why weren't Sylvia and I sent for," asks Qasean.

"Because you two will be sent to the compound in South America if we determine that that is where those two yachts are headed if they get out of the harbor," replies Chance. "The two of you know that jungle better than anyone, so we want to keep the two of you rested now so that you will be fresh if we have to send you there."

Before Qasean can say another word, a communication is received from Joshua and Juilete so everyone turns their focus to the message.

> *Their plan is to leave the compound at first light as they don't want to draw attention to themselves by leaving at night. They are loading the yachts under the cover of darkness so as not to draw scrutiny by doing so in daylight hours.*

Chance sends a message back telling them to make an encampment for the rest of the team will be joining them so that they can apprehend the criminals as they attempt to board the yachts. He then orders the rest of the team to get ready to head to the island. However, before Chance leaves the room, he receives another communication from Joshua and Juilete. The message gives him a pause, and he makes a last minute decision and he must catch Qasean before he reaches Sylvia.

Doing double time down the corridor he catches up with Qasean a few doors from Sylvia's room. He puts his hand on Qasean's shoulder as a cue for him to halt, and as Qasean turns around he notes the tight look on Chance's face and cocks an eyebrow at him.

"I received another message from Josh and Juile," he states. "Mr. Red and the Cartel heads somehow have received word that someone is on to them, and plan to ambush anyone who tries to apprehend them."

"How," asks Qasean now worried himself.

"Don't know, but I don't want my sister on the island."

"You can't stop her from going."

"I can if she doesn't know that we've left."

"You know that she will make our life a living hell when she finds out about that."

"I'm willing to risk it. How about you?"

Qasean looks around to make sure that no one can overhear his next words, "I asked your sister to marry me earlier tonight, so of course I don't want her in harm's way. But I'm not sure if I want to endure her wrath when she finds out that we left her behind on this ship."

Chance doesn't seem surprised by Qasean admission, and at the moment it's not as important as keeping his sister safe. "I should be able to spare you some of her wrath by saying that I gave you a direct order to leave her behind on the ship."

"Fine," Qasean states between clenched teeth. "I'm going to hold you to that when this over."

"Go get your gear so we can be dropped off," states Chance before he walks off to get his own gear.

Within fifteen minutes the team is assembled on the flight deck, and ready to board their transport to the island. No one says a word about Sylvia not being present for it's not their place to question their superiors. Once aboard the plane, Chance informs the rest of the team about the last communication that he received from Josh and Juile, and that they will have to revamp their strategy. Instead of waiting until the men are boarding the yachts to make their move, they will do so an hour before first light. He informs them that Lucas and Henry have been apprised of the new plan, and should be at the encampment with Josh and Juile by the time they arrive.

Just as Chance finishes bringing everyone up to date, they receive the signal that they are over their drop location and each one of them parachutes out of the plane. They arrive at the encampment in record time, and get right to business mapping out the paths each of them will take to the compound and their strategy for capturing those at the compound.

Gingerbread Man

One of the heads of the Mexican Cartels receives word that a group of people have parachuted down to the island, and that they should be careful when making their departure from the island. He informs the other heads, as well as, Mr. Red, and they are all glad that they have made provisions to destroy the compound upon their departure. They are also hoping that whoever has been tracking them believes that they all died during the explosion that takes place. While Mr. Red and the Mexican Cartels double check their plans to blow up the compound, the Marines work on their strategy to take them down unaware that their prey has no intentions of being captured.

"Are you sure that the artillery you have planted is good," Mr. Red asks Alejandro, head of one of Mexico's most notorious arms cartels, through the bandages covering his face.

Somewhat offended by the question, Alejandro responds in an angry voice, "Of course they're good," he practically yells. "I would be out of business if my product was not the best, and I'm offended that you would ask me that."

"Calm down my friend," responds Mr. Red, "I meant no offense. I just want to make sure that we all make it out here without any of our friends being able to follow us."

Snake Chaser

"I understand being cautious, but I don't take to kindly to my reputation being questioned."

"I apologize dear friend."

"Apology accepted."

"Good! Now let's make sure that everything is in place and ready for our escape and the demise of whoever is out there in the jungle," states Mr. Red as he pats Alejandro on the shoulder.

As they head to the surveillance room to view the compound to make sure that they traps they set up are undisturbed, Mr. Red gives a silent signal to his men to put in place his alternate plan. He has had enough of the Mexicans and they have served their purpose, so they will be meeting the same fate as those tracking him. He can't have anyone trying to blackmail him into any future deals because they helped him out of the hangman's noose this one time.

They enter the room and take a seat around the large monitor mounted on the wall. "Turn on the infrared," states Alejandro to the man working the panel off to the side of the monitor. "The green squares you see on the screen are the underground mines that we have planted around the perimeter of the compound, and those will be detonated once we are sure that each member of the enemy team has entered the compound," begins Alejandro. "By our count there should be seven of them, and they will show up on the monitor as red," he continues. "We have loaded the crates of explosives on the yachts, and they will be activated shortly after the mines are detonated to destroy all evidence of our presence here," he adds. "Make sure that you and your men are ready to enter the underground tunnels at precisely 3 A.M. for we will need time to make sure that we are as far from the compound as possible before the fireworks begin."

"We will be ready," replies Mr. Red. He then reaches for the handheld device that will be used to detect anyone's presence at the compound and to detonate the mines and explosives, "Let's go over the process for operating this one more time just in case I end up having to operate it," he states.

"Why would you end up having to operate the device," asks Alejandro a little apprehensive about the request.

"People are unpredictable," replies Mr. Red. "What if they decide to make their move earlier than planned, and I'm closer to the device than you are and end up having to execute our plan," he continues. "I want to make sure that we have a contingency plan in the event that happens for I do not plan on being captured by anyone. Do you want to take that chance?"

"No," replies Alejandro. "I like the way you think," he adds. So he covers the complete operation of the device with Mr. Red in the event that he is the one who ends up with the device.

Once everyone is satisfied that their plan is a solid one and that everything is in place to make sure that they are able to handle their problem, they pour themselves a drink to toast their partnership and the success of their mission. While they're enjoying their drink, one of the security lights starts blinking on the monitor indicating that they have an intruder. Alejandro is the first one to jump out of his chair to look at the monitor.

So as not to give anything away, Mr. Red follows closely on his heels, "What is it," he asks as though he doesn't already know.

Snake Chaser

"The system is indicating that someone has breached the perimeter, but there are no red dots on the screen which would show the intruder's body heat so we can know exactly where they are," Alejandro states frantically.

"I thought you said this equipment was all in working order," barks Mr. Red. "What if it's they arriving earlier than expected?"

"The equipment is in working order," yells back Alejandro. "It must be an animal that the system isn't picking up for there is no way that a human could be this close and the system wouldn't know it."

"That's what you say," states Mr. Red. He turns and heads for the door as he barks over his shoulder, "I'm getting my gear just in case we have to slip into this tunnel earlier than expected."

"Go ahead. I'm going to keep an eye on the system to see if it happens again."

Mr. Red lets his men know that his plan is in motion, and that they should be ready to go at the alternate time. He knows that he has nothing to worry about with Alejandro for he will spend the next couple of hours in that surveillance room with his equipment, and he has a plan that will ensure that he will have plenty to check out.

At the specified time, Mr. Red and his men head to the tunnel to make their escape with Alejandro still monitoring his monitoring equipment. He never even noticed that the handheld device left the room the same time as Mr. Red. Once they are inside the tunnel, one of his men secures the entrance to the tunnel so that it can't be opened from the other side and turns on the handheld device. Then he and his men follow the original plan so that they are as far from the compound as possible when he detonates the explosives and mines.

No sure what is happening with the security system Alejandro decides that they should head for the tunnel now, so he leaves the surveillance room to tell everyone to get ready and then goes into a panic when he can't find Mr. Red and his men. He runs back to the room to grab the handheld as he plans to detonate the explosives as planned, however, when he gets there it's missing. He goes to his men to see if one on them have it, and when they don't he goes into a fit of rage. They head to the tunnel anyway as he doesn't want to be anywhere near the compound when the explosives are set off, where he discovers that he can't open the hatch.

"That double crossing son of a bitch," scream Alejandro. He then turns to his men and says, "When need to get out of here and quick. I have no idea what that asshole is planning to do, but I'm not staying around to find out." So he and his men head to the garage to get in the vehicles they have stored in there, and load up to ride out of the compound. However, the cars won't start, and they have to figure out another way to get away from the compound. One of his men suggests that they use the boats after they dump the crates of explosives into the water, so they head to the boats.

However, the time it takes them to get to the boats and dump the explosives gives Chance, Zaire, and their team the time they need to access the compound. They see the men on the boat dumping the crates over the side, and wonder what type of double cross is taking place. Thinking fast on their feet, they send half of the crew inside the compound and the other half of the crew approaches the men on the boats.

Neither group is prepared for what happens next. A massive explosion from the compound rocks the ground and water, and disorients the men on the boat. However, before they can

Snake Chaser

recover, both boats explode. The crew on the carrier is momentarily stunned as the watch both explosions, but they quickly recover and send out the distress signal on the ship to mobilize a rescue crew to head to the island to see if there are any survivors.

ReGina Crawford

Devastation

The distress signal on the ship jars Sylvia awake, and she immediately heads to the communications room to find out what is going on. When she enters the room, the crew there is stunned to see her, and the ship's commander asks her, "Why are you not on the island with your team?"

"What," she asks still somewhat disoriented. "We're not supposed to be on the island yet. What are you talking about?"

"You don't know that your team left for the island a few hours ago," asks the puzzled commander.

"What," Sylvia shrieks. "What the hell is going on here? Why the distress signal?"

"How about you take a seat right here," suggests the commander as he directs her to a chair out of the way of his crew, "and I'll catch you up as soon as we are able to dispatch a rescue crew to the island.

Sylvia blindly takes the seat she's directed too as her head is swimming in confusion. She watches the commander organize his men for the rescue in a daze as she tries to process what he has and hasn't told her. If her team is on the island and they're dispatching a rescue crew to the island, something went terribly wrong and she doesn't even want to fathom that something has happened to her brother or to Qasean and Joshua.

When the rescue crew reaches the island there is nothing left of the compound or the boats, the Marines or the criminals. Based on the total devastation that they see all around them, it's going to be quite a while before they are able to sort through the body parts to determine who is who.

The crew returns to the carrier to give their report to the commander, but stop dead in their tracks when they see Sylvia sitting in a chair in the communications room. Since it doesn't appear as though she has noticed their arrival, they suggest that they give the commander their report in his quarters. They leave the room undetected, and once they reach the commander's quarters the rescue team informs him that anyone that was within the compound or in the vicinity of the boats was killed. They let him know that they will be picking up body parts for a few days, and it would probably be longer than that before they were able to say for certain what body parts belong to who.

"Shit," the commander grounds out between clinched teeth. "What the hell am I supposed to tell the woman sitting in my communications room," he asks the room at large.

"I suggest you drug her until we can get her back to DC," replies his Executive Office. When the commander looks at him as though he has lost his mind, the XO adds, "From what I understand her commanding officer was her brother and Joshua is the only child of the man who raised her after parents died, so if they have both died on that island she is going to be devastated. Do you want to have to deal with a hysterical woman who has just lost the rest of her family? Especially one with the skill to kill a man with her bare hands?"

"You do have a point," responds the commander. He takes a few moments to contemplate what her reaction might be, then says, "Notify the ship's doctor that we need something to knock out Sgt. Williams until she can be transported back to DC."

The XO notifies the ship's doctor of the situation, and tells him to meet him in Sylvia's stateroom. He then heads back to the communication room to escort Sylvia back to her room and since she is still stunned that her team left her on the ship while they went to the island, she blindly lets him lead her back to her room where the doctor is waiting for her. The doctor is able to sedate her with no problem, and once they get her securely in bed the XO goes back to the communications room so that he can help direct the recovery efforts taking place on the island.

The recovery crew focuses on locating body parts that have military issued clothing first, and once they believe that all eleven members of the Marine squad have been recovered they head back to the ship so that the remains can be shipped back to DC along with the remaining living team member.

*****

Sylvia and the remains have been back in DC for three days before the powers that be determine that it's time to longer keep her sedated as they have been able successfully ID all eleven members of her team. When she comes too, the first person she sees is the Marine Commander and right over his shoulder is Quintana who looks like she's been crying for days. By the look on his face, Sylvia knows that the commander is about to deliver some dire news so she tries to brace herself for what he's about tell her.

Snake Chaser

Not wanting to prolong telling her the devastating news, the commander just comes out with it, "It is with deepest regrets that I must inform you that your brother and the rest of your team were killed on Cuba four days ago." When she doesn't say a word, he adds, "We will give you a few days to process this news and deal with your grief, but after that it is imperative that we debrief you so that we can figure out what happened on that island and why you weren't with your team."

Sylvia then sits straight up in the bed, and with lightening speed grabs the commander by the throat and grits out between clinched teeth, "You and your military can go straight to hell! I have just lost every member of my family and my fiancée, and you want to debrief me! Me! I wasn't there! They left me behind on that damn carrier and got themselves killed, and you think I have something to tell you!" She leans in so that they are nose to nose before screaming in his face, "Go to hell!" She then throws him to the floor, and jumps out of the bed while he's lying on the floor gasping for air. Quintana is so stunned by Sylvia's actions and words that she is frozen in place, and speechless. Sylvia runs from the run and out of the medical facility, and doesn't stop running until she reaches her apartment. Since she doesn't have her belongings, she is forced to break into her apartment through a window off her balcony. Once she's inside, she climbs into her bed, curls up in a fetal position, and cries herself to sleep.

*****

Quintana eventually recovers her wits about her, and calls for help for the commander. After aiding the commander, the head of the hospital starts to call the Military Police to locate and apprehend Sylvia, however, the commander tells him that that's not necessary. He understands that Sylvia is under duress, and he will give her a couple days to recover before seeking her out and he has no intentions of pressing charges against her. After thanking Quintana for her assistance, he asks her to let him know if she hears from Sylvia. She agrees and then leaves the hospital.

When Quintana hasn't heard from Sylvia after three days, she goes to her apartment to see if she ever returned there and finds her in her bed curled up in the fetal position with dried tear tracks on her face. She attempts to wake her, but she doesn't respond. She checks her breathing and her pulse and finds both to be weak and thready, so she calls for an ambulance. The ambulance transports her to the military medical center, and they immediately place her on oxygen and IV fluids as it appears that she hasn't eaten or drank anything in the days since she fled the medical center after receiving the news about the death of her family and team.

After three hours of oxygen and fluids, Sylvia's eyes flutter open and the first face she sees in Quintana's. Tears immediately flow from her eyes as she knows that they both have lost someone who meant the world to them. She reaches up to hug Ana, but finds that she can't move her arms as they have been strapped to the bed. She tries to speak, but she has no voice.

"Shhhhh," states Quintana as she sees Sylvia desperately trying to talk. When Sylvia looks down at the straps on her wrists, Quintana tells her, "They have you strapped to the bed as a result of your attack on the Marine Commander the last time you were here. They just want to make sure you that you don't harm yourself or anyone else." Sylvia closes her eyes as the memory of that day floods her mind. "Don't worry," begins Ana, "The commander doesn't plan to charge you with anything as he understands that you were under duress on that day. He just wants to make sure that you are safe, and that you heal." Sylvia simply nods her head indicating that she has heard Ana's words. "The ceremony for our family members and the rest of the team is in two days time, so I need you to

Snake Chaser

rest and get healthy so that you can attend. So you must do whatever it is that the doctors tell you to do, do you understand?" Sylvia again nods her head. "No G.I. Jane stunts, okay?" Sylvia opens her eyes and gives Ana a pointed look. "Okay," prompts Ana. Sylvia briefly closes her eyes before nodding in agreement again. "Good. Now I'm going to go check on my parents, but I will be back later this evening." Ana leans over and kisses her on the cheek before leaving the room so that Sylvia can rest.

ReGina Crawford

Grief and Recovery

Twenty-four hours after Sylvia has been in the hospital, she has recovered enough to have the oxygen and IV taken away. They have unstrapped one arm so that she can feed herself the clear foods they are allowing her to have in order to build up her strength. She has just finished her lunch of clear broth and crackers when the Marine Commander enters her room, and she is instantly contrite over her behavior during his last visit.

He is able to quickly ascertain her mood, and puts up his hand in an attempt to reassure her that he is not there to sanction her. "I'm glad to see that you are following orders Sgt.," he states as he pulls a chair up to her bed and takes a seat. "I'm sure that Ms. Richardson has told you that I do not plan to have you charged for the incident that took place on my last visit to your hospital room." Sylvia simply nods her head. "Good. It was not my intention to upset you during my last visit, and after talking to the carrier's commander it is no longer necessary for me to debrief you concerning the events that took place that fateful day in Cuba. However, I would still like to talk to you about the mission that your team was involved in leading up to that day. We have a very clever and sadistic criminal on the loose, and I would like to ensure that he is captured sooner than later."

Snake Chaser

"I plan to ensure that he is captured," states Sylvia. "He took away everything that I had left in this world, and for that he will spend the rest of his life in jail," she adds.

The commander nods before saying, "He also took out some very powerful Mexican Cartel members as well during that explosion, so I'm sure that he will be lying low for quite some time. So as a result, I need all the information you can provide so that we will know when he emerges again."

"I'm willing to do whatever I can to help, Sir. You can count on me."

"Good. Now get some rest." With that, the commander gets up and leaves the room.

Sylvia spends the next twenty-fours getting her strength back, along with planning how to bring down the elusive Mr. Red who she has dubbed the 'Gingerbread Man' since no one has able to catch him.

The day of the memorial ceremony arrives, and Sylvia is released into Quintana's care mere hours before the ceremony is scheduled to take place. Having already gone by Sylvia's place to get her clothes to wear to the ceremony, Ana takes her directly to her parent's home to get ready. Once everyone is dressed and ready to go, they all get into the limo that was sent to transport them to the cemetery where the ceremony will take place.

When they arrive, they are escorted to the front row of seating where the family members of the other fallen Marines are already seated. Seeing the closed caskets with the pictures of each one of her team members behind them has a profound effect on Sylvia, and Ana and her father have to catch her before she falls to the ground. They get her into a chair, and Ana has to put an arm around her to keep her upright as silent tears cascade down her face. She sits there caressing her engagement ring which she has placed back on her finger as she morns the loss of her fiancée along with the last of her family members.

At the conclusion of the formal ceremony, the families are permitted to approach the caskets to say their final good-byes to their loved ones. Ana and her parents escort Sylvia first to her brother's casket, then to Joshua's, and finally to Qasean's. Sylvia lays her head on the casket as she talks to Qasean's memory.

> *My Love, I will forever carry you in my heart as I have done since I was fourteen. I miss you terribly, but I am grateful for all the memories that we created together for they shall help me deal with not being able to hear your voice, your laughter, or see your smile, or hold you in my arms. And I promise you that I will bring down the man that took away our forever.*

She then kisses the casket and backs away so that the rest of his family can say their good-byes as well. While she's standing there, she sees a couple who have to be Jules and Juilete's parents and makes her way over to them. "I am so sorry for your loss. I didn't know them long, but I liked them both," states Sylvia to the couple.

"Thank you," states the woman. "We saw you stop at three caskets, who did you lose?"

"I lost my brother, my cousin, and my fiancée," replies Sylvia. "They were the last of my family," she adds. "I have no one

Snake Chaser

left except for the family of my fiancée," states before she breaks down in body-racking sobs. The man has to catch her before she falls to the ground, and Qasean's father rushes over to her to help stabilize her.

"Oh dear," states the woman. "Maybe you should take her home. I don't think she should stay here any longer."

"Thank you," states Mr. Richardson. "We will take her home immediately."

Ana and her father help Sylvia back to the limo, followed by Mrs. Richardson, as she continues to sob uncontrollably. When they arrive back at their home, Ana immediately takes Sylvia up to her room and puts her in the bed. She then goes and gets a glass of water to give Sylvia the sedative that the doctors gave her just in case Sylvia was unable to handle the reality of her loss after seeing the caskets. She has no problem getting Sylvia to take the sedative, and sits with her until she goes to sleep. She then goes downstairs to see about her parents.

When she walks in the living room, her parents are sitting on the couch holding on to each other but when they hear enter the room, her mother asks, "Did you know that your brother and Sy were engaged?"

"I didn't know that he had asked her yet, but I did know that he had planned to ask her," replies Ana. "He called and told me while they were in the Philippines. He must have just asked her before his death, cause I'm sure Sy would have called me to tell me that he had proposed."

"I'm sure she will tell us everything once she is done grieving," states Ana. "I'm very worried about her though," she adds. "She didn't grieve this hard when her parents died or even when Uncle Chappy died, and she thought she was without family those times as well."

"At those other times, she knew she had other family out there. She just didn't have contact with them," states her father. "This time is different. She knows with complete certainty that she has no one left."

"She has us," responds Ana.

"I think she knows that in the back of her mind," comments her mother, "but right now she's feeling completely orphaned. We will have to mindful of that, and just keep supporting her until she has recovered from her loss."

"Okay Mom," Ana says before walking over and hugging both of her parents. She then announces that she is going for a walk, and then heads out the front door. She is gone for over an hour, and when she returns she notes that Sylvia is still sleeping so she decides to go over to her place and gather some of her things since she doesn't think she should be left alone for a while, and especially at her own place where she is sure memories of Qasean will bombard her friend.

When she returns home, Sylvia is just coming around and is still a little groggy. "What did you give me," she asks as Ana walks in the room with her bags.

"I gave you a sedative that the doctor gave me for you so you could rest and not cry yourself sick," she replies as she sets down the bags and walks over to the bed. "You are still weak, and all the crying you were doing was going to land you back in the hospital. So I gave you the sedative so that you could rest peacefully, and allow your body to continue to recover."

As she thinks about what Ana has just said, she looks towards the door and notices her bags. "Why are my bags here?"

Snake Chaser

"We think it's best if you stay with us for a while as you recover from your hospital stay."

"We?"

"Mom, Dad, and I."

"I don't know about that," states Sylvia as she gives Ana a squinty eye look.

"Sylvia, you don't have a choice. You have always been like family to us, and we are not leaving you alone. Besides with that ring on your finger, it seems my brother planned on ensuring you were a member of this family in every way."

Sylvia looks down at her engagement ring, and tears once again flow from her eyes.

Ana sits on the edge of the bed and wraps her arms around Sylvia, "I didn't mean to make you cry." As more tears flow from Sylvia's eyes, Ana squeezes her even tighter, "You are going to make yourself sick. Please stop crying."

"I know . . . you're right," states Sylvia between sobs, "and I . . . promise . . . this is . . . my last . . . hard cry."

Ana lays her head on top of Sylvia's, and they sit there and cry together until Sylvia falls asleep. Ana lays her down in the bed, and then goes to sit in the window seat in her room to think about her own future, as well as, the future of her friend.

Back To Business

It's been three weeks since the ceremony, and Sylvia is ready to get back to business and track down the man that irrevocably changed her life. She packs her bags, tells Qasean and Ana's parents that she is going back to work and for them to tell Ana that she will call her later.

Her first stop is to her apartment where she unpacks her bags, checks her mail and voicemail messages, and then places her engagement ring in her jewelry box along with the jewelry that she received from her parents and Uncle Chappy. Ready to take back her life, she calls the Marine Commanders' office and requests a meeting which he readily agrees to so she heads over to his office.

Upon her arrival, his secretary informs her that she can go right in as the commander is awaiting her arrival. When she walks in the commander stands up and extends his hand as he says, "It's good to have you back Sgt."

Sylvia shakes his hand as she states, "It's good to be back. Now where do we start with taking down the Gingerbread Man?"

"The Gingerbread Man," asks the commander as he cocks his head to the side in confusion.

Snake Chaser

"Your reports probably call him Mr. Red, but since he seems to think he's unstoppable I've dubbed him the Gingerbread Man," is her response.

"I see," replies the commander. "First things first, despite having read all the reports completed by Chance and Zaire, I would like to ask you a few questions about the missions that you participated in. Then I would like for you to help me put together a Black Ops team dedicated to bringing this 'Gingerbread Man' to justice."

"Okay. What would you like to know?"

He pulls out the reports and photos that have been turned over to him from all the missions carried out by Chance's and Zaire's teams, and the both of them go over them with a fined tooth comb for the next three hours. Once the commander is satisfied that he has a clear picture of what took place over the course of all the missions involving Mr. Red, he then pulls out the personnel files of ten Marines he's considering for this new team. He and Sylvia spend the next three hours reviewing their skill sets and past missions to determine who would work best together. They are both in agreement on four of the candidates, however, they are split about who would best fit the role of the fifth team member. So they decide to call all six candidates in so that they may interview and take an assessment of their skills. They schedule the interviews two days out to give those that are not already in the area an opportunity to arrive in DC.

When the Marines arrive, they are directed to the training facility where Sylvia and the commander are waiting for them. They have already made up their minds that Fredrick "Stoney" Blackstone is in as the electronic equipment specialist, along with Gunther Albrecht who comes with phenomenal underwater skills, and Natalia "Nat" Rousseau who will be the navigation expert on the team. Although they both agree that Alrik "Rik" Stein is a match for the team with his skills in hand-to-hand combat, stealth, and marksmanship, they will still evaluate him along with the other two that have hand-to-hand combat skills. Unbeknownst to them, Carlina "Lina" Hernadez and Rocco "Roc" Esposito will be competing for the last spot on the team as their skill level in marksmanship seems to be even, however, Lina has the added skill of hand-to-hand combat while Roc has superior stealth skills.

"Alright Marines, you know why you're here, and I'm sure you're wondering why there are six of you present when teams are made up of only six," begins the commander. "Five of you are locked in, however, the remaining two will be put through a series of simulations to determine which of you will best fit the team and its mission," he continues. "Before we begin the simulations, I want you all to meet Sgt. Sylvia Williams who will be your team leader," he states as he motions for Sylvia to come stand beside him.

"Greetings Marines," states Sylvia. "We need to get on top of this mission fairly quickly, so we are going to begin simulations to determine the last member of the team and then the team will be briefed on the details of the mission we will undertake."

"Rik you will participate in the hand-to-hand simulation with Lina, and the stealth simulation with Roc," states the commander. "While we are assessing the simulations, the rest of you can review these briefs," he adds as he hands the other four a folder containing all the background information they have on Mr. Red and his criminal enterprise. He then turns and heads towards the simulation room followed by Sylvia and the three other Marines.

Snake Chaser

"We'll start with Rik and Roc in the stealth simulation," states Sylvia as they enter the simulation room. "Your gear for this exercise is in the locker room, go ahead and change."

When Rik and Roc reemerge from the locker room, they enter the simulation booth after receiving their instructions, and Sylvia and the commander enter the observation booth. As they watch both men tackle the exercise, Sylvia comments, "Rik is really good."

"That he is, but Roc isn't doing too badly," remarks the commander.

When the simulation ends and both me emerge from the booth, Sylvia is the first to speak, "Great job Marines. Roc you can go change back into your regular uniform and join the others in the conference room." She them turns to Lina, "Your gear for your simulation is in the locker room. Once you've changed, we'll begin your simulation."

Lina emerges from the locker room, and she and Rik enter the simulation booth to see how they fair with the hand-to-hand combat scenario that has been programmed for them. As Sylvia and the commander watch them in action they are still torn as to who should make the team.

Once the simulation is complete, Sylvia instructs Rik and Lina to go get changed and meet them in the conference room. When they join the others, the commander commends the three Marines on their performances in the simulation booth. "However," he adds, "your performances have left us with a dilemma as to who would best fit the team." He pauses as he looks them all in the face before continuing, "Rik, you are in." Then he looks at Roc and Lina, "As you know our teams are made up of six Marines, and the goal of today's exercises was to determine which of you would make the team and which of you would be sent back to your previous assignment. Sylvia

193

and I have decided that due to the nature of this mission we will put together a seven member team, so the both of you are in. Congratulations."

Lina and Roc look at each other before turning back to the commander and Sylvia and saying simultaneously, "Thank you Sir, Ma'am."

"Just make sure you live up to everything that you showed us today," states the commander. "Sylvia will continue the briefing today, but I will see each of you before you leave DC." With that he turns and exits the conference room.

After the commander's exit, Sylvia turns to her team, hands the remaining three the same briefing folder the other four received earlier. "Familiarize yourselves with every photo in the folder, for we will find each one of them and bring them to justice. We will meet back here at 0500 tomorrow to formalize our first mission." With that she too leaves the conference room.

Happy to have the opportunity to be a member of an elite team, the six Marines read every word of the briefs they have been given and memorize every facial feature of every photograph in the folder.

When Sylvia arrives at the training facility at 0500 the next morning, she is impressed that all six Marines are present and ready to go. She spends the morning reviewing the activities of Mr. Red and Hassan, for she is certain that Hassan will continue to make deals with Mr. Red and she's hoping that he will be a great source of information on his activities and movements. She spends the afternoon interrogating Genevieve who had been transported to DC after the death of her team in Cuba, and she learned from her that Hassan has connections in the US Military which is how he has been able to remain at large and continue is criminal activities.

Snake Chaser

She spends her evening getting up to speed on the larger cartels in Mexico as they too are on the hunt for Mr. Red for what took place in Cuba, and she is hoping that keeping tabs on them will help her get a lead on Mr. Red and that she is able to get to him before they do.

The next day and the days following that, Sylvia and the team work on drills and simulations together so that they can learn to read each other without having to have verbal communication while carrying out their assigned missions for that will be critical to their success.

ReGina Crawford

Unexpected Break

Three months after the team has been formed and training together, Sylvia receives word from the commander that he has received reports that Hassan is in Vietnam attempting to take over Genevieve's brothel business. He is claiming that he has paperwork from Genevieve stating that he is to take over the running of her business in the event that she is unable to do so. He has also been able to gain information about her capture and subsequent incarceration which makes his claim appear to be legit, however, the Vietnam government is fighting his claim as they want to put an end to all the foreign women infiltrating their country.

So the team packs up to head to Vietnam to see if they can apprehend Hassan as a means of garnering information about Mr. Red and his whereabouts. The team arrives in Thailand to set up an operations center before venturing into Vietnam for they know that even though the Vietnam government doesn't want Hassan doing business in their country they want the United States doing business there even less. Once the operations center is set up, Sylvia, Rik, Roc, Lina make their way into Vietnam to apprehend Hassan. Stoney stays at the operations center to monitor their activity, as well as, the activity of the Vietnam government and Hassan. Since Gunther's water skills are not needed in Vietnam, he stays behind to assist Stoney.

Snake Chaser

The team arrives in Vietnam after dark, and stealthily makes their way to one of Genevieve's brothels where Hassan has been spotted in recent days. They position themselves around the perimeter of the building for they are not sure which door he would use to enter and exit the brothel. Sylvia admires Genevieve's set up as she has doors for each type of clientele she serves to provide the maximum about of discretion possible. They have been maintaining their positions for three hours when Sylvia sees Hassan arrive at the entrance she's monitoring. She wastes no time in leaving her position to apprehend her prey.

Before he can even ring the bell announcing he requires entrance, Sylvia sneaks up behind him and places a black hood over his head and cinches it tight around his neck. As he reaches up to the back of his neck to loosen the rope holding the hood around his head, Sylvia bounds his wrists as she whispers in his ear in a deadly voice, "Don't make me have to kill you by fighting me." Hassan instantly freezes at her deadly tone. "Good boy," she says as she pushes him to the ground face down. She then bounds his legs together before dragging him back to her hiding place before signaling her team that she has captured the man they are looking for. The rest of the team joins her, and they drug their prey so that they can sneak him into Thailand.

After arriving back at the operations center in Thailand, Sylvia places Hassan in the interrogation room minus the hood, and shackles him to the table while they wait for him to regain consciousness. In the hour between their arrival and the time that he's fully awake, Sylvia reports back that they have him custody. Once he's fully awake, Sylvia and Rik start their interrogation while Stoney makes sure that every minute of it is recorded.

As Hassan eyes begin to focus clearly, Sylvia says, "Well, Well! Look who we have here." She then chuckles at the frown on his face, as he realizes that Americans have captured him.

"What the hell is going on here," he yells. "You Americans have no jurisdiction in Vietnam! They don't even like your kind here," he adds.

"You can stop yelling Hassan," states Sylvia in a calm yet deadly sounding voice. "We are no longer in Vietnam, and no one outside this room can hear you anyway."

"What do you mean we are no longer in Vietnam," he asks with obvious concern in his voice even though he is still yelling. "If we're not in Vietnam, then where are we?"

"Where we are doesn't concern you," replies Sylvia in a menacing voice, "What we want does though." She opens the folder on the table in front of her and takes out a picture of Mr. Red, and slides it across the table. When Hassan doesn't even look down at the picture, still speaking in the same menacing tone and with fire in her eyes, she says, "Look at it!"

Hassan jumps slightly at her tone, and looks down at the picture. "Who is that," he asks with more bravado in his voice than he's really feeling. When she doesn't respond and just keeps looking at him with the same fire in her eyes, he states, "I don't know who that is."

Not wanting to give him the satisfaction of letting him know that he's pissing her off even more, she simply takes another picture from the folder and slides it across the table. The picture shows him shaking hands with Mr. Red at the conclusion of their last arms deal. "Know who it is now?"

"Who are you," he asks.

Snake Chaser

"Who I am is even less important than where we are," she replies. "Do you know him now?"

"You can't charge me with anything," he states confidently. "That deal was not on American soil."

"You're right, I can't charge with a crime," she responds before standing and leaning over the table so she's right in his face. "But I can kill you and no one will be the wiser since no one knows that I have you." She holds her position until she sees fear rise in his eyes before taking her seat, and asks again, "Do you know him now?"

Suddenly unsure of himself, Hassan starts stuttering, "He's . . . an arms dealer." When she continues to stare at him unimpressed with his words or his behavior, he adds still stuttering, "It's not . . . like we're . . . friends . . . or anything. He . . . sells . . . arms. I buy . . . them."

"How can we get in touch with him," asks Sylvia.

"I don't know." Sylvia gets up out of her chair, and Hassan attempts to raise his hands but can't because they are shackled to the table. His fear gets the better of him, and yells, "Look lady, I can't help you!"

Still standing, Sylvia states with a wicked grin on her face, "Too bad. Guess we'll have to kill you then. Can't have you telling him that we're looking for him." She then turns to Rik and says, "Take him to the disposal room and dispose of him." Then she heads to the door to exit the room as Rik gets up and starts to come around the table towards Hassan.

"Wait," he yells as he eyes Rik. Sylvia stops but doesn't turn around. "When I need guns or Ammo, I place a post on a message board that he monitors, and then he contacts me."

Sylvia turns around with the same evil smile on her face, and still feeling uncertain, Hassan adds, "But you should know that he's suspended all of his dealings indefinitely."

"And how do you know that," she asks not moving from her position.

"Everyone who buys items from him on the Black Market knows that," he responds a little too cockily for her tastes, so the menacing look returns to her face. Not liking how she's looking at him, he loses the cockiness from his voice as he adds, "He hasn't responded to any posts for over three months, and the rumors we've heard . . .," he begins but his voice trails off when he realizes that he is about to share information that he probably shouldn't as it could possibly implicate Mr. Red in what the Americans consider an act of terrorism.

When he doesn't immediately continue, Sylvia walks back over to the table only this time she comes to stand directly beside him. "What rumors," she asks as she places her face within a breath of his.

Picking up the menacing undertone in her voice, Hassan quickly swallows before replying, "Before I say anything more, I need some assurances for my safety."

Exasperated by his words, Sylvia walks away from the table throwing her hands up while nearly yelling, "Why the hell does everyone who knows anything about this man need assurances for their safety?"

"So Genevieve asked for the same thing, did she?"

When Sylvia quickly spins and starts angrily striding in his direction, he goes into a panic and almost breaks his wrists as he tries to move away from her. Sylvia grabs him by the collar and brings him nose to nose with her before saying through

Snake Chaser

clenched teeth as she barely holds on to her rage, "What hell did you just say?"

Hassan darts his eyes in Rik's direction who has been quietly watching the scene unfold, and Rik simply puts his hands up to indicate that Hassan is on his own. He swallows a few times as his mouth and throat suddenly feel dry, then he responds, "A few of my men watched Genevieve's capture, and I assume that she asked for protection before she would give anyone any information on The Archman."

Since Sylvia is aware that is the name that Hassan knows Mr. Red by, she knows that they are still talking about the same person. "And did you tell anyone about Genevieve's capture," asks Sylvia with a sick feeling in the pit of her stomach.

As she hasn't changed her stance or the tone of her voice, Hassan quickly makes the decision to tell her everything for he's not sure that he'll make it out of the room alive if he doesn't.

Confessions

"I told The Archman about her capture, and sold him the pictures that my men took of the people that captured her," he says barely above a whisper.

Enraged by that bit of information, Sylvia tightens her hold on his collar to the point that he's barely able to draw a breath, and since he's still shackled to the table there is nothing that he can do to stop her. Rik notices that the man is near to passing out, so he intervenes by prying Sylvia's fingers loose from the man's collar. Hassan immediately starts taking in gulps of air now that his collar has been freed, while Rik walks Sylvia to the other side of the room so that she can collect herself as well.

When Sylvia feels that she has regained some semblance of control she walks back over to the table, and gives an evil laugh as Hassan cringes in his seat at her approach. "Don't worry," she begins. "I'm not going to kill you," she continues. "At least not until you tell me everything that you know about The Archman," she adds. She gives him an evil smile before saying, "Spill it! And I mean everything!"

Fearing for his life, Hassan starts talking even though his throat feels as though it's on fire. "I've never trusted Genevieve, so I left some of my men behind to observe her deal with The

Snake Chaser

Archman, and they watched her capture by the group that emerged from the brush and were able to get photos of their faces," he begins but his voice is raspy due to him not being able to breathe.

Sylvia looks in Rik's direction, and he immediately assesses her silent look and looks at the camera indicating that they needed a glass of water for their guest. In short order, there is a knock at the door and Rik takes the glass of water from Lina. He gives it to Sylvia, who in turn places the glass up to Hassan's lips. He drinks too fast and immediately begins choking. She pats him on the back while telling him to sip the water instead of gulping it. Once his choking subsides, she places the glass up to his lips once more and he takes several small sips trying to soothe his burning throat. Sylvia then sets the glass on the table while saying, "Continue."

Hassan swallows to test his throat before speaking again, "I sold those photos to The Archman hoping to gain an even better footing with him, and possibly gaining a possible position within his organization. He paid me for the photos, but quickly let me know that the photos didn't make him look upon me any more favorably than he had in the past. As a matter of fact he told me that if word leaked out about the transaction, that he would take out my whole family and the families of anyone who worked for me. Having heard about previous families that he has wiped out as a result of being double-crossed, I took him at his word. See why I now need protection?"

"I see, but still not sure if I'm going to give you any other than a six-by-six jail cell," replies Sylvia. "Continue."

"I'm not saying that it was intentional, but some of the faces Marines that I heard were killed in that explosion in Cuba match the faces of some of the faces that were in those photos," continues Hassan. Sylvia has to work hard at not letting her emotions get the best of her so that he can continue telling her what she wants to know. "I know he has connections in various Mexican Cartels since some the guns and ammo he has sold me in the past came from Mexico," he adds. "I also know that his connections with those cartels are how he has been able to avoid being stopped as they have connections inside your government, and they keep him updated on your governments movements," he goes on to say. "I think he knows that your government has dubbed him as enemy number one which is why he has stopped making deals these past months, but I don't think that it will stop him from picking back up once he feels the coast is clear," he further adds.

"Does he know that we have pictures of his face," asks Sylvia.

"It wouldn't matter if you do," replies Hassan.

"Why wouldn't it matter?"

"Cause when he purchased the pictures from me, he suspected that those tracking him may have gotten a good look at him at his compound in South America so he was planning on having his face altered," he responds, "and not the subtle alterations that he has periodically done in the past."

"And you know this how?"

"He told me when he bought the pictures."

"Do you happen to know where he could possibly be holding up while he waits for our interest in him to wane?"

"Not exactly."

"Not exactly?"

Snake Chaser

"Well, I know that he has compounds in both Madagascar and Saudi Arabia, but I don't have any specifics that would help you pinpoint a specific region in those countries," he responds. He then looks pointedly at the glass of water. Sylvia picks up the glass and lets him take several sips of water. "Now that I have told you all that I know, can we discuss how you're government is going to protect me in the event he gets the drop on you guys again?"

"Well since you won't be around to feed him information or pictures, I doubt he'll be able to get the '*drop*' on us again," responds Sylvia a little more menacing than was probably necessary, but since he's the reason her whole family dying in that explosion in Cuba she's taking great pleasure in scaring him every chance she gets. She then signals to Rik, and they both leave the room so that she may report back to DC what Hassan has told her.

After relaying to the commander everything that she learned from Hassan, she asks the commander what she should do with him and he tells her to bring him back to DC with her. He would like to keep Hassan as close as possible to avoid him being able to share any more information with any other criminal masterminds. He tells them that he will be sending transport for them in the morning, and for them to get the operations center packed up.

While they go about getting their gear packed up, they leave Hassan in the interrogation room still shackled to the table. When Sylvia and Rik return to check on him several hours later, they realize that they have left him alone for too long as he has gone to the bathroom on himself.

Hassan is in a rage at the fact that he was forced to soil himself because no one checked on him for hours on end. "This is the thanks that I get," he rages as they enter the room. "I tell you everything that I know, and you leave me in here to soil myself like an infant," he yells. "Not to mention that you have brought me no food or water! Not that I would be able to eat or drink as you have me chained to this table like some kind of animal!"

Not at all fazed by his anger, Sylvia simply looks at him and asks, "Are you done?"

Further enraged by her attitude he makes a move to stand, forgetting that both his hands and legs are shackled to the table, and yells out in pain as the metal from the shackles cuts into his skin and he's force to sit back down. "Lady, you are so lucky that I'm in these shackles," he yells. "Otherwise I would take you down a peg or two! I've had enough of your condescending attitude! Now take this shit off and get me some clean clothes!"

Snake Chaser

Accidental Break

Sylvia lets out an evil laugh at his tirade, before sobering quickly and saying in a tight voice that even scares Rik somewhat, "You have definitely been left alone too long for you seem to forget where you are, and whose in control here!" She then walks over to the table, "I'll gladly take off your shackles and let you have first crack, but know this if I kill you right here right now I will not be punished for it," she growls out in his face.

To enraged to recognize that he has overstepped his bound, Hassan growls back, "Take these shackles off lady, and we'll see who's really in charge! That's what's wrong with your country! Your men have let you women think you are equal to men!"

That was the last straw for Sylvia. She directs Rik to remove the shackles from Hassan's hands and feet, and she even gives him a few minutes to work the circulation back into his arms and legs before she tells him, "Now get up and show me whose boss!"

Rik is standing on the sideline hoping and praying that the man backs down for he has heard stories of her skills in hand-to-hand combat, and he doesn't think that this pampered criminal has a snowball's chance in hell of surviving a confrontation with Sylvia.

Hassan stands and tests his legs before making a move in Sylvia's direction. True to her word, she lets him make the first swing. She catches the punch he throws in the palm of her hand, and pushes him backward. He stumbles a few steps, but quickly comes back to take another swing. Again, Sylvia catches his punch in her palm, only this time she grabs his wrist and twists his arm backwards before pushing him across the room. This only enrages Hassan, and he charges at her like a raging bull intent on tackling her to the ground. Sylvia sidesteps him at the last minute, and he goes crashing in to the wall behind her. He crumbles to the floor, but doesn't stay down for long.

Sylvia allows him to stand up before asking, "Are you sure you want to continue this?"

Hassan doesn't respond. Instead he starts circling her trying to distract her so that he can make his next attack. Sylvia moves with him keeping her eyes on him for she knows he's trying to figure out a way to come at her from behind. After a few minutes of this, she becomes bored and tells him so, "I've had enough of this. Sit your ass down before I put you down."

"Are you backing down bitch," growls Hassan.

"I never back down from a fight, but you should. You've made three attempts, and haven't even touched me."

"You got lucky! That's all! But you're going down, and I'm walking out of here!"

"Um . . . yeah . . . no. I wouldn't hold your breath waiting for that to happen."

Snake Chaser

Tired of her cocky attitude, Hassan makes his next move. He tries to trip her to the ground, however, Sylvia anticipated his move and jumps up over his leg and kicks him the chest at the same time. Hassan flies across the room and crashes into the wall behind him so hard he loses his breath. While he lays there trying to recover, Sylvia takes a seat on the edge of the table. She turns to Rik to tell him to pick up Hassan and re-shackle him. Hassan, who has been watching her every move, quickly gets up from the floor and charges in her direction. Sylvia catches his movement out of the corner of her eye, and snakes out her arm at the last minute. She catches him in the throat, but instead of letting him drop to the floor she wraps her arm around his neck and turns him around. With his back to her front and her arm securely around his neck, she tells him in a harsh tone, "Enough!"

In an attempt to dislodge himself from her hold, Hassan twists his body to the left as she has her right arm wrapped around his neck. In an effort to hold to him Sylvia twists her body to the right while bringing her left arm up and around the other side of his neck, and they hear a snap just before Hassan's body goes limp. His neck has been broken. "Shit," hisses Sylvia at the same time that Rik says, "Damn."

Sylvia lowers his lifeless body to the floor, and then looks at Rik as she says, "It was not intentional. He did this to himself."

"I'm aware of that, but I still think there is going to be hell to pay from the Brass," responds Rik.

"I have no doubt that you're right about that, so let's go make the call to see how they want us to proceed."

They leave the room, locking it behind them, to go make the call from the operations room. They get the commander on the phone and relay to him the events that took place leading up to

Hassan's death, and then ask what they should do with the body. After cussing a blue streak through the phone, the commander tells them to bring the body with them and they will decided what to do with him after they get back to DC.

Rik and Sylvia return to the interrogation room to bag Hassan's body after getting off the phone with the commander. Once their task is complete, Rik places his hand on Sylvia's shoulder as she moves towards the door to stop her from walking. She looks at his hand before looking up at his face, and arches her eyebrow at him.

"I know that this is your team and that you are continuing the mission that was your brother's, but are we going to have more situations like this," he asks as he removes his hand from her shoulder.

"Like what," she asks as she folders her arms over her chest.

"Where you're going to challenge prisoners and they end up lying lifeless on an interrogation room floor?"

"You were here the whole time," she begins. "You know that I did not instigate this situation, and nor did I intend for him to end up with a broken neck," she continues. "I would have preferred to take him back to DC alive and breathing for he could have proven to be an asset to us finding this Mr. Red, and bringing an end to his criminal reign," she concludes.

"I just had to make sure that you do not have another agenda to take out everyone that had anything to do with the death of your family and fiancée," he states.

"Trust me, I am strictly out for justice and not just for me, but for all the women that are sold, all the people who are killed by illegal militias, all the people whose lives are destroyed by illegal drugs. That is my only agenda. Got it?"

Snake Chaser

"Got it," he responds.

The Next Move

The next day the team and the body of Hassan arrive in DC. The team is given the rest of the day off while Sylvia and Rik go with the body to the morgue, and then on to the commander's office. Rik give his accounting of the events that took place in the interrogation room first, and then it's Sylvia's turn. Both of their stories match, so the commander is willing to chalk up the death of Hassan as an accident. Once that business is complete, they go to the communications center to have them direct satellites over Madagascar and Saudi Arabia to see if they can locate either of Mr. Red's compounds and then determine which of them he is hiding out in.

The team has been in DC for three months before the crew monitoring the satellite footage of Madagascar and Saudi Arabia believe that they have located the compound of Mr. Red in Madagascar based on the movements of some well-known plastic surgeons that have recently been frequenting the facility. They report their findings to the commander who tells them to still keep an eye on Saudi Arabia for the presence of the surgeons doesn't necessarily mean that Mr. Red is in residence, they could just be getting ready for his arrival or hiding out themselves.

The commander, however, does inform Sylvia and her team of what the satellite footage has revealed. He doesn't want them

212

Snake Chaser

making a move until he is certain of who is actually present at the compound, and he makes a few calls to other agencies that he knows monitors activity in the region of the compound. It takes a few days for him to receive any information about the compound, and is disappointed to learn that they missed Mr. Red as he was spotted leaving the compound just that day. Pissed that they have missed an opportunity to capture her nemesis, Sylvia asks if they have an idea of where he was headed and learns that they lost track of him when he arrived at the water port in Toliara. They believe that he is on a boat, but they are not sure where the boat is headed. Sylvia asks for permission to go to the compound in Madagascar to see if they can find any evidence of where he might be headed and what his next move will be. She's granted permission for the government is tired of him slipping easily from country to country, and continuing his criminal enterprise.

In two days time, the team arrives in Madagascar near the compound recently vacated by Mr. Red, and set up camp so that they can observe what activities are still taking place there and if there is anyone that they can question about their elusive criminal mastermind. During the three days that they have been watching the compound they see nothing unusual taking place by the men, women, and children living at the compound, and DC has not been successful in locating Mr. Red after he boarded a boat in Toliara. However, on the fourth day a caravan of trucks similar to the ones that use to arrive at the compound in South America arrives, and out of the back of the trucks emerges groups of women and children and they appear to have been trucked in from impoverished regions. In the next two days, they see these women and children cleaned up and fed and Sylvia wonders if these women are being groomed so that they can be later sold when Mr. Red gets back to business.

On the seventh day, they observe a single truck pulling up to the compound and a group of girls appearing to be between the

213

ages of fifteen to eighteen being loaded up in to the back of the truck. Sylvia takes Lina, Rik, and Roc with her to follow the truck when it pulls out of the compound, while giving Gunther, Nat and Stoney instructions to pack up their camp and proceed to their extraction point. While they are following the truck, one of the tires blows and the truck is forced to stop so that the tire can be repaired. They watch as all of the girls are unloaded from the truck, and the truck is up on the jack and the blown tire is removed. Since there are only four men on the truck and two of them are occupied with changing the tire, Sylvia makes the decision to approach the truck. The men do not have their weapons drawn, so it's easy for Sylvia and her crew to make them stop dead in their tracks as they already have their weapons drawn as they approach. The men instantly freeze in the presence of the eight guns whose barrels they are staring down as the two women and two men approach them. Since Roc doesn't have the hand-to-hand combat skills as the others he is instructed to keep his guns trained on the men as Sylvia, Lina, and Rik approach the men to unarm them and place them in restraints. After securing the first man, Sylvia moves on to the man that is staring down the barrels of Roc's guns. Once all the men are secure, they finish the job of replacing the tire, and load everyone up into the truck as they contact DC to let them know what has transpired and find out the closest facility they can travel to with their cargo. They are told that there is a carrier in the Indian Ocean that has a cargo plane upon it that can transport them and their cargo back to DC, so they travel to their designated extraction point where a helicopter from the carrier will pick them up to transport them to the carrier. The cargo plane is ready for take-off, so once they are all aboard the carrier they board the plane with only a moment to spare.

Back in DC, the young women are taken to an unoccupied female dorm building while a decision is made to determine what should happen to them, and so that they try to locate a translator so that they can ask them how they came to be at the compound. The four men are taken to the main building, and housed in individual cells while Sylvia and the commander plot out a plan for their interrogation.

"To be honest, they seem to be transporters only," states Commander Sullivan. "I don't think that we're going to be able to get any useful information out of them."

"I agree," states Sylvia. "I'm hoping the women can shed some light on what our elusive Mr. Red is up to."

"They might inadvertently be able to shed some light on his activities, but I doubt they know too much either."

"If we can find out where they are all from and how they came to be at the compound, we might be able to figure out what he's up to and be able to know where to look for him next."

"That's a possibility, but in the meantime I still have satellites watching the compound in Madagascar and looking for the compound in Saudi Arabia."

"Let me know if they spot anything."

"Will do. Get some rest while we wait for the translators to arrive."

Sylvia leaves the facility and heads to her apartment with the intentions of taking a long hot bath. The events that have take place over the past three months are really wearing on her, and she wants nothing more than an evening to relax and clear her mind. However, when she arrives home, she finds Quintana standing outside her door similar to the way she would find Qasean after a day at the training facility, and she knows that her bath will have to wait.

"Hello Ana," she greets her, "Come on in and tell me what's on your mind."

As Sylvia unlocks the door, Quintana asks, "What makes you think that something is on my mind? Maybe I was just coming to check on you."

"One, you were standing just like Qasean when he had something on his mind," she begins. "Two, you went to a lot of trouble to know that I was back in town," she continues. "And three, if you just wanted to check on my, you would have just called," concludes Sylvia.

Snake Chaser

Quintana

Once they are inside, they both head to the kitchen and Sylvia grabs wine glasses from the cabinet as Quintana grabs a bottle of wine from the fridge. Quintana pours them both a glass of wine, and then takes a seat at the table. She takes several sips before asking, "How are you?"

"I'm fine. Just a little tired," responds Sylvia as she takes a sip from her glass.

"Sy, this is me Ana. How are you really?"

"I miss him so much Ana, but I can't focus on that right now," she replies. "My singular focus is on bringing his killer to justice. Not only did he take away Qasean, but he wiped out my entire family."

"So what am I," asks Ana with a little heat in her voice.

Recognizing that she has hurt her friend's feelings, Sylvia sets her glass on the table and walks over to Ana and pulls her into her arms. "I'm sorry Ana. I didn't mean to hurt your feelings. You know you are my sister in every sense of the word except for shared DNA." Sylvia pulls back and looks Ana in the face as uncontrollable sobs break free from her throat, and she sees a look of deep pain in her face. She immediately walks her into the living room, and sits on the couch with her friend still in her arms. She wants to ask her what's wrong, but she knows that she will not understand a word she is saying until she stops crying. After a few minutes, the sobs simmer down to a whimper, and Sylvia leans back to look her in the face before asking, "Okay, Quintana Michele, what the hell was that all about?"

"I'm sorry," replies Ana as she tries to wipe the tears from her face. "I told myself that I wouldn't break down like this, but . . ." Her voice trails off as she takes several deep breaths, and once she feels somewhat in control again, she continues, "I miss my brother as much as you do, and there are just so many reminders of him in this city. I can't talk to my parents because they're still grieving his loss as well, and as a result they are smothering me." She pauses to take several more deep breaths because she fears her next words are going to send Sylvia into a fit of yelling and cussing. "I need some peace of mind, so I've decided to move to Dallas and start my own restaurant." She said it, and now she's holding her breath waiting for Sylvia's reaction.

"Really," asks Sylvia somewhat in disbelief.

"That's it? No screaming? No cussing? Just a '*really*'?"

Sylvia chuckles before responding, "Is that what the deep breaths were for? You were getting yourself ready for my reaction?"

"Uh, yeah."

Sylvia breaks the hug to sit back on the couch, and talk with her sister friend. "Sorry Sis, but there will be no screaming or cussing coming from me." She gives her a heartfelt smile

Snake Chaser

before asking, "So why Dallas? Do you have the money to pull this off?"

Ana leans back on the couch, before responding, "A friend that I went to culinary school with is moving to Paris with her fiancée and is selling her restaurant, and she asked me if I would like to buy it. The timing couldn't be more perfect as I think I have reached my peak at the restaurant that I'm currently working at, and Mom and Dad have been helping me invest my money so I have enough money to buy the building. Then there's the money that Qasean left to me, which will help me with the first six months of expenses if I need it." She then moves into her favorite position of sitting Indian style on the couch to finish telling Sylvia her plans. "I created a business plan for my restaurant months ago with the idea of opening it here in DC, however, I believe that the restaurant will still be a success in Dallas as the dynamic of the city is almost identical to the dynamic of DC." She then proceeds to give Sylvia a high-level summary of her plans for the restaurant. While she's talking, Sylvia retrieves their glasses and the wine from the kitchen and before they know it two hours have gone by.

Sylvia's need for rest over takes her as a big yawn takes over her, "I'm sorry Ana. I love your ideas, I guess I'm just beat."

Ana looks at her watch, "Oh God, I have been talking your ear off for over two hours, no wonder you're yawning." She leans over to give her a kiss on the cheek, "Go get a shower and go to bed. We can talk more about this at a later time. How long will you be in town?"

"At this point, I'm not sure. The trail on Mr. Red is lukewarm at best now, so we are waiting on a sighting of him somewhere but in the meantime we have several people to question once we can find a translator."

"Okay, I'll give you a call after I get home from work tomorrow to see what's going in."

"Okay," states Sylvia as she lets out another yawn.

Ana chuckles as she says, "Go get that shower and go to bed."

"Will do." They hug one another just before Ana walks to the door to leave, and Sylvia heads to the bathroom to take a shower as she is too afraid she would fall asleep and drown if she took a bath.

Over the next several days as Sylvia waits on Commander Sullivan to find a translator that understands the women and for any word of a Mr. Red sighting, she spends all her spare time with Ana discussing her plans for the restaurant and her move to Dallas.

During one of their conversations, Ana just blurts out, "I'm going to miss you when I move."

Sylvia smiles at her as she says, "I'm going to miss you as well, but depending how things go I may not be in town much anyway."

"Sy, I know how much Qasean meant to you and I know you were just getting to know your brother and Joshua, but please don't let this quest to find this Mr. Red consume you. Please?"

"I wish I could assure you that it won't, but you know me when I sink my teeth into something," she pauses and takes a deep breath, "I have to resolve this in order to be able to move on with my life."

"Then I hope you find him soon. You deserve to be loved, and as long as you are on this quest you are going to keep your heart shut off from the rest of the world."

Snake Chaser

"I have never loved anyone but Qasean, and I doubt that I ever will." She closes her eyes and takes a deep breath to steady her emotions, then she says, "You deserve love more than anyone else I know, when are you going to stop keeping yourself shut off from the world."

"I'm not keeping myself shut off from the world. No one has sparked my interest, but believe me when they do I will be open to it."

"You promise?"

"I promise. Now it's getting late, and we both have to go to work in the morning."

"Okay. Be safe getting home and let me know when you get there."

"Will do," states Ana as she hugs her friend good-bye.
Two weeks have gone by since Ana announced her plans to go to Dallas, and now it is time for her begin her drive to her new home. Since there have been no new developments with Mr. Red, Sylvia is still in town and is there to see her friend off on this journey of her life. There are a lot tears and hugging as Ana says good-bye to her parents and her sister friend.

ReGina Crawford

Tired of Waiting

It's been two weeks since Ana left town, and at this point Sylvia has reach the end of her patience in waiting for a lead on Mr. Red without her friend to keep her company. So she goes to Commander Sullivan's office to have a word with him, "There has to be a way to make this snake come out of hiding," she states as his secretary closes the door behind her after seeing Sylvia inside.

"And what do you suggest we do," asks Sullivan a little weary of Sylvia's obsession with finding Mr. Red.

"I say we set up black market deals for guns, women, and drugs, and see if he bites since we're not sure if he's still dealing in all three markets. We should be able to come up with a deal big enough to spark his interest, and make him want to come out of hiding."

"You know that is not under our jurisdiction."

"Well it doesn't seem like the ATF, DEA, or the Attorney General are on top of things. It's been weeks since they have said a word to us about their efforts."

"Sylvia relax. Sometimes these things take time."

Snake Chaser

"The more time we wait, the further he gets from our reach. We already know that he keeps plastic surgeons at his disposal to change his appearance. Who knows what he looks like now. The pictures we have of him could bear no resemblance to what he looks like now." She jumps out of her chair and begins pacing the room in her frustration. "He cannot get away with taking my family from me."

"Sit down Sylvia," states Sullivan in a commanding voice that stops Sylvia in her tracks. She returns to the chair she vacated, but displays her displeasure on her face.

"If you want to continue to be lead on this mission, you are going to have to place your emotions on a shelf. Understand," he states as he leans over his desk in her direction, his voice no less commanding than when he told her to sit down.

"Got it," she states reluctantly as she knows that she is lying to the highest-ranking officer of the Marines. Wanting to maintain her position so that she is the one to take down Mr. Red, she changes the direction of the conversation. "So there has been no new chatter about Hassan's disappearance?"

"No one seems overly concerned about it, and his next in command has taken over his businesses and is being very cautious in his dealings. It seems he thinks that Mr. Red or The Archman, as they call him, had something to with Hassan's disappearance so he is steering clear of any deals that remotely look like The Archman might be involved in."

"And the women we brought over from Madagascar, they still haven't said anything that could provide us with a lead?"

"No. We are still monitoring the bunkhouse that we have them in just in case they finally breakdown and say something useful when they think that no one is listening." Anticipating her next question, he says, "And no, Genevieve has not given us any more useful information either."

"All these people in custody, and no one has any useful information that could lead us to Mr. Red," she says more to herself than to the commander.

"Sylvia, be patient. We will eventually bring him to justice. Now I have work to do."

Knowing that she's been dismissed, Sylvia gets up and leaves his office. She heads over to the training facility to see what her team is up to, and is not surprised to see Roc looking up at Lina from the mat. She chuckles as she continues walking into the room, "She's still getting the best of you I see," she states to Roc when he looks in her direction.

Roc, not too pleased with her laughter, states, "I've managed to take her down a time or two," as he picks himself up off the mat.

"You have to stop seeing her as a woman, and start seeing her as a threat," states Sylvia. "Once you do that, you'll have more success in dealing with her. But I hear that you are picking up quite a few skills in the hand-to-hand combat arena, so keep up the good work."

"Any new developments," asks Rik who is also frustrated with all the waiting.

"No. The commander tried to assure me that the ATF, DEA, and Attorney General are diligently trying to flush Mr. Red out of hiding with no success, but I wonder how much they are really doing." She pauses and cocks her head to the side as she remembers that she has a friend in the FBI that might be able to help her out with some information. "You guys keep up with your training, and I'll see you tomorrow," she states over her shoulder as she heads to the exit door.

Sylvia tries not to speed as she makes her way back to her apartment to look up the contact information for her friend in the FBI. When she arrives she unlocks her safe, and finds his number and retrieves her personal secure phone to place the call. The phone rings twice before there is a voice on the other line, "Excalibur," answers the voice.

"Snake Chaser."

"Problem?"

"Need info."

"Logistics?"

"Criminal Mastermind. Known as Mr. Red or The Archman."

"Depth?"

"Maxium."

"Peace Time tomorrow."

"Out," states Sylvia just before the line goes dead. Feeling better, Sylvia goes in the bathroom to make a bath for she really needs to relax. While the water is running in the tub, she goes into the kitchen and pours herself a glass of wine to sip while she soaks in the tub. Once the tub is filled to capacity she strips down and gets in, and leans her head back and closes her eyes.

An hour or so later, the water has cooled and she steps out of the tub and heads to bed for she's exhausted yet filled with great anticipation about tomorrow's call with Excalibur.

The next day time seems to drag by as she waits for the appointed time she can call Excalibur to see if he has any information for her, and when the time arrives she anxiously dials the number.

"Excalibur," states the voice on the other end of the phone.

"Snake Chaser."

"You're gonna owe me big time for this."

"Whenever. Wherever. Details."

"He doesn't stay in any one spot for longer than two days which is why your team hasn't been ordered to make a move on him," begins the voice. "He's only making small drug deals to keep himself afloat, so the agencies are just keeping tabs on him for the moment," he adds. "It's believed that his next move will be to San Miguel in El Salvador as he just left Granada in Nicaragua, and he has been moving north but staying close to the ocean."

"He must have ships close by that he can hop on if anyone gets too close," absently states Sylvia. "We're not the only ones looking for him," she states.

"We are well aware that the Mexican Cartels are curious about his whereabouts as well."

"Can you keep me posted on his movement?"

"Until you're found out."

Sylvia chuckles, "You know me to well."

Snake Chaser

"Be careful," states the voice on the other line before it goes dead.

Sylvia sits in the middle of her bed trying to come up with a good reason to leave the city for a few days while she travels to San Miguel for she knows Sullivan won't approve a mission to go there, and she can't tell him where she's really going or why she's going there. Unable to come up with a good story after a few hours, she finally decides to sleep on it and hopes she'll come up with something by morning.

The next morning as she is on her way to the facility, she still hasn't come up with a story that won't make Sullivan suspicious about what she's up to, and it's frustrating the hell out of her. As she enters the training facility in a sour mood, she finds her team assembled with Sullivan standing in front of them.

"Right on time Sgt. Williams," he states. "I've gathered your team together to inform you that you are being granted a week furlough since we haven't been able to get any solid information on Mr. Red, and we don't want to wear you down by having you sit around here waiting," he adds. "Just make sure that you have your secure phones with you and on at all times in case we have to call you back if there are any developments on his whereabouts," he concludes.

Internally Sylvia breathes a sigh of relief as her problem has been solved for her, and she doesn't have to lie to the commander. Externally she states, "Thanks commander." Then she turns to her team and says, "Stay out of trouble this week kids. Don't need you returning worse for wear."

The team nods at her, then expresses their thanks to the commander before filing out of the facility. However, before Sylvia can make her exit, the commander places a hand on her shoulder, "That goes double for you," he states. "As a matter of fact why don't you go visit Quintana in Dallas."

"That's exactly what I plan to do," she responds grateful that he has given her an excuse for being out of the city. He nods at her, and they both exit the facility.

Snake Chaser

Flying Solo

Sylvia does her best not to break any speeding laws as she races back to her apartment to pack her gear for her trip to San Miguel. It takes her no time at all to get her mission pack ready or to make arrangements to leave the country under an already established alias.

Upon her arrival in San Miguel, she checks into a hotel and assumes the role of a tourist as she checks out the city and asks questions about places to visit off the beaten path with the excuse that she wants to experience the 'real' culture of the city. What she's actually doing is looking for places where Mr. Red may be hanging out undetected, and as she is shown around by a tour guide she makes mental notes about a few places he may choose to hold up in.

She arrives back at her hotel a few hours later, and takes a shower before lying down to take a nap before she ventures out later that night to investigate the locations she's got in her head under the cover of darkness. When she wakes up several hours later, she dresses for her mission and gathers her gear. An expert at appearing invisible, she has no problem getting out of the hotel without drawing attention to herself, and she makes her way to the first location on her list. Once there, she creates her hideout, and settles in to watch the activity taking place.

The first hour she's there there is little to no activity taking place, however, during the second hour she sees a truck pull up and the men that exit the vehicle look like mercenaries and appear to be inspecting the building and the area surrounding it. Not wanting to be detected, she slips into her underground nest to wait them out as she watches them on her infrared camera. By their movements, she is certain that they are assessing the area for someone's who arrival whom doesn't want to be observed. They spend an hour inspecting the building and the grounds before they get back in the truck and leave, and wanting to know where they're going next she exits her nest and attempts to follow them on foot. However, as they reach an open area that won't provide her with cover, she has to fall back and let them continue their journey without her tailing them. Knowing there is nothing more she can do on this night, she makes her way back to her hotel to get some rest.

The next day she ventures out into the village, exploring the markets and sights so that she can maintain her image as a tourist on vacation. Later that afternoon, she returns to her room to take a nap for she plans to venture out under the cover of darkness to conduct surveillance on the next location on her list of possible hideouts for Mr. Red. In the three hours she spends at this location she doesn't see any unusual activity, nor do the men from last night appear at this location and she wonders if they were here last night. Since it appears she's not going to learn anything at this location, she heads back to her hotel.

It's day three and she repeats her activities of the previous day, however, today she sees the truck from the first location she had under surveillance. She tries to appear uninterested in them even as she intensely watches their every move, however, she still catches the eye of one of the men and he walks over to where she is inspecting native crafts at an outdoor stand. He doesn't say anything at first, just stands to the side watching

Snake Chaser

her and she acts as though she doesn't notice his presence until she accidently bumps into him. She mumbles that she's sorry in a mixture of English and Spanish so as not to give away how fluent she is in Spanish. The man appears to lose interest in her at that point, and tells her no problem in English as he goes back to join the other men at the truck as they have completed their purchases and are ready to leave the area.

Sylvia continues perusing the items at the various carts long after the men have left the area so as not to bring any more attention to herself for she noticed that quite a few people in the area froze in place when she collided with the man, which leads her to believe that they frequently visit the village and have struck fear in the natives. She returns to her hotel room at the same time she has the past two days. No need to change her routine because of the run in with the mercenary, and besides she still has one more location to check out while she's in town.

That night, she once again ventures out under the cover of darkness, and to her disappointment there is no activity at this location either. So she returns to her hotel room with the intentions to take one more look at the first location once more the following night. Oh the next day she once again explores the sights and sounds of the area during the light of day, and that night she returns to the first location to see if there is an activity taking place there. While surveying the area, she once again sees the truck that appeared on the first night pull up to the building and the same mercenaries exit the truck, and the one that she bumped into in the market suddenly stops and tilts his head back as though he is smelling the air. Not sure what that means, she immediately climbs down into the underground nest she didn't have the time to conceal on her first night there. Via her infrared camera she is able to watch the man walk over to the very location where she was lying in cover, and by his body language he is once again smelling the air. Believing that he has picked up the scent of someone, he begins a thorough inspection of the area, however, he is unable to locate her so he heads back to the truck. As Sylvia continues to watch the camera, she sees an additional person join them and by the way they are walking they are carrying heavy bags or equipment. She fumes because she knows that she cannot come above ground to see who the additional person is or what they are carrying, but she knows in her gut that it's Mr. Red. She stays put for another forty-five minutes after they leave the area before she ventures above ground, and heads back to her hotel room.

Back in her room emotionally exhausted, she takes a shower and goes to bed having made up her mind to head back to DC in two days time, and with plans to contact Excalibur to see if he can confirm her belief that Mr. Red was indeed here, and if he has information on the next location they expect to see Mr. Red.

The next day she starts packing her bags for her return home, and waits until Peace Time to contact Excalibur. Again the phone rings twice before it's answered, and the voice on the other end of the line says, "Excalibur."

"Snake Chaser."

"No luck?"

"Not exactly. Think I missed my opportunity to see his new face."

"You? Really?"

"Don't be cute!" He chuckles at the mock venom in her voice. Choosing to ignore his laughter, she asks, "Next location."

"Even though it's on the Gulf of Honduras, we believe that he will next appear in Puerto Barrios in Guatemala."

Snake Chaser

"That's a lot of land to cover be truck," speculates Sylvia out loud.

"True, but we think he's trying to make new contacts and connections so that he can get his business back up and running. A lot of people are steering clear of him as a result of him being on the hit list of some of the Mexican Cartels and the US government, so we believe he's targeting small time criminal enterprises with the promise that he can elevate their status on the Black Market."

"Let me know if anything changes."

"Will do," states Excalibur before the line goes dead once again.

As Sylvia sits in the middle of the bed, she tries to come up with a believable reason for her and the rest of her team to make a trip to Guatemala. She eventually falls asleep without coming up with a good reason for them to make the trip.

Positive Interference

The next morning Sylvia begins her trip back to DC, when she gets a message from Sullivan. Even though they have two days left on their furlough, Sylvia and her team are being ordered to report back to DC immediately. Pissed that she might have to put her plans to travel to Guatemala on hold, Sylvia arrives in DC at the same time as her team and they all head to the commander's office.

"Glad you all were able to return so soon," states Sullivan as they enter his office and close the door behind them.

"And why were we ordered to return so early," asks Sylvia with a little impatience in her voice.

"We have received a tip about our elusive Mr. Red," Sullivan responds.

Sylvia's eyes widen in surprise at the same time her heart begins to race at the thought that she can continue her quest to bring Mr. Red to justice. "And just where did this tip come from," she asks.

"It seems that we have an ally in the FBI who found out we are interested in capturing Mr. Red for acts of terrorism," he begins as he gives Sylvia a pointed look, "and the head of the

234

Snake Chaser

FBI called me to tell me that they have been tracking his movements. And that they believe that he is headed to Puerto Barrios on the east coast of Guatemala." He continues to look at Sylvia who feigns a look of innocence, and so he continues, "They believe that it will be another three days before he reaches that city, and thought that we might like to be in place there when he arrives."

"So does that mean we are headed out to Puerto Barrios immediately," asks Sylvia trying to hide the excitement in her voice.

"Yes you will leave at 0300, so I suggest you get busy getting your gear together for your next trip," he responds. However, as the rest of the team files out of his office, he calls Sylvia's name. She stops and turns towards him and he walks over to her until they are standing toe-to-toe, "Since we were able to get some valuable information, I'm going to over look your rogue behavior this time but don't test me. Clear?"

Knowing she is walking a tightrope, Sylvia simply responds, "Clear."

"Dismissed."

When the commander turns his back to her and heads back to his desk, Sylvia doesn't say a word and exits his office glad that she doesn't have to lie to him in order to get her team into Guatemala. She will deal with whatever fallout she has to deal with after Mr. Red is captured and brought to justice. She joins her team in the supply room to gather their gear for their next mission as she works hard at not showing her joy over the gift that Excalibur has given her for she knows that this is handiwork.

At 0300 the team is on the tarmac ready to catch their ride to the carrier that will get them close to their destination. After landing on the carrier, Sylvia and Jules head to the communications room to view the satellite footage of the region and to plot the path of travel they will take once they are on dry land. Once that is complete, they head to their staterooms so that they can rest up for their mission like the rest of their team.

Under the cover of darkness, the seven member team heads to Puerto Barrios so that they can set up their underground encampment 500 yards from the compound that they believe is the next hideout of Mr. Red. When they complete that task, Nat and Stoney venture out to set up surveillance equipment around the compound and the roads leading up to the compound. Satisfied that they have everything in place to capture their prey, the team settles in to get some rest for they know that they will be going non-stop once he arrives at the compound.

The next morning they are monitoring the activity of the compound from their underground nest, and by the way the natives are running to and fro they know that they are expecting someone they consider of great importance or someone that they fear. Either way, all indications point to the fact that Mr. Red is due to arrive sometime that day, so they wait. They don't have long to wait as a truck pulls up two hours later, and Sylvia recognizes the mercenaries from San Miguel. However, she doesn't immediately recognize the last man to exit the vehicle, but based on his stance and the fear he evokes she's sure that it's Mr. Red with his new face.

Wanting to know what he's up to, the team monitors the activity of the compound for the rest of the day. No one leaves or enters the compound that day, however, that's not the case on the following day when another truck pulls into the compound. A well dressed man and a couple of bodyguards exit the truck and are greeted by four of the mercenaries that arrived the day before, who proceed to pat down the new arrivals. Once they are satisfied that they don't pose a threat to the man inside the compound, they are led inside the main building. They are inside for several hours before they exit the building, and based on the smile on the well-dressed man's face they assume that the meeting pleased him. While the meeting was taking place, Stoney runs the face of the man through facial recognition software so they can see if they can determine whom Mr. Red is meeting with in an effort to find out what he's up to. The man turns out to be on the FBI list as a gunrunner, but what they weren't expecting to find was that the man has quite a few connections in the US.

It becomes obvious to Sylvia and the rest of the team that Mr. Red is looking for new suppliers for his Black Market deals, and they wonder if he plans to move his operations to the States. He has to be careful of the Mexicans who would like nothing more than to dispatch him to hell where he rightfully belongs, so maybe he's looking to set up shop in the states as he knows they would have a hard time getting into the country undetected. Sylvia decides not to interfere in their deal, and lets the man and his bodyguards leave the area without attempting to apprehend them. There is no activity the rest of the day, so as darkness descends the team takes to their bedrolls so that they can repeat the same actions the next day.

On their third day of surveillance, another truck pulls into the compound and another well-dressed man emerges from its interior. He and his men endure the same treatment as the previous guests to the compound, and after passing the test are allowed to enter the main building of the compound. Stoney once again executes his magic, and discovers that the man meeting with Mr. Red is also on the FBI's surveillance list and is believed to be a major player in the drug trade.

Sylvia reports their findings to the commander, who instructs her to continue monitoring Mr. Red's activities but not to attempt to apprehend him. So for the next two days they follow the same routine, however, no one else visits the compound. Then on the fifth day, it appears as if Mr. Red is ready to make his departure, and Sylvia is disappointed that she's not alone and can't make a call to Excalibur to see if knows of Mr. Red's next destination. However, her spirits pick up as she hopes that Sullivan has reported their findings to the FBI and that they in return tell him where they believe Mr. Red will be traveling to next. After the vehicle carrying their prey departs the compound, Sylvia and her team begin breaking down their nest for their departure.

When they arrive at the harbor to make their departure, they run into a snag when they encounter the mercenary that Sylvia had her near run-in with while in San Miguel. He picks up her scent as they arrive at the boat dock to hitch a ride out to where the carrier is waiting for them, and she knows he recognizes her by the look on his face. She pretends as though she doesn't know him even though they notice that he's following them to last boat slip on the dock to catch their ride. Sylvia instructs her team to board the boat first, and that she'll handle the gentleman if he tries to stop her from boarding the boat. Even the team is at a loss as to why the man is following them or why he would try to detain Sylvia, but they do as instructed.

Even though she looks like a tourist along with the other people that she is with and they are boarding a charter boat that conducts tours of the waterways of Guatemala, the man is not accepting it as coincidence that he has spotted her twice while escorting his employer through Central America. So he plans to find out who she is, and grabs her arm just before she attempts to board the boat.

Anticipating an attempt to stop her from boarding the boat, Sylvia is ready when he grabs her arm and makes a move to counteract his grasp. Unaware of her skill level in hand-to-hand combat, the man is momentarily taken by surprise but that doesn't stop him from making another attempt to grab her.

238

Snake Chaser

Sylvia is able to avoid his second attempt, and fully aware that he doesn't plan to let her go freely she begins her own assault against the man. Not too shabby in hand-to-hand combat himself, it takes Sylvia several attempts to get the upper hand and subdue the man. With him locked in a submission hold, she asks, "What do you want?"

"Who are you? You're not a tourist as you would like me to believe."

"Who I am is none of your business," she hisses in his ear. "Now what do you want?"

"Lady turn me loose before I'm forced to cause you bodily harm!"

"Since I have the upper-hand here, how do you plan to accomplish that," she asks with her voice dripping with sarcasm.

Not wanting to play this game with her anymore the man makes a move to break free of her hold, and in the process of trying to keep him pinned Sylvia ends up breaking his neck. Knowing that she can't just leave his body lying lifeless on the boat dock, she drags his body onto the boat with her. Once on the boat and Rik sees that the man's neck is broken, he looks at her and asks, "Another one?"

She shrugs her shoulders as she says, "It couldn't be helped.

ReGina Crawford

Interrogation

After they arrive at the carrier, they immediately board the transport plane that is scheduled to take to them back to DC. Sylvia calls Sullivan from the plane to let him know about the unexpected turn of events, and he tells her that he will be on the tarmac waiting for them and the body and he doesn't sound too happy about this turn of events.

The team disembarks from the plane with the body in tow the moment the plane taxis to a stop on the tarmac, and are immediately escorted to the commander's office. Sullivan questions each member of the team separately, saving Sylvia for last. Based on what the other team members have reported, Sullivan knows that the confrontation was unavoidable up to a point. However, he wants to know why the man took such an interest in Sylvia, and brings her into his office to get some answers.

The moment she walks into his office and takes a seat, the commander starts throwing out questions, "Why did this man single you out of the crowd of people headed to the boat? Did you know this man? Did the man know you? How would the two of you know each other? I need answers and I need them now Sylvia."

Snake Chaser

"Are you sure you want me to answers those questions, Sir," comes back Sylvia.

"I know you did not lie low during the time off I gave you, but what I don't know is what you did during that time," responds the commander. "And now I'm wondering if you had a run-in with this man during that time, and that's why he was following you. Now if you want me to, I can create my own scenario of what took place during the five days you were out of DC. Is that what you want me to do?"

"No Sir."

"I told you before you left on this latest mission that I would not tolerate any rogue behavior from you, and I meant that. So tell me what transpired during those five days so I can determine if there is anything I can do to keep you from being called on the carpet about this."

Knowing she has no other choice at this point, Sylvia takes a deep breath before giving the commander a run down on her time in Central America. Once she has told him every detail about those days, she concludes with, "So since he saw me as a tourist in San Miguel, I don't know why he wouldn't think that I was a tourist in Puerto Barrios. It just doesn't make sense to me."

"I agree he was stretching in approaching you, however, I'm sure he didn't accept it as a coincidence that you happened to be in two separate countries at the same time that his employer was in those countries," replies Sullivan. "However, this Mr. Red knows that he is on quite a few hit lists, so I'm sure that the men he's hired to protect him were told to investigate anyone that is seen more than once during his travels. So I can cover your ass this time using the scenario that while on furlough you went to San Miguel to relax and was seen there by this man, and when the man saw you again while on this mission he became overly suspicious and approached you," he continues. "But know this Sgt. Williams, this is the last time I am covering your ass for bringing home a body in a body bag, clear?"

"Thank you, Sir," responds Sylvia. She then adds, "Yes Sir. Clear."

"Dismissed," states the commander with a pointed look.

Not wanting to press her luck, Sylvia leaves his office as fast as she can, and is surprised to see her team waiting for her in the outer office. Without saying a word she heads for the interrogation room, and her team quietly follows behind her. Once inside the room, she nods to Stoney to make sure that all monitoring devices have been disabled before she begins speaking.

"I apologize to you all for having to endure an interrogation by the commander," she begins. "I didn't anticipate the man in Puerto Barrios recognizing me from when he saw me in San Miguel a few days before."

"What were you doing in San Miguel," asks Rik. And before she can answer, he asks, "And why were you there alone?"

Knowing she needs to come clean with her team as their careers and lives are on the line with every mission that she leads them on, Sylvia takes a deep breath and then proceeds to tell them about her contact in the FBI, the information that he gave her, and how she came to be in San Miguel on a solo mission. "Since I didn't know if anything would come of my mission to San Miguel, I didn't want to involve any of you since you would have had to pay for your own travel. Plus I didn't want to draw any unnecessary attention to any of us if something was going on there."

Snake Chaser

"Seem you failed at that last part," replies Roc. Sylvia gives him a pointed look, and he counters her look by saying, "Apparently you did garner some unwanted attention from the man we brought home in the body bag."

Sylvia gives him a pointed look as she states, "Thanks for pointing out the obvious." Roc simply shrugs his shoulders.

"So what's next," asks Nat.

"We'll wait until we are given a directive on our next mission," Sylvia responds. "I'm hoping that my contact in the FBI continues feeding information to Sullivan on the movements of Mr. Red, and that we'll be able to apprehend him before too long."

"What I want to know is what you would have done if you could have gotten close to him," asks Roc.

Sylvia once again turns to him with a pointed look, "I probably would have killed him," she states with quite a bit of sarcasm in her voice. "Is that what you wanted to hear Roc?"

"I'm just trying to figure out what your agenda is here," he begins. He then spreads his arms out to encompass the rest of the team, "All of our lives are on the line with every mission we embark on with you," he adds.

"This man killed my brother, my cousin, and my fiancée," she practically yells at him. "So yes I want him off the streets by any means necessary," she adds. "But I would never endanger the lives of any of you which is why I went to San Miguel alone," she concludes.

"I think that everyone should take a deep breath and calm down," interjects Nat. Everyone swings their heads in her direction for she says very little. She stands her ground even with everyone's eyes on her, "I understand your concerns Roc about Sylvia going rogue and then being seen with the rest of us, and how that could jeopardize the safety of the rest of us," she begins. "However, I understand that this personal, as well, as business for Sylvia. She lost her whole family at the hands of a madman, and I feel she's entitled to some empathy from us," she adds. "Now what we need to do is find a happy medium that will allow Sylvia to utilize whatever resources she has, and not jeopardize our safety as we try to complete the mission we've been assigned," she concludes.

"I agree with Nat," chimes in Lina.

"I'm in agreement with that," states Rik and Stoney at the same time.

When Gunther doesn't speak, Roc turns to him and asks, "Do have an opinion?"

"I'm all for getting this guy off the streets, and whatever it takes to do that," he shrugs his shoulders while adding, "I'm cool with that."

"Well since it seems you all are in agreement, I guess I have no choice but to go along with program as I'm not willing to walk away from this mission," responds Roc.

"I appreciate your wanting to stand by my side during this, and I'll try not to do anything that will place your lives in danger," responds Sylvia. "Go get some rest, and we'll report back here in the morning." They all nod their heads, and exit the facility.

Snake Chaser

Questions II

When Sylvia arrives home, she heads straight to her bathroom to take a long hot bath for it has been a grueling few days. While she is relaxing in the tub, she replays the events of the day or so in her mind for she knows that she needs to make a decision of how she plans to achieve her goal of getting Mr. Red off the streets. The mercenary approaching her was a little unsettling for she doesn't want anyone to know that she's on his trail, and she wonders what Mr. Red will think when the man never returns. Will he go further underground? Or will he become enraged because he's lost his best man? Knowing that she will never get the answers to those questions will lounging in her tub, she switches her thoughts to what her next move will be.

She doesn't want to endanger her team but she also wants Mr. Red with a vengeance, and she plans to take advantage of every clue and tip that she receives. Yet, the question remains does she stay with her team and elicit their help? Or does she go it alone? While she knows she could avoid all the red tape by going it alone, she knows that having additional people with her will be to her advantage. After playing out several scenarios in her head, she decides that she's not going to be able to answer her own questions without talking to Excalibur.

So decides to put the questions on hold for the night, and pick them back up the next evening.

*****

After an uneventful day at the training facility, Sylvia wastes no time getting home so that she can place a call to Excalibur. At the appointed time, she dials his number.

Two rings, and then the voice on the end of the phone says, "Excalibur."

"Snake Chaser." She gets nothing but silence, but she knows that he's on the line. She gives a few seconds more, and when she continues to get nothing but silence she hangs up. She stands there looking at the phone in her hand confusion as to why he's stayed silent, then questions starting flying around in her mind. Has he gotten into trouble with his superiors for feeding her information? Is he currently in trouble? Does he need rescuing? Where is he? How can she find out? She knows that there is no one that she can contact to ask after him, so she continues to sit in the middle of her bed trying to figure out a way to get information. Then it hits her, there is another time that she can make a call to him. So she looks at her watch to see the current time, 7:37 pm. In two hours and thirty minutes it will be St. Stephen's time, she will make the call then. So she decides to take a nap until then just in case she gets the same response, and if she does she will make a move to find out where his last known location was and go and find him.

Her alarm goes off at 2200 hours, and she has exactly seven minutes to wait to make the call. So she goes into the bathroom to wash her face, and then sits in the middle of her bed waiting for the exact time she can place the call.

Snake Chaser

Once again, the phone rings twice and the voice on the other end of the line says, "Excalibur."

"Snake Chaser. Secure?"

"Safe."

Sylvia breathes a sigh of relief that he is safe and secure. "Problems?"

"It seems your commander is not pleased with your trip to San Miguel, or the two bodies he has on ice at your hands. Literally."

"They couldn't be helped, but neither one of the bodies came from San Miguel."

"Regardless, you need to be careful before you're dishonorably discharged."

"I'm aware that I'm on thin ice."

"Good, and you should know that I'm skating close to the edge as well so you'll have to be extremely cautious with any info I give you. Now what do you want to know?"

"Didn't mean to place you in the hot seat. How bad is it?"

"Nothing I can't handle. Now what do you want to know?"

"Does Mr. Red AKA The Archman know that his man has been taken out of service?"

"From the reports we have received, he seems to think that the man got a better offer. So no, he doesn't know that he was taken out by the hands of the American Military. Why?"

"I'm fearing that he will go deeper into hiding, and if he believes the man defected that's a strong possibility."

"Since he seems to operate on a need to know basis and last minute notification, I don't think he's worried about the missing mercenary giving away his next location. The only information he could have possibly shared would have been the previous hideout, and possibly the names of those he met with if he even knows their real names."

"Really?"

"Yeah. He's not a very trusting man."

"Do you have any idea where he might be headed next?"

"Although my superiors think that the information is wrong, we received word that his next stop was New Mexico."

"New Mexico? New Mexico as in the New Mexico that is located in the United States?"

"Do you know of another New Mexico?"

"No, but . . . ," her voice trails off as she processes this information. "Doesn't he know the risk he'll be taking by being on American soil?"

"When you think you're above the law, I don't think that risk factors into your plans."

"Will the FBI know when he touches American Soil?"

"Not sure, but when he touches American Soil the case will be handed off to the CIA."

"Really?"

Snake Chaser

"Yes."

"Okay. Take care," replies Sylvia, and the line goes dead.

"What the hell," states Sylvia to her bedroom. Then she starts racking her brain for any contacts she could possibly have in the CIA, but she can't think of a single soul. Filled with questions and no answers, she heads to her kitchen to grab a beer. She's hoping it will help her sleep for she knows she's not going to get any more answers tonight, but tomorrow is another day.

ReGina Crawford

Decisions

The next couple days are rather mundane with no new information as to the whereabouts of Mr. Red, and the team is tired of standing around waiting so Sylvia asks Sullivan if the team could be given some time off and he agrees. While the rest of the team goes to visit family, Sylvia stays put in the city trying to figure out how she get find out what, if anything, the CIA knows about Mr. Red to no avail. However, on the second day of her furlough, Sylvia's secure line buzzes at Peace Time. Slightly stunned by the incoming call she almost misses the ring cut off of five rings.

She answers on the fifth ring, "Snake Chaser."

"I don't have a code name, but I do have information for you," states the unfamiliar female voice on the other end of the line.

"How did you get this number? Who are you?"

"I was close with your brother, and he gave me your number in case of an emergency."

"You were close with Chance?"

"Yes. Listen, the man that you are looking for is setting up a stronghold in Las Cruces, New Mexico."

250

Snake Chaser

"Are you with the CIA?" Silence. "I'll take that as a yes. Am I the only person outside of the CIA that has this information?"

"Yes."

"The CIA doesn't plan to tell the Marine Commander about this?"

"No."

"Stay safe."

"Will do."

The line goes dead, and Sylvia stands there for several moments just staring at her phone. Once she gathers her wits about her after being stunned by the anonymous caller, her first move is to go through her brother's belongings to see if she can figure out who he was close to in the CIA. She's been going through his things for over an hour before she thinks that she has stumbled upon a name. It appears that he had some type of relationship with Zakiya who is the Assistant of Brad Davidson who is the head of the CIA. At the very least they were friends since he sees her name in his personal calendar on several dates over the past year, but she is unable to determine if they were just colleagues or involved personally. She then determines that the nature of their relationship is not important.

What she needs to do now is decide if she will be sharing this information with Sullivan and the rest of her team and possibly getting Zakiya in trouble with her boss, or acting on the information solo. The problem with acting solo is she will have to give up her career as a Marine, and that's all she's ever known – life as a Marine.

ReGina Crawford

As she sits there contemplating which direction to go with the information that she has received, she make a very startling revelation – she has no way of knowing if her anonymous caller is really Zakiya or a way of contacting her to double check any of the information that she was given. "Damn," she states out loud. She shakes her head at herself for letting herself get caught up in this type of blind situation. So now she needs to decide if she will act on this information now, or wait until she is able to gather more information about Mr. Red's movements and if he is indeed setting up shop in Las Cruces. She decides that she needs more information before she can make a decision on which way she will proceed, so she hops on her laptop to begin doing research on Las Cruces as she would like a layout of the land on the off chance that she ends up traveling to the city.

Something that could work to her disadvantage is the presence of the White Sands Missile Range that is located in the city as she is sure that the government will have beefed up security in the area, even underground which is where she generally sets up her bunkers. She will the Organ Mountains, aside from offering her an alternative place to bunk down above ground, they will also provide her with great vantage points to observe the city. Mr. Red won't have the advantage of having a major airport close by, but the government structure of the city may allow him to get away with keeping a private plane at the small airport that is located in the city and that concerns her. Also, the fact that the city sits right on top of the Rio Grande River causes her concern as far allowing Mr. Red to slip in and out of the city undetected. Knowing that there is nothing she can do about the geographic makeup of the city, she decides to concentrate on the Mayor and the six City Councilors that make up the government of the city to determine if they would be allies or foes in her quest to put a stop to Mr. Red's activities.

Snake Chaser

She wakes up the next morning in an upright position with the laptop still in her lap as she fell asleep while still doing research on Las Cruces. Her body is protesting any and all movement as she sets the laptop to the side, and makes her way to the bathroom. She goes through her morning ritual and gets dressed before venturing to her kitchen for a quick breakfast while she contemplates what she is going to do with the rest of her day. She could only gather so much information on the public internet about the missile range and the government officials of Las Cruces, and she didn't want to draw attention to herself by using her government credentials to login to any of the government sites since she's not sure who knows what or who, if anyone, is watching her movements.

After having breakfast, she decides to head over to the training facility to work off some of the frustration that she's feeling by going through some of the hand-to-hand combat simulations. After about two hours in the booth, she's feeling a little less tense so she heads to the locker room to take a shower. When she returns to her locker, which she is sure that she locked before going into the shower, it is standing wide open and she stops dead in her tracks. She takes the time to look around the locker room to see if she sees anyone lurking in the area, and once she's satisfied that there is no one in there with her she cautiously walks over to her locker to see if anything has been taken from or added to her belongings. Right off she sees an additional cell phone on top of her bag, and even though she's curious about it she's a little apprehensive about picking it up. So she stands there for several minutes staring at it trying to make up her mind about whether she's going to pick it up of not.

Her curiosity finally gets the best of her, and she walks over and picks it up. Underneath the phone is a note that reads:

Listen to the voicemail.
Look at the pictures.

ReGina Crawford

Sylvia does as instructed, and the voice on the voicemail is the same voice from her anonymous call the night before. The message tells her that Mr. Red is planning to stick to domestic sales in the US and Canada for he feels that the international market is too hot for him right now, and that he plans to stick to guns and drugs for there are too many risk is selling human flesh in the States. As she scrolls through the pictures she's not sure who she's looking at until she sees the main character in a picture with the mercenary whose neck she broke in Guatemala, and then she realizes that it has to be Mr. Red. He looks quite different from the pictures her and Qasean took of him in the jungle of South America.

She now knows where he plans to set up shop, what he's dealing in, and what he looks like. Is that enough information to warrant a request that she and the team be sent to Las Cruces? Or will Sullivan tell her it's now in the hands of the CIA, and that they will let them know if they need additional help? She's again feeling as frustrated as she was when she first arrived at the training facility, and she's not sure what she should do about it. Knowing that her body needs a rest even if her mind is in turmoil, she decides to head home to evaluate the situation so that she can make a decision as to which way to proceed.

Snake Chaser

Decisions II

After exiting the training facility, she makes a stop by the information disposal site and adds the phone to the barrel containing other electronic devices that are scheduled to be destroyed. She wants to be sure that she follows the instructions she was given, and besides she doesn't need it as she has Mr. Red's face committed to memory. When she arrives home, she goes right to her bedroom and sits in the middle of bed with her laptop, and continues her research on Las Cruces.

She takes note that the major interstates in and out of the city are Interstate 10 going east and west, and Interstate 25 going north and south. However, she can also utilize US Route 70 which travels east and west for a less popular travel route which would limit her chances of being spotted if she has to make a hasty escape. Although the railway doesn't offer passenger service, she could always stow away in a cargo car for even more concealment if she has to leave the city undetected.

Now that she has compiled all of this information, what is she going to do with it? She was hoping that she would have heard from Sullivan that he was contacted by the CIA and fed more information about Mr. Red's movements, but she hasn't heard a peep out of him. She decides to have a glass of wine and sleep on it, and then go see Sullivan in the morning to see what information he has.

The next morning after breakfast, she heads over to Sullivan's office and his secretary escorts right in which makes her hopeful that he has information for her about Mr. Red.

"I'm glad that you stopped Sylvia," he states as she takes a seat in the chair in front of his desk.

Unable to contain her excitement she blurts out, "You've received information on where Mr. Red is hiding out?"

He shakes his head as he says, "No, I haven't received any information on Mr. Red's location, but I have received a directive from the CIA."

"What kind of directive," she asks with obvious disappointment in her voice for she fears she's about to hear the same words that she heard from Excalibur.

"Now that it is believed that Mr. Red is on US soil, the Marines are no longer involved," he replies. "The CIA will take over the investigation from here on," he adds.

Sylvia jumps out of her chair and begins pacing back and forth in front of his desk because she doesn't trust herself to speak without screaming at the top of her lungs, and since Sullivan doesn't want to hear her scream he just sits at his desk and watches her. Eventually she stops directly in front of his, places her hands palms down on his desk, and leans in as she states through clinched teeth, "This is bullshit!" She pauses and takes a deep breath before continuing, "Are you just going to sit there and let this happen? Let them push us out of the way after all the time we've spent tracking him, and the Marines we've lost?"

Snake Chaser

"I understand your anger and your frustration Sylvia, but my hands are tied on this," he responds. "Sec Def has made it clear that we are to back off and let the CIA run with this."

"What the hell does he know about combat today," she nearly yells. "It's been years since he's been in the middle of a battle!

"Enough Sgt. Williams," counters Sullivan as he rises up out of his chair and places his own hands palms down on his desk. "You are bordering on insubordination, and don't think for a minute that I won't charge you with it!" He leans in closer to her, "I told you I could only cover your ass so far, and your second body was enough for the CIA to say they didn't want you involved with tracking down Mr. Red anymore. They feel you're too emotionally involved, and I agree!" His words feel like a slap in the face, and Sylvia staggers backwards until she falls into the chair that is directly behind her. "Nothing is going to bring them back Sylvia. Accept it and move on," he adds in a slightly calmer voice.

In what sounds like a far away voice to Sullivan, Sylvia states, "A Marine is all I have ever been, then Qasean came into my life, then my brother came back into my life, and then Joshua came forward as Uncle Chappy's son, and then they were all taken away in one explosion. If I can't be a Marine, what do I have left?" Without saying another word, she simply gets up out of the chair and heads for the door.

"Sylvia," calls Sullivan but she keeps walking to the door as though she hasn't heard him. "Sylvia," he calls again but she just opens the door and walks out, closing it softly behind her.

Once the door clicks close, the door at the back of his office opens and CIA director Brad Davidson walks into his office. "Will she be alright," he asks.

"She's a true Marine. I have faith that she will snap out of it, and be just fine," replies Sullivan. "I'll give her a few days to work through whatever she needs to, and then I will send her out on another mission."

"I hope you're right because her voice at the end sounded like the life had been sucked out of her," responds Brad.

"It had to be done."

Brad simply nods at him as he takes his leave, but he makes a mental note to assign one of his agents to keep tabs on her. He's not sure why, but he intends to do it anyway.

****

Sylvia comes out of her daze, and finds herself at home in the middle of her bed even though she doesn't remember how she got there. She makes a decision right then and there, she's going to follow Mr. Red and she doesn't care if she has to enter the belly of hell in order to bring him to justice. Having made that decision, she begins putting together her game plan to leave DC and set up shop in La Mesa which is fifteen miles south of Las Cruces via New Mexico Route 28. She makes a list of supplies that she will need to sustain her while she's there, as well as, the things that she will need to battle Mr. Red. She also checks the amount of funds in her untraceable off shore accounts for she will need funding for this mission, and she doesn't want anyone to be able to track her down and throw a monkey wrench into her plans.

Her conscious rears its ugly head, and whispers '*What about your career as a Marine?*' "I'll deal with that after I have taken down Mr. Red," she says out loud to the room. '*Are you sure you want to go AWOL?*' her conscious asks. "I don't have any other choice." She then shakes her head at herself as she is

Snake Chaser

speaking out loud in a room that is only occupied by her. Refusing to believe that she is out of control, she continues outlining her plans for bringing down Mr. Red. She's confident that he doesn't know who she is and that he doesn't have any other men that would recognize her, and she feels that her chances of catching him are better if she operates solo as opposed to having a complete team with her. She knows that she will have to carve out a life for herself there and live that life for a while before she actively pursues her mission to stop this criminal mastermind in his tracks.

Once she believes she has a solid plan, she calls it a night for she has a long To Do List to complete tomorrow before she can leave town.

ReGina Crawford

Leaving The Nest

The next morning, Sylvia is up bright and early putting her plans in order. She is able to secure a postal box address over the phone, and then prepares her supplies and belongings to be shipped to La Mesa. She also secures herself a place to stay at a boarding house in La Mesa which she will use while staying in the city as she establishes her new profession as a handmade jewelry maker which will give her a creditable reason for 'hanging out' in various locations in the city of Las Cruces.

Not entirely sure if she's already being monitored, she books a flight to Dallas hoping that everyone will believe that she is visiting with her best friend Quintana. From there she will take a flight into Juarez, Mexico and then drive north from there to La Mesa. She plans to lay low for two weeks making jewelry, and monitoring CIA, FBI, and military communications to see if they are looking for her and where they are looking. She's counting on Mr. Red to occupy their time with his activities so they won't spend much time looking for her.

The next day as she's boarding her flight to Dallas, she catches a glimpse of a military police officer watching her from across the airport. She thinks to herself, maybe they'll fall for her ruse and by the time they figure out that it is a ruse she will be so far underground they won't be able to locate her. When she arrives at the Dallas Airport sure enough there she spies

Snake Chaser

another MP near baggage claim as she reclaims her luggage, and is grateful that she made plans to take a charter flight to Juarez instead of flying commercial. After retrieving her luggage she heads to the taxi stand and hails a cab, and she tells the driver to take her to the restaurant that Quintana has opened in downtown Dallas just in case someone is following her from the airport. Unbeknownst to the cab driver she has a surveillance device that is letting her monitor the traffic around them, and since she doesn't notice anyone following them she tells him to take her to the small charter airport just on the outskirts of downtown. Although he thinks that it's strange that she has changed her destination when they are so close to her original destination, he makes the lane changes necessary to take them out of the city and Sylvia is still monitoring the traffic around them to make sure that she didn't miss a tail. Satisfied that no one is following her, Sylvia begins to relax a little for the rest of her taxi ride.

At the next airport, she boards her charter flight and begins to mentally prepare herself for the changes her life is going to take as she sheds her old life and becomes a one woman mercenary determined to take down a dangerous criminal mastermind. When her flight lands in Juarez, she grabs her luggage, and heads to the car rental counter to pick up her car. After securing all of her belongings in the car, she begins the drive to La Mesa to put into motion the first phase of her plan to capture Mr. Red and bring him to justice. Her forty-six minute drive across the border and into La Mesa is uneventful, and she is extremely grateful that she ran into no issues at the custom's checkpoint.

She arrives at the boarding house and checks in, and then proceeds to unpack her luggage before going to the post office to pick up the packages that she had shipped there before leaving DC. She spends the rest of the day separating her jewelry making supplies into the organizers that she bought to store them in, and that takes her well into the wee hours of the morning. Feeling stiff and sore from sitting on the floor and the traveling she did that day, she crawls into bed to get some rest grateful that she doesn't have to keep a structured day at the moment.

When she awakens and looks at the clock, she sees that it's noon and almost goes into a panic before she remembers that her life is her own and she doesn't have a schedule to keep. She lies back down until her stomach reminds her that she hasn't eaten in quite a while, so she gets up, gets dressed, and goes in search of food. She finds a little restaurant to have lunch, and while she's eating a gentleman sits down at her table, "You must be new in town," he states.

Sylvia looks up from her plate and arches her eyebrow at the man hoping that if she doesn't say a word he'll take the hint that she doesn't want company, and gets up from the table and walks away. When he doesn't, she finishes chewing the forkful of food she had placed in her mouth prior to him sitting at her table before responding, "What makes you think that I'm new in town?"

"I make it my business to know everyone who lives here, especially attractive unattached women. And since I haven't seen you before, you must be new here," he responds with what she assumes is '*knock-a-woman-off-her-feet*' smile.

"Well you are correct, I am new in town," she begins with a half a smile on her face. "I've been diagnosed with an incurable disease, so I came here to spend my last days in peace and tranquility," she adds at the same time she drops the smile from her face.

The gentleman immediately stands, and begins to walk away while staying over his shoulder, "Enjoy your time here."

Snake Chaser

After he leaves, her waitress comes over to her table with a smile on her face, "How did you manage that," she asks barely able to suppress her laughter.

"I take it he believes himself to be irresistible," states Sylvia. At the waitress' nod, she adds, "I told him I came here to die."

The waitress is unable to contain her laughter at this point, and erupts into a fit of laughter that Sylvia can't help but join in on. Once her laughter dies down, the waitress tells her that her meal is on the house, and then walks away to wait on a customer who was just seated.

Sylvia finishes her lunch, and then returns to her room to begin working on the jewelry that she will be selling in La Cruces as her front while she tries to get a handle on Mr. Red and his activities.

The next ten days of her life are spent exploring La Mesa and making jewelry, and monitoring what she can of CIA, FBI, and military chatter to see if they have gained any more information about Mr. Red's activities. The chatter regarding Mr. Red is minimal, but she's hoping that he has arrived in Las Cruces and has made progress to get his criminal enterprise up and running again. She needs him to be back to business as usual so that she can build her case against him, and justify her going rogue in order to take him into custody. That is if she doesn't have to kill him first which she is truly hoping and praying doesn't happen, otherwise she will have to live the rest of her life underground for she knows that the powers that be will believe she killed him out of revenge.

Once she believes she has enough jewelry completed to begin marketing her wares in Las Cruces, she contacts the vendors office there to get a permit to set up shop in the open market that takes place there. After securing her vendor's permit, she makes plans to spend the weekend in Las Cruces by securing a room at a bed and breakfast there and packing up her display stands, completed jewelry, and a few supplies so that she can make jewelry in her booth so that the citizens can see her handy work in hopes that will entice them to make purchases. She needs sales to be successful to legitimize her presence in the city.

Friday morning arrives, and she is up early loading up her car for her drive up to Las Cruces to begin her surveillance of the area. When she arrives in town, she parks her car in the designated parking area for vendors, unloads her wares, and gets her booth in order. She receives a lot of traffic from the start, which pleases her immensely for the traffic gives her ruse creditability. In the ten hours that she's open she sells most of the pre-made jewelry that she brought with her, and even takes a few orders for some custom made pieces which she makes while sitting in the booth.

Even though she's happy with her sales, she's a little disappointed that she wasn't able to pick up any information about a new criminal element being in town but then tells herself this just her first day in the city and she's not even sure that Mr. Red has arrived yet. At the end of the day, she breaks down her booth, and as she is heading back to her car she swear she sees one of the men that she's seen with Mr. Red in the past but he disappears before she can get a good look at him. As she loads up her car she keeps her eyes open for any other signs that her nemesis is in the area.

As she makes her way to her room at the bed and breakfast, she wonders if it was just her imagination playing tricks on her and that she didn't really see the man that she thought she saw. Maybe it was more wishful thinking than reality. After arriving back at the bed and breakfast, she unloads her car and takes the evening meal with the rest of the guests before retiring to her room. As it's still early, she spends the rest of

Snake Chaser

the evening making new jewelry pieces for her time in the market the next day.

ReGina Crawford

Waiting Game

The next day in the market place, it's more of the same as the previous day but she's enjoying meeting and conversing with the citizens of La Cruces. As she talks with the people who stop by her booth, she scans the rest of the area hoping to see the man that she thought she saw the previous day, however, she doesn't. In the midst of her disappointment, she has to remind herself that this only her second day in the city, and although her CIA informant lead her to believe that this is where Mr. Red was headed she could have been wrong or Mr. Red could have changed his plans at the last minute. Then she wonders if her informant is aware that she has left DC and is supposedly in Dallas, and maybe that's why she hasn't tried to contact her anymore figuring she was on a furlough and therefore should not be disturbed.

Following those thoughts is the thought '*I wonder if Sullivan has come to the conclusion that I'm not coming back? I mean, I've been gone two weeks which is much longer than any furlough ever granted, and he hasn't tried to contact me once during this time.*' She then shrugs her shoulders at her thoughts, and continues working on the bracelet that a male customer asked her to make for his wife.

*****

Snake Chaser

Meanwhile back in DC, Sullivan is aware that Sylvia is no longer in Dallas, and he is furious with himself that he allowed her to give him the slip while he waited for her to accept the fact that she was no longer assigned to bring Mr. Red to justice. He knows that she never met up with Quintana, and that Quintana was not even aware that Sylvia had even been in the city of Dallas. Hoping that she just went off to be alone and grieve, Sullivan decides to patiently wait for her to resurface although he plans to keep in tune with CIA chatter on the off chance they pick up on her presence while they track Mr. Red's movements. When she didn't make contact or resurface within seven days after having left the city, Sullivan had no choice but to declare her AWOL. He then called Brad, and asked him to come over to his office for he knows that he needs to notify him that she is possibly trying to track down Mr. Red on her own. Trying to keep her sanctions to a minimum, he thought that it would be best to notify Brad in person rather than over the phone.

When Brad enters his office, he greets him with, "Thanks for coming Brad. Please have a seat."

As Brad takes the offered chair, he responds with, "What's going on William?"

Sullivan runs a hand down his face before he proceeds, "I felt it was only fair that I inform you of what's occurred in person."

"And just what has occurred?"

"It seems Sylvia has gone rogue."

"What," yells Brad as he jumps up out of his chair to begin pacing. "How did this happen?"

"Once the MPs spotted her claiming her luggage in Dallas and hailing a cab to take her to Ms. Richardson's restaurant, I took the tail off of her."

"You did what?"

His yelling is starting to aggravate Sullivan who in turn stands and places his hands flat on his desk, "Can you lower your voice," he asks before responding, "I realize now that that was a mistake, but I thought I was doing the right thing for her mental health." He pauses as he and Brad take their seats once again. "I really didn't think that she would go off on her own, and with her skills at camouflage and stealth she is going to be as hard to track down as this elusive Mr. Red that she's determined to bring to justice."

"Shit! This is just what I need, having to get a handle on Sylvia, as well as, Mr. Red," states Brad more to himself than to Sullivan.

"One thing in our favor is now that I have officially declared her as AWOL, no one will risk their jobs by feeding her information so she is truly flying solo if she's still trying to track down Mr. Red," states Sullivan.

"Why doesn't that make me feel any better," asks Brad.

"Well it sounded good any way," responds Sullivan.

"That it did. That it did. Thanks for the information William, now I need to get back to my office and figure her presence into my game plan," says Brad as he stands to leave. The men shake hands, and Brad leaves Sullivan's office.

Back in his office Brad sends out a communication to his teams in the field letting them know that there might me another person they need to watch out for while they are tracking down Mr. Red. He sends them her skill set, as well as, a picture of her hoping that she hasn't decided to alter her appearance.

*****

As the market day comes to a close, Sylvia once again packs up her belongings still slightly disappointed that she hasn't gained any new information concerning the activities of Mr. Red. She returns to the bed and breakfast, unloads her car, and then joins the others for the evening meal. At the end of meal a few of the other guests mention that there is a free outdoor movie in the market place tonight, and that they were going to go take in the show. Tired of living the solitary life that she's been living the past few weeks, Sylvia asks if they mind if she tags along and they assure her that they would love to have her tag along. She goes to her room to get a light sweater and her purse, and then meets them back in the dining room. They all load up in the van that the bed and breakfast uses for the tours that they offer their guests, and they all head to the market place to take in the movie.

Just as the movie ends, they hear a commotion at the other end of the market place from where the movie was being shown. The group that she's with becomes very nervous as the voices take on an angrier and louder tone, and want to rush back to the van to head back to the bed and breakfast. Sylvia wants to linger and see what is going on, and is kicking herself for not driving herself. However, as they make their way back to the van, Sylvia catches a glimpse of one of the men in the midst of the commotion, and it's the same man that she thought she saw the other day while loading her car. '*Damn*' she says in her head, and is now really kicking herself for not driving her own car. Then she thinks to herself, maybe it's better that she is with a group for if she was alone she might be tempted to walk right into the middle of the commotion to see if Mr. Red was among the men arguing. They reach the van, climb inside, and head back to the bed and breakfast. Everyone is speculating about what the commotion was about, but each one is glad that they were able to avoid coming in direct contact with the men involved in the argument. Well, everyone except for Sylvia who's job up until almost a month ago was to jump in the middle of a conflict with both feet, and put an end to it.

Once they are back at the bed and breakfast, everyone retires to their rooms for the night. Back in her room, Sylvia is pacing as she tries to figure out how she is going to go about finding if the man she's seen twice is here solo or here as security for Mr. Red. There is no easy solution to her dilemma without bringing unwanted attention to herself, and it's frustrating her to no end. Coming to the conclusion that she will have to be patient and continue to wait, she stops pacing and sits on the bed to continue to think. It's just her first weekend in Las Cruces, and she believes that she has evidence that Mr. Red is either in the city or planning on arriving soon so she should be content for the moment for she knew that this wouldn't be an easy mission to complete. Having made that decision, she prepares for bed for tomorrow is another day and she wants to be well rested for she knows she is going to have to be more alert than ever tomorrow. At least that's what her instincts are telling her.

Snake Chaser

Making Contact

The next morning she has breakfast before heading to her booth in the market place. She spends as much time scanning the faces of the people in the marketplace as she does making jewelry, and is quite disappointed when she doesn't see a face she recognizes by the time the market shuts down for the day. She packs up her booth, and begins the drive back to La Mesa as she has already checked out of the bed and breakfast. When she arrives back the boarding house, she unloads her bags, takes a shower, and then gets in the bed. She'd forgotten how exhausting it was mentally and physically to be constantly on alert. She's asleep as soon as her head hits the pillow.

The next morning, she awakes feeling somewhat refreshed for she is able to relax knowing that she doesn't have to stay on the constant lookout for Mr. Red or his henchmen. After getting dressed and having breakfast, she takes a seat on the floor to calculate the money she made from her weekend sales, and is surprised to see that she made a tidy sum selling her handmade jewelry. Next she takes inventory of her supplies, and takes note of what she needs to reorder in order to keep her business going. If sales keep going the way that they went this first weekend, she may not have to touch the money she has on stand-by offshore.

ReGina Crawford

With her list of needed supplies in hand, she makes the thirty-five minute drive to El Paso, TX to pick up what she needs to replenish her supplies. After making her purchases at the craft store, she finds a quaint little bistro to have lunch before heading to her temporary home. As she drives she contemplates where her actions have landed her, and is a little taken aback at the realization that she is technically homeless for she is sure that Sullivan has declared her AWOL by now. She wonders what her team had to say about her disappearance, or if they even care that she has disappeared. Finding her thoughts a little depressing, she tries to focus on something a little more cheerful. She begins replaying in her mind all the unique and colorful beads she purchased, and begins planning in her mind the jewelry she would make this week. She even planned to make a few special pieces for a few of the women who had made purchases over the weekend while she was in Las Cruces.

Back in her room, she begins the process of organizing the beads, stones, clasps, and wire that she purchased. Once complete, she makes herself a sandwich for lunch for she figures she'll work better on a full stomach. With her stomach full, she begins working on the jewelry, and just as she did the week before she spends the entire week turning her visions into spectacular works of art.

On Friday morning, she makes the drive up to Las Cruces, checks in at the bed and breakfast, and then heads to the market to set up her booth. Once again she spends the weekend selling her wares in the marketplace, and taking her morning and evening meals with the other guests at the bed and breakfast. This weekend is less eventful than the weekend prior, and she has a hard time keeping her disappointment at bay on the drive back to La Mesa Sunday evening. However, she has no plans to abandon her mission, and to distract herself she switches her focus to the sales that she made on this particular weekend and the bright smiles on the faces of the women for whom she made special pieces.

The next three months drag by as she has seen no evidence that Mr. Red is in the city of Las Cruces nor has she picked up any clues that he plans to arrive in the city, and she's starting to think that she turned her life upside down for no reason at all and that her anonymous informant may have been fed false information. She examines that possibility as she sits on the floor of her room at the boarding house making new jewelry. Who could have planted false information where she would have found it? And could they possibly know that she would give that information to Sylvia? The more she thinks about it, the more ludicrous the idea sounds, so she abandons the idea yet she can't help but wonder why she hasn't seen anything that could confirm that Mr. Red was in the city of Las Cruces. She hasn't even seem the man that she saw on her first weekend in the city, and then she wonders if she missed Mr. Red and if he has moved on to a new city.

Needing confirmation that her mission is indeed legit, she takes a chance and turns on her secure line two minutes before St. Stephen's time hoping that someone has been trying to make contact with her and will try again tonight. Sure enough at 22:07, her line buzzes, and her hand shakes slightly as she proceeds to answer the phone for the call could provide her with new information or provide the military with the means to locate her and take her into custody.

"Snake Chaser."

"Yes," states the voice on the other end of the line. "I have been trying to reach you for weeks."

"Been keeping a low profile under the circumstances."

"I understand, but I'm glad you turned your phone on tonight."

"Why?"

"Mr. Red was delayed arriving in Las Cruces due to a few of the Mexican Cartels picking up his trail, so he had to lead them away from his true destination."

"Do you know when he will arrive?"

"In two days time. Are you still in the area?"

"Yes."

"Be careful as a team of agents from the agency will be arriving as well."

"Good to know. Thanks for the update."

"I want him to pay for taking Chance away from me as well."

The line goes dead, and Sylvia has a reason to smile. To amped to work, she gives up jewelry making for the night, and decides to check her 'Go Bag' to make sure that it has everything that she might need just in case she has an opportunity to bring down Mr. Red. Once that's complete, she goes to take a long relaxing bath hoping that it will enable her to sleep for she wants to make sure she is well rested when she arrives in Las Cruces this coming Friday.

She wakes the next morning with more energy than she's had in a while, and is amazed at the creative vibe that over takes her as she completes making the jewelry pieces that she didn't complete the night before. In her excitement over finally getting a lead on Mr. Red's movements, Friday can't get here fast enough even though it's less than 24 hours away.

Snake Chaser

Déjà Vu

She arrives in Las Cruces on Friday at her usual time, and goes about her normal routine of checking into the bed and breakfast and setting up her booth in the marketplace. As she sits there talking with regulars, as well as, new customers, she doesn't see anyone who looks like they may be working for Mr. Red or Mr. Red himself. The rest of the weekend proves to be uneventful as well, and camouflaging her disappointment she packs up her things on Sunday and heads back to La Mesa. She knows that she must continue with her regular routine so as not to draw any unwanted attention to herself.

The next couple of weeks are uneventful as well, however, a month after Mr. Red was supposed to have arrived in Las Cruces, Sylvia spots a couple of men that she's seen before. One is the man whom she saw in Las Cruces before, and the other is a man she recognizes from South America, so her spirits begin to pick up. That night they are showing a movie in the marketplace again, and she declines to go with the group from the bed and breakfast with the excuse she needed to work on some new pieces of jewelry. After the group leaves, she gets dressed in her camouflage gear to go scope out the town to see if she can find out where Mr. Red is making camp.

ReGina Crawford

When she reaches town, she makes it a point to steer clear of the marketplace and heads to an area of town that very few people venture to figuring that was the most likely place for Mr. Red to take up residence. She creates an underground hideout not far from a few of the houses that are spread out in the neighborhood, and pulls out her infrared camera to see if she can determine which houses are occupied. The first couple of houses appear to be the homes of 'normal' families, however, the house at the end of the street appears to be occupied by large group males and she figures that this is Mr. Red's residence so she makes it the focus of her surveillance. Now that she knows the location of his hideaway, she makes other arrangements to keep tabs on his movements and activities. Just as she was considering packing it in for the night, she notices some activity around the perimeter of her underground hideout and is extremely grateful for her suit that limits the amount of body heat she emits so that she can't be detected by infrared cameras.

As she watches the movement of the bodies above her, she instantly knows that those are the agents that her contact told her to watch out for while she was there. She watches them as they spread out from her location to circle around the house trying to assess the property, and she sincerely hopes that they have no plans to breach the house, at least not tonight for they would find nothing out of the ordinary going on inside and would not be able to make a case against him at this point. They spend about an hour doing recon around the house before leaving the area, and she waits a half hour after they leave before she leaves the area. When she arrives back at her room, she sits in the middle of her bed to think about how she wants to proceed to with her surveillance of Mr. Red, and not be spotted by the CIA agents in the area. She's let her hair grow since leaving DC and added red highlights to camouflage her appearance, but she wonders if she should do something else to alter her appearance without it being too obvious to those who have seen her at the market place for the past two months.

Snake Chaser

Then she figures the agents wouldn't want to draw attention to their presence in Las Cruces, so she probably has nothing to worry about. *'Besides they are probably singularly focused on bringing down Mr. Red, and could care less about me.'*, she thinks to herself. Deciding that she can't do much about the agents, she focuses her time and energy on developing a plan to bring him down herself just in case the CIA is unsuccessful.

Knowing she can't alter her previous behavior, she plans to follow her normal weekend routines when in Las Cruces, and she will spend her evenings during the week to do recon and surveillance on Mr. Red's house. She knows that she will have to also figure out how the CIA plans to keep tabs on the residence so that she doesn't draw their attention to her. Once she's satisfied with the plan of action she develops, she goes to bed for she still has another day in the marketplace tomorrow. At the close of the market on Sunday, she packs her car and heads back to La Mesa as per her usual behavior.

Once back in La Mesa, she unloads her car and unpacks before checking for any government chatter regarding Mr. Red and the CIA's activities on the networks that she can access undetected. The chatter is minimal so she knows that she's going to have to do her own recon on both the CIA agents and Mr. Red. With that thought firmly planted in her mind, she goes to bed for she knows that she has her work cut out for her.

Monday morning she gets up and works on creating enough jewelry for the upcoming weekend's market, and that evening she makes her way to Las Cruces to begin her recon work on the CIA agents. She sets up a sniper's perch five hundred yards away from Mr. Red's residence in hopes that she can catch a glimpse of the CIA agents so that she knows who she's working with or against in an effort to bring down Mr. Red. She gets lucky in that the agents are doing recon, and so she puts down her rifle and picks up her camera to snap photos of the agents. She waits the normal thirty minutes after the agents have left the area before she comes down from her perch, and heads back to La Mesa. Once back in her room she uploads the photos to her laptop to get a better look at the agent's faces to see if she recognizes any of them from past missions, and as luck would have it she knows three of the six agents from having worked on joint missions in the past. With that task accomplished, she turns in for the night for tomorrow is another day of recon and since she now knows a few of the agents she might be able to access their chatter.

Tuesday proves to be less productive as she is unable to gather any information on the agent's mission, so she's unaware if they are merely there to observe or to capture their prey. She takes up her perch again outside the house, however, there is no activity during the four hours she's there. Wednesday and Thursday end the same way as Tuesday, so she's hoping she's able to gain more information while in the marketplace over the weekend.

When Friday morning arrives, she packs up her car and heads to Las Cruces hoping that she is able to make more progress than she has since Monday. Friday's market proves to be uneventful, but she has to maintain hope that she will get a break soon. Saturday she receives a break, however, she's not sure it's the break she was hoping for as she sees several known members from various Mexican Cartels and assumes that they are not there on friendly terms. Her assumption proves to be correct near the end of the day when as she's packing up she witnesses an encounter between the members of the Mexican Cartel and some of Mr. Red's henchmen. The exchange doesn't appear to be friendly, and it appears that the Mexican Cartel takes the upper hand for they appear to be forcibly leading the henchmen away from the marketplace.

Feeling she needs to be on hand for whatever is about to take place but not wanting to appear obvious, she pulls out of the marketplace parking lot and heads towards the bed and

Snake Chaser

breakfast. However, when she feels it's safe to do so, she pulls her car off the road and down a path that doesn't see regular traffic, changes into her camouflage, and does double time to get to her sniper's perch. She arrives just in time to see a commotion taking place in the courtyard of the house as more of Mr. Red's men join the men from the marketplace. As she scans the area around the house, she sees the CIA agents making their approach to the house, and she hopes that they don't plan on breaching the perimeter of the house at this point for they still don't have enough evidence against Mr. Red to put him in jail for life.

Just as she moves her focus back to the inner courtyard, she sees one of the members of the Mexican Cartel fall from a single shot between his eyes. Having nerves of steel she doesn't flinch, however, the CIA agents do double time towards the house and a couple of the Mexican's show surprise on their faces as their comrade hits the grown. Then they hear the voice of Mr. Red say, "The rest of you can be taken down just as easily, so I suggest you drop your weapons and release my men." The members of the Mexican Cartel do as instructed, and once their weapons hit the ground and his men are released, Mr. Red speaks again, "Now all of you put your hands behind your heads and get down on your knees." By this time the agents have taken up position right outside the wall surrounding the house, and are at the ready to breach the interior. As the remaining members of the cartels do as instructed, Red's henchmen begin making their way inside the house one by one. Soon after the door closes behind the last man, the whole house explodes right before her eyes, and this time her nerves fail her as she imagines this is exactly what happened to Qasean, Chance, Joshua, and the rest of her team. She bites her lips to the point that she draws blood to stop herself from crying out in pain and anger, but she remains focused on the house for she is certain that Mr. Red has not killed himself or his men. The only thing that she isn't certain of is if he knew that there were CIA agents close by, and if he meant to kill them as well. At any rate, he's killed eighteen US service members who were simply doing the job they were assigned to do all so he can continue operating his illegal businesses.

Snake Chaser

Gingerbread Man II

She maintains her position as she watches the local firefighters and police, and a military rescue team descend upon the property to determine if there is anyone left to save. Through her binoculars she sees them shaking their heads indicating that there was no one left alive after the explosion. She closes her eyes, and tears silently fall from her eyes as she offers up a prayer for the families of those lost today. Once her prayer is complete, she wipes the tears from her eyes and continues to watch them put out the last of the smoldering embers and gather up the bodies of the fallen.

What she doesn't know is that while she's watching the action at the house, someone has picked up on her presence. Brad Davidson, the head of the CIA, caught a glimpse of someone as his helicopter was flying over the area prior to landing in Las Cruces, and he made a note of where the person was located. Now that he's on the ground, he's using a CIA satellite to watch the lone figure and to figure out who it is.

When everyone leaves the house, Sylvia climbs down from her perch and looks up at the sky with her eyes closed to offer up one final prayer. Brad is extremely grateful that she does, as he is able to capture a clear picture of her face. He takes the picture of her face and runs it through the facial recognition software, and when her information pops up on the screen he lets out a low whistle before saying out loud, "So you're the elusive Sgt. Sylvia Williams." He can't wait to get back to DC to formulate a plan that will involve Sgt. Williams for he is determined to capture Mr. Red, and feels that Sylvia just might be the 'man' he needs to make sure that that happens and soon.

Sylvia heads back to her car so that she can head back to the bed and breakfast, and prepares herself to be bombarded with questions since she's sure that the news of the explosion has reached the other guests and they'll probably be wondering if she saw anything. As soon as he walks through the door, the owner of the bed and breakfast rushes over to her, "Thank God you're alright," she gushes as she tries to wrap her arms around Sylvia but finding it difficult with the bags of jewelry and supplies that she's carrying.

"Why wouldn't I be alright," Sylvia asks seemingly oblivious to what the woman is talking about.

"You don't know?"

"Don't know what?"

"There was an explosion on the other side of the city. Didn't you hear it?"

"I was out in the countryside trying to get some inspiration for some new pieces and I thought I felt the ground shake and I heard a noise, but I just assumed it was something that took place at the missile station," responds Sylvia as she works to keep the emotion from her face and voice.

"Oh no. It's been all over the news. A house on the other side of town exploded and a bunch of men were killed," she states. "The media is speculating that it was the work of some

Snake Chaser

criminal mastermind as CIA agents are being reported as having been at the site of the explosion," she adds.

"Wow," exclaims Sylvia. "That sounds like something we should steer very clear from," she continues. "Since I don't get involved in politics, I'm going to my room to work on the new pieces that I have in mind. I'll say a prayer for those who lost their lives today," she adds as she heads towards her room.

Once inside her room, she turns on her secure phone hoping that she'll be contacted by her contact from in the CIA with details about has taken place in Las Cruces. Unfortunately, both occurrences of St. Stephen's time takes place without a call, so she turns the phone back off and begins working on some new jewelry pieces since she can't sleep. She finally crawls into bed in the wee hours of the morning for she is emotionally and physically drained. When she does awaken the next morning, it's way past the time she should have left for the market so she rushes to get ready to at least get a few hours in at the marketplace, and to see if she can pick up any information about what took place yesterday evening. As she rushes down to the foyer with her bags, she runs into the owner who attempts to stop her from leaving. "I'm super late," she says as she tries to sidestep her. "Why didn't you wake me," she asks as she takes another sidestep.

"The market is shut down for today in light of what happened last night."

Sylvia stops dead in her tracks, "Oh," she says as she stands there looking at a loss of what to do next.

"Even though it's close to checkout time, you can sit down and have lunch before you get back on the road home." Sylvia stands there staring out into space without answering, so the owner touches her on the arm as she asks, "Are you okay?"

Sylvia shakes herself loose from her thoughts, "Yes. Yes, I'm fine," she replies. "Thanks for the offer, but I think I'll head on home."

"Okay," states the owner as she heads back towards her office. "Have a safe trip," she throws over her shoulder.

Sylvia doesn't say another word as she walks out the door, and loads her bags into her car. Her mind is spinning like a whirlwind as she drives back to La Mesa for she wonders if she's lost Mr. Red once again, and if she'll be able to find out where he's headed next. When she arrives at the boarding house, she unloads her bags and then falls across her bed for she doesn't know what to do next. She just lays there for hours thinking that once again Mr. Red has turned into the Gingerbread Man, and wonders if she will ever be able to catch him

*****

Meanwhile, Brad returns to DC and works on getting updated information on Mr. Red and a plan to involve Sylvia without her or the agency knowing that he's behind it. He pulls out the file that he has on Mr. Red while he waits on the arrival of Sylvia's complete file to be delivered to his office. He wants to make sure that he is not going to secretly solicit the help of an unstable individual for he would hate for his plan to backfire on him down the road. As he reads over the file on Mr. Red, he comes to the conclusion that New Mexico was not his final destination based on the way the residence he was staying was structured. "The question remains was he only intending to take out the members of the Mexican Cartel or did he know that we were on his tail as well," Brad asks out loud unaware that there are ears in his office just before there's a knock on his door. "Come in."

Snake Chaser

"Here's the file that you requested from personnel," states his Administrative Assistant.

"Thanks Zakiya," he states as he takes the file from her. "This will be it for the day," he tells her as she makes her way to the door, dismissing her for he doesn't want to take the chance that she may overhear any plans that he may make concerning Mr. Red. The less who know about what he's planning the better.

"Good Night Sir," she states as she walks out of his office closing the door behind her.

*****

Since no answers are forthcoming as she lies in bed trying to figure out what her next steps should be, Sylvia gets up off the bed takes note of the time and turns on her secure phone hoping that she gets a call for her informant. As luck would have it, her phone rings exactly at Peace Time. Even though she's dying to answer it, she waits the required number of rings before picking it up, "Snake Chaser."

"It's me," says the female voice on the other end of the phone. Sylvia lets out the breath she didn't realize she was holding hoping that she would hear the voice she actually hears on the other end of the line. "I know you know about what happened in Las Cruces, but what you don't know is that the head of the CIA requested your personnel file when he returned to DC after visiting the site of the explosion."

"He was here," Sylvia nearly shrieks into the phone. Her mind is reeling as she conjures up an image of her sniper's perch to determine if she could have been spotted by anyone. She is very familiar with the rumors that Brad Davidson could spot an ant in the woods from 500 yards, and is hoping she wasn't an ant that he spotted.

"Yes he was there. Whenever he loses men he makes it a point to travel to the site where their lives were taken to see if they have left any energy for him to absorb."

"I've heard that he does that," responds Sylvia as she continues to hope against hope that he didn't pick up her vibe. "Anything on Mr. Red?"

"Brad is also reviewing his file as well. My advice, stay where you are for the time being. I'll try to get you information, but I can't say how quickly I'll come by it."

"Since I have nothing else to do at the moment, I'll be here," responds Sylvia before the line goes dead.

Snake Chaser

Unauthorized Mission

For the next two months, Sylvia remains in La Mesa, and continues to sell her jewelry in Las Cruces on the weekends so even if Hawkeye himself saw her the day of the explosion and is keeping tabs on her, he won't suspect her of being in the area because of Mr. Red. She has just finished unpacking her belongings upon returning to La Mesa when her secure phone rings, "Snake Chaser."

"It's me," states the voice on the other end of the phone. "Sorry it's taken me so long to get back to you, but they have been keeping everything concerning Mr. Red under lock and key, and even the meetings have taken place in secure locations so it's been hard to gather any information," the voice states all on one breath. She then takes a deep breath before continuing, "However, a file was left unsealed, and I was able to skim through it without being seen. It seems you're out of the eye of the hawk since you have stayed put since the explosion, and you don't have to worry about anyone coming to look for you."

Sylvia breathes a sigh of relief at that news before saying more to herself than her caller, "So he did see me when he arrived in Las Cruces."

"Apparently so."

"Was there anything in there on Mr. Red?"

"I can't say for certain that the file was referring to Mr. Red as his name was not mentioned specifically in the file, however, from what I read I'm thinking that he does have something to do with him."

"What did it say?"

"It said that the person of interest set up a fake residence to conceal the construction of his actual residence, and that the fake residence was destroyed when the person of interest left."

"And the actual residence is located where?" There is a long pause. "Where," repeats Sylvia.

"Dallas."

Sylvia grins as she knows she can go to Dallas under the guise of visiting Quintana while she investigates the area to see if Mr. Red has indeed taken up residence in the area. "Will make arrangements to relocate to Dallas within three weeks time."

"Be careful," states the voice, and then the line goes dead.

Sylvia immediately begins working on a cover for herself as she readies herself for the move to Dallas, but knows that she must maintain the cover she is currently in just in case she is still being watched. She'll use her knowledge of vegetation and water to set herself up as a conservationist which will give her an excuse to travel to remote locations in the city of Dallas and the surrounding areas, for if she knows anything about Mr. Red she knows that he will not set up his operations in the inner city.

Snake Chaser

For the next three weeks, she puts everything into place in Dallas while at the same time continuing to make jewelry and selling it in the marketplace of Las Cruces. She gives the owners of the boarding house and the bed and breakfast the excuse of needing to help a friend with her restaurant as her reason for leaving the area and moving to Dallas, and since Quintana has made quite the name for herself with her restaurant it will seem valid to anyone who decides to investigate her reason for leaving. On her last day in the marketplace, there are some tearful goodbyes between Sylvia and the other vendors, as well as, amongst her loyal customers. She promises to come back whenever she can even though she's not sure that she can make that a reality.

She arrives in Dallas on a commercial flight from El Paso so that no one will know that she's been in New Mexico all this time, and after retrieving her luggage heads to the taxi stand to hail a cab to the hotel where she wants anyone who's looking to believe she is staying while in town. After giving the check in clerk her name, she is told that there is an envelope waiting for her, and the clerk goes through the door behind her and comes back with a thick manila envelope that she hands to Sylvia before completing the check in process. Use to concealing her emotions, Sylvia takes the envelope as though she knew it would be waiting for her, and once the clerk hands her her room keys she heads directly to her room anxious to open the envelope to see who the sender is and what they have sent her.

After tipping the bellhop that brought her bags to her room, she grabs her gear and goes into the bathroom with the envelope just in case she needs to quickly dispose of its contents. Before breaking the seal on the envelope she quickly scans it with her infrared camera to see if it picks up anything that might generate heat that would indicate that there was something explosive inside, and once that test is passed she examines the envelope with a mini x-ray device to further inspect it before

289

breaking the seal. Feeling confident that there is nothing intended to harm her in the envelope, she opens it so that she may examine its contents, and is a bit shocked by what she finds inside. She takes another look at the outside of the envelope looking for possible clues as to where the envelope came from, but there are no obvious markings on the envelope and her name was typed on the front and not hand written. As that realization hits her, she instantly freezes for she knows very few entities have the ability to print on envelopes of this size, and the US Government is one of them.

"So," she asks out loud, "who in DC is sending me mission documents on the sly?" Knowing she is not going to get an answer to her question at this moment, she leaves the bathroom and sits in the middle of the bed to examine the documents that she has pulled from the envelope. She finds updated pictures of Mr. Red and the men that are guarding him, as well as, a list of names of black market dealers that he is believed to be working with to purchase guns and drugs. She also finds a list of his enemies, and a satellite map of the compound that he's built in Mesquite which is only fifteen minutes from Dallas and can be accessed by three major interstates, one being a US highway and one a Texas State highway. There is also a list of people who have the ability to distribute guns and drugs all over the US, and some even have international connections.

After reviewing all of the documents multiple times, she places them on the bed, and says out loud to the room, "My contact doesn't sound like she has access to this type of information, so I know it didn't come from her." She continues to think as to where the documents could have come from, "I really doubt that Sullivan sent them to me for if he knew where I was, I'm sure he would have been waiting for me in the lobby instead of the envelope," she states. Staring up at the ceiling, she continues to rack her brain for an answer as to who could have sent her the documents, and constantly comes up empty. Finally after an hour of thinking and coming up with nothing,

Snake Chaser

she states, "I'm guess I'm in an unauthorized mission as someone knows where I am, and wants to see Mr. Red taken down and must feel that I'm their best asset to make that happen."

Figuring that someone is going to want to feed her regular updates, she turns on her secure phone so that they will be able to reach her. Then she takes a shower before ordering room service, and while eating her dinner she goes over the documents from the envelope once more. Just as she finishes eating she looks at the clock on the nightstand just as her secure line begins buzzing, it was Peace Time. "Snake Chaser."

"It's me. I take it you made it safely to Dallas."

"Yes I did, and there was an envelope waiting for me when I got here."

"There was," the voice asks, but before Sylvia could say a word, she asks, "What was in it?"

The tone of her voice clearly indicates that she is genuinely surprised by Sylvia's announcement, so she confirms that her informant knows no more about the envelope than she does. "It appears to be a mission brief without specific orders."

"Really?"

"Really."

"What the hell is going on?" There is a brief pause before the voice adds, "No one knows about my secure phone or that I've been in contact with you, so who the hell could have known you were going to Dallas? And why would they send you a mission brief?"

"I was really hoping that you could tell me."

"I have no clue. Tell me what was in the packet, and I can tell you if I've seen them and maybe together we can figure out where they came from." Sylvia gives her the rundown of what she found inside the envelope, and the voice states, "I haven't seen any of that information in my office, so I don't think it came from someone in the CIA and frankly that someone has had access to that type of information and hasn't dispatched a team to the area to handle Mr. Red is a mystery to me."

"Maybe they feel as if we have lost enough men at his hands, and thinks that maybe I have a better chance of bringing him down on my own."

"Hmmm. I guess that's possible the voice states. I will keep my ears and eyes open. You stay safe. Be in touch when I have info." And then the line goes dead.

"She should be an agent," states Sylvia as she looks at the now dead phone in her hand.

Snake Chaser

Unfriendly Invasion

For the next two weeks, Sylvia continues putting everything in place for her cover identity now that she's actually in the city, while at the same time keeping her ears and eyes open for any activity by Mr. Red. If he is indeed in the city, he's keeping a low profile for the moment. However, she is not discouraged for she has received regular deliveries that have kept her updated on any new contacts that Mr. Red makes although her informant hasn't been able to pin down where this information is coming from.

She is able to locate a two-story building that is ideal for housing her office on the first floor, and that will allow her to set up a military bunker on the second floor as all of the windows had been bricked in years ago. She even had enough room to create a mini workout area to keep her skills sharp. Once she has her office set up, she sets about making connections with city and county planners so that she will have free reign to travel all over the city without being questioned. Once everything is in place, she begins traveling all over the city so that she can become familiar with the streets and possible locations for black market transactions, and so that when she eventually ventures into Mr. Red's neighborhood it won't seem out of the ordinary. She has also secured a permanent residence in a building containing four large condos, so she won't have to worry about too many neighbors watching her comings and goings. She is lucky in the fact that she the condo she secures is on the first floor of the building, so she can keep track of her neighbors and their guests, as well as, offering her the advantage of being able to slip in and out at various times of the day without drawing attention to her movements.

*****

She's been in the city for six weeks, and feels that now is the time to venture into Mesquite to see what she can learn about Mr. Red's activities. She rides through his neighborhood, and is grateful that there is an abandoned field near his property which gives her an excuse for being in the area for extended periods of time. On day three as she is cataloging the vegetation that is growing in the field and keeping a watchful eye on the compound at the same time, she notices one of his bodyguards heading her way but pretends that she hasn't noticed him. When he touches her on the shoulder to get her attention, she jumps as though he has scared the living daylights out of her, "Oh," she shrieks as she turns to face him while placing a hand over her heart. "You scared the shit out of me," she says in a breathless voice. She takes a few deep breaths as he stands there just looking at her before asking, "Is there something I can do for you?"

He cocks an eyebrow at her before replying, "This is the third day you've been in this field. What are you doing here?"

Pretending she's taken aback by his question she answers with sarcasm in her voice, "Working." Then she cocks her head to the side as though she is replaying his words in her head, "How do you know that this is the third day that I've been here," she asks. She then removes her sunglasses from her eyes and narrows them at him, "Are you following me," she asks.

Snake Chaser

Surprised by her response, he cocks his eyebrow again before replying, "Lady I live in the house adjacent to the field," he states as he points to the compound. "That's how I know you've been out here for three days. What exactly are you doing?"

"I'm a conservationist, and I'm logging the vegetation that is growing in this field to determine if it is native to this area or was brought in my someone or something else," she responds testily. "What difference does it make to you? I'm nowhere near your house."

"My employer, the owner of the house, doesn't take to kindly to unfamiliar people lurking about."

"I'm not lurking," she states indignantly as she places her free hand on her hip. She waves the hand holding her tablet around the field, "And this field is city property, and I have permission to be here," she adds as she waves the permit around her neck in his face. "Now if there is nothing else that you want, I have work to do," she states as she turns her back to him and kneels back down to finish examining the plant she was inspecting when he put his hand on her shoulder.

Satisfied that she is not a threat to his boss, the man turns from her, and heads back towards the house. Sylvia breathes a sigh of relief as he walks away for she wasn't expecting anyone from the house to come over and confront her about her presence in the field. She figured that they would just continue to watch her, and use their connections to see if she was connected to either the Mexican Cartels or the US Government. Knowing her cover was firmly in place, she wasn't concerned about them investigating her.

She spends another ninety minutes in the field cataloging the plants that she found there before she takes her leave, making a point to not look in the direction of the house knowing without a doubt that they were watching her every move. When she arrives home, she spends the next hour inputting the data on the plants she looked at today into her database so that she can see if there was anything interesting growing in the field. While the software she was using did its thing, she takes a shower and orders dinner. Just as she finishes eating, she notices that the computer screen is flashing a message across the screen, and she walks over to it see what it's telling her. It seems that one of the plants that she inspected today is not native of the area, and based on everything that she's reading on the screen the plant should not be able to survive in this area. She can't wait to take her findings to the city planners in the morning, and she hopes and prays that they give her clearance to set up a study area in the field as she could keep better tabs on Red's movements with a valid reason to set up camp right outside his door.

The next morning her prayers are answered, and she is given the clearance that she needs and she makes moves to set up a temporary field office in the field to see how many of the plants are growing in the field. It takes two days to get the equipment she needs and to find students of botany to help her explore the field, but she is soon setting up her field office.

As they are setting up the tents and equipment, she sees the same gentleman who approached her three days ago striding purposely across the field in her direction. "What is all of this," he asks with more than a little annoyance in his voice as he waves his arms in the direction of the tents and equipment.

However, before she can answer him, the head of the planning office speaks, "And you are?"

"I live in the house over there," he begins as he points in the direction of Mr. Red's compound, "And I demand to know what is going on here!"

Snake Chaser

"You have no grounds for making any demands as this is city property, and we have every right to be here," responds the city planner. "You, however, are trespassing. So why don't you head back to your house, and make it a point to stay out of our way."

The man looks back and forth between the smug look on Sylvia's face and the angry look on the face of the man who was just speaking to him. "And you are?"

"Mr. Walker, head of the City of Dallas Planning Office. I have complete jurisdiction over this area, and I suggest that you not interfere with the workers as they go about their jobs." As the last words leave his mouth, he turns back to the workers and students and tells them to continue with what they were doing as they have all frozen where they were standing to watch the exchange taking place. Sylvia follows suit, and goes back to overseeing the setting up of the equipment.

Feeling dismissed, the man heads back to the house, and Sylvia has a hard time keeping a smile from her face. She is going to enjoy annoying the hell out of Mr. Red and his men. Once everything is set up, the off-duty officers tape off the area, and then take up their posts around the perimeter to keep any would be thieves from attempting to walk off with the equipment that they are leaving behind. Mr. Red and his men watch as the woman and the rest of the people with her load up into the vehicles, and drive away.

"Damn," Mr. Red spits out between clenched teeth. "Their presence here is going to be a problem," he continues. "We are going to need to secure a location to conduct business since they will be leaving those cops here overnight," he adds. Knowing that that was a direct order, a couple of his men go about finding an available warehouse to conduct business despite the lateness of the hour.

ReGina Crawford

By late afternoon of the next day, they have found what they believe to be the perfect location to conduct business. However, they are unaware that the building that they have chosen is directly across the street from Sylvia's office.

Snake Chaser

Secrets and Revelations

Sylvia and her crew of students spend the next five days in the field studying the plant life that is growing there, and are a little disappointed that they only find one other plant that is not native to the region. They take down their tents and pack up all the equipment, and leave the field pretty much the same way that Sylvia found it. The next day Sylvia returns to her office building, and as she reviews the surveillance tapes for the days that she was in the field she sees several unexpected faces arriving at the building directly across the street from her. "Well I'll be damned," she states as she stares at the screen. "Make it easy for me to keep tabs on you," she adds as she pauses the footage and stares into the eyes of the elusive Mr. Red.

She downloads the footage onto an external hard drive to make sure that she has plenty of room to record all future comings and goings of Mr. Red and his crew, and any potential visitors that he might have. She also makes sure that her cameras are positioned so that she can capture all traffic to the building across the street, as well as, all traffic to each intersection near the building. Feeling a burst of energy as a result of the latest developments in her quest to bring Mr. Red to justice, she heads upstairs to work out for she knows that she will have to be patient as she waits for him to show his hand.

It's a week later after discovering that he's utilizing the building across the street from her office before Sylvia gets a clue as to what Mr. Red is up to, and who's he's dealing with for his black market deals. As she's sitting in her office, she sees a known rebel leader enter the building across the street, and a half hour later she sees Mr. Red and his visitor exit the building and get into a vehicle sitting outside the building. She knows that he's unaware that she is across the street from him and she doesn't want to give away her location but she doesn't want to lose track of them either, so she uses her secret escape route at the back of her building and attempts to follow them. However, she loses them as they have a head start on her but she doesn't give up, and the universe is on her side as she is able to pick up their trail again as she heads to a location that she believes would be ideal for black market dealings. When she sees them pull off the main road onto a cleverly concealed off road path, she drives past the road only to drive off road five hundred feet from the path and doubles back on foot. She arrives at the location of the deal just as the purchaser fires off a test round from one of the guns, and the bullet whizzes right past her head as she takes up her post to watch the deal go down.

"Damn, that was close," she whispers as she conceals herself in the dense foliage surrounding the abandoned building where the deal is taking place. She pulls out her long-range camera, and captures footage of the rest of the deal. She waits thirty minutes after Mr. Red and his guest leaves the area before she leaves, and heads back to her office. When she arrives back at her office, she downloads the camera footage before she heads home to get a shower. After her shower and deciding that she's not in the mood for cooking, she heads over to Quintana's restaurant figuring it was time to let her friend know that she had taken up residence in Dallas just in case they run into each other. "I can't have her calling out to me, and unconsciously giving up information about me to my nemesis or any government officials who may still be looking for me," she states out loud as she grabs her purse to head to the restaurant.

When she arrives at the restaurant, there is a long line of customers waiting to be seated and she wonders if she will be able to get a table since she's dining alone. However, as fate would have it, Quintana comes to the front of the restaurant to offer free appetizers to the waiting patrons and sees her. "Sylvia," she states as more of a question than a statement.

"Hi Ana," she replies.

"As soon as I am done here, follow me inside," states Quintana as she continues offering the appetizers to her customers. Sylvia simply nods her agreement, and waits for Ana's tray to be emptied and then she follows her through the restaurant and back through the kitchen to Ana's office.

Unbeknownst to Sylvia, Mr. Red, his henchmen, and a potential customer are dining in a back corner of the restaurant, and she doesn't see them but they see her. Mr. Red cocks an eyebrow as he watches the conservationist follow the owner of the restaurant through the crowd, and into the kitchen. "Now just how does a city employee afford the meals in this place," he muses out loud. "And she must eat here frequently to know the owner well enough to be allowed in the kitchen," he adds.

"You know the woman," his client asks.

"Not as well as I'm going to get to know her," he states absently as he continues to stare at the door to the kitchen. After a few more moments of staring at the door, he shakes himself loose from his musings and gives his full attention back to his client.

When they reach her office, Quintana closes the door and then pulls Sylvia into a big hug, squeezing her so tight Sylvia is finding it hard to breathe. After a few minutes, Sylvia pries herself free of Ana's embrace and looks in her face. The tears that are silently flowing down Ana's face alarm Sylvia, and she leads her over to the sofa she sees against one wall of the office. "What's wrong Ana," Sylvia asks with fear in her voice as drastic scenarios play out in her head.

"You're alive," she states in an almost whisper fearing that if she spoke too loud that Sylvia would fade away, and that she would find that seeing her was just a figment of her imagination.

"Of course I'm alive. Why would you think that I wasn't?"

"You've been declared AWOL, and no one has seen or heard from you in almost a year. Mom, Dad, and I feared the worse when none of us heard from you." Sylvia frowns at her friend, confused as to why they would think that she was dead. Quintana quickly interprets her friend's frown, and answers her unspoken question. "We figured that you were tracking Mr. Red, and when we heard about the explosion in Las Cruces we thought that you might have been there and that no one would know to look for your body as no one would have known that you were there.

It's Sylvia's turn to hug her friend and damn near stop her from breathing for she knows that that must have been hell on earth to believe that they lost her the same way that they lost Qasean. Her heart is constricted by the pain she feels for causing them needless worry, and she hugs Ana a little tighter. "I . . . can't . . . breathe," states Quintana breathlessly. Sylvia relinquishes her friend, and watches her take several deep breaths. Once she has recovered, Quintana gets right in Sylvia's face and asks, "Where the hell have you been all this time? And why didn't you at least keep in touch with me?"

Snake Chaser

She skips over the first question figuring the less Ana knew about her whereabouts the better, but she does answer her second question, "I couldn't Ana. I have no idea if anyone is monitoring my movements or the movements of those that I have left on this earth, and I didn't want to put anyone in danger by letting them know where I was or what I was doing."

By her response, Quintana knows that her assumptions were correct and that Sylvia has been tracking Mr. Red, and she can only hope and pray that she plans to bring him to justice and not kill him. However, she is not beyond trying to convince her friend to put an end to her dangerous endeavors. "Nothing is going to bring them back Hon, and what you're doing just might get you killed. Please just let it go."

"I wish I could," states Sylvia for she sees the anguish in her friend's eyes that she is unable to hide. "This is all I have left to live for." Fresh tears flow from Quintana's eyes at her words. "Don't cry," whispers Sylvia as she embraces her friend once again. "I promise to be careful, and besides Mr. Red doesn't know who I am or that I'm tracking him."

Quintana leans back from Sylvia's embrace as she states with anger in her voice, "You hope he doesn't know." She stands up and begins pacing her office, "No one has proven that he didn't know about your team tracking him before, yet he killed everyone but you. And who's to say that he didn't know about the CIA agents that he killed in Las Cruces." She stops right in front of Sylvia and her anger is evident in her face and her voice, "You are not invincible," states Quintana.

Sylvia closes her eyes knowing that her friend is concerned about her safety, but also knowing that she will not stop until she is able to bring her nemesis to his knees. When she opens them, she simply states, "I just came here to get something to

303

eat, and to let you know that I'm in town so that if you see me on the streets you don't attempt to speak to me."

"Fine," states Ana angrily. "Wait in here, and I'll bring you your food shortly." With that she leaves the office, and proceeds to prepare one of Sylvia's favorite dishes for she assumes it's been a while since she's had a decent meal, and knows that's what really drove her to come to the restaurant.

Sylvia eats her dinner, and then leaves via the backdoor at the insistence of Quintana for she figures the least amount of people that see them together the better.

Snake Chaser

Crosshairs

Mr. Red concludes his business and finishes his dinner, and heads home to immediately begin digging deeper into the life of the woman who seems to keep crossing his path. He takes some snapshots of her face from the surveillance footage that he has of her from when she was working in the field beside his house so that he can pass them on to his contacts hoping that they will be able to find out exactly who she is.

The next morning just as Mr. Red and his men are entering the building that they have chosen for their business dealings, he spots Sylvia entering the building directly across the street. "Damn it," he hisses as he walks through the door. "I need to know who this woman is, and now!"

Sylvia sees Mr. Red and his men entering their building just as she is entering hers, but acts as though she doesn't notice them. "This couldn't have worked out any better if I had planned it myself," she states out loud to the empty room. Just as she is about to sit at her desk to check her security footage, there is a knock at her door. At first she simply looks at the door in rapt curiosity for she hasn't told anyone about this place, so she has no idea who could be knocking on her door. Then she goes on high alert thinking that it could be Mr. Red or one of his men at the door with less than honorable intentions. She grabs one of her twin desert eagles and turns off the safety as she approaches the door, "Who is it," she asks as she crouches beside the door.

"Secure Delivery for a Ms S. Chaser," states the voice on the other side of the door.

She tucks the gun in the back of her waistband as she stands to open the door, but she never takes her hand off the grip. When she opens the door, she sees a delivery guy holding a large manila envelope and one of those handheld signature devices. He hands both to her, and she lets go of the gun to take them tucking the envelope under her arm before signing the tablet. The man heads back to his truck as soon as he has her signature, she closes the door and looks at the envelope. She instantly freezes for the manila envelope is an exact duplicate of the one that she received when she checked into the hotel when she first arrived in Dallas. "Who the hell knows that I'm here, and what I'm doing," she asks out loud. She takes a seat at her desk, and opens the envelope to see what she's been sent this time.

There are pictures of her at the field taking to the man who approached her from the compound, as well as, pictures from Quintana's restaurant showing Mr. Red and several other men dining at table in the corner of the restaurant. She gasps as she never noticed him while she was there, but it appears that he noticed her and followed her with his eyes as she enters the kitchen with Quintana. "Thanks for the warning," she states as she continues to look at the pictures, "whoever you are."

Several weeks go by with no real interaction between her and Mr. Red and her security tapes reveal nothing about what is taking place in the building across the street. Feeling restless, she gets in her car and drives around the city hoping to pick up on any clues as to what her nemesis is up to. While driving past an abandoned lot, she notices someone she hasn't seen

Snake Chaser

before scoping out the lot, and he makes the hairs on the back of her neck stand up so she decides to keep tabs on him.

It isn't until he's out of the hood that he picks up the tail behind him. *'Let's see who is interested in me, and what they have in mind,'* he thinks to himself. He leads the tail through a maze of streets before pulling up to his new offices. *'They need to know where to find me when the time comes to make some contacts with the underground,'* is his thought as he gets out of the car and heads for the front appearing to be oblivious to the tail. Just as he reaches the door and is about to insert the key in the lock, a female hand covers the key hole. He slowly follows the hand up the arm across bare a shoulder, and up the neck to a gorgeous face. He whistles unable to help himself. "I'm not officially open yet, but for you I'll make an exception." She doesn't say a word, just merely arches a perfectly shaped eyebrow.

He moves her hand and opens the door before turning and saying, "Come on in." He opens the blinds slightly to let in some light, before pulling his chair around to the front of his desk since it's the only chair in the place. Only his things from New York have arrived already, the rest of the furniture should arrive in three to four days. "Have a seat," he states as he moves the chair next to her before having a seat on the corner of his desk. "I'm Quentin McNair, and you are," he asks after she takes a seat in the chair.

"My name is Sylvia Williams."

"Well Ms Williams, what brings you to my doorstep since I'm neither open nor advertising?"

"I followed you from the last vacant lot you were looking at, didn't you see my Mercedes behind you?"

"No, I'm afraid my mind was preoccupied with the buildings and land I saw today," he responds while thinking to himself why she would want him to know that she was following him. "Then I went sightseeing through the city to get a feel for the type of architecture used here. That must have been a really wild drive for you if you followed me from South Dallas. Why did you follow me?"

"Obviously, I thought you were someone or something you're not."

"Excuse me? Could you clarify that for me?"

"I thought that you were one of those alphabet boys," she responds, "or at least a real player looking for some action." At his raised eyebrow, she answers what she believes to be his question, "Alphabet boys, you know FBI, CIA, DEA, ATF, but since you don't notice when people are following you I guess you're none of the above. Although for a while during your sightseeing, I thought you were trying to lose me."

"Like I said, I didn't even know you were behind me, and I know I glanced in my rear view mirror quite a few times. I think I would have noticed you if you were behind me," he states out loud while thinking *'Why would I want to lose my first contact to the underground'*. "But why would you think I was one of the 'Alphabet Boys' as you call them?"

Ignoring his question, she responds, "Well I wasn't directly behind you, but that's not the point of my visit. Just exactly who are you Mr. McNair and what are you doing in my city?"

"I am merely a real estate broker whose company is expanding to this area, and since I have been broker of the year for the last two years I got first shot at this office. I can turn abandoned buildings and vacant lots into big money projects in no time at all. My boss says I have a great knack for seeing the potential

Snake Chaser

in various locations. I told him it's because I get a vibe from the people of the city, and can feel what they want or need." Seeing that she is not impressed by what he has told her by the scowl on her face, Quentin states, "I get the feeling that you don't like me Ms Williams. Have I done something to offend you?"

"No, but keep in mind that I'll be watching you," she states just before she gets up and leaves.

When the door closes behind her, he states out loud, "I'll be watching you too." He reaches inside his pocket to turn off the tape recorder that he had running, and hopes that the surveillance camera got a good shot of her and her car. He locks the front door before going into the hidden back room to check the recording. "Great, I got a full facial view of you Ms Williams and your plate number," he states out loud. He removes the DVD and replaces it with a new blank one before leaving the room to send the audio and video off for identifying purposes.

As she pulls away from the curb, Sylvia states out loud, "Well obviously you're not here to bring me in since you showed no reaction at all to my name, or you're damn good at hiding your thoughts." As she continues to drive and think, she continues her one-person conversation, "Just who are you Mr. McNair, and what are you doing here? You better believe that I'm going to find the answers to my questions."

Necessary Deception

Needing some comfort food and wanting to see if Mr. Red would be meeting with any more potential clients, she heads over to Quintana's restaurant.

Just as she's being seated, Quentin and Quintana enter the restaurant from the kitchen. "Hi Sylvia," states Quintana as they reach the table. Quentin is shocked into silence that Quintana knows this woman.

"Hi Quintana, Mr. McNair," replies Sylvia camouflaging her surprise that they both know Quintana.

However, Quintana is not as successful as Quentin and Sylvia at hiding her surprise that they have met. "You two have met," she asks looking back and forth between the two of them.

"We met this morning at my as yet unopened real estate office," volunteers Quentin.

"I saw him driving through the neighborhood, and decided to follow him to see where he would end up. Imagine my surprise when he stopped in front of what appeared to be an abandoned office building," adds Sylvia looking a little displeased at finding the two of them together.

Snake Chaser

"Oh. Well just so there's no misunderstanding, I saw him first," states Quintana while smiling at Sylvia.

"As much as I'm enjoying this conversation, I need to get going," Quentin states to the ladies. Then to Quintana, "I'll see you after work." He smiles revealing his dimple before turning and walking out of the restaurant. As he gets inside his car he wonders to himself, "Is it just coincidence that you showed up at the restaurant today, or were you still following me? And how in the hell do you know Quintana? How is it that she doesn't know who you are? Well I plan to get to the bottom of this, and soon."

"Just how do you know this McNair person," asks Sylvia after Quentin walks through the door to the outside.

"He's the brother of the bride whose wedding I'm catering in a few months," answers Quintana. "Why?"

"Nothing that I can put my finger on. There just seems to be more than meets the eye with him. He claims to be a real estate broker and nothing more, but I just feel like he's hiding something."

"Why do you feel like he's hiding something?"

"Like I said I can't put my finger on it, but I will figure it out. Trust me on this one."

Quintana walks away, leaving Sylvia to her thoughts, hoping she doesn't find out who Quentin is if he doesn't want her to know. Then she wonders if Quentin can find out who she is, and if he even cares who she is. That's a stupid question, she thinks. If she followed him around town, he probably already put the wheels in motion to find out who she is, and if she can be of any use to him. Quintana wonders if she will be caught in between them since one is her friend and the other is her lover.

By the time Quentin makes it back to Indigo's there's a message waiting on him from headquarters. He calls in to see if they have any information on Ms. Williams. The phone is answered on the second ring. "Hey Brad, got your message," states Quentin. After listening to Brad's reply greeting, Quentin asks, "Anything on Ms Williams?"

"Yes, and you're not going to believe what I'm about to tell you. I just want you to know I had to pull a lot of strings to get this information," states Brad feeling bad that he has to lie to one of his top agents. When he sent Quentin to Dallas he didn't think that his path would cross with Sylvia's, but as luck would have it they did.

"Just spit it out," returns Quentin impatiently.

"She's an ex-undercover military operative. Apparently a few years ago a military unit was taken down by some South American drug lord, and her fiancé, brother, and a cousin were all a part of the unit. She has made it her mission in life to bring to justice all who were involved. She does not tolerate interference from anyone including the CIA and FBI, so be very careful around her my friend. We will do everything possible on this end to make sure your cover isn't blown, because if she finds out who you are she will put it on the local news so that no one will deal with you. She doesn't want anyone taking these guys down, she wants to be the one to do it and will get rid of anyone that she thinks is a threat to her mission. She's become somewhat of a renegade, and is somehow funding her own operation since her government funds were cut off ten months ago."

Snake Chaser

"Well I certainly wasn't expecting that bit of news, but it certainly makes things a little more interesting."

"Be careful man. I've talked with a couple of agents who have crossed paths with her before, and they say she's vicious and determined that no one else takes these guys down."

"Believe me I plan to keep both eyes on her. She let me see her claws this morning though she didn't use them. I think she just wanted me to know that they were there. If there's any other information about her out there I want it. Friends, family, enemies, favorite restaurants, her gym, etc. I want it all since that is the only way I can keep from crossing her path accidentally. I especially want to know what her relationship is with Quintana Richardson."

"Sure thing man. I'll get right on it. Talk to you later." Brad hangs up even though he has all that information sitting right smack in the center of his desk, but if he had given it to Quentin right then and there he would have been suspicious as to why he had that information already.

The next morning after showering and changing clothes, he does another drive through the city looking at vacant lots and abandoned buildings in an effort to maintain his front as a real estate broker. As he pulls up in front of the last property he plans to look at today, whom does he see in his rear view mirror? None other than the unconventional Ms Williams.

He steps out of his car and walks towards hers, as she rolls down her window he asks, "Are you following me again Ms Williams?"

"No, but I wonder if it's coincidence that we keep turning up in the same places," she states in a somewhat irate voice.

He keeps his composure, pastes on a smile, and asks, "What is it about me that you don't like?"

"I don't like anyone who pretends to be something that they're not," she responds.

"I assure you, Ms Williams, I am a real estate broker. One of the best in the business too, I might add."

"You may be that on the surface, but there's more to you than meets the eye and be assured that I will find out what that is," she states as she rolls up her window and puts her car in reverse.

Snake Chaser

Unexpected Run-In

Just as Sylvia arrives home up pulls Mr. McNair and he gets out of his car carrying a couple pails of paint, and she wonders if he's now trying to turn the tables on her and is following her. However, before she can open her mouth to say one word, he speaks, "Okay lady, I've had just about enough of your stalking. You need to back off," he states very irritated at this point.

Taken by surprise, Sylvia cocks an eyebrow before stating in a surprisingly calm voice, "I wasn't following you this time. I happen to live in this building. So are you now masquerading as an interior designer so that you can turn the tables on me?"

"Sorry for snapping at you," he replies, "and I happen to have just bought a condo in the building. I'm painting the walls, thus the paint," he continues holding up the buckets in his hands. "I'm normally not this grouchy, it's just been a grueling couple of weeks moving here and trying to get my condo livable and my office workable. I really am sorry for snapping at you," he states again.

"Not a problem. I usually have that effect on people since I tend to rub them the wrong way," she responds around a ghost of a smile.

"You enjoy rubbing people the wrong way." It wasn't really a question, more of a statement really.

"I'm really not into bonding with people, so my technique works for me."

"That seems like it would be a very lonely existence, but you seem to have bonded with Quintana."

He thinks he sees a flash of pain in her eyes before she speaks, but he's not quite sure. "That's different. We became friends when I was different," she states in a somewhat far away voice. However, she quickly regains her composure and adds, "I just hope our paths don't keep crossing like this. It just seems too much of a coincidence." She walks off into the building before Quentin can make heads or tails of this latest encounter.

Deciding that now is not the time to try to figure out the puzzle that is Ms Williams, Quentin heads inside to his condo to begin painting. After getting everything set to go, he decides to turn on the radio for some mood music. Less than thirty minutes into painting, the radio broadcast is interrupted by late breaking news.

'Important News Flash – An abandoned building on the city's south side has just exploded. Firefighters are on the scene, but are having very little success in getting the flames to go out. It seems the blast rocked about two city blocks as the building exploded. We'll keep you updated as more news becomes available.'

"Damn, what the hell is that about," Quentin asks out loud. "Let me call Brad and get him on this in case it has something do with what I'm working on," he continues. However, before he can pick up his phone and dial the number, there's a frantic knock on his door. "Who the hell could that be," he asks as he

Snake Chaser

heads to the door. Upon opening the door, he sees a visibly upset Sylvia Williams.

"Okay buster, tell me who you are and tell me now," she states angrily as she pushes past him into the condo.

"Look here Lady, you have no right to come barging in here like this," he responds just as angrily. "Besides what have I done now to have you screaming at me like this?"

"I don't know how you know, but you obviously know who I am and what I'm doing, and you're trying to stop me. But blowing up my base of operations will not stop me from completing my mission," she throws at him at the top of her lungs.

"Okay, what kind of drugs are you on? I have no idea what you're talking about."

"The building that is all over the airwaves. The one that just blew up. It was my base of operations," she responds as she continues to look at him as though she is ready to kill him at the slightest provocation.

"The news flash that just came over the radio about the explosion, that's what you're talking about? I have nothing to do with that. I don't know who you are, nor do I care who you are. And frankly, I have had enough of you to last me a lifetime. So please do me a favor, and get the hell out of my home so I can get back to work," he states as he makes a move to reopen the front door.

'Important update – It seems the explosion was a miniature bomb set off to be a warning as the firefighters discover a message carved into the only wall left standing after the blast. 'We know who you are Ms Williams. Back-off or you'll meet the same fate as your family' is the message that was left. The

ReGina Crawford

FBI and CIA have been called in to try to figure out who this Ms Williams is, and who wants her dead. Stay tuned for further updates.'

"Okay Lady, that's it. Like I said, I don't know who you are, and I'm convinced more now than ever that I don't want to know who you are. If someone is trying to kill you, I don't want them to think that I know anything about you and what you are doing. Now, get out," he shouts as he opens the door.

"Look, I'm sor . . . ," Sylvia begins.

"Save it Lady, and just get out," he states in a very angry voice. Sylvia drops her head, and walks out the door. Quentin slams the door behind her, and takes a seat in the middle of the floor. Before he can even get his thoughts in order, his phone rings. "Yeah," he barks.

"Whoa," states Brad on the other end. "What the hell bit you in the ass?"

"Sorry man. Some weird shit just happened here. I was trying to get myself together before giving you a call."

"That's exactly what I'm calling you about. The building was being used by Ms Sylvia Williams as her base of operations, and the bomb that blew it up has the same signature as bombs used in the past by a guy who uses the code name Mr. Red."

"Shit! Shit! And more shit," hisses Quentin.

"What," shouts Brad into the phone.

"Remember the conversation that I overheard when I first got here," asks Quentin.

"Yeah, what about it?"

318

Snake Chaser

"Mr. Red was paying someone to scare someone else. I wonder if the person he was talking about is Ms Williams."

"Shit! Shit! And more shit," shouts Brad on the other end of the line.

"Exactly," shouts Quentin.

"Okay, let me put some things in motion regarding Ms Williams, and see what information I can find on this Mr. Red since no one seems to know his true identity. I'll get back to you when I have more info." The line goes dead for Brad knows that he must be careful how much information he feeds to Quentin at any one time. His hand was forced to send an agent to Dallas to see if they could get a handle on Mr. Red, and he couldn't very well refuse since no one knows that Sylvia is in Dallas and still pursuing him.

Quick Exit

Sylvia goes to her condo to contemplate what her next move should be since Mr. Red has obviously found out who she is, about her presence in the city, and the fact that she's tracking him. Just as she settles herself in the middle of her bed and begins exploring the idea that maybe her CIA contact is used her to force Mr. Red's hand and provided him with information on her, she receives an SOS message on her phone. She retrieves her phone, and upon seeing the message she makes a call to the sender. The phone rings three times before it's answered, and the person on the other end of the line doesn't say a word letting her know that it's safe to talk.

"Snake Chaser."

"Excalibur."

"Troubles?"

"Info."

"Post."

"Dakar."

Snake Chaser

"Players?"

"Sending photos."

"Double Time?"

"Precisely."

"Two Clicks."

Sylvia receives the photos, and can't believe who's the main subject of them. Zahara, an African Princess in hiding. "What in the world are you doing in your native country," she asks the photo. "And Excalibur how did you end up there with her?" As she continues to stare at the photos, she makes the assumption that the family that wanted her to marry their son must be still after her country. "Damn," she states. However, as she continues to think about, she decides that this couldn't have developed at a more opportune time for she's not sure who's feeding who information. All she knows is that her identity has been compromised, and she needs to protect herself. "I need to get out of the country for a while, and this is the perfect excuse to leave," she states out loud, "especially if someone in the government is watching me as they won't question why I'm going to Africa to help Zahara." She makes the call to let Excalibur know what's going on, and that she will be on her way to assist.

"Excalibur."

"Snake Chaser."

"Info."

"How did you get involved with this case?"

"My art background, why?"

"Assassination plots in that country are not easy to stop, damn near impossible. And it seems that the female agent on your case has angered some very influential people by pretending that she is not Princess Zahara."

"If she is Princess Zahara, she's not pretending. She really doesn't know who she is. Apparently her parents never got around to telling her her real history before they were killed. Maybe they thought that their trip here two years ago would be successful and they would tell her when they regained control of their country."

"I tried to tell Zarif and Zarina that it wasn't a good idea for them to go to Africa themselves. They should have sent someone else to negotiate the return of the artifacts. They should have at least let me return with them."

"What? You knew the King and Queen?"

"No, Zarif and Zarina were servants to the King and Queen, and where charged with getting the princess safely out of the country. I was assigned to them when the Princess was recognized by one of her countrymen who was an exchange student at her high school. I was with her until her second year in college when all interest in her ceased. The King and Queen were really killed in the plane crash, but Zahara wasn't with them. The child that died in the crash was the child of a servant."

"So Zamora is really Zahara?"

"Yes she is, and I think you're going to need some invisible help with this case. I can be there in three days. Let you know when I've arrived and I will fill you in on all the details when I get there."

Snake Chaser

The line goes dead, and Erik sits in stunned silence. He is unsure of what to do with the information that he has just been given or who he should share it with. He then decides he doesn't want anyone to know about his connection to rouge agent Sylvia Williams, so he better keep the information to himself. He will just have to make sure that any plans they make during the course of the case involve strict security for Zamora.

Sylvia goes to her closet, and pulls out her luggage to pack for her trip to Africa. Once her luggage is packed she makes plans to drive to Houston where she will catch a flight to Atlanta, and then a connecting flight to Africa.

Just as Quentin is pulling up in front of the building the next afternoon, he sees Sylvia loading luggage into the trunk of her car, and thinks to himself *'Good move lady. Go underground for a while so I can find out what's really going on.'* He doesn't look her way as he is getting out of his car, then heads straight for the front door of the condo building.

Sylvia sees Quentin pull up to the building, but doesn't stop loading her luggage. *'I wonder if he will stop and say anything to me before going inside'*, she thinks to herself. As he makes his way inside the building without so much as a glance in her direction, she further thinks, *'I guess he wasn't joking when he said he doesn't want anyone to think that he knows me. Maybe I'm wrong about him. Maybe he's not more than he appears to be.'* She shakes her head as if to clear it, *'I can't start doubting myself now. I've got too much invested in this,"* she thinks to herself. After loading her luggage, she gets in her car to head to parts unknown while she tries to figure out who has found out about her, and how they found out about her.

Once inside his condo, Quentin peeks through the blinds just in time to see Sylvia pull off and to see the car that pulls off behind her. He quickly jots down the license plate number to see if he can find out who's tailing her. He needs to get a handle on all the players, and quick.

He pulls out his phone to call Brad to give him the plate number. It takes Brad less than ten seconds to tell him that the car tailing Sylvia is one of theirs giving him the excuse that they want to keep an eye on her in case there are any more threats sent her way, as the agency wants to know what happened to Sylvia's team as much as Sylvia does. The real reason Brad has a car tailing her is that he wants to know where she plans to hideout, for he knows that he can't afford to lose track of her for picking up her trail is almost as difficult as picking up the trail of Mr. Red.

Snake Chaser

Initial Meeting

Sylvia arrives in Africa three days after leaving Dallas, and immediately creates an underground bunker for herself for she wants to maintain a low profile while she's there. She sends her coordinates to Excalibur, and requests that he come meet her alone for this initial meeting so that they can coordinate a plan of action.

Erik reaches the rendezvous point, however, he doesn't see his contact person. He double checks his phone to make sure that he is in the right spot, and just as he raises his head he sees the sand in front of him shifting. He is momentarily stunned as he sees a figure emerging from the shifting sand, however, he quickly recovers as he notices that the person is his contact.

"Snake Chaser," he states when she moves to stand in front of him.

"Excalibur," is her response. They hug each other in greeting before they get down to business. "I thought I taught you never to show emotion when on a case," she admonishes with very little heat in her voice.

"Sylvia, you never cease to amaze me with your abilities to camouflage yourself in your surroundings," states Erik.

"And you are still a Green Horn," she responds with laughter in her voice. "I have secured us a private location where we can talk," she states as she turns and walks towards what appears to be a mound of sand.

When they reach the mound of sand, he sees the opening from which Sylvia emerged. They both enter the hole, and she proceeds to lead him to her underground hideout. Anxious to know the full story and Sylvia's plan of action, Erik wastes no time in speaking, "First tell me your plan of action, then you can tell me the story from the beginning."

Sylvia chuckles before asking, "What makes you think I have a plan of action?"

Erik cocks an eyebrow before responding, "Cause I know you. And I'm sure that you already know all the players on the continent, and what their roles are. So again, what's your plan of action?"

Sylvia chuckles again before asking, "You think you know me quite well don't you?" At the nod of his head and his smile, she continues, "In this case you do. I do have a plan of action, but it's going to require some highly qualified individuals to pull it off. Who is here on this case with you?"

"Heading up the case is Rick Price," he responds.

"Rock is good. Glad he's here."

"Then there's Giovanni . . ."

"Swamp Rat," shrieks Sylvia before Erik could finish saying the name. "Definitely glad that he's here." Sylvia chuckles at the scowl that Erik is giving her for interrupting him. "You may continue without further interruption," she states.

Snake Chaser

"Thank you," he states sarcastically. "There's Enrique Whittmore, a new guy Marquise McMillan, and of course the princess who is known to the agency as Zamora Richardson and as Zariah Robinson on this mission."

"Pathfinder is with the agency now," asks a slightly stunned Sylvia. She quickly recovers, however, as she ponders the other name Erik gave her. "Not excited that Sidewinder is here though."

"Who don't you know," asks a slightly surprised Erik.

"There are a few people out there that I don't know, but good people I tend to make sure I know and know well, as well as people that I need to keep both eyes on and Sidewinder is one of those you should keep three eyes on," she responds. "But if I know Pathfinder as well as I think that I do, he has just the crew that we need close by," she continues. She begins pacing as she reviews her plan in her head and how to get Pathfinder on board without him being pissed about being asked to go off the grid with being new to the agency. "Do you think you could get Pathfinder to come meet with us without telling him who he's meeting with?" At Erik's cocked eyebrow, she continues, "He's somewhat of a straight arrow, and I'm not sure if he would be willing to go off the grid if this is his first major case with the agency."

Understanding where she's coming from, "I don't think that you will have any problem getting him to go off grid on this case," he states. At Sylvia's cocked eyebrow, he elaborates, "He's in love with the princess." At Sylvia's stunned silence, he adds, "I don't know the whole story of how they met, but they know each other quite well. I think that she is as much in love with him as he is with her."

"I'm not sure if that's a good thing or a bad thing," muses Sylvia out loud. "Pathfinder in love, never thought I would see the day that would happen," she continues musing. However, she regroups quickly, "We might be able to make that work in our favor," she states. "Now here's the plan," she states as she sits down and begins pulling documents out of her duffle bag.

They sit down for an hour going over everything that Sylvia has brought with her. Just before leaving, Erik states, "I think Marquise will be on board without a problem, and will be able to handle it without love clouding his thoughts." At her nod, he continues, "I'll bring them back in an hour." He then leaves the way that he came.

Erik returns to the hotel just as Marquise is emerging from Zamora's room. "Hey man," states Erik, "I need to talk to you." At Marquise's nod, he continues, "I just met with a friend of yours, and she's here to help."

"A friend of mine," asks Marquise skeptically.

"Snake Chaser," is Erik's simple response.

Marquise lifts an eyebrow in surprise, "That's a name I haven't heard in years," he responds. "How do you know her, and why is she here?"

"We met years ago when I was a kid on the streets of DC getting into trouble. She changed my life," he answers. "I sent for her. And before you go Rambo on me, I would trust her with my life and I thought that we might need her expertise on this mission. I've seen her in action."

"Not going Rambo," responds Marquise on a chuckle. "I'm actually glad she's here. We're going to need all the help we can get, and she's one of the best. Have you set up a meet?"

Snake Chaser

"Yes," is Erik's automatic response. "This was a lot easier than I thought that it would be. I think Zamora should come to the meet as well."

"I agree. She needs to be a part of everything from now on. Her life depends on it."

*****

Erik takes them to the beach where he and Sylvia met earlier that night, and simply grins at the blank look on Zamora face. Neither he nor Marquise so much as twitch when the sand starts to shift, but Zamora has to use her hand to cover the small gasp that came across her lips. When Sylvia emerges, Zamora feels a twinge of recognition but has no time to dwell on it as everyone starts moving in Sylvia's direction. Once inside her hideout, Sylvia introduces herself to Zamora while wondering how long it's going to take her to remember when and where they have met.

Sylvia and Marquise share a hug of friendship and remembrance. "Long time Pathfinder."

"Yes. It has been Snake Chaser. When are you going to stop being a chameleon and start to heal?"

"I won't be able to heal until he is caught. You know that," she responds before turning to her make shift table and the papers laid out on top of it.

Sylvia clears her throat of the emotion she is feeling at the memory of losing her fiancé. "I assume Cockroach is aware and nearby," states Sylvia while turning in Marquise's direction.

"You assume correctly," responds Marquise.

"Great! His team will become critical in order for us to pull this off, and for me to remain off the grid." She then tilts her head in what Marquise knows to be her *I-will-not-be-swayed* position. What Sylvia and the rest weren't prepared for was that it would spark recognition in Zamora.

Before she could catch herself, Zamora yells out, "YOU!" She quickly clamps her lips shut when everyone turns in her direction at her outburst.

Before anyone can say a word, Sylvia moves directly in front of Zamora before stating, "Yes Czar, it's me. I was wondering how long it would take you to recognize me." On a chuckle she states, "Should have known the look would have done it since I perfected it while watching out for your safety." The chuckle is quickly cut off as Zamora grabs her in a big bear hug, and nearly squeezes the life out of her. "Czar," she barely gets out, "I can't breathe."

Zamora quickly let's her go, "Sorry. I'm just so happy to see you. I was actually praying for you when I found out that I was the missing princess, and here you are."

"I told you that I would never be far, and would always be there for you if you ever needed me," states Sylvia.

"Yes, yes you did." Quickly recovering from her shock and relief, Zamora states, "What's the set up?"

"Hold on," states Marquise after recovering from the shock that Sylvia and Zamora know each other. "Care to explain that little exchange," demands Marquise with a scowl on his face.

Sylvia and Zamora look at each other and chuckle, then Zamora nods to Sylvia who explains how they know each other. "I was assigned to Zamora while she was in high

330

Snake Chaser

school, and one of her country men recognized her on campus. We needed to protect her identity, and discourage any unwanted interest in her." At Marquise's raised eyebrow, she adds, "As I'm sure you discovered, Czar is a handful, and she was probably even more so back then hating all the restrictions that were placed upon her with no explanation. She knew her parents were wealthy, but she didn't think that it warranted all the extra security that was around."

"We can get to everyone's story after the mission is over," interrupts Zamora, "Let's get to the plan so we can end this thing, and I don't have to sleep with one eye open."

"See what I mean," states Sylvia on a chuckle. At Zamora's glare, she holds up her hands, "Okay, I give. Let's get to it."

Game Plan

Sylvia looks at Marquise and Erik to fill her in from their end. Marquise takes the lead and speaks first, "These are the people we believe we have to watch out for when on the streets," he states as he pulls up the pictures on the handheld device he received from Rock.

"I see they're still using children to do their dirty work," states Sylvia as she goes through the photos. "Tell me what events have taken place since your arrival," she then asks.

Marquise and Erik inform her of all the events that have taken place, and the measures that they have taken to keep Zamora safe. Marquise also informs everyone about the Navy men he has positioned nearby lead by one of his most trusted soldiers, codename Cockroach for his ability to survive just about anything and penetrate any structure undetected. "Rock cannot know of Cockroach's presence or yours for that matter," states Marquise directly to Sylvia.

"I'm well aware that he cannot know that I am here," states Sylvia somewhat annoyed. "I am here because Excalibur sent for me, and because Zamora needs me. And believe me I plan to make sure that she remains safe, as well as, maintaining my invisibility with the agency until I find Qasean's killer and do what the agency refuses to do," she ends on a near growl.

Snake Chaser

"Settle down Sylvia," begins Marquise, "I just want to make sure we are all in agreement as to who needs to know what in this case. Things are going to get decidedly more complicated before this thing is over, and I plan to make sure that we all make it out of here alive and in one piece. Okay?"

"Fine," responds Sylvia, "Let's get back to the plan."

"The artifacts are due to arrive in this country in 11 days, right," asks Sylvia.

"That is correct," answers Zamora.

"We know that there are five possible assassins, and the fact that they are all children will make it difficult to apprehend them without arousing suspicions. However, I think I can work an angle I've used in this country before," begins Sylvia. "I've posed as a photographer documenting African Culture in the past, so I think I can resurrect that role as my reason for being in the country right now," she continues. "You probably won't recognize me on the street if you see me, but I will make it a point to be in the village anytime that you are out and about," she adds. "I think it's best that Swamp Rat and Sidewinder not know that I am here, and on the case," she concludes.

"What about Cockroach," asks Marquise.

"Yes, let him know as he will be critical to the plan, and we need to coordinate our efforts so that he can take credit for the takedown if it comes down to that," she responds.

"What is your plan," asks Zamora.

"I don't think that they will make anymore attempts on your life until the artifacts arrive since they believe that the US

Government is closely watching them after Sidewinder and Swamp Rat's visits to the Museum Curator," responds Sylvia. "However, I will arrive in the country in two days time with my journalism credentials in place. I will get a room in the same hotel as Swamp Rat so that I can have a clear view of your hotel," she adds. "Upon my arrival, I will begin photographing children from various villages, but will eventually take a keen interest in these five children from the Gamboto tribe. If I'm successful in convincing the tribe that I can gain interest in their country by capturing the lives of these children, I will be able to make sure that they are out of the area the day the artifacts arrive. However, that may lead the Gamboto leaders to look to older assassins to go after Zamora, so you will have to be watchful of every member of the tribe at that point."

Zamora, Marquise, and Erik all nod in understanding, as Sylvia continues, "That's where Cockroach comes into play," she states in Marquise's direction. His team will need to position themselves throughout the city from the docks to the museum, and at your hotel. They should divide up into teams of three with at least one sharp shooter on each team, as well as, someone who can blend into the surroundings undetected."

"I don't think that will be a problem," responds Marquise. "I'll let him know of the plan when we return to the hotel."

"In the meantime, stick with your original plans while waiting for the artifacts to arrive," adds Sylvia. "Don't want the natives to think that we're on to them or that we're even here."

"No problem," responds Marquise before turning to Zamora and Erik, "I think it's time that we head back to the hotel."

They nod in agreement, and take their leave of Sylvia.

Snake Chaser

Two days later, Sylvia heads over to the museum that is supposed to display the artifacts to see what she can learn about the players on the other team. Sylvia arrives without so much as a ripple, and immediately begins surveillance on all parties involved beginning with the curator and his staff while she photographs the children that are begging on the steps of the museum. She is somewhat surprised to see Sidewinder entering the museum on the third day of her stakeout, but what shocks her most is that the head of the Gamboto tribe enters the museum less than five minutes later.

"What the hell is going on here," she mutters to herself. Determined to get some answers, she enters the museum. "Greetings," she states to Sareena who rolls her eyes at the thought of another American being at the museum. Choosing to ignore the sarcasm dripping from the young woman, Sylvia asks, "Are pictures allowed to be taken inside the museum?"

"Why would you want to take pictures in here?"

"The architecture of the building is amazing, and I would like to capture it on film."

Not really caring about the American or her camera, Sareena simply waves her on, "Take all the pictures you like."

Sylvia, pleased with being dismissed by the woman, begins exploring the museum snapping pictures until she is completely forgotten about. Relying on her ability to blend into her surroundings and already having a layout of the museum, she makes her way back to the office of the curator since she's sure that's where the men are meeting. Once there she overhears a heated conversation taking place between Enrique "Sidewinder" Whittmore and the Head of the Gamboto tribe.

"I thought that you were going to make sure that the American woman was taken care of," she hears Sidewinder say heatedly.

"The first attempt brought a lot of attention our way," replies Gamboto, "We are going to have to bide our time, but she will be taken care of," he adds. "Besides you were supposed to be getting us inside information on her movements. Are you doing your part?"

"Unfortunately, I have been left out of the loop at the moment," Enrique responds. "I have been left out of the last few meetings just in case your people get too close to her, as my government doesn't want your people to know what my true role is here."

"Well, that is unfortunate. You are not proving to be as useful as you claimed you would be when you first approached us," responds Orogotto.

"I will get you the information that you require to dispose of the woman, you just make sure you have my money when this is over," Enrique heatedly responds. He then storms out of the office without noticing the young woman with the camera in the hallway.

Sylvia quietly follows him out of the museum, and notes that he is headed in the opposite direction of his hotel. "Hmm, seems there is another snake in the grass surrounding the Princess. I'll have to make provisions for him," she says to herself. Feeling as though her work at the museum is complete for the day, she heads back to her hotel room as she needs to get this new bit of information to Marquise and Erik.

Snake Chaser

Deceptions

Meditating in his room, Erik is surprised when he hears the faint chirp of his cell that connects him to Sylvia. He picks it up and enters the code to open up communication.

"Excalibur."

"Snake Chaser."

"Development?"

"New snake in the grass."

"Who?"

"Hideaway. Nightfall. All hands."

The line is disconnected, and Erik simply stares at the phone for a few minutes before putting it away. He then seeks out Marquise and Zamora.

"It seems Sylvia has uncovered another player, and wants to meet with us at nightfall."

"Shit," hisses Marquise. "Who the hell could this be?"

"I guess we'll have to wait for nightfall to find out," states Zamora a lot calmer than she's actually feeling. When both men turn in her direction, she simply shrugs her shoulders, "Until we know who it is, there's not much we can do. So I'm not going to get upset about it in the meantime."

*****

Nightfall arrives, and the three of them make their way to Sylvia's hideout.

"I'm going to come right out with it since time is of the essence here," begins Sylvia. "Sidewinder has plans to steal the artifacts and sell them to the museum curator."

"What," yell Marquise, Erik, and Zamora at the same time.

"Are you sure," asks Zamora who is having a hard time maintaining her temper.

"Yes, I overheard him, the head of the Gamboto tribe, and the monsieur discussing it at the museum earlier today."

"Shit," Marquise mutters heatedly.

"So what can we do to stop him," asks Erik trying to remain calm with this latest bit of news.

"I can take him out of the equation, and force the hand of the Gambotos," responds Sylvia. As the other three turn in her direction with raised eyebrows, she continues, "The artifacts are due to arrive at the museum in six days, so we don't have a lot of time to figure out how he plans to get his hands on them. However, if we get rid of him, then Gamboto and the curator will have to find another way to get their hands on them." She pauses for a few minutes knowing that her next words are not going to be received well, "However, once he is out of the picture, I'm sure that the efforts to assassinate Zamora will more than double."

Knowing that the words just spoken are extremely accurate, the room becomes deathly quiet. Everyone is lost in their own thoughts of how this could play out, and no one is pleased by the most prevalent thought – these people want Zamora dead so that they can claim the rights to her country.

After having explored their own personal thoughts for some time, Marquise speaks first. "How do we dispose of Enrique without informing Rock?"

"That does pose a problem," states Sylvia, "for he cannot know of my involvement."

"I think we should leave Enrique in play so as to flush out everyone involved in the deal he's made, and then we don't have to tell Rock anything," states Erik. "Our main focus here should be to keep Zamora alive which means we need to know everyone who would stand to gain something from her death. We also don't need to spook any of the players into acting hastily, and try to take Zamora out of the equation."

"I agree with Excalibur," states Sylvia. "Protecting Czar and the artifacts should be our number one concern. Sidewinder can and will be dealt with, and Rock doesn't have to know that I was involved."

"I know that you're right," states Marquise, "However, these new developments are not sitting well with me at the moment. But I am willing to hear you out Sylvia."

Still stunned by all she has just heard, Zamora remains quiet and that concerns the other three. However, they will have to deal with her silence later. Right now they need to make some decisions, and they need to be the right decisions.

Sylvia begins to outline her plans on how they should proceed. "I will need to know every detail of the plans currently in place from the time the artifacts touch ground in Dakar to the time they are turned over to the museum. I need to know the names of every person involved with the case from top to bottom, and I will make sure that nothing happens to the artifacts before they can be secured inside the museum."

"Erik and Marquise, it will be your job to make sure that no harm comes to Zamora. And you might want to let Swamp Rat and Cockroach know about the latest developments as they will be critical to the plan's success."

"Once I have the details about the artifacts and everyone involved, I will come up with a plan to protect the artifacts and dispose of anyone not on our side. Once my plans are put into place, I will let you know what they are, so that you can be prepared for whatever happens."

Sylvia pauses before making her next statement, "Once my plans are in place, you will not see me again. You will not even know when I have left the country."

Understanding the need for her to remain a ghost, Marquise and Erik simply nod. Zamora still has not spoken, and all three turn in her direction.

"I'm fine. I just needed to organize some things in my head," Zamora states. "I think that you all should know that I will do my part in making this mission a success, while at the same time making sure that I stay alive."

Grateful that she is on board, Marquise walks over to her and gives her a quick hug before sitting down with Sylvia and
340

Snake Chaser

giving her all the information that has requested. Once that is complete, Marquise, Erik, and Zamora make their way back to the hotel.

*****

Unaware that he has been seen meeting with the enemy, E-Dub continues his preparations for getting his hands on the artifacts so that he may sell them to Orogotto. He schedules a meeting with the forger to make sure that the paperwork will stand up to scrutiny by the governments of both countries, for the paperwork is crucial to his plan.

As he arrives at the building being used by the forger, the hairs on the back of his neck stand up. He scours the surrounding area looking for unwanted visitors, but sees no one. He continues his walk to the back door of the building still feeling a little uneasy, and as he raises his hand to knock, takes one more look over his shoulder. Still seeing no one, he knocks and enters the building once the door has been opened.

Sylvia, true to her name of Snake Chaser, is watching his every move from her camouflaged location only fifty feet from the door. Knowing that E-Dub would need the best paperwork to pull off any type of coup, she has been staking out the forger's place for the past two days as he is the best in this part of the world. Knowing she can't anticipate his every movement, she places a tracking device on E-Dubs car once he enters the building. She then pulls out a small parabolic microphone to hear what is taking place inside the building.

Once inside the building, E-Dub questions the forger, "How is your surveillance around this place?"

"I assure you that my surveillance is top notch," he replies in an agitated voice. "No one could get within 200 feet of this place without me knowing about it!"

"Are you sure? I could have sworn I felt someone watching me as I walked up to the door."

"Paranoid much," asks the forger. "I can show you the footage from the cameras for the last five days," he continues. "You would then see that no one has been near this place except for me."

"Fine! Show me the paperwork," states E-Dub still feeling a little uneasy.

The forger unlocks a file cabinet, and pulls out the paperwork in question. "Look it over," he states while handing the papers over. "You will find that they are flawless, and will pass any scrutiny by any authenticator in the world. I would not have been able to stay in business as long as I have if I was not the best at what I do. Even your government has solicited my services a time or two."

"Oh shut up and let me look them over," states an aggravated E-Dub. He pulls out a small magnifying glass so that he may look at the intricate details of the documents. Half an hour later, E-Dub has completed his review of the documents, and is satisfied that they indeed look authenticate. He hands the forger an envelope containing his payment, and places the documents inside his coat. "It was nice doing business with you," states E-Dub as he takes his leave.

Once again the hairs rise on the back of his neck as he walks back to his car. He again scours the countryside, and still sees nothing amiss. "I'll be glad when this is all over," he mumbles to himself. "I've never been this paranoid in my life. This just

Snake Chaser

goes to prove it's time for me to get out of the spy business."
He gets in his car and drives away.

Taking Care Of Business

Sylvia waits thirty minutes after E-Dub has driven away before approaching the door of the forger, and knocking. He opens the door expecting to find the ungrateful American standing there, and is stunned to find a woman at his door holding two large guns on him. "Shut up and walk backwards slowly," she hisses before he can say a word.

He does as he's told, and she kicks the door closed behind her. Once inside, she holsters her weapons before laughing at the frown on the man's face. "Come on Ivan," she states. "Loosen up a little."

"Little girl, I should thrash you," he states. He then bursts out laughing and gathers her in a big bear hug. "What are you doing here?"

She hugs him in return before responding, "It seems the gentleman who just left here is trying to bring harm to a friend of mine, and I just cannot allow that to happen."

"So he was right. There was someone watching him," states Ivan the forger. "You're ability to show up undetected still amazes me," he adds. He shakes his head before asking, "Who are you protecting now?"

Snake Chaser

"Someone I've been protecting for many years . . . Zahara."

Stunned by the revelation that the princess is still alive, Ivan is rendered speechless for several moments. "She's still alive," he asks his voice barely above a whisper.

"Yes, she's still alive. And she is in possession of the royal artifacts that the American is trying to steal and sell to Orogotto."

"Damn," he hisses. "I assumed he got his hands on the artifacts after that couple was killed two years ago. I never dreamed that Zahara was still alive and now in possession of them."

"It's okay, dear friend. No one was to know that she was alive, and I have made sure that her identity has been kept secret all these years. Even when she traveled to this country two years ago after the death of the Richardsons."

"So what's your plan now that he has the documents that show him to be the rightful owner of the artifacts?"

"What I need to know is where you camouflaged your signature on the documents," she responds. At his stunned silence, she continues, "I know that you sign every document that you make, and since time will be of the essence when I take him down I need to know where it is as I will not have time to search for it myself."

"How . . . How do you know that," he asks.

"I have studied your documents for years, and it was only two years ago that I discovered your distinct signature in one of the documents. After I discovered it, I looked over every document you have made that I could get my hands on, and discovered that you put the same signature on every document that you make. Now, tell me where I can find the signature on the documents you just handed over."

"You are so lucky that I love you Sylvia, otherwise this meeting would not have a happy ending for you."

She throws her head back and laughs, before saying, "All of your weapons have been disabled, Ivan. You couldn't do me in if you wanted to."

He shakes his head and gives her the information she has requested. They give each other a giant bear hug, and she takes her leave.

Upon arriving back in the city, Sylvia pens a message to Excalibur to inform him of the forged documents, and drops it off at the hotel in which they are staying. Just as they are about to break for the afternoon, they receive a call from the front desk that a message has been left for them. Unsure who or what could be waiting for them down in the lobby, E&J and GL take separate paths to the lobby while Marquise stays in the suite with Zamora who is in her room unaware of the current events. GL enters the lobby from the stairwell on the opposite side of the lobby from the elevators just before the elevators open and E&J steps into the lobby. GL calls E&J's cell phone just as he steps off the elevator to give him a reason to pause and check his surroundings before approaching the desk. E&J is on the phone less than ten seconds before he spots Sylvia in the far corner of the lobby, and lets GL know that the message is legit. He hangs up the phone and approaches the front desk to retrieve the message. Once he places the message in his jacket pocket, he returns to the elevators to go back to the suite. Just as the doors open, he turns back to see that Sylvia has left her post in the lobby. GL makes his way back to the suite the same way he came, and meets E&J at the door to the suite. They enter the suite to find Marquise on the sofa just staring at the door to Zamora's bedroom. They know that he heard them enter the suite, but he never removes his eyes from her door. They take the seats they vacated to go retrieve the message, and simply wait for M&M to acknowledge their presence. It's five minutes later before he breaks eye contact with door and turns to them.

"Where's the message," he asks.

E&J retrieves the message from his jacket pocket, and hands it over as he states, "I believe it's from Snake Chaser as she was in the lobby when I stepped off the elevator."

Marquise simply nods as he opens the envelope. He begins to read the message out loud, "When the forged papers are presented, there will be the picture of a phoenix in the dot above the third I on every page. This is the forger's signature."

Marquise and GL speak at the same time, "Micro dots."

"Even with as long as I've known her, I'm still amazed at her ability to gain information that no one else is able to get," adds Marquise.

"She is very crafty," adds GL.

"That's why I called her in," states E&J. "She was able to find out my next move even before I knew what my next move was going to be." He pauses as he remembers his first encounters with Sylvia. "I can't tell you the number of times she saved my life on the streets of DC."

Even though she left the lobby of the hotel, Sylvia didn't leave the vicinity for she knows that there likely more snakes in the grass than she's already detected. While she's conducting surveillance around the backside of the hotel, she sees a lone female figure exiting the service entrance and determines that it's Zamora so she follows her. As she follows her, she picks up the presence of someone else following her, but relaxes as she realizes that it's Cockroach. Figuring that the rest of Zamora's team doesn't know what she's about, she places a call to Excalibur to let him know that she and Cockroach are watching over Zamora.

"Excalibur."

"She's safe. Cockroach and I have eyes on her."

"We know. Cockroach already informed Pathfinder. We're staying put. You guys just make sure she returns safely."

"Will do, young'un."

He hears her laughter just as she disconnects the line. "Sylvia's on top of her as well," he states to the room before he takes a seat. "I guess there's nothing for us to do but wait for her to return."

Sylvia and Cockroach take up spots out of sight as they wait for Zamora to exit the residence of the Xaliifa, the priest in residence at the kingdom. They both ensure that she arrives safely back at the hotel, which involves them having to take out a band of three men who began following her after she left the perimeter of the village. After which Sylvia returns to the village to have her own visit with the Xaliifa for she believes that she knows why Zamora went there to visit with him. Upon being granted entrance, she discovers that her assumption is correct and completes a promise she made to Zamora's caretakers years ago which is to provide Zamora's chosen betrothed with the Royal Engagement Ring.

On her way back to her hideout, she gets a page from Cockroach telling her to get to him as soon as possible. She does double time as she heads to the location where she is to meet him, and when she arrives she is pissed to find that

Snake Chaser

someone has taken out the museum curator that was meeting with Zamora, as well as, the young woman who worked as the museum greeter. "It seems someone is getting desperate, and has thrown a monkey wrench into our plans," begins Sylvia. "We should probably inform the others of this latest development, and see how they want to proceed," she adds. Cockroach simply nods his agreement. Sylvia sends a message to Excalibur while Cockroach sends a message to Pathfinder.

*****

The next morning Sylvia receives a message from Excalibur informing her of the new game plan that have put in place as a result of the events that took place the night before, and she willingly accepts her role in their plan.

ReGina Crawford

Saying Good-Bye

The day to put their plan in motion has arrived, and Sylvia is busy executing her role of following Enrique "E-Dub" Whittmore. Once she becomes aware of where Sidewinder is headed, Snake Chaser speeds ahead to the airstrip to take up her hiding place. She plans to let Cockroach and his men handle the thieves that E-Dub has hired, but she herself will take down Sidewinder. She watches him arrive and take up his hiding place, and she waits to see what his next move is going to be.

Just as the plane taxis to a stop, a truck pulls up to collect the artifacts. Once the plane comes to a complete stop, the door of the plane opens and two men emerge from the plane to check the perimeter. Seeing nothing out of the ordinary, they lower the ramp and begin unloading the crates. E-Dub is hoping his men don't jump the gun, and wait for the artifacts to be completely loaded into the truck. He likes his odds; he has twelve men to the eight men protecting the artifacts.

As the last crate is being placed in the back of the truck, E-Dub's men emerge from their hiding places only to fall flat on their faces. "What the hell," shouts E-Dub from his hiding place. The shots fired were quiet yet accurate, and each one of his men has been subdued. As Cockroach and his men emerge from their hiding places to check on the band of thieves, E-Dub

Snake Chaser

leaves his hiding place and heads to his vehicle. He believes he is unseen as everyone is occupied taking care of his band of thieves. "I will not lose," he shouts as he heads to his car. "I will have to hijack the truck with the artifacts in it myself!"

Just as he opens the door to the car, he hears a familiar voice, "Not so fast Sidewinder." As he reaches for the gun on his hip, the voice speaks again, "Unless you want to hear from the twins, I suggest you place both your hands in the air."

Knowing how deadly accurate his nemesis is, he does as he's told and turns in the direction of the voice. "I am so tired of you dogging my every move," he hisses.

"I believe this will be the last encounter that we have," replies Sylvia.

"I wouldn't be so sure of that," Sidewinder counters.

"And why is that?"

"I will not be so foolish as to tell you how I plan to get out of this!"

"If you think you can, go for it," Sylvia states in a deadly calm voice.

Sidewinder touches the palm of his right hand with two fingers, and shots ring out from Sylvia's right. Her right thigh is hit by one of the bullets and she falls to her knees, yet she manages to get off a shot. The round hits him in his right shoulder, yet he remains standing. "You little bitch," he says between clinched teeth as he reaches for his gun with his left hand. Sylvia lets another round fly, and this time she hits him dead between the eyes. He falls to his knees with a look of disbelief on his face before falling face down on the ground

Cockroach enters the hanger at that moment. "Snake Chaser," he calls out.

"Here."

He walks around the vehicle and sees her struggling to get to her feet. "Damn it, stay down!"

"It's a flesh wound, I can still walk."

"You are way too hard-headed for your own good. Let me help you."

"Fine," she says as she places her right arm around his shoulder. He helps her to stand, and together they walk to the waiting vehicle. All of the thieves have been bound, and loaded in the back of the truck. "I need to get bandaged up and over to the palace," she states as he helps her inside.

"Not a problem. We're headed to the palace anyway to lend our help to the security team there if anything out of the ordinary arises. However, before we leave I need to bag the trash," he states as he looks at Sidewinder lying on the ground.

"I can't be seen at the palace. You'll have to let me out before we get there."

"How do you propose to get there with a bullet hole in your leg?"

"I have a rabbit hole close to the palace. Drop me off there. I can patch myself up, and then make it to the palace on my own." She sees he's ready to protest. "Are you sure you want to battle me on this?"

He sighs, and gives in for he knows how pig-headed she can be. "Fine. Have it your way." He gets her settled in the truck,

Snake Chaser

and then returns to tie up Sidewinder and alert Rock that the body is available for pick up.

As they are underway to the place, Sylvia contacts Excalibur to give him the update on E-Dub.

"Excalibur."

"Snake Chaser. Mission complete. Sidewinder slithers no more."

"Not the desired outcome, but expected."

"No choice. Took one in the thigh."

"Serious?"

"No. Flesh wound. This will be our last communiqué before I leave the country. Good Luck."

Before he can say another word, the line goes dead.

*****

Sylvia patches herself up in her hideout, and then makes her way to the palace. She immediately goes to Zahara's room. She smiles as she thinks '*I can now safely call her by her rightful name since she now knows who she is.*' Zamora is lying on the bed trying to absorb the reality of her situation when she swears she hears a faint swish as though a door has been opened. She sits up, and sure enough she sees Sylvia entering the room. She is too stunned to say a word. Sylvia walks over to her, sits down beside her, and takes her hands in hers. "Czar, I know this is all new to you, but you were born into this. And while it may take you a minute to assimilate, you will do well in your role as princess. If at any time you need me, here's my direct contact number," she states as she passes her a business card. "I have watched you grow up into a wonderful woman, God bless you on this new journey in your life. I will remain on the grounds until you are recognized as the Princess and the rightful governing factor of the kingdom, and then I will be gone."

Czar gives her a great bear hug, and then releases her. "Thank you for all you have done for me. I will never forget you. God speed as you continue your life's journey, and may you one day find the peace you so desperately seek."

Sylvia leaves the same way that she came, and Czar lies back down to continue her meditation about the new journey she is about to embark on as Princess Zahara of Umboto. She is eternally grateful that she will have Marquise by her side during this journey.

She makes her way to the room occupied by Pathfinder. Just as she enters the room, she hears him talking out loud, and when he remarks that he's talking to himself again she lets him know that he's not exactly alone.

"That's not entirely true," says a voice from a shadowed corner of the room. Marquise immediately jumps from the bed and grabs his weapon from the bed's nightstand. "Relax Pathfinder, it's only me," states the voice as the person moves into the light.

"Damn it Snake Chaser! You know I hate it when you do that!" He places the weapon back on the nightstand as she moves closer to him.

She chuckles before giving him a big bear hug. "Czar has not come to the realization that she will indeed be queen when the two of you marry," states to his amazement. At the stunned look on his face, she states, "That is the only thing that would

354

Snake Chaser

make her freak out at this point." She then adds, "When she does, she will indeed freak out, so you will need to be her rock until she accepts that fact. I have watched over her for many years now, but as of today I am entrusting her to your care so don't disappointment me," she smiles as the last words leave her mouth.

"I will not disappoint you for she is my world, has been since the day we met on that Georgia highway two years ago."

"Glad to hear it. She knows how to reach me if you find that you need my help, and if you don't want her to know I'm being summoned there is always Excalibur."

"Duly noted. God speed Snake Chaser. May you soon find the peace you are searching for." They embrace once more, Sylvia leaves the way she came, and Marquise again lies down on the bed.

Divide and Conquer

Three days after leaving Africa, Sylvia is back in Dallas. Her first order of business is to find a new place to live and a new base of operations, then figure out what Mr. Red has been up to, and she still wants to know who Quentin McNair is and what he's really doing in the city while not letting him know that she has returned to the city. From what she's been able to gather, Mr. Red has abandoned the city as his compound is empty, and no one seems to have heard a word from him since he blew up her building almost a month ago. She's pissed that his trail seems to have gone cold once again, but she refuses to keep searching for information on his whereabouts

She becomes extremely agitated when after being back in the city for two months she is unable to pick up his trail, however, there seems to be a new player on the scene who is going by the name of Charles Givens. While trailing Mr. Givens, she ends up in front of Mr. McNair's office as he and his men go inside. By the amount of time they spend, it's obvious to Sylvia that they are in a meeting and she's curious as to why a drug lord is meeting with a real estate broker, and sinks her teeth into her theory that Quentin is more than he claims to be. However, she's not sure what side of the legal line he's on, but she's determined to find out and so she stands her ground until Mr. Givens and his men leave the area figuring it's time to let

Snake Chaser

Mr. McNair that she was back in town and would be keeping a close eye on him once again..

Sylvia waits until she is sure that they are out of the area before she approaches the door to Quentin's office, and just as she reaches it she hears him locking the door. Not wanting him to look out the blinds and see her, she quickly and quietly moves away from the door, but she doesn't want to leave the area so she posts up next to the building. While waiting she thinks to herself, '*Why the hell did he just lock his door? The amount of time he waited to do so is an agency move. What the hell is going on here?*' As she stands there pondering all of these questions, her anger level increases by the minute as she waits for him to emerge from his office. She doesn't have too long to wait before she hears the locks pop on the door, and she quickly moves to the door and find herself looking in his eyes as he opens the blinds over the door.

Even though he's a little startled to see her standing there, he opens the door, "Good afternoon, Ms Williams, I haven't seen you for quite a while. Thought you had left the city."

"I bet," she states sarcastically as she walks through the door. Once Quentin has closed the door, she spins on him and starts firing questions at him. "Why were you meeting with Charles Givens and his crew? Why did you lock your office door after they left? I know I've asked this before but just who are you? And why are you in my city?"

Surprised and angered by the venom in her voice, Quentin barks back just as harshly as he approaches her, "I don't know who you think you are and why you feel you have the right to barge into my office and question me about anything. I don't have to answer to you, and I trust that you will remember that in the future." He is now standing nose-to-nose with her, and both are shooting daggers at each other with their eyes.

"Besides shouldn't you be more concerned about who's trying to kill you?"

Not the least bit intimated by his size or his anger, Sylvia stands her ground, "I would like answers to my questions, and I want them now."

Not willing to back down either, Quentin answers, "Who I have meetings with is none of your business. Why I close my office is none of your business. As I've said before, my name is Quentin McNair and I'm a real estate broker here to do business in real estate. That's what real estate brokers do." He then heads to the door and opens it as he says, "Good day Ms Williams."

Walking in the direction of the open door, Sylvia states, "I will get answers to my questions one way or the other."

"I wish you the best of luck with that," he states while still holding the door open.

Walking out the door, Sylvia states, "This is not over."

Quentin doesn't say another word as he closes the door behind her. "That woman is working my last nerve. I need to call Brad and see if he can do something about her." He places the call to Brad, before finishing up the rest of the paper work sitting on his desk.

As she gets in her car, her anger with him continues to increase as she knows that he's not being honest with her which probably means he's not being honest with Quintana. "I need to find a way to make her stop seeing him, she states out loud, and focuses her attention on devising a plan to make that happen. Even though she knows that the plan she has concocted will distress Ana, she puts it into motion anyway for she knows that it will accomplish her objective.

Snake Chaser

*****

Quintana arrives home to find the place filled with officers, and is livid after the long day that she had today. "What the hell is going on here," she asks as she walks through the door.

Quentin quickly walks over to her to explain, "When I got here your door was broken in. I called Kyle, and he and Keith came over to investigate. When we found your office had been searched, they called forensics to see if they could get any information on who broke in here."

"Why would anyone want to break in here," she asks shaking. "I don't have anything that anyone would want to steal."

"I don't think they were here to steal anything sweetheart. There was a search screen on your laptop when we got in here." At her questioning look, he continues, "They were searching for documents with my name attached."

"Why would anyone be looking for documents on my laptop that have anything to do with you? We aren't in the same business. We don't even do business together."

"I know sweetheart. I don't know why this happened."

Needing time to think, Quintana asks, "How much longer are they going to be?"

"They shouldn't be too much longer."

"I'll be in the kitchen until they finish. Please let me know once everyone has left." As she turns to leave, Quentin reaches for her and she jumps back. At his questioning look, she states, "I need a minute to process this. Just let me know when they are done." She turns and walks from the room.

ReGina Crawford

By the time the scene is wrapped up, Quintana has decided that she needs space, and once everyone has left her apartment see lets Quentin know how she feels. Sylvia, who has been monitoring the activity taking place in the apartment, is pleased that her plan worked even though she doesn't like seeing her friend this stressed and unhappy. However, she learns that her plan is not as foolproof as she thought as she receives a call from Quintana later that evening.

"Hello."

"I need you to be straight with me," responds Quintana.

"I'm always straight with you," she says. "What is this about?"

"I need to know what you know about the break-in at my home tonight."

"Why would I know anything about it?"

"Sylvia, don't bullshit me. I want answers and I want them now."

"Alright Ana, your boy is meeting with some heavy hitters from the underground, and I need to know what he's up to. And I will find out what he's up to whether you and he want me to or not."

"Why is that so important to you? And why are you willing to put me in the middle of it? I thought that we were closer than that."

"Ana, you know you mean the world to me. You are all that I have left of my life with Qasean, and I would never do anything to intentionally hurt you. But I know that you and your boy are keeping something from me, and you know that I
360

am like a dog with a bone when it comes to stuff like this. I can't let it go even if it brings tension between the two of us, but I do know that our bond is strong enough to endure this just as we have endured in the past."

"Sylvia, I wish you would let go of all the anger and pain you are still feeling after all these years. I think that the pain of the day we lost Q is clouding your brain, and it is turning you into a very bitter person. I love you and I will always love you, but as in the past I will not get caught up in this game of danger and intrigue that you are playing. I just want to know one thing, why did you make it look like a regular burglary? I know how good you are, and you could have come into my home and no one would have been the wiser."

"It's very simple really. If I did find something out about him, I had planned to leak the information to the underground, the media, and law enforcement, and when that happened I wanted him to think that one of the people he is in bed with leaked the information. If he's undercover which I truly believe he is, he probably knows all about me and would have figured out that I was the one that leaked the information."

"Let me state this one more time, there is nothing to find out about Quentin. He has nothing to do with the people that you are searching for, and I don't know why you won't let it go. I do not want to be a pawn in the middle between you, and I don't appreciate you involving me in this."

"Ana I'm not trying to upset you, but there is more to your boy than you want to believe. And you know I can't let this go, there is no reason that Q should have died the way that he did not to mention the rest of my family."

Cutting Sylvia off, Quintana interjects, "It was their time to go, accept it and move on. I have, and it's time that you did too.

You don't know how much you've changed over the years Sylvia, and to be honest you're starting to scare me."

With irritation in her voice, Sylvia responds, "Fine Ana. Live your life how you see fit, and I'll do the same. Talk to you later." Sylvia hangs up the phone leaving Quintana staring at her cell phone like it had suddenly morphed into some alien creature. Even though she doesn't believe that she is in any danger, she maintains her resolve to stay away from Quentin for she knows how unpredictable Sylvia can be and she doesn't want to get caught up in the middle of the battle that she is sure going to erupt between the two of them.

Snake Chaser

Hook, Line, and Sinker

Knowing that she is going to have to extra careful now that she's back in the city and she's not positive that this Mr. Givens is not connected to the elusive Mr. Red, she alters her appearance once again by cutting her hair changing the color, as well as, her eyes color with contacts. Over the next couple of weeks, Sylvia channels all of her energy into finding out who this Mr. Givens is, and avoiding Quentin for she's not sure if he's figured out that she was behind the break-in at Ana and she doesn't need him to know that she's investigating his new business partner until she finds out if he's clean or dirty.

So it seems that Mr. McNair decided to build a business complex while she was in Africa, and that Mr. Givens is one of his top investors. She devotes all of her time to trailing Mr. Givens and his men, and even though all of his business dealings seem to be legit there is something about him that bothers her so she continues her surveillance of him even though she hasn't found anything that indicates that he's dirty dealing. She has to give the man credit, for if he is involved in anything illegal he keeps his hands clean.

A few times her investigation of Givens have come close to having her path cross with McNair, and she's impressed that he's not taking the man at face value and is conducting his own investigation of the man. On one particular day as she is cruising the city, she comes across Quentin looking at a recently vacated building next to an empty lot and can't resist approaching him.

"Scouting property for your next project already," she asks sarcastically.

Quentin spins around as though he is surprised to hear her voice even though he knew she was following him, and was hoping that she would approach him since she's been keeping her distance from him since the break-in at Quintana's. "Where did you come from," he asks.

"Since you're back to cruising my neighborhood and already doing business with the shaky Mr. Givens, yes I am following you."

"What is it you don't like about Mr. Givens?"

"He's as dirty as they come, and if you're not careful, you're going to get buried beneath his dirt."

"Why do you think he's dirty?"

"I don't think that he's dirty, I know that he's dirty. I just need to prove it, but he's as slippery as he is dirty."

"I've seen no evidence of him being dirty, but there is . . .," begins Quentin, "No I don't think he has anything to do with that."

"To do with what? What are you talking about," asks an animated Sylvia.

"It's probably nothing," states Quentin.

Snake Chaser

"Just spit it out," counters Sylvia.

"Well my night security guard thinks that he's been slipped something to put him out for a few hours a couple of times, and he says he always feels that way after a visit from Mr. Givens. But we have found no evidence of anything strange going on after he feels that way."

"That's exactly what I'm talking about, dirty and slippery," comments Sylvia. "I'm telling you now, you are going to wind up on the wrong side of the law dealing with that man."

"If he is doing something illegal, I'm not involved so I have nothing to worry about," states Quentin indignantly. "Besides there is no evidence that he's doing anything. He tells the guard that he just likes to make sure that his investment in the project is well guarded. They talk a little sports, and then he's gone. They only thing he's ever done is shake the man's hand, so how could he have slipped him something?"

"It was on his hand," states Sylvia out loud.

"How is that possible? Wouldn't he have been affected by it as well if it was on his hand?"

"Not if he took something to counter act the drug before applying it to his hand," responds Sylvia.

"How can I prove that's what happened? And how can I find out what he's up to? I don't want to be caught up in any illegal dealings," states Quentin.

"Would you like my help Mr. McNair?"

'I knew you would not be able to resist the bait Ms Williams,' Quentin thinks to himself. "How can you help," he asks.

"You may not want to get too involved with this, so I don't think I'll tell you want my plans are. I just need some information from you." Sylvia then proceeds to shoot a dozen or so questions at him about the project and Charles Givens involvement in it.

After Quentin has answered all of her questions, Sylvia gets back in her car and pretends to drive away when in reality she has driven a around the block, and taken up a perch in another building across the street from the building Quentin is standing in front of for she spotted one of Mr. Givens' men in a car on the street. Quentin continues to scope out the building just in case anyone saw the two of them talking, and wanted to make it look like they were working together. A few moments later as he approaches his car, Quentin is glad that he didn't immediately leave the area at the same time as Sylvia for one of Givens' henchmen is leaning against it.

"Hey Jason, what's good man," asks Quentin smiling.

"Ain't nothing good when it comes to Sylvia Williams. What were the two of you talking about?"

"You know that crazy lady too," asks Quentin. "That woman has been dogging me since I first arrived in this city, asking me questions like she has a right to be all up in my business. And she doesn't like being told that something is none of her business."

"Yeah, that's Sylvia. Once she sinks her teeth into something or someone, it's hard to get her to back off."

"Then how do you get rid of her," asks Quentin.

"You don't," states Jason.

Snake Chaser

"What do you mean you don't? I don't plan to spend the rest of my days telling that lady to get out of business, and I'm tired of her just popping up out of the blue."

"She's been dogging us for some years now and even though she may lay low from time to time, she never goes away."

"Damn, that's the last thing I wanted to hear," states Quentin as he looks at his watch. "Oh shit," he states, "I'm going to be late for lunch with my lady, man. I've got to go." As he opens the door to his car, he calls over his shoulder, "See you later." As Quentin pulls off from the curb, he wonders of Jason realizes that he slipped, big time. Sylvia has only been working domestically since she went AWOL, so she can't have been dogging Givens for years. "Are you really the elusive Mr. Red," Quentin asks out loud. Knowing that there is nothing that he's going to do about it at the moment, he continues his drive to Quintana's restaurant leaving that investigation in the very capable hands of Sylvia Williams.

As Quentin drives away, Jason gets on his phone to let his boss know about seeing Sylvia talking to Quentin. "Yeah boss, I think we need to move up our time table as well. See you at the office in thirty." Jason hangs up and makes his way to his car unaware that Sylvia is watching him.

Sylvia is able to read his lips, and knows that she is going to have to keep closer tabs on Mr. Givens if she intends to catch him in the act of anything illegal. With that in mind, she moves in double time so that she can get to their office the same time that they do.

Jason meets Charles at their offices away from the project site. "Hey Boss," greets Jason. "It looks like Ms Williams is crawling back out of her hole, and is planning to harass Mr. McNair. Apparently today is not his first run in with her, and he asked me how to get her to stop dogging him. When I told him you can't, he didn't seem too happy about it."

"Which makes me think that Mr. McNair isn't as squeaky clean as he appears. If he didn't have anything to hide, he wouldn't be so concerned about her being in his business. Maybe we can kill two birds with one stone," Charles thinks out loud.

"How so Boss?"

"We can make Mr. McNair look like he's the illegal arms runner which would get Ms Williams off our asses, and we can let her uncover what illegal activities he really has going on. This way, if he doesn't get busted, we could possibly get in on his business dealings in the future."

"Great idea Boss. So are we just going to lay back and see what develops between Williams and McNair?"

"Yes, I think that's best for now."

Snake Chaser

Eavesdropping

After eavesdropping on the conversation between Jason and Charles Givens at his office, Sylvia heads over to the development that Quentin is building to plan how she is going to sneak in later that night. She needs to get a full layout of the project in the daylight before she makes her foray on to the project at night. She notices the normal security camera setup, the guard station, the entrances and exits for the construction crews, as well as, the entrance she assumes is used by McNair and Givens. After getting the 'lay of the land', she hacks into the security firm being used by McNair to find out who will be on duty tonight so she knows who she's dealing with in the event she runs into the guard later tonight. Once she finalizes her plans for the evening, she sits back and waits for nightfall.

*****

At precisely midnight, Sylvia enters the construction site unaware that Quentin, Keith, Kyle, and Kendrick are watching her on the surveillance cameras. Believing that Givens is either Mr. Red in the flesh or his front man, Sylvia searches for a secret room in Givens off, and once she finds it she takes snapshots of his gun shipment before breaking into his file cabinets to find out who the guns are meant for. Unfortunately, she isn't able to find the information she's looking for so she adds her own "party favor" to the crates, a prototype of a new barely there surveillance device.

*****

The next day as Sylvia is monitoring the construction site since both McNair and Givens are on site, she witnesses a heated exchange between them and the local police. Although she doesn't know what took place in McNair's office between him and Givens, what she picks up from the surveillance equipment she installed in Givens' office lets her know that it wasn't a pleasant exchange and that he plans to execute his plans that night and she'll be ready to take him down when he does.

Less than thirty minutes later, Sylvia gets a call from her contact within the bureau letting her know what has just transpired in Dallas. "I know all about it. My contact on the DPD already called me with the information, and I'm set and ready to go. I just want to know McNair's position in the play."

"As I've already told you, McNair is not a player in this game. In fact, from what I've learned he is the one that actually tipped off the police when his security staff tipped him off about the extra nighttime activities of Charles Givens and his crew. I just hope this is the guy you've been after, I want this whole thing over with. I've never wanted to be a spy, just an efficient administrative assistant."

"You lost someone just like I lost someone, and we both agreed that the person that took them away from us should pay. This was the only way to make it happen," states Sylvia with more than a little tension in her voice.

"I know Sylvia, I know. It's just that sometimes I feel like such a traitor helping you this way since the government cut

Snake Chaser

you lose. I just hope this is the end, and then maybe both of us can get on with our lives."

"I hope so too. I'm actually tired of living like this, but I need closure for Q and the rest of my team. If everything goes as planned you will probably be rewarded for helping me, if not then you won't hear from me again after today. So, let me take the time now to say thank you for all you have done for me and my team, and I wish you all the best with the rest of your life. Gotta go." Sylvia disconnects the call before her friend could say another word. She needed to keep her mind clear and focused. She could reminisce about her friend after she completed this one last mission on behalf a country she might soon have to leave behind.

Later than night Kyle and his crew are suited and booted, and ready for action. Thanks to Quentin's secret room and passageways, they are able to position themselves at the site without being seen. They also know that they are not to interfere with Sylvia Williams should she appear on the playing field. The feds have given them clearance to let her handle this situation as she sees fit just so that they can put an end to her clandestine activities.

Sylvia has her game plan down, and her crew is at the ready. She can't wait to look into the eyes of the man who killed her team, and most importantly her family and turned her world upside down. The only part of her plan that is not finalized is whether or not she will kill him, or let him take his chances with the court system. "I guess I'll have to play it by ear," she says out loud to herself.

The Takedown

As soon as nightfall arrives, everybody goes into motion. Charles and his crew begin loading their merchandise into one of the construction trucks even though they would have preferred to use their own trucks, but they don't want anyone to be able to trace their actual mode of transportation. Once they are away from the site, they will transfer their product into one of their own trucks for delivery to their buyer.

Just as soon as the last crate is loaded on the trucks, Kyle puts his team on first alert on the off chance that Sylvia doesn't show up, or isn't able to handle the situation. Little does he know that Sylvia and her team have been on first alert as soon as the first truck was completely loaded, just on the off chance they were going to move the trucks out one at a time.

"Alright," begins Charles, "everybody knows what they have to do, right?"

"Yes, Boss," is the chorus from his crew. However, the next words out of their mouths are "What the fuck," as Sylvia and her crew surround each and every vehicle with guns at the ready.

"I would advise everyone to take shallow breaths and make no sudden movements," instructs Sylvia as her crew makes their
372

Snake Chaser

move. "This is not a drill, and each and everyone one of my men are trained snipers and will not hesitate to shoot anyone of you if so much as take a deep breath."

Kyle and his crew whisper a collective '*Damn*' as Sylvia makes her move. They quickly realize that she doesn't need their help, but they still remain at the ready just in case she's willing to let the law in on a piece of the action.

"Bitch, you . . .," is all Charles is able to get out of his mouth before Sylvia has her Desert Eagle imbedded in his cheek.

"You might want to choose your words carefully, Mr. Givens," begins Sylvia, "as I have an itchy trigger finger and a hair trigger on this weapon." She takes a second to remove her cap and glasses so that she can look directly into his eyes. "I've been waiting three long years for this moment," she states. "This is your last move as a free man, and if you don't cooperate it could be your last move as breathing man. So, if I were you I would carefully plan my next move and my next words." Still looking in his eyes, Sylvia gives her crew their instructions, "Alpha Team disarm and subdue the men you have surrounded." Once they have completed their objective, she gives Teams Bravo, Delta, and Omega the same instructions. Once every member of Charles' crew has been disarmed and detained, she states out loud, "Lieutenant Wright, your men may now retrieve your prisoners since I know you are on the scene."

"How the hell did she know we were here," Kyle asks out loud. However, before anyone can say a word, he gives the order for his crew to move out. "What do you plan to do with him," Kyle asks Sylvia once he has all the prisoners loaded into the transport vehicles.

"He and I are going to go to his office, and have a chat. If I like what he has to say, then we will meet you at the station," she states while never taking her eyes off Charles. "However, if he feeds me some bullshit, you'll never see him or me again. No matter what, it's been a pleasure working with you Kyle, and I wish you the best." She then pulls a second Desert Eagle from her back as she tells Charles to turn around. As he does as asked, she points one at Charles' head while placing the other in his back and they walk towards his office.

Kyle and his crew move out with their prisoners and the cargo. Quentin has been watching the events take place on the security monitors in his office, and is amazed at how efficient Sylvia and her team were when taking down Charles and his crew. Knowing he's going to have to give a full report in the morning to his superiors, Quentin tunes into the events taking place in Charles' office between him and Sylvia. While he's listening, Brad shows up at his office, tells him to turn on his handheld monitor, and then they head over to the construction site for he wants to be on hand to stop Sylvia from killing the man she's spent years chasing.

Once inside his office, Sylvia holsters the gun she had placed in Charles' back, and hands him a set of handcuffs telling him to handcuff his hands in front of him. Once the handcuffs are secure she sits him down in one of the guest chairs in front of his desk. She then haves him handcuff each of his legs to the legs of the chair, before she retrieves her second weapon from her back and takes the chair behind his desk.

"Now Mr. Givens, Mr. Red, or whatever your name is, I need you to answer a few questions for me. And let me caution you up front to be honest with me, because I am not in the mood for bullshit after three years of waiting. You've got to know that your career as a gunrunner is over, so you might as well tell the truth. Especially since I was telling the truth when I told Lieutenant Wright that if I don't like what I hear no one will see you ever again, and my two friends here Desert and Eagle will make sure of that. And just like you are able to go underground for years and years, I too can go underground. And I will have no problem going underground for the rest of my life after this."

Charles remains silent as Sylvia stares at him looking like the devil reincarnate armed and ready for war.

"Silence. Not exactly what I expected from you," comments Sylvia. "If you don't just want to come clean on all your activities, I guess we can play twenty questions," she continues. "Let's start with the most important question first, how did you know about my teams plans to take you down three years ago?"

Charles debates on whether he should tell her anything until she starts attaching a silencer to one of her weapons. "Slow down you crazy bitch," he begins. Sylvia attaches a silencer to her second weapon. "Okay, okay," states a now nervous Charles. "I knew that someone was on to my operation, and was trying to cover my tracks so I had my warehouse rigged to blow to throw whoever it was off track. The death of your squad was simply a bonus, no one knew they would be there. Although, I'm wondering why you weren't there with them as their Capitan."

"That's none of your concern," states Sylvia is a deadly voice. "But how do you know I was their Capitan?"

"When their bodies were found, their fingerprints were taken and your database hacked to find out who they were. I was able to get their names, ranks, and the details of their mission. You were listed as the capitan of the mission they were assigned to, so why weren't you with them?"

"I told you that was none of your business," she states as she leans over the desk with both guns pointed in his direction.

"I'm the one asking the questions here," she continues. "Now, I want to know every asshole you've sold guns to. Every one."

"Why is this so important to you? You've been dogging me for six years, and I won't answer another question until I get some answers. You won't kill me until you get everything you're looking for, so I'm not worried about you shooting me," states Charles displaying more bravery than he was actually feeling at the moment.

It's obvious to Sylvia that some of the information he's been fed is incomplete because even though the Marines and the CIA have been tracking him for six years, she's only been tracking him solo for three years. However, she doesn't feel the need to explain herself to him, so she doesn't correct him. However, to answer his question, Sylvia puts a bullet in his right shoulder. Charles screams in pain as the bullet enters his flesh. "Still not worried," she asks.

Quentin and Brad arrive at the site just as Sylvia shoots Charles, "Damn," states Brad out loud. "I was so hoping he wouldn't give her a reason to shoot him. It's going to be difficult to get him to help us if he is filled with holes from those twins she calls friends."

"What do you want to do," asks Quentin. "I still don't want her to know who I am, just in case this isn't the last mission she decides to undertake."

"Don't worry, I'm going to handle this one myself," responds Brad.

"Wait man, you haven't been in the field in over ten years," begins Quentin, "do you think you're ready to take on the likes of Sylvia Williams?"

Snake Chaser

"What are you trying to say Quentin? You don't think I can handle myself or her?"

"I'm just saying, you've been behind a desk for over ten years and she's been in the field all that time. Hell she's been a rogue agent for three years, and there's no telling what new skills she's picked up in all that time."

"What you don't know is that I take field training every year, so I am up on all the new tactics and am in excellent shape. Don't worry, I've got this."

"If you say so boss," responds Quentin.

Quentin heads to his offices on the site, while Brad makes his way to Charles' office. When he is five feet from the door, Sylvia calls out, "Stop right there Capitan Davidson."

"Shit," whispers Brad angrily as he freezes in his tracks.

"Are you here to apprehend me? Or to help with the interrogation?"

"I'm here to help you Capitan Williams," responds Brad. "I know how important this is to you, and I just want to make sure you don't end up a fugitive after this is over."

Unexpected Developments

Not really wanting to go into hiding after this whole ordeal is over with, Sylvia concedes and allows Brad to enter the office. "Come on in Capitan Davidson, but remember this is my interrogation."

Brad enters the office, "Deal," he states. However, he takes a half a second pause as he finally gets an up-close and personal look at the elusive Sylvia Williams. *'Damn, she looks better in person than in any of the photos that I've seen of her,'* he thinks to himself. After making a quick recovery, he takes a stand behind her and allows her to continue her interrogation.

Charles takes advantage of the disruption, and makes a plea to Brad, "Man, this bitch is crazy. Get me out of here."

Sylvia takes another shot at him, but Brad interferes and she misses his other shoulder. She stands up and faces him, afraid that she might try to shoot him next Brad places her in a bear hug to keep her from raising either of her friends. What neither one of them is prepared for is the spark of electricity that passes through both of their bodies. Knowing that now is not the right time to investigate that little surprise, Brad looks her in the eyes and says, "We don't need him full of holes when we take him in, so take it easy with your friends there, okay?"

Snake Chaser

Needing a little more time to recover, it's a minute longer before Sylvia responds. "Fine," she states a little softer than she intended.

"Do you two need a moment alone," Charles asks sarcastically.

They both turn to him with their guns raised, "Don't push your luck," states Brad with deadly intent in his voice. He then turns to Sylvia, "Carry on Capitan," he states as he takes up his previous position behind her chair.

Sylvia sits back in the chair, and returns her attention to her hostage. "Ready to answer my questions now," she asks as though there was not a break in the interrogation.

"You're going to let her get away with this," Charles asks Brad. When Brad doesn't respond and Sylvia aims her friends at him again, Charles starts stuttering, "I can't . . . uh . . . just give up . . . the people I've dealt with."

"Yes you can, unless you want another hole in you. I have no problem with it, but you might," comes back Sylvia as she takes aim at his left shoulder again.

"Alright, alright, but what am I going to get for my cooperation?"

"Fewer holes in your body," quips Sylvia.

Charles looks at Brad and seeing that he is not going to get any help from him, he states, "I've sold guns to any and every one who had the money. Iraqis, Saudis, Germans, Asians, Cubans, Columbians, Niggas in the hood. You can't expect me to remember each and every one of them."

"I don't really care about the niggas in the hood, but I am concerned about those who have waged war against American Troops."

Charles runs down every radical military group he's ever sold weapons to, along with the dates and types of weapons sold and any other information he had about their organizations.

Once he's dumped his brain, Brad asks Sylvia if he can have a word with her in private. She agrees and they step out into the outer office. "I want to help you as much as I can Sylvia," begins Brad. "We've been wanting to put an end to this guy's gun running as much as you have, and I don't want you to have to go into hiding. So we need to put together a plan of action together to turn him, and make sure you don't end up behind bars yourself."

"What do you have in mind," asks Sylvia a little more breathlessly than she intended.

"Sit down, and let me lay it all out for you."

After outlining the plan to Sylvia, Brad calls in transport for Charles. Once they arrive in Washington with their prisoner, Brad escorts Sylvia to his office while MPs take Charles to the infirmary to have his wound treated.

"Have a seat Capitan," Brad tells Sylvia. "First, I would like to congratulate you on the success of this mission. You have proven to be a first rate soldier. However, there will be some sanctions against you as this mission was not authorized by any government official, and your little help mate will also find herself punished for her part in your activities."

"Wait just one damn minute," yells Sylvia as she jumps to her feet and touches her nose to Brad's. "You said you weren't there to apprehend me. I should have known better than to

380

Snake Chaser

trust a paper pusher like you to do the right thing," she continues. However, that damn spark flares up between them again, so she pulls back and starts pacing the room as she puts together a plan to get out of his office and out of the country. Everything is already in place for her life in hiding, she just has to get to her boat in the gulf.

"I'm not letting you out of here Sylvia, so stop running options in that head of yours," he states. Undeterred by the angry look she sends his way, he continues, "You will not be doing any jail time for this, but you will have to resume your role as an operative for the government," he stops speaking as she turns to him with fire flashing in her eyes. "It's the only way, I can let you get away with everything you've done for the past three years and for stealing government property and funds."

Sylvia walks around his desk to confront him face-to-face, and when Brad sees her intent, he immediately stands so as not to give her an advantage. "If the government hadn't abandoned me, I wouldn't have had to "steal" anything. Zakiya wouldn't have felt compelled to help me, and she wouldn't be in trouble right now."

Brad is overwhelmed by her presence and fire, and reacts without thinking. He grabs her in a bear hug and takes the kiss he's being dying to take since first laying eyes on her. Sylvia is first stunned by the kiss, then overwhelmed by the electricity passing between them. Before she knows it, she's returning the kiss whole-heartedly. Once the need to breathe becomes paramount, Brad breaks the kiss. "I'm sorry," states Brad. After a few more gulps of air, he continues, "No I'm not. I've been wanting to kiss you from the moment I laid eyes on you tonight." He feels her fighting against his hold on her, but refuses to let her go. "I would let you go, but I'm afraid you might shoot me."

"They took my guns when we entered the building, remember," responds Sylvia still trying to regain control of her breathing.

"You got me on that one, but I'm still not letting you go. I know you are deadly even without a weapon in hand, and I really don't want to fight you right now. I'd rather make love to you, but somehow I don't think you'll let me."

"Are you sure about that," asks Sylvia breathing a little more steadily now. But his hold on her and his words are making her head spin, and her heart race. She's not sure what to do since she hasn't been this affected by a man since Qasean.

Snake Chaser

New Beginnings

Quickly recovering from the shock of her response, Brad kisses her deeply one more time. When he's finally able to break the kiss, he lets her go and quickly moves away from her and braces himself for any assault she may decide to make.

To his surprise, Sylvia simply takes her seat as she tries to recover from his touch and his kisses. "Sit down Brad. You are in no danger from me. At least not at the moment."

Brad eases into his seat still on alert. "Look Sylvia, I know you weren't expecting me to attack you that way and it certainly wasn't planned on my part, but I don't regret one second of it. But that's not why I brought you here. I want to make sure that we have an agreement before I take you to the General for him to give you the details of your new position."

"Brad, you might be surprised to hear this, but I have no more fight left in me. This mission has been my life for the last three years, and I was prepared to go into hiding after it was over and live a life of leisure. I don't want to be a field agent anymore."

"And you won't be."

"What? Wait a minute. I know you don't think I'd be happy as a paper pusher do you?"

"No Sylvia, I know you won't be happy behind a desk, but I think you will be happy as a trainer and consultant."

"What?"

"Your new position involves you training recruits that have been assigned to clandestine missions so that they will know how to survive in the wild, and especially if they get disconnected from their team. Plus, you will serve as a consultant when those missions are being planned, helping with the strategy and attack methods. I think you'll be very happy in that position. You'll even get to travel."

"I don't know Brad."

"You don't have a choice Sylvia. It's the only way to save your hide and Zakiya's."

"Shit," curses Sylvia. She leans her head back and closes her eyes to digest what Brad has just told her.

Brad, in the meantime, is studying the length of her neck and fantasying about placing kisses down that neck as well as other places on her body. As his arousal becomes uncomfortable, he shifts in his chair which makes Sylvia look in his direction. He is unable to mask the desire in his eyes, and he notes the surprise in hers. He cocks his eyebrow at her, before shyly smiling. He knows that his reaction is a surprise to her, and frankly it's a surprise to him as well.

"How closely will we be working together," she asks.

"If I have my way, we'll be working very closely together."

Snake Chaser

"I mean in my new position," clarifies Sylvia.

"I am talking about your new position," he responds with more than a little subjectiveness in his voice.

"I'm serious here Brad."

"I am too," he responds.

Sylvia rolls her eyes before closing them again, and is saved from having to respond as Brad's phone rings. "Yeah," he barks into the phone.

"Interrupting, am I," quips Quentin on the other end of the phone.

"As a matter of fact you are," Brad barks.

"Take it easy," quips Quentin. "I was just checking in."

"Check in tomorrow," states Brad, and then he promptly hangs up the phone.

He then turns back to Sylvia and says, "It's been a long day. Let's get you checked into your temporary quarters," states Brad.

Sylvia doesn't say a word. She simply gets up from the chair, and lets Brad lead her out of his office and out of the building. She does, however, retrieve her friends on the way out.

Once they arrive at the safe house that Brad has arranged for, he tells her to go get a bath while he sees what there is to eat. Still pondering the events that took place in Brad's office, Sylvia makes her way to the bathroom and takes the suggested bath. Twenty minutes later, Brad enters the bathroom with a nightgown and robe, as well as, a glass of white wine. Sylvia doesn't acknowledge his presence, hoping he'll turn around and leave.

"I know you know I'm here, and I'm not leaving so you might as well open your eyes."

"Why can't you just be a gentleman and leave?"

"Because I don't want to be a gentleman. I want to make love to you." Sylvia's eyes pop open at his comment, but before she can say a word he hands her the glass of wine. "This should help you relax, as well as, the fact that I'm not going to make love to you tonight since I don't think you're up to it. There'll be plenty of time for that." After she takes the glass from his hand, he makes his way to the door throwing over his shoulder, "Your nightgown and robe are draped across the commode."

"What the hell is wrong with me," Sylvia asks out loud once Brad has left. "I've never been this affected by the presence of a man, not even my beloved Qasean. She takes a deep drink from the glass before sitting it on the floor, and leaning back against the back of the tub.

Another thirty minutes have gone by, and Sylvia hasn't emerged from the bathroom. Brad wonders if she escaped out the window, or drowned herself in the tub. "Only one way to find out," he states out loud as he makes his way to the bathroom. He pauses just inside the door, Sylvia looks like a complete angel sleeping in the tub, a very desirable angel since all of her bubbles have dissipated and he has a clear view of every inch of her voluptuous frame. After looking his fill, he scoops her up in his arms and carriers her to her room. He can't resist taking one last look at her before covering her with the sheet. "She's probably going to be mad as hell that I put her to bed wet, but if I dried her off I'd be in that bed with her and we wouldn't be sleeping," he states as he pours himself a drink in the sitting area.

Sylvia wakes up ten minutes later as she notices she is no longer floating in water. It takes her a minute to remember where she is, but once she does she takes note of the fact that she is in bed completely nude and there is only one way she got there. Letting her anger get the best of her, she quickly gets out of the bed and marches into the sitting area to give Brad a piece of her mind. "You had no right to remove me from the tub. I have no intentions on drowning myself," she rants as she enters the sitting area. "I will not be treated like a child," she continues.

Displaying an outward calm he is far from feeling, Brad takes a sip of his drink to keep from tasting her skin, "Believe me Sylvia, I have no intentions of treating you like a child. As a matter of fact, if you continue to stand there as bare as the day you were born, I may show you exactly how I plan to treat you. Right here. Right now."

"You cannot intimidate me with your sexual innuendos. As a matter of fact, if you lay one finger on me you'll . . .," her voice falters as Brad leaves the chair and is a hair's breath away from her.

"I'll what Sylvia," asks Brad standing nose-to-nose with her. The manly scent of him, the heat of his body temporarily disorients her, and she is unable to finish what she was about to say. Brad takes her silence as acquiescence, and takes control of her mouth with his. She returns his kiss without hesitation, and Brad takes that as her consent to let him love her.

He carries her to his bed, and tastes every inch of her bare skin. Her moans of pleasure only add fuel to his fire, and the scream of her climax nearly does him in. He quickly removes his clothes as she rides out the climax, and then rejoins her on the bed. If his suspicions are right, she hasn't made love since the death of her fiancé, and he knows he's going to have to take it easy with her this first time. He slowly kisses her breasts before making his way slowly down the rest of her body. He knows he has to get control of himself, so he makes love to her with his mouth again to calm himself down. While she is riding out the waves of her second climax, he makes his first tentative entrance into her depths. Even as wet as she is from his mouth and her first two orgasms, he is not able to penetrate her fully. He pulls back and makes another attempt, but he is still unable to achieve full penetration. On his third attempt, he is finally able to bury himself to the hilt inside of her. He becomes so overwhelmed by the sensation of being inside her he freezes as he tries to adjust himself to what he's feeling.

"Don't stop now," whispers Sylvia. "Please," she pleads a few seconds later.

"I have no intentions on stopping Sylvia. I just want to savor being inside you," he replies. "You have no idea what being inside you is doing to me right now," he adds.

"If you being inside me is affecting you the same way it's affecting me, then I think I have a pretty good idea how you feel," is her response.

Her response breaks his control, and he begins moving in and out of her at a frantic pace. The moans and sighs that escape each of their lips sends them both into overdrive, and the pace of their lovemaking gets faster and faster. Her scream of ecstasy mingles with his roar of completion as a powerful orgasm slams into both of them at the same time. Neither of them are able to move or speak for quite some time as they try to calm their racing hearts and labored breathing.

Snake Chaser

Brad is the first one to regain his voice, "I didn't want our first time to be like that," he begins. "It was supposed to be slow and easy not hard and frantic."

"I didn't want slow and easy," states Sylvia. "I needed hard and frantic," she adds before taking a deep breath. "This is the first time I've felt alive in three years," she states before breaking down in tears. Brad cradles her in his arms and rocks her as she cries. Once the tears are almost over, she asks, "What am I going to do now?"

"What do mean," asks Brad.

"Qasean and my team and our missions were my life. When I lost them, finding their killer became my life," she begins. "That's over now, and I have nothing to drive me. Nothing to live for," she states as she lays her head on his shoulder and starts crying again.

Not wanting her know how much her words angered him, he pulls her closer and rocks her in his arms. After giving her a few moments to let her tears free fall, he lifts her head and looks her straight in the eyes, "You do have something to live for," he states in a voice that sounded a lot angrier than he intended. He takes a deep breath, and begins again, "I know this might sound crazy, but I love you and I'm not letting you go." She starts to shake her head, and he grabs her chin. "I do love you. I don't know why or how, but I do. Please, just don't walk away from me. Give us a chance."

"I'm scared, Brad."

"I know sweetheart, I'm scared too. I've never been in love in my life," he states. At her surprised look he adds, "No woman has ever moved me the way that you do, and no woman has ever moved me the first time I laid eyes on her."

ReGina Crawford

Not knowing what to say, Sylvia simply kisses him senseless and they make love into the wee hours of the morning.

Snake Chaser

Tying Up Loose Ends

Brad wakes up several hours later after making love to Sylvia all night, and makes a few phone calls. Once she wakes up he lets her know that everything is in place for her professionally, and that he plans to take of her personally. He is surprised at how quickly she accepts his words, but doesn't question her decision.

At noon he receives a call from Quentin, "What's up," he answers the phone.

"You tell me man. You sounded quite busy last night, but you seem to have survived the night. Guess the lady didn't do you in," states Quentin trying to keep the laughter out of his voice.

"No, the lady didn't do me in the way you think," states Brad not trying to hide the laughter in his voice while winking at the smile that Sylvia has on her face.

"Sounds like an interesting story. One you'll have to tell me about when you don't have an audience. I just wanted to make sure everything ended as planned last night."

"Everything is as it should be. No worries."

"Glad to hear it. We'll talk tomorrow."

"Yes we will," responds Brad before hanging up the phone.

*****

One of the conditions of her punishment is that she must make amends with those that she offended in Dallas, and Brad has arranged for a charter flight to take them there to do just that, as well as, make arrangements for all of Sylvia's belongings to be shipped back to DC. When they arrive in town, they find out that the people she needs to see are headed over to Quintana's restaurant. Just as they are about to walk in the door, who is walking in their direction? None other than Brad and Sylvia, both smiling ear-to-ear. Quentin is praying that Brad doesn't acknowledge him since that would give him away. He has nothing to worry about as Brad notices the large group standing in front of the restaurant. Sylvia greets them all, and introduces Brad.

Kyle then invites them to have brunch with their group. "We would love to," replies Brad. "Sylvia tells me that you helped with the sting last night."

"Yes sir, we did."

"Did a good job too from what I hear."

"We'd like to think so," states Keith. "But I don't want to talk shop, I want to eat the incredible meal that is waiting on me on the inside."

"Then follow me," states Quintana.

"Ana," begins Sylvia, "can I talk to you for a minute?"

Snake Chaser

"Sure." Quintana then turns to her hostess and lets her know to add two more settings to her table, and that she would be right there. "I'm glad this is over for you, and that you're okay," states Quintana as she turns back to Sylvia.

"Are you really?"

"Of course. Why wouldn't I be?"

"You don't think I'm betraying Q by being with Brad?"

"Honey, we lost Qasean three years ago. You have mourned his loss long enough. I've always wanted nothing but the best for you, and you know it. Be happy."

"I am," responds Sylvia.

"You sound surprised by that."

"I am. I've been so driven by finding his killer that I never took a close look at my personal life. That's not true. I actually felt like I had no life after I lost him, but Brad has convinced me that I do have a personal life and a new professional life thanks to his connections with the government."

"That's great Sylvia," states Quintana as she gives her friend a big hug. "Will you be moving to Washington?"

"Yes, I will. I'll make the announcement at brunch. Now let's go join the others." The ladies walk to the table hand-in-hand.

The sit down at the table with the others and the conversation gets kind of loud and rowdy, but Sylvia is enjoying being in their company. However, there still another thing that she needs to take care of before moving back to DC. Once all the excitement dies down and everyone goes back to their lunch,

Sylvia leans over to Quentin and asks him if she can talk to him privately.

Quentin nods his head in agreement as his curiosity gets the best of him. They get up from the table and head towards the lobby of the restaurant followed by the curious stares of the rest of the table.

"What can I do for you Ms Williams," asks Quentin in a not so friendly voice as they reach the lobby.

Undeterred by the slight hostility that she hears in his voice, Sylvia replies, "I would like to call a truce between us." Still undeterred by the skeptical cocking of his eyebrow, she continues, "I'm sorry that I suspected you as a possible adversary to my mission. Now that it is over, I realize that you are who you say you are and I would like for us to at least be civil with each other. Especially since you are about to marry my best friend."

"I'm glad to hear that you have changed your mind about me, and I guess we can put the past behind us," responds Quentin. He then adds, "I hope that you will be happy with your new life, and try to stay out of trouble." The smile on his face takes the sting out of his last words, and Sylvia smiles back as she extends her hand to seal their truce. Quentin shakes her hand then leads her back to the table to join the others.

Once they take their seats, Quintana leans over and asks Quentin what happened between him and Sylvia. "We called a truce," he whispers in her ear. Quintana smiles and leans over to kiss him on the cheek, but he turns his face to her and takes the kiss full on the lips. The kiss heats up quickly, and goes on so long that the table at large clears their throats to remind the two that they are not alone. Sheepishly Quentin mutters, "Sorry bout that. I kinda got carried away."

Snake Chaser

"We could tell," states Kyle and Keith at the same time.

"There goes that stereo thing again," quips Quentin, and the table at large bursts out laughing.

Once the laughter dies down, Kyle asks Brad what brings him and Sylvia back to Dallas. "Sylvia had some unfinished business to conclude," responds Brad while looking pointedly at Sylvia.

"I just wanted to tell you and your men thank you for allowing me to take down Charles, and to apologize for being such a pain in the ass while I was here in the city," states Sylvia as the whole table looks her way.

"You're welcome," states Kyle. "No apology needed though," he adds. "We knew what this case meant to you, and you provided us with information that probably would have taken us a lot longer to get if we had to deal with departmental red tape."

"I know you're right about the red tape, but I still feel like I could have been a little less hostile to you and your men," responds Sylvia.

"She was a real pain in the ass sometimes," comments Keith. The table looks at him with censure, and he responds, "What? She said the same thing, and no one looked at her sideways."

"That was different," states Jade. "She can say it. You can't," adds Jade looking more than a little pissed with him.

"I don't see what the difference is," begins Keith, but at the look Jade sends his way he changes his tune. "I'm sorry Ms Williams. I didn't mean to sound ungrateful."

Sylvia smiles in his direction, "No harm done since I know you were just stating the truth." She then turns to Quintana, "Ana, I want to thank you for staying my friend throughout all this. I know it was hard for you, and hope I didn't cause you too much heartache while I pursued what had become my life's mission."

"Sylvia, I love you and will always love you. I know how what happened all those years ago destroyed your life as you knew it, and I knew you needed closure. I'm glad you have it, and I wish you all the best as you start your next life."

The women have tears in their eyes, and the men interfere as they don't relish the thought of having to deal with a table full of crying women. "What's with the service in this place today," asks Keith.

"Yeah, where's my food, I'm hungry," chimes in Kyle.

Before Quintana can say a word, their waitress arrives with their meals. Quentin takes the moment to place a shrimp in her mouth to keep her from lashing out Kyle and Keith. Kyle and Keith follow his lead, and do the same thing to Indigo and Jade.

"That's what I'm talkin' bout," states Keith and Kyle at the same time as they take a bite of their food.

"Can someone please turn off the surround sound," quips Quentin, and the whole table bursts out laughing again.

Once the laughter dies down, they finish their lunch, and then each of the couples head their separate ways to enjoy the rest of their day.

Snake Chaser

Life Anew

Brad escorts Sylvia back to their hotel room for they are not flying back to DC until the morning. Once they get inside the room, he leads her over to the couch and pulls her into his lap. As he wraps his arms around her, he kisses her on the forehead before saying, "I'm very proud of you." She leans up and looks at him with a puzzled look on her face, so he adds, "You handled the situation with Keith, Kyle, Kendrick, and Quentin very well." He settles her back against his chest as he states, "I must admit I wasn't sure that you wouldn't come at them with both barrels."

She settles even further into his embrace before responding, "I feel like a different person now." She closes her eyes and takes a deep breath, "But I'm still scared," she adds.

"I know you are," he replies. "If it makes you feel any better, I'm scared too." She tries to lean up out of his arms, but he refuses to let her out of his embrace. "Just let me hold you," he states. "This is all new to me as well, Sweetheart. I never thought that I would ever find someone that makes me feel the way that you do, and I never thought that it would happen this quickly either," he continues. "I want to get to know you outside of what I know from your file. All I'm asking is that you give this a chance. Give us a chance. Do you think that you can do that?"

"I want to," she says barely above a whisper. "I'm just not sure I know what do, but I do feel differently," she states a little louder. "And I like the way I feel, the way this feels, the way we feel," she adds.

"That's good to know," he responds. "We'll take it as slow as you need to as long as you stay in this with me."

"I'd like that," she states.

"Thank you," he says against her lips before kissing her slowly yet deeply. The kiss quickly turns passionate, and before she knows it he's stripped her completely naked. When she begins to reach for his clothes, he pins her arms over her head while shaking his head, "Tonight, let me do this my way." She smiles as she nods her head giving her consent. He gives her a slow, long, drugging kiss before trailing kisses down her neck to her collarbone, before settling his open mouth on the nipple of her left breast and suckling. Once the peak of her left breast is a hard little nub, he moves his mouth to her right breast and gives it the same attention that he gave her left breast. When he's had his feel of her breasts, he moves his mouth down her stomach kissing and licking her flesh, and when he reaches her belly button he dips his tongue inside absorbing her trembles in his mouth.

"I'm going to let your hands go," he states in between kisses, "but I need you to keep them where they are." He then slides further down her body, puts his arms under her legs as he spreads her thighs wide before dipping his tongue inside her love cove to taste her essence. Her hips buck off the couch, and he places his palms flat against her stomach to press her back down on the couch but he never stops what he's doing to her. It's not long before he feels her thighs tighten signaling

398

Snake Chaser

that she is on the verge of a climax, so he increases the speed of his tongue while at the same time getting a tighter grip on her hips to keep her from moving. She grabs a hold of his head, to do what she doesn't know, she just knows that she needs to hold on to something. And before she can make up her mind what she wants to do, her orgasm crashed down on her causing her to scream out his name.

Once her trembles subside, he removes his mouth from her body and lays his chin on his hands that are resting on her stomach and stares at her until she opens her eyes. "That's how it was supposed to be the first time," he states around a smile. She can do nothing but shake her head, and smile back in return. He gets up and reaches his hand out to her while saying, "Let's go to bed so that I can love you properly." She puts her hand in his, lets him help her off the couch, and lets him lead her to the bedroom. Once they are inside the room, he picks her up, and gently lays her on the bed before removing his clothes. When he is as bare as she is, he joins her on the bed and gives her another slow, long, drugging kiss. Before she knows it, he's slowing burying his manhood inside of her, and she is so blown away by the sensuality of it that she is unable to move. Once he is buried to the hilt inside of her, he stops moving so that he can savor the feel of being inside her.

After several moments, she clinches her inner walls around him causing him to suck in a deep breath. "Make love to me," she whispers. Unable to resist her or the words she's spoken, he begins a slow rhythm of moving in and out of her body, and the sweetness of it his movements causes both of them to suck in a deep breath. He loves her at that pace until he feels his own release upon him, "Come with me," he states between clinched teeth for he doesn't think he's going to last much longer. She eagerly complies with his request, and they both let go and scream each other's names as they are consumed by the maelstrom of their joint orgasms. They make love until they both fall into an exhausted yet content slumber.

*****

The next morning they catch their flight back to DC after making arrangements to have all of her belongings packed up and shipped to DC. When they touchdown in DC, he reluctantly lets her go to her apartment for some alone time for he knows that she needs process all that has transpired between them, and the new life she is about to begin.

As she sits in her living room contemplating the turn her life has taken, she comes to the realization that she doesn't want to spend the night alone, so she takes a shower, gets dressed, and heads to Brad's home on the other side of town. When she arrives, she parks, gets out of her car, and rings his doorbell. As she stands there waiting for him to answer the door, she realizes that she feels no reluctance at being there, and knows that she has once again found love and is ready to begin her life anew. Brad opens the door and although he is surprised to see her, he is so overjoyed that she came to him that a big smile spreads across his face as he opens the door wide enough for her to walk inside. After he closes the door behind them, he leans back against it and just looks at her. "I've thought about it, and I know that this is where I am meant to be," she responds to the unspoken question in his eyes. "In this moment I begin a new journey in my life, and I know that I want to share this journey with you," she adds with the sheen of tears of joy in her eyes and a smile on her face.

Brad lifts himself off the door and walks until he is standing toe-to-toe with her. "I hoped you would eventually come to that conclusion," he begins. "I just didn't think that it would happen this soon," he adds.

Snake Chaser

"As I sat in my apartment, I felt incomplete and I thought long and hard about what I felt was missing," she states, "and it was you."

Brad kisses her forehead before taking her hand, and leading her up the stairs to his bedroom. He makes slow love to her in the same manner that he did in the hotel room in Dallas, before pulling her into his arms for them to get some much needed rest.

The next morning, they have breakfast, get dressed, and head into the office so that Brad can layout the duties of her new position with the agency. Once that is complete, he lets her know that he has a meeting with the upper brass that he must attend and tells her to go check out her new office in the training center. When she exits his office, she stops at Zakiya's desk for this is the first time she has seen her anonymous accomplice in person. "I would like to apologize to you for any trouble that I've caused you in my quest to bring down the man who killed my family."

Zakiya shakes her head as she says, "No need to apologize. I knew what I was getting into when I contacted you, and I needed justice for the loss of Chance." She then stands and comes around her desk, and pulls Sylvia into a big hug. "Thank you for bring him in, and for the bullet wound to his shoulder. While it won't bring Chance back to us, it gives me a reason to smile every day," she states.

As Zakiya releases her from the embrace, Sylvia looks at her and says, "I can see that we are going to become great friends." And then she walks away to go check out her new office feeling even better about the new life she has been given.

Upcoming works from the author:

Icing On The Cake

For those of you who have asked what happened to Jade and Kyle, and Ebony and Kendrick, their stories will be completed in this book. You will also receive updates on Quentin and Quintana, as well as, Sylvia and Brad.

www.ingramcontent.com/pod-product-compliance
Lightning Source LLC
Chambersburg PA
CBHW060141260626
47160CB00001B/77